DUCHESS OF AQUITAINE

DUCHESS OF AQUITAINE

A Novel of Eleanor

◈

Margaret Ball

ST. MARTIN'S PRESS ❧ NEW YORK

www.stmartins.com

Design by Susan Yang

Library of Congress Cataloging-in-Publication Data

Ball, Margaret, 1947–
    Duchess of Aquitaine : a novel of Eleanor / Margaret Ball.—1st ed.
        p. cm.
    ISBN-13: 978-0-312-20533-1
    ISBN-10: 0-312-20533-3
    1. Eleanor, of Aquitaine, Queen, consort of Henry II, King of England, 1122?–1204—Fiction.
2. France—Fiction. 3. Crusades—Fiction. I. Title.

PS3552.A45535D83 2006
813'.54—dc22

2006042221

First Edition: June 2006

10 9 8 7 6 5 4 3 2 1

Duchess of Aquitaine

Prologue

"A l'entrada del tens clar, eya,
Per joia recomencar, eya,
E per jelos irritar, eya,
Vol la regina mostrar
Qui es si amoroza."

The queen is dancing to bring the sun back.

Although it's still cold, the earth damp and soggy from winter rain, the bare trees dripping overhead, she dances barefoot in a thin green gown. Where her feet touch the ground, fresh grass comes out, and where she passes under the trees, tight-furled buds of leaves appear on the branches. Waves of deep rich color wash across the world with each turn of the circle, cloud-white sky turning blue, black bare trees hazed over with green, brown earth sprinkled with white and yellow and pink of little spring flowers. Around her, the young men and the girls dance and sing to bring back the sun.

"See the queen, see the queen," they sing, "the queen who brings back joy."

Each year the sun must be danced back into the sky, to make the land warm and fertile again, to bring back life and joy. Nothing must stop the circle. They dance in the churchyard: the priest curses them to dance all year until they sink into the earth from weariness. They dance in the fields: they call up too much strength from the earth and become a ring of standing stones, gray and weathered with the changing of innumerable seasons. They dance in the dark forest where boars root and snuffle in the damp rotting leaves: their linked hands become the entangled branches of tall young trees whose strength renews the forest. None of this and nothing else can stop the dance, for they are the land and the change of seasons, and they must circle and renew the earth year after year, as the sun passes through the Houses of

Life and Death, as the wheel of Fortuna turns and casts one down who even now was riding high; so the dancers circle forever.

And at their center is the April queen. Today she is a girl of fifteen, flushed and bright-eyed and breathless with the endless spiral of the dance. Her young face is serious as she goes carefully through the steps and turns, lifting her feet gracefully, taking care not to stumble or to lose the chaplet of flowers that covers her unbound hair. She has known this dance in a thousand lives, but in this life, in this spring, it is new again to her and the chaplet is heavy as a crown. She must make joy begin again. It is not a light thing.

> *"A la vi', a la via, jelos!*
> *Laissaz nos, laissaz nos*
> *ballar entre nos, entre nos!"*

> Away, away, jealous ones!
> Let us alone
> let us dance among ourselves!

The bare feet of the dancers thud down on the packed earth of the churchyard, the best dancing circle in the village. The rhythm beats like a pulse through the earth, calling, drawing forth life from the winter-chilled ground. Even the carved stones of the church quiver with life under the insistent beat of bare feet on earth. The stone forms come slipping free from the portal, grotesques with the heads of birds or the claws of beasts, demon-masks, and malformed bodies. They are old men in masks now, breaking into the circle, scattering the dancers, who shrink back before them. Only the April queen, eyes half closed, keeps to the rhythm of the dance as the old men close around her. Their cold hands reach for her trailing gown, brush across her cheek. She is theirs now, and their circle croaks a harsh victory chant as the scattered dancers vainly rail against them.

A cloud comes over the sun. Fat, cold drops of rain fall in the churchyard, turning the packed ground to mud again. The flowers wither on the April queen's chaplet and it becomes a wreath of dry branches. The old men take up the next verse with cracked triumphant voices.

"Lo reis i ven d'autra part, eya,
per la dansa destorbar, eya,
que el es en cremetar, eya,
que om no li voill' emblar
la regin' avrilloza."

The king comes on from the other side,
so as to break up the dance,
for he is all aghast
lest someone wants to rob him of
the April queen.

The dancers part to let the king in his black cloak pass through, the young girls and men drawing back with fear, the old men in their grotesque masks bowing with respect. The king is tall and strong, but he dances like a bent old man, black cloak wrapped about him, hood drawn low over his face. He sidles and minces through the path made for him until, with one last bound, he reaches the April queen and throws his cloak over her. They sway back and forth, locked in an embrace under the black cloak, while the old men croak their chant of triumph and the dancers sing in vain:

"A la vi', a la via, jelos!
Laissaz nos, laissaz nos
ballar entre nos, entre nos!"

Away, away, jealous ones!
Let us alone
let us dance among ourselves!

The queen stands as if asleep, or in a waking dream, under the black cloak of the winter king. Finally she hears the chorus of the dancers. She pushes the king away from her and runs around the circle of old men, beating with her hands at their linked arms. Their masks of bird and monster faces peck at her bare hands.

The outer ring of dancers sings louder and louder, and their feet pound out the dancing rhythm until the ground trembles with it and the sky is full of their music.

The clouds shake and the sun pours through again, gilding the ground. The old men are weak; the old king cannot pursue the queen. She breaks through their circle and runs to the outer ring of dancers, where a young man seizes her by the waist and lifts her joyously to the sun. Flowers spring up where her bare feet have left prints in the mud; her wreath of bare branches blooms again, turning into a chaplet of flowering vines that grow to cloak her from head to feet before the song is ended. The old men shrink back into the shadow of the church door, become still, become gray, become stone. No one sees the departure of the winter king. He has been vanquished for another season. The earth is renewed; life begins again.

For every rebirth, there must be a death . . .

Chapter One

SANTIAGO DE COMPOSTELA, 1137

Saint James of Compostela looked down approvingly on the glitter of candles about his cathedral. It was Good Friday, a day of mourning, and the high altar was shrouded in black; but there were green branches strewn about the pavement, to remind men that death was only a passage to a fairer world, and there were candles and incense and the twinkle of gold and silver, jeweled reliquaries and gold-plated altar frontals and statues bright with new paint. All of which Saint James approved, for he was not only a Christian saint but also the Lord of the Far Country. Here at the western end of the world he presided over the land of the dead and the trail of stars where the new-dead souls set out on their journey. He loved lights, did Santiago Matamoros, Saint James the slayer of Moors, and, like most saints and spirits, he appreciated a proper show of respect from the mortals whom he had chosen to honor with his presence. William, duke of Aquitaine, was showing the right degree of respect by coming to die here, and Saint James intended personally to set his feet on the trail of stars when the man's soul departed his body.

That would not be for some hours yet, however, and there were other worshippers to attend to. On this Good Friday of April 1137, the cathedral was crowded as usual with pilgrims of a dozen different nations, from sober English to peacock-gaudy Sicilians. From nearby there were mozarabs, Spanish Christians with Arab blood in their cheeks and Arabic words lisping through their prayers. From farther parts had come Poitevins, Auvergnats, Franks, Burgundians, Germans, and even a dozen dusty-footed Flemings who had walked, so they said, all the way from their northern homeland to celebrate Easter with Saint James. Presently they would march back the long road that led through fertile Galicia, up into the high passes of the Pyrenees where Roland died for Charlemagne, through the sandy wastes of southern Gascony and so on back along the pilgrim road, this time with scallop shells in their hats to show that they had made the long march to Compostela.

Just now, though, the Flemings were too caught up in the glorious display of the cathedral to think of shopping for souvenirs. Like all the other new arrivals of that day—all but one—they shuffled around, admiring the altar frontal of gold with its adornment of antique gems and cameos, praising the delightful lines of the eight Virtues figured as women who supported the base of the tabernacle, asking each other where one might go for the certificate of confession and where for the certificate of communion and who might be the great lord whose retinue was rudely crowding around him, taking up all the good space in front of the high altar?

"Get on with your business," snapped the man of whom a Flemish pilgrim in- nocently made this last inquiry, "and leave my lord to his!"

"And what may that be?"

"Can't you see? He's dying."

Guilhem de Herbert, chamberlain to the duchy of Aquitaine, turned his back on the curious pilgrims and knelt again beside his master. The duke of Aquitaine was dying more rapidly than a man of his size and vigor had any right to do. Only two nights past that fool of an innkeeper had been swearing the fish he served them was fresh-caught from the little stream that flowed through the Wood of the Lances. William of Aquitaine had been hungry enough to take him at his word. His fol- lowers, more prudent, made a sparing meal of bread and beans.

The night had been a demon's holiday of retching and sighing and prayers for grace. There was no physician in the little village. Guilhem and the rest of the duke's men could only watch helplessly through the next day and the next long night as their master turned from a strapping young giant, golden and untouchable as the sun, into this gray-faced man who clutched his belly and sweated like the river itself and whose body seemed to be rotting off his bones while the stars wheeled through the night sky.

With the dawn he surprised them all by demanding his horse. "I vowed to be at the shrine of Saint James by Easter, and so I will be."

"My lord, the ride will kill you," Guilhem had protested, knowing already it was in vain. When had his master forgone anything he'd set his will upon?

The duke of Aquitaine bared his teeth under the sweat-darkened hair that clung to his pallid face. "I'm dying anyway. I may as well do so where I can get the most forgiveness for my sins."

It was, Guilhem later reflected, the most realistic thing he'd ever heard his master say.

Those last eight miles to Compostela had seemed a longer journey than the two months of travel that lay behind them. The duke had refused a litter; when he grew too weak to sit a horse, he'd walked, or rather stumbled, supported by two of his men, stopping every few paces when his death sickness overcame him. There were times, sweating and struggling along that last eight miles of the road, when Guilhem thought from the stench that his lord must already be dead, only that the spirit was too stubborn to leave his body until he had fulfilled his vow to Saint James.

And his earthly duties? He had no right to die like this, thought Guilhem, leaving his followers in a strange land, with only two girl children to inherit his realm. Aquitaine would shatter like the church window at Anjou when Fulk Nerra's demon wife burst through it. Today a great dukedom, glorious as any of the windows of colored glass that spread their jewel-toned radiance over this cathedral; tomorrow a handful of glittering shards to be fought over by a dozen quarrelsome vassals. And God knew what would happen to those two girls—seized and married to the first of William's vassals to get the news of his death, no doubt, as was the common lot of heiresses.

And the duke of Aquitaine was wasting his last moments listening to the Mass, instead of planning some disposition of the estates he'd neglected all his life!

"My lord, you must make your will," Guilhem prompted him.

"Not now. Praying." And the duke rolled his eyes back toward the altar, where the priest was going through the Great Litany of prayers for the church and the pope and the bishops and the deacons and all the holy people of God.

"*Flectamus genua*," the priest commanded, and those of the faithful who had crowded around the high altar to hear the service sank to their knees. Guilhem knelt too. "To purge the world from all errors," he followed the words of the prayer under his breath, "to take away diseases; to keep off famine; to open prisons; to loose chains; to grant to travelers return, to the sick health, to mariners a port of safety."

Amen! "And Lord, keep Aquitaine from falling apart after my lord dies," he added quietly.

"*Flectamus genua.*"

The next prayer also was one in which Guilhem could heartily join. "May the prayers of those that cry to thee in any tribulation reach thy ears . . ." There would be tribulation enough when his lord's warring vassals tore Aquitaine and Poitou into a network of little, troublesome fiefdoms, with no law and no rule but that of the strong man in his castle.

"*Flectamus genua.*"

Mechanically, Guilhem bent his knees and murmured the responses through the rest of the litany, while he brooded over the problem of what could possibly be done to safeguard the land he loved from the time of troubles he saw coming. He was so absorbed that he almost knelt during the obligatory prayer for the Jews, when the congregation was supposed to stand and refuse the priest's command in memory of the Jews' betrayal of Our Lord upon this day.

"*Flectamus genua.*"

At last the prayers were over. Those who had listened to the Mass this far crowded in even closer for the Adoration of the Cross, some of them nearly trampling the sick man's bier. The band of Flemings had grown bored and wandered away to inspect the saints' altars some time previously; now, in a burst of religious enthusiasm, they broke into a spontaneous chorus of the marching song that had carried them all the way down the pilgrim road. The Latin verse was a low melodious background to the solemn ceremony, but when they reached the swinging chorus, their Flemish voices burst out in unrestrained exuberance, drowning out priest, people, and even the perpetual call of the verger who stood by the ark to solicit offerings.

"*Herru Sanctiagu!*"

"*Grot Sanctiagu!*"

"*E ultreja, e sus eja!*" bellowed the pilgrims.

"*Zee larcha de lobra monseñor Samanin,*" droned the verger in what he believed to be French.

"*Popule meus, quid feci tibi?*" chanted the deacons behind the cross in memory of Christ's agonized question. "O my people, what have I done to thee? or in what way have I grieved thee? Because I led thee out of the land of Egypt, thou hast prepared a cross for thy Savior."

"Sanctus Deus."

"O my people, what have I done to thee?"

The duke clutched at Guilhem's gown, and he knelt by his master's side. "My people . . ." whispered the duke.

"Sanctu Deus. Sanctus fortis. Sanctus immortalis, miserere nobis." The chanted response swept over the duke's halting words.

Guilhem held his lord's sweaty hands and tried not to think about the stench of death and illness that even the clouds of incense about them could not disguise. "Yes, my lord. You are ready to make your will?"

"Popule meus, quid feci tibi?"

"For my soul's sake . . ."

He wanted land given to monasteries, endowments for clerks to pray after his death. Guilhem nodded, barely concealing his impatience, and the clerk scribbled frantically. Sometimes the dying man's whisper was drowned out altogether by the chanting of the choir, the scuffling and gossiping of pilgrims, and the loud voices of the guides who showed them around the church. *"Sanctus Deus. Sanctus fortis. Sanctus immortalis . . ."*

"What happened to *him?*" a Lombard demanded.

"He ate the fish."

"Ah! Warned not to do that, we were."

The verger switched to his Italian voice. *"O Micer Lombardo, questa larcha de la lavoree de Micer Sajocome."*

"To my younger daughter Petronilla, my lands in Burgundy."

He didn't hold much in Burgundy, barely a respectable dowry, but at least Petronilla would be safe from heiress hunters. "And to Eleanor . . ."

"Popule meus, quid feci tibi?"

". . . Aquitaine and Poitou . . ."

"No, sirs, first you look at the ark, then you make your offerings at the altar." A self-important guide pushed a party of English pilgrims around the bier where Duke William lay dying.

"Ate the fish, did he?" one of them asked incuriously in passing.

"My lord, you cannot leave your lands to the child! She'll be seized by the first baron to hear of your death!" Guilhem protested involuntarily, as though he hadn't feared just this from the moment when he realized that the duke wasn't going to recover. Petronilla, the frail younger daughter, was Duke William's petted darling, but his respect, even a little fear, went to Eleanor, whom he proudly said to have the brains of a man and the soul of a warrior. All of which might be true enough, but it wasn't enough to enable a girl of fifteen to hold the richest dukedom in the Languedoc.

"My lord?"

But William, tenth duke of Aquitaine, was rapidly passing beyond all worldly cares. His eyes were fixed on the blaze of candles about the altar; his breath came in shallow gasps, and he seemed not to hear his chamberlain's protests or anything else that went on around him.

"Sanctus immortalis, miserere nobis."

Guilhem made the sign of the cross.

The news of Duke William's death was bound to spread outward from Santiago de Compostela like ripples on a pond, borne by returning pilgrims across the length and breadth of Europe. It would be Guilhem's task to see that he outdistanced that news, to bring warning to Bordeaux that the girl in the archbishop's palace was now the richest marriage prize in Europe, to be guarded against every one of her vassals and neighbors until someone chose a man for her. He wondered how many horses he would have to kill.

While the Mass ended and the solemn service of Tenebrae followed, while the pilgrims wandered out of the church in search of their dinners and the verger put up the relics, William Duke of Aquitaine panted out his last breaths, dying with the slow stubbornness that had characterized him in life. Toward the end, with the ritual extinguishing of candles that marked the close of the Good Friday services, he was no longer conscious, and some of the men who knelt around his deathbed were growing restive.

"Shouldn't we go on?" whispered one of them to Guilhem. "Those who are to carry the news? We could start now. If we wait much longer, the light will be gone."

Guilhem shook his head, too tired to explain his reasoning. It was important to make good speed, yes. But it was also important to be with the duke to the last. What if Saint James worked a miracle, and the duke recovered even now? What then would be done to the messengers who'd sped north with false assurances of the duke's death?

And beyond that . . . he had not left his master in twelve years of service, and he would not leave him now to die alone in Galicia.

The last candle was extinguished, leaving the church in darkness, and the clerks who had sung the service closed their books all at once, with a thunderclap like the sound of Saint James himself galloping through the night sky to slay the enemies of Christendom. Duke William started up at the sound, then sank back. His open eyes reflected nothing but the green twilight glimmering in at the open doors.

"Now," said Guilhem, rising to his feet and nodding to the two men he'd picked to accompany him. The rest could stay here to see the duke buried beneath the high altar, then make their way back at their own speed.

At the same time, though Guilhem and the rest of the duke's men could not see him, Saint James himself cupped the duke's soul in his two hands and set the wandering, naked soul on the trail of stars that it must follow to God's feet. The memories of life fell away and became trivial before the shimmering immensity of the empty sky. With his last mortal thought, the duke prayed Saint James to have a care for the daughters he'd left behind in Bordeaux, and the saint answered his prayer in a wind that whipped through the hills of Galicia and up over the passes of the Pyrenees. Peasants startled and crossed themselves, murmuring that such a wind must surely portend the death of some great man, or the beginning of something equally great.

An hour later, before the sun had quite set, Guilhem and his companions were back at the inn from which they had set forth that morning, with the little stream running by the road and the shivering wood of trees sprung from the lances of men who died in battle against the Moors. Behind them the city of Santiago de Compostela lay all gray and lavender in the last light of evening, and in a meadow beside the stream a girl's voice rose clear and pure in a shivering lament of love.

"Que farayu, o que serad de mibi, habibi?
Non te tolgas de mibi!"

What shall I do, what will become of me, beloved?
Don't leave me!

Chapter Two

Eleanor sat in the great hall of the archbishop's palace at Bordeaux. It was only the end of April, but already the promise of spring was trickling through the stone walls, white dust and warm light under the massive ill-fitting doors where a sharp wind whistled through to bite the ankles in winter. She knew this country of the Bordelais in summer and winter, spring and fall, as she knew every part of her father's domains in every season: the gray stone abbey of Fontevrault, the green roads through Poitou, the curiously carved church portal of Notre-Dame-la-Grande of Poitiers with its dancing grotesques, the armory at Blaye and the mint at Melle and the college of Limoges where Saint Martial blessed the sweet singing of the boys in choir. Her life since the age of seven had been the ceaseless round of travel to move the duke's household and hold the duke's court and fight the duke's wars. There were places she might have chosen to spend the spring, but this heavy stone palace in the middle of a noisy harbor town was not one of them; it was what the duke chose for her. A safe place, he said, to leave his treasures—Eleanor and frail Petronilla—while he went south to cleanse his soul at the shrine of Saint James of Compostela.

At the end of the great hall, the archbishop Geoffrey du Lauroux was haranguing her grandmother, his narrow hands darting in and out of the fur-trimmed sleeves of his gown as he gestured and lectured. Archbishop Geoffrey was always upset about something; just now he was complaining about the Rogation Days.

Last week had been a church festival, the ritual blessing of the fields that the grain might grow fresh and clean without the rust-blight that so often poisoned it during a damp spring. The church had ordained prayers and processions and solemn fasts for this festival. The peasants, unfortunately, had other plans.

"I am certain, madame, that there had been a cart preceding us on the road!" Geoffrey du Lauroux complained shrilly.

Dangereuse of Châtellerault inclined her head courteously. "Indeed, my lord archbishop, there have doubtless been a number of carts on the road that passes your manor. The peasants *will* keep using the roads. Annoying of them, no doubt, but what can we do?"

The archbishop seemed unaware of the flicker of amusement in her face, a secretive gleam that Eleanor recognized. Now in her seventies, with her long braids turned to silver and the flesh of her face fallen in to reveal the sharp lines of her bones, Dangereuse of Châtellerault still showed traces of the mischievous beauty that had gotten her in so much trouble with the church in years past. Eleanor looked at her grandmother and saw, for a moment, the laughing black-haired beauty who had ridden away from Châtellerault on the saddlebow of William IX, then duke of Aquitaine. The church had never blessed those two, the duke with his living wife in the abbey of Fontevrault and Dangereuse with her living husband the viscount of Châtellerault. But their children had married with the church's blessing: William's son by Philippa and Dangereuse's sweet Aenor by Châtellerault were no blood kin, even though they'd been raised in the same scandalous household. No priest in Aquitaine was bold enough to forbid that wedding, and very few looked askance at the children of it: Eleanor and Petronilla and their little brother who had died of the fever with Aenor.

"Yes, madame," Geoffrey du Lauroux all but stammered in his zeal and rage, "yes, there have been carts, and there will be carts again, but *this* cart, madame, bore a very particular burden. I think you know to what I refer!"

Eleanor bent over the cope she was embroidering and shook her own long golden-brown braids forward to hide her smile. *Grandmère* knew very well what the archbishop was fulminating about, and she had no intention of admitting her knowledge or of seeing the peasants punished for a little harmless play. Of course they drew the Lady of the Cart about the fields in spring. Who'd want to risk offending the Lady so that she drew her skirt over the fields and left the black trail of horned grain behind her? And who'd be fool enough to tell the priests about it? Most priests, Eleanor thought pityingly, had sense enough to pretend ignorance of customs that were older in the land than any church. But the archbishop was a very virtuous man and most concerned with the dignity of his church—and he had very poor judgment about where and how to uphold that dignity.

Now, as Dangereuse of Châtellerault blandly pretended ignorance of any special rites about the Lady of the Cart, the archbishop branched forth into a mighty fulmination about the pagan ways of these Bordelais. They looked to the moon instead of to the proper saints' days to decide their times of planting, they concealed the host under their tongues at time of Communion and used the consecrated wafers as magical charms, they concluded their bargains at crossroads and spilt wine into the dirt for the demons who bore witness, they went into the forest to conduct rites of unspeakable vileness.

And through it all Dangereuse of Châtellerault sat straight-backed, listening and nodding and murmuring little words that could have signified assent or shock or utter boredom.

Eleanor laid down a line of gold thread and couched it with tiny, almost invisible stitches. The slanting lines of the stitches made a herringbone pattern on the gold couching of the panel. Ten more lines, and she could begin embroidering the figures: the coronation of the Virgin, with Mary seated beside Christ as His heavenly bride. The crowns would be made of seed pearls, to match the pearls decorating the Jesse Tree on the lower panels of the cope. She had worked the tree last year, when she was fourteen and impatient, and the stitches were uneven.

Eight more lines of couching to go, and the gold thread blurred before her eyes. She laid aside the unfinished panel and stretched her arms up over her head, hoping to alleviate the cramping ache in her back. The small, annoying pain didn't go away; it only shifted position, clutching her just under the broad girdle of silver-gilt brocade that held in the fullness of her gown. She leaned forward, elbows on the table, and trailed one finger through a sticky puddle of spilt wine that should have been scrubbed away after the morning meal. If she had charge of this household, no servants would get away with such careless ways.

A fly buzzed hopefully around the moving finger; when Eleanor's hand slowed and stopped, he lit in the middle of the face she had drawn in the sticky lees. Two eyes, a curved line for the nose, another squiggle for the mouth, a long swoop of braided hair. It could be anyone or no on one, but as the spring sun danced through the windows and slanted across the table, the random splashes of wine winked in the light and for a moment a pert young woman smiled up from the puddle. Eleanor's hand lifted and came down flat, obliterating the fly (and, incidentally, the picture that had accidentally formed in the drying wine). *So,* Emma of Limoges was out of the game, anyway, another man snatched her up while the duke was thinking about his courtship. No heirs for Papa out of Limoges, not this time, too bad, too bad. For a breathless week everybody thought Papa was going to make war over the insult, but ever since the finger of God felled him through that preaching monk of Clairvaux he'd had no spirit for war; instead of calling for trumpets and destriers, he'd gone south to shrive himself in the drone of psalms. Easter at the holy altar of Santiago de Compostela—that should set a man's soul aright. But when he came back all fresh and clean he'd be looking around for another wife, because at thirty-eight it was time for a man to forget Eleanor's long-dead mother and get himself a son to rule Aquitaine after him.

Eleanor scrubbed the last of the wine off the table with the trailing edge of her long sleeve, careless of the stain, and dropped her needlework on the bench. Her head ached. She wanted to be out of this long chilly hall where the spring sun had to fight its way in past tall guards of stone and wood. She wanted to lie down, to cry, to dance, to sing. She wanted some wine for herself, a warming drink to spread into her belly and soothe away this ache that came and went.

A clerk trotted into the hall and interrupted the archbishop's oration, speaking deferentially, head bent. Eleanor could catch only a few phrases. Geoffrey du Lauroux looked irritated. But then, he usually looked like that.

"William of Lezay? Talmont? What does he want now?"

The clerk buzzed and murmured around the subject, insistent as the flies circling the table above Eleanor's head. William of Lezay had a widowed mother who had retired to the convent of Saint-Medard, within the diocese of Bordeaux. Now, to settle an argument about a mill, Lezay wished to gift some lands to the church of Saint-Jean-d'Orbetiers in his home district. The lands in question came from his mother's dowry, and her consent was required. She objected. Lezay wished to lay the matter before the archbishop for his decision. The nuns of Saint Medard were not likely to protest the archbishop's ruling, and in gratitude for the expected support, Lezay offered to the archbishopric of Bordeaux the metairies of his villages in the

Gâtine of Poitou, with hunting and hawking rights through the adjoining forest . . . .

"Hawking rights?" The archbishop's pinched mouth relaxed slightly, and his eyes brightened. "I hear Lezay has some Iceland gyrfalcons. White ones. If he's willing to give up one of those in the bargain . . ."

"With respect, my lord archbishop." The big blond man had entered behind the clerk, moving on soft cat feet so gently that no one paid heed to him until he knelt before the archbishop. "The gyrfalcons are not mine; I house them for Duke William. They are not mine to give . . . at present."

"At present," Geoffrey du Lauroux repeated. He played with his rings, heavy gold bands that hung loose on his long, bony fingers. He twirled the one on his forefinger and sparks of sunfire dazzled within the rounded surface of a ruby. "Equivocations, Lezay?"

"Arrangements might be made. Once the duke returns from his pilgrimage, the matter could be discussed. He does not care overmuch for hawking, I think; he has never asked to see the gyrfalcons." Lezay lifted his head and looked past the archbishop, down the long shadowed hall. His eyes met Eleanor's. She caught her breath and looked away. He looked bold and demanding, like Papa when he'd set out to court Emma of Limoges. *I'm too young.* But she wasn't, not now; the cramp in her belly was proof of that. *Grandmère* had told her more than two years ago what to expect; it seemed she'd been waiting forever for this.

She felt dizzy, almost too dizzy to stand. *"Grandmère . . ."*

Dangereuse was by her side. The gaily painted roof beams with their images of sun and moon and stars seemed to tilt and sway above her. A dry hand on her forehead. "Child, you're not sick?"

Eleanor smiled through stiff lips. "I think . . . only with the sickness that comes to all women. I should like to retire to my chamber now, *Grandmère.*"

Away from the hall and the buzzing flies and the dry buzzing irritation of Geoffrey du Lauroux with his greed and his perpetual fear that somebody was doing something he oughtn't behind his back, away from the big blond man called Lezay who looked at her as a hungry man looks at a feast. Eleanor lay back in the big carved bed she shared at night with Dangereuse and Petronilla, One of her ladies combed out her tight braids until the honey-brown hair was spread like silk over the pillow, rustling and glinting with captured sunshine; another brewed a cup of hot spiced wine and brought it to her. Eleanor sipped slowly at the steaming cup of *vin cuit,* tasting the herbal tang of galingale and rosemary for her cramps, mint to clear her head, honey to sweeten the mixture. A folded pad of linen beneath her thighs caught the first rush of bright blood.

"It's like preparing her for her wedding night," whispered one of the ladies.

"And we'll be doing that soon enough," whispered another. "She'll make a good alliance for the duke. Where does he most want support, do you think?"

"Did you see the way the lord of Talmont looked at our little lady?"

"He'd not waste her on one of his own castellans. Toulouse, maybe . . . he'd be happy to win back Toulouse without a war."

"And then she wouldn't have to leave the Languedoc. Poor child . . . what if he wants to make an alliance with the Hohenstaufens? She might be better off at Talmont."

"She'll have to go where she's told, like any other woman."

Eleanor raised herself on one elbow. The pampering and the attention were agreeable, but this chatter irritated her. "Nothing will be said or done in this matter without the word of my father the duke," she said clearly. "Now leave me. I wish to rest."

"Yes," Dangereuse seconded her, "out, all of you. You too, Petronilla! It's a lucky thing, becoming a woman on May eve. We'll brew the posset you know of for her tonight. She must rest until then."

"What is that?" Intolerable that Petronilla, who was still a child, should know what she didn't. But the wine she'd already drunk was having its effect. Eleanor slipped into sleep without the energy to nag her grandmother for an answer she wouldn't have gotten anyway. Dangereuse never answered questions she found inconvenient.

The garden that Master Alluis of Caen had designed for the archbishop's pleasure was set out like a series of boxes, each wall and each high locked gate giving onto a smaller and sweeter world than the one outside. In this, Master Alluis had explained, it was a copy of the mysteries of faith, which was hard to those who believed not but became sweeter the closer one penetrated to the true light of Our Lord. The outer garden held useful herbs and garden plants: Mary-gold against pestilence and painful stings, sage to cleanse the body of venom and to whiten the teeth, hyssop for bruises and catarrhs and to remove ill humors from any part of the body, tall elecampane staked against the garden walls until its roots could be dug up and dried in the summer sun for sweets and cordials. Dangereuse and the midwife Aielle knew the uses of all these good herbs and had taught them to Petronilla, who ran free with them while Eleanor followed her father's court to learn justice and letters.

Within this circle was a second walled garden where flowers, some useful and some merely beautiful, made a carpet of blue and white and red: periwinkle, white violets for Our Lady, poppies, and daisies. The pasqueflowers had bloomed and withered early in April, but the yellow flowers of the Lenten lilies still made a brave show. Here, beside the single pear tree in the center (symbolizing, with neat medieval economy, both the Tree of Life and the Holy Rood), a bower of woven twigs gave the ladies a place where they could sit and enjoy the luxuries of shade and cool water and water-growing plants in the warm southern spring of Bordeaux.

The woven arch gave shade but no real privacy. Tired from the wine and the afternoon's heavy sleep and the bustle about her first woman's bleeding, Eleanor could sit in the freckled shadows of woven twigs and listen to the castellan of Talmont with perfect propriety. Her ladies were gathered about Petronilla and Dangereuse at the far end of the pleasaunce, stitching fine girdles of gold thread and chattering about the marriage alliance the duke would surely make for his oldest daughter, now that she had at last become a woman. Closer still, on the lily-starred dark green grass, her father's Gascon troubadour plucked at his lute and sang love songs in a low voice, stopping and repeating himself and trying out different rhymes until he found a sequence that pleased him. When he was especially pleased with his rhyming, his voice rose for the benefit of Eleanor and William of Lezay, who were occupied with other matters than poetry.

"Talmont's a small holding, but a good one, and in a strategic place," Lezay informed Eleanor unnecessarily. She knew exactly where Talmont lay on the coast of Poitou; her father had held the ducal court there in the autumn of 1133, when she was eleven. Doubtless Lezay did not remember that she had been in the duke's retinue; he did not seem the sort of man to pay much attention to children. "Your father does well to have a man of proven loyalty there."

Eleanor's lap was full of the yellow Lenten lilies, plucked for her and showered upon her skirts as an offering from Lezay, like the gold that rained upon Danaë in her tower. The dried flowers would make a golden dye to brighten her hair; until they wilted, they could as well become a chain or a chaplet. She split one juicy green stem with her thumbnail and inserted another stem through the slit.

"I think my father would not waste a great alliance upon Talmont," she said, her eyes fixed on the golden flowers and their dangling stems. "By my faith and Saint Radegonde, *I* would not do so!"

"Your father might wish his daughter's happiness," said William of Lezay.

His voice was soft as the late afternoon breeze; above it rose the troubadour Cercle-le-Monde's joyous verse.

> *"Ab lo temps qes fai refreschar*
> *lo segle e'ls pratz reverdezir,*
> *vueil un novel chant comenzar*
> *d'un amor cui am e dezir."*

"A song of love is my desire," William of Lezay repeated softly, half singing, "a song for her whom I desire."

Eleanor threaded three more golden lilies through the stems of the previous ones and let the chain dangle from her upraised hands.

"When your father the duke returns from Compostela, he will look for a new young wife," William of Talmont suggested. "Your position in his household will not be so pleasant then. Even a small holding might be preferable."

"My father's last search for a wife ended ill," Eleanor remarked. She looped the green and gold flower chain about her wrist. "When his household changes, then will be time enough to discuss these matters."

William seized the dangling end of the flower chain and wrapped it about his own arm. Their hands lay side by side for a moment; Eleanor studied the dusting of golden hairs on his broad knuckles as though she were learning the map of a foreign country.

> "Alas, so far is she from me,
> I dare not reach so high,
> Nor can she hear my words,
> Nor pities she my sigh."

William ignored Cercle-le-Monde's song. "When the duke of Aquitaine has a son to inherit after him," he suggested, "you may look more favorably upon a little castle by the sea. There is a secret garden there, lady, safe from the salt spray, where roses grow, and where I would see a golden lily as well. And there are six white gyrfalcons of Iceland, waiting for a lady young and sprightly who will ride with a hawk on her wrist to take game in the forests of Talmont."

"I hear that the walled gardens have already a lady to decorate them," said Eleanor. She withdrew her hand with a quick decisive movement that broke the chain of flowers and left the greater part of them dangling over William of Talmont's muscular arm. "And the gyrfalcons are my father's in any case."

"A mistress is not a wife," William replied. "Many things can change in a short space. Remember this, lady: I speak now, before I know what dowry your father may settle on you after his sons are born."

"Sons to a wife as yet unknown!" Eleanor laughed and took the dangling flowers. "Allow me to save these, my lord of Talmont; you can have no use for them."

"Nor you," said William of Talmont. "Why do you want to capture the sunshine, you who have honey in your hair? There is nothing about you that I would change."

His eyes were too intense, too hungry. Hunger for her—or for Aquitaine? He spoke as though her father's remarriage were a settled thing. Maybe he meant to gamble that it would never happen, or that no sons would come of it.

"I think I hear my grandmother calling," Eleanor said.

It's great good fortune, to become a woman on May eve," Dangereuse said. "You must honor the Lady and show your gratitude for this sign of her favor."

A plain wooden cup was on the bench beside her, half full of the same sweet spiced wine that Eleanor had drunk earlier. Petronilla and Eleanor's ladies were clustered about the archway that led to the outer garden, framed by the green garden hedges and the golden walls of the Ombrière Palace, within sight but not in hearing. William of Talmont had been banished so courteously that Eleanor doubted he understood, even now, that he had been sent away; he probably thought that he had grown tired of courting a half-grown girl who might inherit no particular fortune.

The afternoon sun was sinking into the western sea, gilding the high church towers and spires of the city and casting long shadows across the pleasaunce; a cool breeze whispered through the leaves of the pear tree and ruffled the white blossoms like foam upon the sea.

"Is this something the archbishop would approve?" Eleanor asked.

Dangereuse's iron-gray glance quelled her impulse to tease. "It is a matter for women, between women."

Eleanor glanced involuntarily at Cercle-le-Monde, who was still leaning against the pear tree, drawing random notes from his vielle like the splashing of water droplets into a secret fountain.

"Well . . . what is a mystery without music?" said Dangereuse with a smile. She reached into her sleeve and drew out a tiny box, carved of the horn of the narwhal, with no hinge or opening that Eleanor could see. Under Dangereuse's fingers, the side of the box slid open. She shook out a handful of blackened, horn-shaped grains.

"*Seigle ivre*," Eleanor exclaimed and crossed herself. Mad rye, horned rye, crazy grain—this was the blight the Lady of the Cart was supposed to avert. But these grains were dry, saved from some other season of blackened rye.

Dangereuse gave her a thin-lipped smile. "It is not either good or bad, except in how you use it. When the Lady draws her robe across the fields and turns all the rye black, it poisons the peasants who must bake bread from it, be the crop good or bad. But a few grains at the right time can help a woman when her time comes. If your father had not insisted on dragging you all over the country with him, to witness his charters and hear his courts, you might have stayed at home in Poitiers with Petronilla and me, and learned something you could use. You'll never hold the right of justice over your vassals, but you will be called upon to help your women on the birthing stool. Petronilla is two years younger than you, but she already knows the dose of the horned grain that will strengthen a woman in her time and bring forth a child without bleeding."

"Is it to stop my bleeding, then?" asked Eleanor in a low voice.

Dangereuse shook her head. "No. That is a gift from the Lady, who made you a woman. We will not seek to stop that before its time. There are other uses for the Lady's gifts. She has favored you by bringing your first woman's blood on this evening. Now you will honor her by seeing with her eyes." As she spoke, she ground the black horn-shaped grains into powder and spilled the powder into the cup of wine.

Eleanor touched the powder that remained and raised the finger toward the tip of her tongue. A bitter, acrid taste assaulted her.

"The wine masks the worst of the taste," Dangereuse said, "and the taste is only the beginning."

"The beginning of what?"

Dangereuse shook her head. "It is different for each of us—yes, I was blessed like you, and I had the drink from a wisewoman of Châtellerault. Take it and learn what you must know."

Eleanor hesitated, turning the cup between her palms. The polished wood felt smooth and heavy and strong, as though she held the trunk of a tree whose roots went through the earth and whose branches raised up into the sky. She sniffed the bitter potion and looked over the rim of the bowl at the flowering pear tree before the bower, where white blossoms like stars were sprinkled against the evening sky.

"Look into the cup," said Dangereuse.

Crushed herbs floated on the surface of the dark, spicy, bittersweet wine; the reflections of white flowers mingled with them. Among herbs and seeds and flowers Eleanor saw nothing but her own face, floating in darkness as if crowned by flowers and pale images of flowers.

"That is what I saw this afternoon," said Dangereuse. "What does the crown mean?"

Eleanor shook her head.

"Drink and learn."

The wine was bitter and sweet, sharp and aromatic. It tasted of old secrets and new mysteries, rich with the grapes of the south, the dried herbs of Dangereuse's still-room, and the spices of distant Constantinople. It slid down her throat in one long, thirsty swallow. Eleanor's head spun; she looked down and stared at her clasped hands, willing herself not to be sick. The world danced around her; she shut her eyes to keep it out. But she could not keep out the knowledge of the dance. Ocean encircled the world, and the sphere of heaven encircled all, and the bright stars beyond took hands with the angels and danced above her head, and in the other half of the circle, to keep the balance, demons capered. At the top of the circle, directly under heaven, the Blessed Virgin sat with her crown of the moon and her cloak of the starry sky, exactly as she was drawn on the panel of the cope that Eleanor was embroidering; but she could not see the matching panel of the spouse, only a blaze of celestial light.

I am not worthy, she thought. And the exterior world was safer than these interior illuminations. She dared to open her eyes and raise her head. The same light that had dazzled her interior vision was here too, real and present in the world and as brilliant as if the sun had chosen to set here in the center of the archbishop's pleasure garden. The long evening light gilded every leaf of every flower and herb in the pleasaunce. The long stems of grass were gold at the center; the Lenten lilies grew fresh and new as if they had never been trodden upon or bruised or plucked. A wind sighed through the garden, and every branch, every leaf trembled with a meaning she could not quite read.

The pear tree in the center of the pleasaunce was covered with white flowers, white clouds, a cloud of white birds. The birds all rose at once from the tree with a great beating and whirring of wings that lifted Eleanor to soar in their midst, white wings beating in her blood, sun warm on her upturned face. The sky swam blue around her, the garden was green below. "Blue and green are the colors of the living world," murmured a voice in her ear.

It was Cercle-le-Monde, her father's troubadour. Eleanor smiled happily at him. She wanted to tell him that she knew his secret now, that he could fly, that was how he circled the earth so many times that he finally took Cercle-le-Monde for his name. But he went on talking, and his words were terribly important, she did not know why, but she knew that she must listen with all her might. "Listen with your heart," Cercle-le-Monde told her. "The heart remembers. In the Breton tongue we call these beads *patteraenu*, blessed. They are found sometimes within circles of standing stones. They must be taken at the dark of the moon by one holding herb-of-the-cross in his right hand, else the stones will fall and crush him. This holds the protection of the stones and those who raised them, the strength of the earth and the freedom of the sky. Keep this to guard you, my queen."

She closed her hand over something hard and cool, opened it to see a blue-green stone, irregular curves polished by time, with a hole through the center to take a thin silver chain. She put the chain over her head, and the stone bead fell down cool and hard between her breasts, and the white doves cooed approvingly about them.

The sky was above her head again, the ground firm beneath her feet. But the clearing where they stood was not the neatly trimmed and tended pleasaunce of the archbishop's garden in Bordeaux. Shaggy trees half choked with climbing vines encircled this clearing, and some of the vines were bare and some were covered with white flowers and some were heavy with ripe red berries and some were flaming with the fires of autumn, all at the one time and in the one place and springing from the one root. Deep in the forest behind the trees there moved strange shapes half glimpsed behind leaves and branches, a deer, a stag, a white hind, a man crowned with horns. Eleanor trembled and put out her hand to Cercle-le-Monde, desiring the touch of human flesh, but he bowed and slipped aside as softly as a wisp of cloud blowing across the heavens.

"The touch of the queen is not for me." He swept off his soft velvet cap and bowed, proud and humble at the same time. "But for the one who comes at the appointed time."

"Three times you have named me queen," Eleanor cried out. "Why do you do so?" The white doves rose into the sky around her, whirring and clucking with disapproval, and scattered before the plunge of a hawk. It came to rest on the stone ledge of the well in the center of the clearing, a white Iceland gyrfalcon, hard golden eyes glaring at her. A moment before there had been no well, only the trees wrapped in their green and burning vines. Now a spring of clear water rose and overflowed the stones.

"What is this place?" she demanded.

"This? This is the heart of the oldest forest," said Cercle-le-Monde, "and it is to be found wherever you seek it."

Eleanor's neat braids had come loose in the flight, and the tangled hair fell across her shoulders and clung damp to her forehead and neck. Only the green stone on its silver chain was cool between her breasts. She pushed the hair from her face. "I am weary of your riddles. I will go back now. Where is the path?"

Cercle-le-Monde strummed the vielle that he had not held in his two hands a moment earlier, and a rainbow of dancing notes glittered in the air between them. "So each entered the forest at a point that he, himself, had chosen," he sang from the geste of the Holy Grail, "where it was darkest and there was no path."

"I weary of riddles," Eleanor repeated. "I'll make my own path, since you'll not show me the way!"

She grasped a flowering vine to break it out of her way, but it coiled about her arm and hissed at her with its flickering tongue, two red eyes as bright as berries in a green head, dry sliver of scales in the green shape wound spiralwise about her wrist.

"Do not be afraid," said Cercle-le-Monde. In his hands the serpent became once again a flowering length of vine. Gently he reached toward the supporting branch, and the vine grasped the branch and lay still again, a wreath of white flowers entwined about the living wood. "It will wither now that you have broken it," he said, gently reproving.

"I am sorry for that."

"No need for sorrow. We all begin dying in the moment of birth. Pity would be to waste what has begun as so fair a flower." With quick, deft fingers he took the broken vine again from its branch and plaited it into a chaplet of white flowers. "Will you wear the crown, my queen? Will you taste the fruit and drink from the fountain? Then you may always find your way here again at need."

The berries were full and ripe with the heat of summer in them. They looked like the wild raspberries that she and Petronilla picked every summer in the woods about Poitiers. Cercle-le-Monde filled Eleanor's cupped hands with the fruit and she ate greedily. There could never be enough of so sweet a fruit. And yet, when her hands were empty, she craved no more. She approached the overflowing well and bowed before the white gyrfalcon, plunged her hands into water as cold as winter and brought them to her face. The water cooled her burning forehead and slaked a thirst she had not been conscious of. And when she looked up, well and forest, falcon and vines were gone as though they had never been.

There was only the gay flowering border and the grass of the bishop's pleasaunce, the white pear tree in the center and Cercle-le-Monde leaning at its base, strumming his vielle and singing a May eve song. At the far end of the pleasaunce, Petronilla and Eleanor's ladies sat plaiting chains of flowers and gossiping idly. Above them, three stars and the tip of a crescent moon showed in the clear evening sky. Behind the high hedge that bordered the pleasaunce, the setting sun still glowed like a fire that is not quite out.

The casual strumming changed to a wild dance tune, and suddenly Eleanor remembered that it was the eve of May, it was spring, and she was young and her feet wanted to follow the twisting, turning, spiraling music wherever it led. She could see her ladies startling up as if from a dream; the music was calling to them too.

"A l'entrada del tens clar," sang Cercle-le-Monde, and Eleanor's ladies came running around her. They joined hands and began the circle of the dance while Cercle-le-Monde coaxed runs and jangles and trills of music out of his battered vielle and lifted up his clear tenor voice to lead the May eve song.

"A l'entrada del tens clar."

"Ey-ye-a," sang Radegonde of Maillezais in her cracked voice.

"Per joia recomencar."

"Ey-ya-a," Petronilla joined in with a little girl's voice, thin and reedy but sweet withal.

"E per jelos irritar."

"Ey-ye-a," all sang together on a rising note that carried them into the last two lines with Cercle-le-Monde's true notes leading the way, like hounds on a scent: *"Vol la regina mostrar / Qui es si amoroza."*

Someone caught Eleanor's hand, and instead of standing in the center of the dancing circle, she was part of it, swaying and singing around and about the flowering tree and feeling the new spring entering into her blood, joy and summer and long lazy warm days ahead.

"A la vi', a la via, jelos!" she sang with the rest of them, while Cercle-le-Monde made a dancing road with his music and the flowering pear tree bent down its branches to join in the dance and Dangereuse looked on from her seat on the marble bench at the far end of the pleasaunce. *"Laissaz nos, laissaz nos / ballar entre nos, entre nos!"*

There was some disturbance over at the arched gate of close-clipped shrubs that led back to the archbishop's palace. Sunset glowed about the walls of the Ombrière palace, a red halo like the flames of a city given over to sack and flames, and in that fiery afterglow a man came forward shouting words that Eleanor could not understand, words that made no sense whatever.

Her ladies let go their hands, the dancing ring dissolved into clusters of girls and women standing uncertainly on the chill damp grass, and the man came forward to kneel before Eleanor.

One man, in riding clothes, so covered with dust that for a moment she did not know him. No. Yes. Guilhem de Herbert. The chamberlain of Aquitaine. Papa was back already, then! But it was too soon—he'd meant to be in Compostela for Easter, just three weeks ago. Had he turned back, then? Surely he had not come all the way from Galicia in three short weeks?

Something soft and yielding, with thorns beneath the softness, pressed into her empty hands. Eleanor looked down, confused. It was the chaplet of her dream, woven of a thorny vine covered with white flowers and green and burning leaves, and

Cercle-le-Monde had given it to her—or had he? He was standing beside the pear tree now, all music stopped, looking alert and respectful as befitted a mere troubadour in the presence of his lord's highest official.

"My lady." Guilhem inclined his head to Dangereuse where she sat like stone on her marble bench, then at last turned toward Eleanor, but without quite looking at her. He was desperately tired; Eleanor could see the lines of deep fatigue under the dust on his face. It was unlike Papa to press his men so hard. An emergency? War?

"My lady duchess."

What was he talking about? There was no one of that rank here.

"My apologies for interrupting you at your recreation, but I bear news that will not wait."

She could not quite hear what he was saying. She did not want to hear it. Someone was screaming in the garden, a thin high wailing like that of a rabbit in a snare. Petronilla. "Someone should teach that child some manners," Eleanor said crossly, but no sound came out of her own mouth. Guilhem de Herbert was going on now, something about bad fish, and a burial of somebody at the shrine of Compostela, and the forgiveness of sins—how confusing! When Papa came back he would explain it all.

No. Papa was not coming back. And something was hurting her hand. Eleanor looked down and saw that she had closed her fingers about the thorny vine; the chaplet was crushed inside her palm. Very slowly, with infinite care, she smoothed out the wreath of green and burning leaves and the bruised white flowers that glowed like stars in the night sky. She raised the chaplet and placed it on her head. It felt very heavy. As heavy as a crown.

Chapter Three

Eleanor lay open-eyed in the darkness off and on all night, listening to the snuffles and rustlings and dreaming murmurs of the ladies who slept around her in this great chamber. Within the great curtained bed she held Petronilla, who wept her way into sleep with her whole body, with a child's self-absorbed and total grief, alternately clutching at Eleanor and burying her tear-swollen face in Dangereuse's bony shoulder. "Who will take care of me now?" she cried. "Who will look after me?"

Dangereuse had only cold truths to offer her, hard and sharp as honesty, as a knife blade. All men die. I wept so for your grandfather; all griefs ease with time. You're not a great heiress, your father's lands in Burgundy will dower you well enough for a good marriage but not enough to make you a prize worth the risk of war. There's time, you're young yet, we will find a good husband to look after you.

She did not make this last soothing promise to Eleanor, lying cold and still within her own self-contained grief. She could not. Eleanor's husband would be marrying Aquitaine and Poitou, Saintonge and the Bordelais and the Auvergne, a land of river valleys and fertile plains, the salt marshes of Gascony and the high mountain passes to the Pyrenees. That was a prize worth fighting for, and unless the right man was chosen to succeed Duke William as Eleanor's husband, there would be war, and Eleanor the prize of battle; Eleanor and Poitou and Aquitaine and all this land of well-watered valleys and high mountain passes, the harbor city of Bordeaux and the trade fair of Poitiers and the tolls on the pilgrim routes.

For Eleanor there was no time, no time at all. She must be married and safe before the news of Duke William's death spread through the land, before any vassal with a mesnie of knights to follow him took it into his head to seize the richest marriage prize of this generation.

Through the long night, Eleanor drifted in and out of uneasy sleep, coming to this knowledge through a crazy tumble of waking dreams and sleeping visions. In her dreams, armies rose from mountains of sand, a parade of skeletons in armor marched across the trail of stars in the night sky, the crescent moon bent down among the bare branches of winter trees to whisper a soothing promise that, once awake again, she could not remember.

Elsewhere in the palace, candles burnt the night through, and a bleary-eyed clerk smeared the ink on the letters that Geoffrey du Lauroux dictated: letters he meant to send to all his vassals, laymen and clerics, calling them to march with their men to Bordeaux, to guard this new young duchess until a safe marriage could be made for her. The archbishop's hounds, sleeping all in a tangle together with the dog boy and two pages before the dying fire in the great hall, snapped and snarled in their sleep at imaginary prey. The archbishop's hooded hawks, blind in the darkness of the mews, ruffled their feathers and dreamed of soaring in the empty blue of the seven spheres. The archbishop's guests dreamed or snored or tossed in their beds, including William of Lezay, castellan of Talmont, whose dreams might or might not be prophetic. He dreamed of one of the white gyrfalcons from Iceland stooping to take its quarry by the neck, talons digging deep into tender flesh, and then he dreamed of the church of Notre-Dame-la-Grande of Poitiers, of incense and hymns and a man and a woman sitting under the golden circlets that crowned them duke and duchess of the realm.

The darkness of the sky just before sunrise differed from the darkness of midnight as a muddy river differs from an inkwell. At one awakening, Eleanor had lain under a night soft and solid as a cloak of black fur, sliced by the hard, crystalline edges of moonlight; at the next, she woke to cloudy confusion and the scent of dew, with no clarity anywhere, but with the sense in the air of mists rising and light coming closer. In that obscurity she found her way from the great sleeping chamber, to the stairs, to the hall where the last embers of the evening fire burned, to a little private door, to the series of gates and enclosed gardens ending in the pleasaunce where Dangereuse had brewed the potion and the leaves on the trees had trembled with light.

Soon the sun would rise over this city of Bordeaux, and it would be the first morning of May. Which was not a festival of the church.

Eleanor paced over the wet grass. The little flowers, white violets and blue periwinkle, were scattered like stars in the darkness that gradually took on form and color: from black to gray to deep rich green in which the shadow of each blade thrust forward like a spear before the rising sun. She walked through narrow paths planted with sweet herbs, and the scent of their crushed leaves rose around her: mint and lavender, rosemary and thyme.

There was nothing in those scents as bitter as the aftertaste of the wine that Dangereuse had given her to drink, and this morning's light revealed none of the certainty that Eleanor had felt, standing in the light of that other wood.

But there was music now, as there had been before. Two birds were joined by a third, and then a whole chorus twittered about her head. And when the birds tired, a single dancing line of melody still echoed across the herbage.

"Cercle-le-Monde, you should not—" Eleanor began, reproving, and then stopped still. The man sitting on the marble bench was taller and broader of shoulder than her father's Gascon troubadour, and the head he bent over the vielle showed golden lights in the rising mists of morning.

"If I did not fear to wake the good archbishop and all his prudent counselors," said William of Lezay very softly, "I would sing for you."

"I have jongleurs and troubadours enough, if I desire them," Eleanor told him. No one could observe them here. But a palace full of sleeping men could be roused by her call. There could be no danger to her in this meeting, chance or not, and no harm in talking to the man.

"Ah," said William of Lezay, "but your jongleurs know only the common songs that they share—is it not so? I would make a new song for my new lady—" He swept his hands across the strings, chanting softly under his breath, "*Quant l'aura doussa s'amarzis . . .*"

"You should know better," Eleanor told him, "than to steal a song from my own man, if you would claim to make your own. Cercle-le-Monde made that song for the lady of Blaye."

"I said I *would* make a new song," William defended himself, laughing softly under his breath, "not that I could do so. I would serve you in any way, my lady."

"By which, I take it, you mean that you cannot do so at all."

"I can at least offer you a dry place to sit," William said, moving aside to make a space for her on the bench. "Your shoes are wet with the dew."

And her feet were cold. Eleanor took the offered seat. Casually, as though it were no more than the continuation of his courtesy, William extended one arm and let his cloak fall about her shoulders.

A bird sang somewhere in the garden. In the brightening light, the pear tree appeared as a white cloud or a crystal shot through with sun.

With one arm about her shoulders, William of Lezay could not play his borrowed vielle. But he hummed the words of Cercle-le-Monde's song under his breath, and he was so close that Eleanor could feel the vibration in his chest.

"*Et ieu de sai sospir e chan,*" he half whispered. "And here I sigh and sing of love."

Very subtly, his arm tightened about Eleanor. She slipped away and left him alone in his broad fur-trimmed cloak. "You are bold, castellan of Talmont, and you have a good singing voice—and a good memory for other men's songs. You should do well as a jongleur, should you ever desire to find a new trade to follow."

"And would my lady of Aquitaine recommend that I take up that career?" His voice was mild enough, but there was a flash in his eyes that made Eleanor glad, for once, of her large, tiresome retinue of waiting women and ladies and clerks and men-at-arms and knights, all within call on the other side of the palace wall. "I had another one in mind, I must tell you."

"You thought to be duke of Aquitaine through me?"

"Any man may aspire," he said. "Does the prospect so displease you?"

He was tall and fair-haired, young and strong, and the skin at the neck of her gown remembered the brushing touch of his broad thumb, so casual it could hardly be called an embrace. Eleanor shook her head. "There are other considerations. . . ."

William threw back his head and laughed, but soundlessly, careful not to alarm those sleeping in the palace. "*Considerations,*" he mocked her, "are for old men and clerks. I had thought there was living blood beneath that pale skin of yours."

She might be married to a Hohenstaufen in Germany, or a Norman or an Angevin:

some foreigner. William of Lezay was only the castellan of a small seaholding, but he spoke with the accents of the south, and he sang like a southerner, with the sun of the Bordelais in his voice and in his hair.

"Come with me," he urged her now. "Or only say the words. Say that you take me as your betrothed, and I'll fight them all to keep you, pretty Eleanor. I will make songs for you . . . or buy them!" he finished on an indrawn breath and a laugh that invited her to enjoy his own dishonesty with him.

She was half tempted. God knew what marriage the old men in the archbishop's palace would make for her!

"Do you really think that the castellan of Talmont could hold Aquitaine?" she asked him.

William flushed. "A man can rise as chances come his way. I've not been lucky."

"But to get the heiress to Aquitaine and Poitou, before the rest of the world even knows of her father's"—Eleanor stopped and swallowed hard on the next word—"death, that would be a fine piece of luck, and a good morning's work, wouldn't it?"

"Need you reduce everything to the political?" He was on his feet now, and forgetting to keep his voice down. Eleanor would not step back. Show fear, her father had told her when at the age of seven she rode before him to the hunt, and the dogs will have you down. They're bred to that kind of fierceness, as are my knights. As are my knights.

"Is it beyond your comprehension," William demanded, "that a man might see you and desire you? You seemed to understand me well enough yesterday."

There was too much hunger in his eyes. "Many things have changed since last night," she said at last.

"You mean that I am no longer good enough for you!"

He took her in his arms then, and she did not fight him but stood passive while his mouth explored her cool, pale face and the white skin of her neck. Only when he slipped his hand under the loose neckline of her gown, his fingers caught in something that pulled hard against her neck, choking and hurting her, and she broke out of her trance and pushed him away. It was the silver chain that held the stone bead Cercle-le-Monde had given her; the bead swung free now, blue-green and cool as the sky. William eyes were blue too, but they burned.

"Come willing or not," he said, "but you'll come with me now, or—"

Eleanor ran without thinking, stupidly, putting the pear tree and the wicker

arbor between them instead of calling for help or running back into the archbishop's palace. She blundered into a hedge—no, only a few loose bushes whose
stems broke and scratched her face and hands. Trees blocked her way; she dodged
among them and ran on, pushing aside leaves and branches with her hands. Something with the shape of a man, but with horns branching from its head, moved in
the shadows behind her. A bodkin stabbed in her side and the breath came raw to
aching lungs. She ran on until a thorny vine wrapped itself around her gown, holding her from feet to knees, knees to waist with a thousand prickling dagger points
that were covered by green leaves and white flowers and burning leaves all on the
same vine and in the same time.

So may you always find this place in need: Cercle-le-Monde's promise.

The flowering vine slithered to encircle her feet, a coil of green loops ending in
two eyes bright as wild red berries. Eleanor stepped over, carefully, and entered the
wild garden where all things bloomed and made new leaves and burned in autumn
at the one time.

There had been a fountain before, or a well. Now she saw neither, but on the far
side of the clearing the land fell away sharply, and she heard the murmur of rushing
waters.

She crossed grass as dark as midnight, soft as a cloak of fur, and looked down
the hillside to the green waters of the Garonne. In the center of the river was a tiny
island, a pointed oval of land rising out of the water, all covered with trees whose
tangled bare branches were just putting on their spring cloak of new green leaves.

A scramble down the hillside, with real rocks bruising her shins and real leaves
catching in her tangled hair, and Eleanor was at the river's verge. But the water here
was cloudy, and farther out she could see it running clear over sand and small red
pebbles. She girdled up her gown and kicked off her ruined shoes—pretty soft cloth
shoes made for dancing or sitting in a bower—and stepped into a current so cold, so
strong, the shock of it took all her breath away. She lurched forward, reached to a
branch for support, and found herself at the little island. Climbing up the steep
curve of the earthen mound was like climbing onto a boat. But this boat could go
nowhere; it was rooted in rock and solid earth.

Loose the knots in your hair and find a wind that will carry you where you will. The voice
was Dangereuse's, but she was alone on the island.

Eleanor combed out her tangled hair with her fingers. There were nine tight snarled knots all filled with twigs and leaves. As she undid each knot, a breeze sprang up, whistling through the bare branches over her head. When the eighth knot was undone, the winds whistled past her and whipped her loose hair about her cheeks. The ship of earth rocked in the channel as if its invisible sails were filled. But still it did not move forward.

The wind that will fill these sails is the wind of heart's desire.

Far away, at the headwaters of another river, Eleanor saw on the horizon a city of gray spires and golden towers, a city lit by the sun that glanced over the river valley without warming the deep shadows of the cold rushing water.

Loose that wind if you dare, if you will pay the price.

Finally, Eleanor smoothed out the last of the nine knots in her tangled hair, while a great wind rose about her and howled through the bare branches. The ship of earth shivered and moved. Slowly, majestically, it cut through the waters that were neither Garonne nor Seine nor any earthly river, carrying Eleanor to a city she had never seen, a city where a king's son awaited her and the church bells rang with joy for her coming.

After a long while staring into the rising mist, tracing the outlines of unknown spires, Eleanor's eyes burned. She became aware that the sense of movement had ceased, and the earth was solid again beneath her feet. She looked down upon a carpet of green grass sprinkled with blue and white flowers like stars. The masts of tree and the sails of bare branches wove themselves together over her head; the spires and towers on the horizon blossomed into a pear tree covered with white flowers.

Eleanor stepped from the bower at the center of the archbishop's pleasaunce. It was May morning, and the garden was golden in the risen sun, and William of Lezay was nowhere to be seen. And she knew, now, what it was she must do.

The clerk from Normandy sipped his host's wine and listened without overmuch interest to the heated discussion going on in the solar of the archbishop's palace. Guilhem de Herbert, chamberlain to the late duke of Aquitaine, was drawing maps in the air with both hands and arguing with the archbishop about how best to settle the new young heiress to Aquitaine and Poitou. The names of southern magnates flashed through the air like sparks from a well-stirred fire, flaring momentarily in the brief wind of the archbishop's interest and then falling dead to the floor as one objection or another was raised.

The argument was of little interest to Arnulf the Norman. His master, Stephen of Blois, was most thoroughly married, and the errand that had brought him to Bordeaux was settled to Stephen's satisfaction, if not entirely to Arnulf 's. He'd been sent south from Normandy because that devil Geoffrey of Anjou was collecting men for another attack on Stephen's lands, and Stephen had some hope that the duke of Aquitaine could be persuaded to stay out of this war. Aquitaine had an inconvenient habit of helping out Anjou in any little war that might be going, but William of Aquitaine had lately been worried about his soul, and King Stephen thought there might be a fair chance of persuading him to remain neutral this time. If Arnulf succeeded in persuading the duke to take Stephen's proffered bribes, there was to be a reward in it for him: archdeacon of Séez.

Well, Duke William's soul—Arnulf crossed himself on the thought—was now beyond such considerations, and there'd be no support out of Aquitaine for this one of Geoffrey Plantagenet's attacks on Normandy, not with the duke new laid in his grave and the duchy handed over to a girl child, and the true rulers of the realm, this archbishop and chamberlain, scurrying like ants out of an overturned nest to find some man to marry the duke's daughter.

That would be news most pleasing to King Stephen. And he would be glad, too, to learn that Aquitaine's neutrality had cost him precisely nothing. But would he consider himself bound to give Arnulf the promised reward? After all, Arnulf hadn't done anything; there'd been no need. Still, if he could take the road today he would be the first man to bring Stephen this excellent news, and that alone might be enough to get him the post to which he aspired.

"My lord archbishop!" He raised his voice to get the attention of the two absorbed men. "My lord, I really should be on the road. King Stephen will wish to hear this news as soon as possible."

Geoffrey du Lauroux glanced over his shoulder. "In a few minutes, Master Arnulf," he said pleasantly but with absolutely no real concern for the fate of a young clerk kicking his heels while his masters debated world affairs. "We may wish your advice and counsel in this matter. If Eleanor marries Ebles de Mauléon, do you think Stephen would see it as a threat? Ebles's lands in Brittany, joined to Eleanor's in Aquitaine and Poitou?"

Arnulf consulted his own mental map. Brittany and Poitou would be poised like nutcrackers over Anjou. Geoffrey Plantagenet would have more to worry about in such a marriage than would Stephen of England and Normandy.

"I think my master would not be actively displeased with such an arrangement," he said cautiously.

Guilhem de Herbert scotched the proposal. "Who cares what Stephen thinks? Louis of France won't stand for it. He'd be a fool to let two of his major vassals combine like that. Better to wed her to young Parthenay; he's young and biddable—"

"And Ebles de Mauléon, not to mention half a dozen others, would promptly try to kill Parthenay and take the widow," the archbishop interrupted. "It has to be someone strong enough to hold Aquitaine, but not strong enough to offend France. Unless, of course, he were strong enough to defy Louis. . . . What if we married her to Geoffrey Plantagenet?"

Guilhem de Herbert's eyes widened at the daring of this notion. "Anjou and Aquitaine together?"

A terrible thought, in Arnulf's opinion. Terrible for his master, anyway. And fortunately, an impossible one. He cleared his throat delicately. "Ahem."

Both men turned. "Yes, yes, I am aware that Stephen would object," Geoffrey du Lauroux said impatiently, "but—"

"So," pointed out Arnulf, "would Geoffrey's wife. Empress Matilda." The bitch, he added mentally. As a supporter of Stephen, he was bound to discount Matilda's claim to the English throne; the epithet came naturally to him. Troublemaking woman. The *bastard* bitch, if you believed those stories about her father Henry I of England hauling her mother out of a nunnery for a "marriage" the church had never approved. And as Stephen's man, Arnulf had every intention of believing those stories, whether they happened to be true or not. But at the moment, Matilda's existence was actually serving King Stephen's interests. He allowed himself a small smile at the irony of it.

"Oh. Yes." Geoffrey du Lauroux subsided. "I had forgotten about Matilda. So, from all accounts," he added, brightening, "does Geoffrey, most of the time. He certainly hasn't done much to support her claim to England. You don't suppose—"

"Even if he were inclined to divorce her and take your young duchess," Arnulf pointed out, "divorces take time. Dispensations take time. And time is precisely what you don't have, my lord—nor I. So if I might just be going—"

Geoffrey du Lauroux waved him back into his seat. "Wait a few minutes. Your advice has been useful. I would be pleased if you would remain until this matter has been settled."

Settled? This argument over the duchess's marriage had begun before dawn; it could drag on for *days*. At the rate these two were going at it, they would still be arguing two weeks after some impatient vassal had raided the palace and carried away the heiress. And meanwhile, every day lost would hurt Arnulf's chances of being the first to bring King Stephen the good news. "But, my lord—"

"*Sit.*"

On the other hand, Arnulf reflected philosophically, a minor clerk who offended an archbishop was unlikely to rise any higher in the church.

He sat.

He was still sitting when, thirty minutes and five or six names later, a slim young girl with leaves in her tangled hair came boldly in without asking permission.

Guilhem de Herbert, who had been lounging on a bench with his boots propped on a windowsill while he ticked off the pros and cons of the Fronsac family as a marriage alliance, swallowed the last of his wine the wrong way and jumped to his feet. The bench rocked to and fro behind him as he stifled a cough and bowed to the girl.

Arnulf concluded that the child must be the heiress whom they'd been discussing. He rose too but kept discreetly to the shadows. He thought of himself as an observer in these affairs, not one of the participants. He would just as soon Geoffrey du Lauroux came to share that view. Quickly.

"No, no." The girl waved away Archbishop Geoffrey's proffered list of names as if they were a tray of honey cakes. "I have had an excellent idea, my lord archbishop."

"If it's about the May Day pageant," said Geoffrey du Lauroux, "I fear it would not be wise for you to go out into the town at this time, my dear—"

"*No.*" Somehow the girl stood a few inches taller, and the reverend archbishop of Bordeaux stopped in midsentence. Arnulf waited, eager in spite of himself to hear what had inspired this young girl to burst in and interrupt men at important business.

In the breath before she spoke again, he realized that all three of them were waiting on her words. How had she managed that? Instead of being turned politely around and told to go finish her needlework, she was commanding them all. When she spoke, he could almost see the letters forming over her head, illuminated in gold leaf and vermilion, stamped with the ducal seal of Aquitaine.

"No man in my realm is strong enough to hold Aquitaine without the agreement of my other vassals," Eleanor pronounced. "Is that not so, my lord archbishop?"

"It certainly is," Geoffrey du Lauroux said warmly. "You see, Guilhem, even the demoiselle here perceives—"

"And if I marry outside Aquitaine—if we ally with Normandy or Toulouse or even Geoffrey of Anjou—Louis of France will perceive the joining of our lands as a threat and may make war on us."

"Geoffrey's *married*," Arnulf put in, but no one paid the least heed to him. He might as well have been on the road at dawn, for all the difference his advice was making to this council. Now Guilhem de Herbert was nodding and commenting on the sagacity of Eleanor's statement. Well, she'd said nothing beyond the obvious, nothing but what these two great men of Aquitaine had been arguing over since before dawn.

"Then," said Eleanor with a dazzling smile that suggested, somehow, how dull must be anybody who failed to appreciate her conclusion, "there is but one marriage possible, is there not? The king of France has a son. . . ."

"A number of them," Geoffrey du Lauroux said dryly.

"Only one suitable for the duchess of Aquitaine," Eleanor responded. "If I marry the heir to France, Louis will not make war on us, and no one else will dare to do so."

In the silence that followed, Arnulf heard shouts and oaths in the courtyard below. There was the jingling of harness and the clash of mail, sounds that should be meaningless to a good clerk of the church, vowed to peace.

But where would there be peace, except in this girl's daring proposal?

"I suppose Louis might agree." Geoffrey du Lauroux rubbed his chin. "If it were put to him correctly . . ."

"He won't *agree*," Eleanor contradicted him. "He will decide on it for himself. We will not go to Louis of France for a favor, gentlemen. We will simply supply him with information; the decision will be all his." Her attention switched from the archbishop to Guilhem de Herbert. "You have ridden hard to bring us this news,

Chamberlain. I am sorry to ask you to take the road again so soon, but my father's will must be brought to Paris, and at once, before the news of his death is spread abroad among my troublesome vassals."

"Your father's will," Guilhem de Herbert said slowly, "makes no mention of your marriage, my lady."

"Nor will the new one," Eleanor told him. "But it will specify that he leaves me and my lands in the wardship of the king of France." Her glance swept the three of them equally now, bright as a hawk's eye, and Arnulf of Normandy perceived that he had been wrong to think himself concealed by shadows. "Louis will wish to secure Aquitaine for France, and what better way to do it than by marrying me to his heir? Anyone else who held Aquitaine could be a threat to him. But with the prize of Aquitaine for himself—to join to France—I think he will be here as soon as may be, and with an army adequate to defend against attack by any of my vassals or any other man who may have . . . ideas above his station."

The shouts from the courtyard grew louder. Arnulf thought he could hear the clang of metal on metal. Squires at arms practice? If so, they should be warned to keep their voices down.

"You speak of forgery!" the archbishop protested.

"I am sure," Eleanor said, "that you will do it very well." She moved then, laying one slender white hand on the archbishop's sleeve. "Let us go and consult as to the wording of this will, while my chamberlain readies himself for the journey."

As she turned toward the door, Arnulf saw her full-face for the first time and finally identified the two jewels hanging from her neck. One was a crude blue-green bead on a silver chain. The other was a round device of cast brass: the ducal seal of Aquitaine.

"Oh, by the way, Guilhem," she said as if on an afterthought, "you do understand that this will work only if we can keep the news from getting out. You must tell no one but Louis himself of your errand."

Guilhem de Herbert bowed. "You may trust me for that, my lady. But what about the others who know?"

"I have given orders," Eleanor said calmly. "The clerks who were to carry the archbishop's letters were . . . not inclined to argue with my good Poitevin knights."

But someone, Arnulf thought as the noise from the courtyard finally died down, had certainly contested the orders.

"No one except yourself is to leave the palace until Louis's army arrives," Eleanor spelled out to Guilhem de Herbert.

Arnulf made a convulsive gesture of denial and then stopped as Eleanor's bright glance trapped him. "Does this inconvenience you?" she asked. "We are sorry for that. You may perhaps be consoled to know that others will be even worse inconvenienced by this necessity."

Instead of leaving with the archbishop, she crossed to the windows of the solar and looked down into the courtyard. "Poor Lezay," she murmured. "If he had thought to depart as soon as I refused him, he might have been troublesome. But since he took his time . . . he is definitely not clever enough to hold Aquitaine. Don't you agree, gentlemen?"

Arnulf managed a confused agreement as Eleanor swept out of the room, bearing the befuddled archbishop with her like a leaf on a flooded stream. Only with her departure did he begin to feel his head clear.

Guilhem de Herbert took a deep breath. Arnulf wondered if this great man had been afflicted in the same way by Eleanor's presence.

He shook his head wonderingly. Everything she said had made sense while she was in the room. Now that she was gone, he could see a dozen flaws in the plan. And the worst flaw of all might be in its success.

He had, after all, had occasion to meet the pious boy who was heir to France.

Chapter Four

The king of France was not in Paris.

Arriving late and sweaty after eleven days of hard riding, with the men from Bordeaux cursing him and his haste, Guilhem de Herbert learned from an underclerk in the chamberlain's offices that the king and his council had retired to a hunting lodge some distance north of the city.

"Béarne—Béthune—Béthisy, that's the name of the place." The clerk scratched a tonsured scalp. "That's where you'll find him. If you hurry. He's fallen ill."

Two days later, Guilhem de Herbert was demanding entrance to the king's sickbed at Béthisy and trying not to let the stench of illness distract him. They said the king suffered from a flux of the bowels, not an uncommon ailment in a man who for years had been too fat to sit a horse.

A plump little man in a monk's habit bustled out of the inner chamber. Courtiers besieged him with demands. How was the king's health? What were the chances of a recovery? Could he sign a charter for a church in the Touraine? Could he hear this petitioner for just one little, little moment?

Guilhem de Herbert raised himself on tiptoes and shouted over the heads of the courtiers. "News for the king from Aquitaine! I must have entrance!" He pushed a few bejeweled lads in long embroidered gowns out of his way, feeling marginally better for the chance to elbow someone, and planted himself before the little monk.

"The king might be feeling better tomorrow. Can't it wait?"

Guilhem was about to shove the monk out of his way like the rest of the courtiers he'd pushed aside; one hand was outstretched to take the little man by the shoulders when the monk raised his own hand. Rings captured light and threw it back into Guilhem's face in splinters of gold and red and blue. Two rubies, by God, and a sapphire in gold, and that was only the left hand.

Only one man would combine a king's ransom in jewels with the plain habit of his order, one who had control of the king's inner chamber and the king's ear, one who for years had fought a battle between his personal love of luxury and the asceticism he knew was proper to a man of God. A jumped-up, puffed-up little peasant fellow with dung under his nails, they called him—but not in his hearing.

Suger, abbot of the royal monastery of Saint-Denis. Schoolfellow, friend, confidant, and chief counselor to Louis, king of the Franks.

"You must judge the urgency of my message yourself, Abbot Suger," said Guilhem de Herbert. "This letter from the archbishop of Bordeaux will explain the situation. It might best be read in private."

Ten minutes later Guilhem de Herbert was in the royal presence, sipping a cup of wine and doing his best not to notice the stinking bucket that stood at the foot of the royal bed.

Louis the Fat heaved his gross bulk under the sheets, suffered his attendants to lift and sponge the huge, flaccid body as if it were a thing not even connected with him, and talked steadily through the convulsions of illness that shook his great belly like a woman in labor. "After due consultation with our advisers we have decided that our ward, the duchess of Aquitaine, can best be safeguarded by an immediate and suitable marriage. Our beloved son Louis will return to the south with you."

Ten minutes, Guilhem thought. His young duchess had been entirely right in her assessment of the king's reactions. Why wasn't he feeling more relieved?

Perhaps because of the youth who stood on the far side of the royal bed, his face half disguised in shadow. Pale, blond, beardless, and soft as a girl, with meek eyes cast down like a novice monk's. This was the next king of the Franks. This was the man who was to master Aquitaine. Nobody in the south knew much about him, except that he'd been intended for the monastery. Fortunately, he had not yet made irrevocable vows when his older brother Philippe rode his horse into a runaway pig that was roaming the streets of Paris in search of a snack. The ensuing fall had broken the horse's knees, Philippe's neck, and young Louis's plans for a quiet cloistered life. He was plucked from the monastery and told to straighten up, learn warfare, and act like a proper heir to the throne. Had he been glad or sorry of this turn in Fortune's wheel? The soft, shuttered face at the far side of the room was telling Guilhem nothing.

The king was still giving his instructions. Guilhem listened with half his mind, trying to read the character of the blond youth who had just had a fortune dropped into his lap. "You will accompany the royal party—or, no—" A movement of Suger's hand, hardly more than a twitch of the stubby beringed fingers, halted the king in midspeech. "What's that?"

Suger murmured in the king's ear, but not so softly that Guilhem could not make out the words. It would take time to arrange a suitable escort for the young prince. An army could not march south overnight. The chamberlain of Aquitaine should return in advance of the army, bearing letters with the royal seal to assure Archbishop Geoffrey of the king's good intentions. A grant to the diocese of Bordeaux might be in order, something contingent on the duchess's remaining safe and unmarried until young Louis reached her.

"Do you really think that is needful?" the king fretted.

Suger nodded. "We do not wish to leave Geoffrey du Lauroux in any doubt as to our good intentions to him, do we, my lord king? Do we?" he repeated insistently as the king's eyes closed and his body rippled with another convulsive movement.

The young prince looked up and answered for his father. "No, indeed, Abbot. Send what assurances you think necessary. We rely on you, as always, not to fail us in this great matter." His eyes were light as the sky in that shuttered room, and his soft lisping voice made Guilhem shiver. He wouldn't like, he thought, to be the man who made a mistake in that prince's affairs.

Maybe, after all, this young prince was man enough to rule Aquitaine. A hint of savagery was no bad thing in a man who would soon have to take the homage of more than a hundred new vassals, all speaking a different language from his and all firmly accustomed to being left alone to do things in their own way, though it was surprising, in a youth who otherwise had the meek and mild manners of the novice monk he'd once been.

And then again, maybe Guilhem was imagining things. The young prince hadn't actually *said* anything threatening. He had only meekly acquiesced in the decisions of his father and the good abbot, as befitted a young man not yet ready to assume his father's crown.

It took until nightfall to prepare the letters, and then they had to wait another day until the count of Vermandois, the king's cousin and seneschal of France, could come to witness them with his own seal.

Raoul de Vermandois, when he did arrive, had Guilhem's instant approval. A wiry middle-aged man with graying hair, the count arrived in riding clothes, knelt to kiss the king's hand, added his seal to the charters, and returned to Paris without delay. Guilhem wished this man were riding south with him, at the head of a good strong troop of French knights and men-at-arms to discourage any untoward ideas that might come into the heads of Duchess Eleanor's vassals. But then, it was probably best that this lean, efficient man should stay in Paris to supervise the organization of the army escorting the young prince south. After all, nothing less than an army would suffice to hold Aquitaine, should any rumors get out about the duke's death.

After Guilhem de Herbert left, Eleanor had nothing to do but wait. May passed in heat and dust, with the chatter of her ladies and the heavy walls of the Ombrière Palace and a land full of her own vassals making a triple circle around the still point where Eleanor waited for somebody to make a move on the board. She had no news; she could do nothing. She dared not leave the Ombrière without an army to guard her; she could not call up an army without starting rumors about the duke's prolonged stay in Compostela. Any day, a returning pilgrim might bring the news that would spread across Aquitaine like fire through the dry stubble of a harvested field.

Most of the archbishop's guests accepted their enforced waiting period philosophically. The Norman clerk Arnulf turned out to have some skill at chess. He taught Eleanor the game and they whiled away long hours at move and countermove while Cercle-le-Monde made slow, sweet music in the background.

William of Lezay, she understood, was being kept under guard somewhere in the Ombrière; he had not been at all philosophical about his imprisonment. Eleanor did not visit him. And she grew impatient with Cercle-le-Monde's songs of love.

"Don't you know anything new?" she demanded.

The troubadour rummaged in his capacious memory and drew out a romance that had been sung in the duke's court two summers past, a tale out of Ireland full of wonders and doomed lovers, magic potions and talking birds.

"It's a silly story," Eleanor said contemptuously, "and Yseult was a silly woman. She had a good marriage to a great king who treated her well, and she threw it away to go wandering in the forest with this Tristran. Sing something else!"

Cercle-le-Monde looked at her with something like pity. "Perhaps someday you will understand the worth of love, my duchess—my very young lady duchess."

"Love is for peasants," Eleanor said. "We make alliances. And I intend to make a very good one." She slid a pawn across the board. "Arnulf, your queen is in danger."

"I noticed, I noticed." Arnulf of Normandy bent over the board, scowling.

Dangereuse remarked that some people managed to spend their leisure time more productively than pushing bits of carved ivory across a board.

"The archbishop dislikes chess, too," Eleanor remarked, knowing that nothing would more rapidly reconcile her grandmother to the game. "He thinks it is a game of chance and that one might as well be wagering on the throw of dice like a common soldier." Arnulf's bishop came forward to guard the queen, and Eleanor moved a mounted knight over the heads of her own pawns to take the bishop. "Of course, the way he plays, that's true...."

Dangereuse sniffed. "It may not be a game of chance, but it's still not useful. Why can't you finish the goldwork on the cope you were embroidering for the archbishop?"

Eleanor looked up with the flashing smile that always took away Arnulf's breath for a moment. "Dear *Grandmère*, I am working on it. You see?" She held up the fabric, stiff with gold and silk thread. "I sew between moves—it takes Master Arnulf so long to decide what to do next." Arnulf scowled. His fingers hovered over the queen. Eleanor could almost see what he was thinking. It would be so easy to take the knight Eleanor had just placed within reach. Too easy. There had to be something wrong with the move. "Clever, Arnulf," Eleanor commented. "You can see the danger of taking my knight, can't you? It's hard to fool a master of the game." She turned back to Dangereuse. "It's more fun to do two things at once. Three. I can listen to Cercle-le-Monde at the same time," Eleanor finished triumphantly, "only I do wish he would sing something more interesting!"

Cercle-le-Monde retaliated with a slow, gliding, sensuous melody that he had picked up from his teacher Marcabru, who had it from the court of King Alfonso in Spain.

> "I sat in the chapel of Saint Simeon
> and great waves crept around me, came on and on,
>> waiting for my love,
>> waiting for my love!"

Arnulf of Normandy left his queen where she was and pushed a pawn forward. Eleanor gave him a three-cornered grin. Her long fingers moved a forgotten castle down the straight path to place his king in check.

Arnulf shrugged and accepted defeat. "What do I owe you now?"

"Burgundy, Berry, and Flanders," Eleanor responded promptly. "Shall we play for the Holy Roman Empire next?"

"What will you offer me against it?"

She tapped one finger against her cheek. "How about . . . Constantinople and the Greek Empire?"

"Done!" But as he began to clear the board for the next game, Arnulf paused and frowned. "I still don't see what you would have done if I'd taken that knight with my queen."

"I'd have lost," Eleanor told him.

"God's bones," Arnulf swore quietly. "And to think I taught her this game!" he appealed to the room at large.

"You taught me only the moves on the board," Eleanor said. "The game's more than that. I've been learning it all my life." *Men. Did they think she'd learned noth-ing in all these years of following the duke's court around Aquitaine and Poitou?*

Cercle-le-Monde rolled his eyes and began a new verse of the slow, sweet Moorish-inspired song.

> "I stood in the chapel, at the altar-side,
> and the waves crept around me, the great sea tide,
>> waiting for my love,
>> waiting for my love!"

Heat and sun and warm nights of the south thrummed behind the melody. Eleanor's cheeks flushed and she tapped one foot absently in time to the song.

"All right," said Arnulf the Norman, "Constantinople for the Holy Roman Empire, and this time you won't trick me like that!"

"Not now," Eleanor said absently. "I'm . . . tired of the game." She leaned back against the wall, eyes half closed.

> "And the waves crept around me, waves so great—
> I have no boatman to row my boat,
>> waiting for my love,
>> waiting for my love!"

G uilhem de Herbert returned before the last day of May, bearing messages from Louis of France to Geoffrey du Lauroux and, almost as an afterthought, to the girl who had inherited Aquitaine. The archbishop was more than pleased with his letters; he actually smiled at Eleanor and for two whole days forbore to complain about her new predilection for games of chance.

She could not understand why she was not more elated at the news, except that it was only what she had predicted, no more, no less. And now there was nothing to do but wait, and chess and music and embroidery and the chatter of her ladies were not enough to fill the long, hot days of June. All these things faded into the background, as inconsequential as the endless sawing of the cicadas in the garden, as trivial as the sluggish trickle of a dying spring through the muddy remains of the archbishop's water garden.

She had always been thin. Now, with heat and sleepless nights and loss of appetite, her face was sharp-featured as a fox's, surrounded by a mass of dry, crackling yellow-brown hair that no one could tame. Her hair squirmed out of its braids, straggled free of coifs, tied itself into a million knots that she had to untangle patiently, one at a time, with the ivory comb that matched her needle case. There was a lion carved on the back of the comb, snarling, and the teeth of the comb were its claws. They broke easily.

At night a fitful breeze gusted in from the sea. "Now we can rest," her ladies said gratefully, and they dropped off to sleep in twos and threes, naked, drawing linen sheets or silk scarves over their bodies as the night air cooled. Eleanor lay awake in the great bed, listening to sobbing voices on the wind, mourning in a language she could not understand. Sometimes a freak of the corner window made the breeze shriek so that her ladies startled out of their dreams.

She paced the innermost circle of the pleasaunce at dusk and sunrise, but she could not find the secret forest again. She stared at Cercle-le-Monde and Dangereuse, whose voices had been with her there. But the courage that allowed her to give orders to an archbishop and her father's chamberlain failed her when it came to speaking of things that might have been no more than dreams.

"Young girls have these fits of fancy at the time of their bleeding," she could imagine Dangereuse saying, cool and dismissive.

While Eleanor waited for news of the French army, her little sister escaped to the orchard around the pleasaunce and lay in the shade of an ancient apple tree, tracing the gnarled lines of bark with one finger and chewing a stem of sweet grass and thinking of everything and nothing. After the first days of endless tears she felt quite empty, cried out and drained of feeling, and as long as she did not think again of Papa, she could float in this safe warm space, encircled by the protective trees of the orchard planted in times too ancient to recall.

She felt sorry for Eleanor and glad that she herself was not to be the prey of some ambitious vassal. Only a little sister, two years younger than Eleanor, Petronilla had never been anybody important; whether or not Papa married again and got an heir made no difference to her lack of standing. So they had always let her go her own dreamy way: dreaming heat of midsummer, dreaming green leaves and secret cool earthy places of the forest, dreaming the sweet juice of a full ripe pear dripping down her chin. She was only a minor character in somebody else's story. And she didn't really mind, not much, anyway; from second place you could see and dream and live. She dreamed castles and cities and empires in the clouds, bit into a tart green apple and tasted freedom on her tongue. Heiresses were never truly free; Petronilla knew from all the troubadour romances that they must always marry the king's son in the end. Petronilla was happy enough not to have Louis. What would she do with a little boy who'd been raised to be a monk? When she took a husband, it would be someone tall and strong who could keep her safe forever, a big armored man like Papa—

Dangerous memories. Petronilla hurled the half-eaten green apple away from her and swallowed down hard on the bitterness rising in her throat. It would not do to think of the past; she had a future to think of. She was lucky, really, free to live and love where she liked. Poor Eleanor, carrying Aquitaine like a crown of lead to press her down.

The only problem with being a second daughter, thought Petronilla, was that sometimes unmarried extra girls got put away in a convent: look at poor Aunt Agnes in Maillezais. Petronilla didn't want a convent; she wanted a man. Even knowing all about the bloody and dangerous and painful business of birthing, even having helped the midwife Aielle dose women in labor with the black grains—second daughters got away with a lot—even so, Petronilla knew that she wanted a man and a cradle with a baby in it. The pain of birthing was soon over, and then there was a child binding you to the future as your ancestors bound you to the past, part of the living world forever and ever, with a safe place of her very own.

And until then, until some man made her the heroine of her own story instead of a follower in Eleanor's story, at least she would be free to do what interested her: to follow Aielle and Dangereuse, to learn the herbs for stopping blood and starting menses and relieving the white flux and all the other ills of women.

And she had one more safe precaution. Eleanor had promised not to let them put her in a convent, and she had promised never to leave Eleanor. They were bound together by blood and birth and the hot summer sun of Poitou, sisters, two flowers on one branch.

Petronilla broke off a leafy branch from the tree above her and leaned against the trunk, absently twirling the green leaves between her fingers. Hard, hard to break the leaves from their stems, and once broken, they blew away in the wind and withered away. How free was she, truly, being born on one branch with Eleanor?

On July 5, four days after the feast of Saint Martial, the advance guard of the French army reached Bordeaux with the information that the rest of the army was following, more slowly, from Limoges. Guilhem de Herbert recognized Raoul de Vermandois with joy and relief, and felt the burden of Aquitaine lifted at last from his shoulders. The count of Vermandois appeared no less relieved to be there. Although he paid due attention to posting guards and sentinels around

Bordeaux, he also made time for a daily visit to Eleanor and her ladies. His relaxed, competent attitude proclaimed, without a word being spoken, that all danger of a revolt in Aquitaine was now past. None of Eleanor's turbulent vassals would dare to move with the French army so close at hand.

As if to underscore his certainty, Raoul countermanded the orders that had kept Eleanor and her people, the archbishop and his guests, virtual prisoners for so many weeks. William of Lezay departed for Talmont without pausing to take leave of Eleanor or anyone else. The archbishop's clerks went on about the various businesses that had been delayed through half the summer. Arnulf of Normandy lingered, to the surprise of everyone including himself, for one final game of chess with Eleanor.

"I had thought you eager to bear your news to King Stephen," Eleanor remarked while taking one of his pawns.

Arnulf shrugged. "He'll be back in England by now. And when he's in England, he doesn't pay much attention to affairs on this side of the water; he's got enough to worry about there, trying to keep the crown on his head. Besides, the news will reach him from Paris faster than I could get to England from here. No, I've given up any hope of reward for that service. Not that it would have mattered much in any case. What the king promised in March won't mean much to him in July. He'll make me archdeacon of Séez, or not, depending on who has the luck to be the last person to speak to him on the subject." He shifted a bishop.

"I think you are not so devoted to the service of Stephen of Blois as you seemed, Master Arnulf." Eleanor's queen advanced far enough to threaten Arnulf's king without being herself placed in jeopardy.

"I should like," said Arnulf slowly, "to be the adviser to a lord who would use my counsel well and wisely. What Abbot Suger has been to King Louis, that I might be—someday—to another king." He laughed at his own naked ambition, self-deprecating, but not denying the fact. "Or count, or duke ... But Stephen takes all counsel, and no counsel, and changes with every wind that blows. As well seek to be adviser to the thistledown."

"Young Louis ..." Eleanor said pensively, without finishing the sentence. "Tell me." It was the first time she'd asked the question in all the weeks of waiting, now that her bridegroom was less than a week's march from Bordeaux. "You've met him. What is he like?"

Arnulf's hand hovered over a castle while he considered, and discarded, several replies. "I think that the young Louis, when he comes to be king, will be guided by Abbot Suger, as was his father before him. Suger's place in the counsels of the Capetians is . . . very strong. You should be aware of that, my lady, when you come to be queen in Paris."

"That will be many years yet." Eleanor's pawn advanced, revealing an avenue by which her bishop, protected on all sides, could take the black king.

"I think . . ." Arnulf searched the board. There was no way out. "I think it is a pity you were not born a man."

Eleanor laughed. "You clerks have no skill with courtly speeches! For myself, I think it is a pity we never played for real stakes."

"That," said Arnulf, "is a matter of opinion." He stretched out one lean fore-finger and toppled his king. "Isn't it fortunate," he said with a smile, "that real kings are not unmade so easily? Farewell, my lady. It is time that I returned to Stephen's service."

On July 11, the main body of the French army arrived in Bordeaux, and Eleanor saw her prospective bridegroom for the first time. There was no privacy in the meeting, nor in the days that followed. She looked at him from a distance, thinking, *At least he is tall and straight.* They shared a bowl at the banquet that night, and she came away knowing little more. Young Louis was fair-haired and handsome. He stared at her a great deal and said little. That was perhaps just as well, since he had no knowledge of the langue d'oc. Eleanor could converse well enough in the northern dialect favored by Normans and Franks, the langue d'oïl, but only if those she conversed with spoke slowly and clearly. Louis hardly opened his mouth when he talked, and the words came out all in a nervous rush so that she had to puzzle over each sentence. Doubtless, she reflected while her ladies chattered around her that night, they would grow to understand one another better soon.

"What did you think of him, Petronilla?" she whispered long after they were in bed, when Dangereuse's snores assured her that their grandmother would not be listening.

Her little sister giggled under her breath. "He sounds funny when he talks. I like the count of Vermandois better."

Eleanor sighed. Petronilla was still a little girl. Raoul de Vermandois brought her sweetmeats when he visited the ladies' quarters and teased her like a favorite niece. She looked for nothing more in a man than a possible replacement for her father.

Not, Eleanor reflected, that she herself was sure how to judge those other qualities. But Cercle-le-Monde's songs and romances, the whole atmosphere of intrigue and mild romantic tension in which the court breathed, had lately begun to afflict her with certain vague longings. *Love is for peasants; we make alliances.*

Her proud statement to Cercle-le-Monde was still true. All the same, she was not sorry that young Louis was tall and fair.

On the edge of sleep it occurred to her to wonder what he had thought of her. After all, he'd had no more choice in this marriage than she; less, really, since he hadn't even had the satisfaction of conceiving the plan.

He stared at me a great deal. On that ambiguously comforting note she drifted into sleep.

On Sunday, July 25, the ships at anchor in the River Garonne blossomed with pennants of red silk and banners of cloth of gold. Green and flowering, branches arched over the narrow streets to create a shaded passageway, and the stones underneath were covered with white and pink flowers. Four jugglers with trained monkeys in scarlet suits turned cartwheels in the square before the cathedral. Six musicians in gold-braided tunics played a dance tune from Poitiers, too slowly and too solemnly. The fountain in the center of the square, dry since the fourth week of the drought, spouted red Bordeaux wine from three of the gaping gryphons' mouths and white wine of Poitou from the other three. The Gascon troubadour from Duke William's court led a chorus of young boys in the song he had composed the night before. The angel over the west portal of the cathedral lifted his stone trumpet and added a counterpoint of dancing notes above the melody, too high for mortal ears to hear. The Poitevin musicians snatched capfuls of wine from the fountain and resumed their dance tune at a proper pace. Citizens crowded into the square and beat out the rhythm of the dance with their wooden shoes clacking on the stones.

Eleanor, by the grace of God duchess of Aquitaine and countess of Poitou, was to marry Louis, the heir to the French throne, in the Cathedral of Saint-André at Bordeaux. And their own Archbishop Geoffrey was to have the honor of performing the ceremony.

From the Ombrière Palace to the cathedral was a short way, but the wedding procession wound through and through the narrow, flower-bedecked streets of the city. The citizens got a good look at their new duke, a tall slim boy whose lank golden hair was put out of glory by the sparkle of gold embroidery and white silk on his surcoat, and they had a chance to cheer the young duchess who rode beside him in a scarlet gown, her hair brilliant with dust of gold and her light eyes brighter than the jewels around her throat. And the noble guests who had been pouring into Bordeaux for the last two weeks, to do their homage to Louis and Eleanor and to see the wedding celebrated, had a good look at the sights of Bordeaux: the fourteen churches with their relics of Charlemagne and Roland, the semi-enclosed gardens with their gates open today to show tiled fountains and banks of flowers, the tapestry-hung housefronts and the ships rocking on the gentle surface of the river with their banners dangling limply in the hot still air.

At the church of Saint-Rémi there was a figure of a horse and rider, all made of flowers, and a boy concealed within the frame who squeaked out a Latin poem composed by the priest. No one could hear the poem for the cheers of the crowd, but the flower statue was greatly admired.

At the Porte Medoque there was a mountain covered with cloth of gold, and on the top of the mountain a tree bearing fruits and flowers of all kinds, and three ladies came out of the mountain and danced a mime to show that Bordeaux laid all its richness of trade and fruit and wine at the feet of the young couple. Some people were trampled in the crowd of onlookers trying to get a better view, and Maître André of Poitiers lifted his little daughter to his shoulders to protect her from the crush.

"Is that lady the queen?" Jeanette pointed at Petronilla. Her thin brown hair was completely covered with garlands of flowers and she had a new dress for the wedding, of pale silk woven with shimmering threads of pink and gold, and her eyes were shining with delight for the day.

"No. That's the queen's little sister. There's Eleanor, on the gray horse, in red." Eleanor was pretending to watch the pageant and stealing glances at Prince Louis whenever the dancers turned away for a moment. She was bored, and her face showed it. "At least, she will be a queen, one day. And she's our duchess now."

Jeanette looked critically at the thin girl who sat so straight. "I like the other one better. She looks too old."

"Hush, love!" Maître André kissed his daughter's palm and swung her down from his shoulders. He had his own doubts about this duchess, though hardly because she was too old! Two weeks he'd been waiting in antechambers of the Ombrière Palace, after traveling the weary road south with the French army, all on the chance that he might get audience with this young new duchess about the grievances of her people in Poitiers. The city could not bear the taxes laid on by Duke William two years previously for his war with Angoulême—and now that the duke was dead and the war never begun, why shouldn't these taxes be remitted? And there was more to discuss, matters of freedom for the burghers to trade in various commodities and to oversee the creation of guilds to keep the quality of goods high. The charter of liberties he'd been sent to show the duchess would benefit her as much as the citizens of Poitiers, in the long run. And a young girl like that should have been easy to persuade. But he'd never so much as had audience with her. What, a merchant talk with a duchess? He'd been laughed at, sent from hall to waiting room to antechamber and back to hall, kicked once and cursed more than once, and never a chance to deliver his petition. Her father, the merry Duke William, would not have treated one of his people so. And *his* father, Duke William the Troubadour, might have refused the petition and hanged the petitioner—but he would at least have given him audience!

"Can't see!" The crowd had moved on while he mused, and now they were at the tail end of the procession, with half the people of Bordeaux between them and the royal couple.

"Never mind, Jeanette," he soothed the whining child. "Shall we go to the lodgings now and find your mother?"

"No! Want to see the monkeys!"

Maître André took Jeanette by the hand and they trailed after the wedding procession, stepping carefully around the discarded flowers and the squashed cakes and the horse droppings, in the hope that the jugglers with their monkeys would still be performing in the square when the great ones went inside.

After Louis and Eleanor took hands and spoke their wedding vows at the door of the cathedral, the nuptial mass was celebrated inside. In the sweet, smoky darkness of the cathedral, candles danced like stars and the gold and silver vessels on the altar threw back the light in sparkling fragments. Eleanor and Louis knelt to be blessed by the archbishop; behind them, the nobles of France, Gascony, Poitou, and Aquitaine knelt in unison, their stiff cloaks and embroidered surcoats and tunics of shining baudekin rustling like the waves of the ocean. The familiar prayers and the long chanted sequences gave each of the participants in the great wedding time to think and dream and hope and maybe even to pray for the future.

With more than five hundred nobles and burghers attending the banquet, plus wives, mistresses, squires, and sons trailing after them, there was no possibility of serving the wedding feast in the rambling halls of the Ombrière Palace. Tables were set up on the flat green meadows on the far side of the Garonne, covered with linen and shaded by tents of silk and gold. All morning, while the wedding procession wound its way through narrow streets under arches of green branches, while the wedding guests knelt and whispered and dreamed and prayed and sang through the service at the cathedral, the preparations for the feast—and for certain other matters ordered by Raoul of Vermandois—had been going on. Flat-bottomed boats from the upper reaches of the river brought flowers to sprinkle over the tables and under the feet of the arriving guests. Servitors from the Ombrière, assisted by townsfolk pressed into temporary service, set up temporary bake ovens in the mead-ows and ferried across the cooked meats from the archbishop's kitchens. The arch-bishop's fine dinner service, the platters of silver and silver-gilt, the cups and vessels of rock crystal bound with gold and studded with rough-cut stones, could not be entrusted to a boat; it went the long way around, by oxcarts creaking over the bridge.

Shortly afterward, the bride and groom and the five hundred noble guests also went over the bridge. The hooves of their horses crushed the flowers and green boughs that had already begun to fall from their hastily tied arches, until the party rode in a sweet green scent redolent of May rather than of a hot dry summer Sun-day. There was music before and behind them: pipes, tabors, tambourines, rebecs, lutes, shawms, and troubadours. Jaufré Rudel, the young lord of Blaye, had com-posed a song of his own in praise of the young duchess and her wedding day. So had the Gascon Cercle-le-Monde. So had the embittered misogynist Marcabru, who had followed her grandfather's court and then disappeared into Spain for un-counted years. They wrangled amiably for a while about which song to sing first, then agreed to compromise by singing something written by the lady's grandfather, the great Duke William, the troubadour duke. Only none of them could remember a single one of Duke William's songs that was fit for a maiden to hear on her wedding day. She'd have known the words to all of them, of course, but somehow it didn't seem appropriate to sing at a wedding about how many times Duke William had laid Lady Ermessen while her husband was away on Crusade, or how hard he found it to choose which of his two "mares" he wanted to ride next.

While Jaufré Rudel and Marcabru were still going over the list of Duke William's songs, Cercle-le-Monde slipped up to the high table and began chanting a tale he'd learned from Bleheris the Breton. It was a pretty story, about a queen named Guenevere who went a-Maying and was carried away to a far country by a knight disguised in a suit of green branches. It seemed eminently suitable: she was his queen and she was being carried away to the far north. Of course he had every intention of following her, but that need not disturb the sweet pathos of the song, the eternal melody of love and loss and longing. He looked only at her as he sang, and sometimes he thought she looked back at him. She was his duchess, and somehow during the long weeks of waiting, in a palace that had been both protection and prison, she had become the queen of his heart—at least for that moment. It was a hopeless love, of course, not to be taken seriously; even in the moment of his greatest poetic sincerity, Cercle-le-Monde knew that much. But the tale of Guenevere was a sad and beautiful story, and he deeply enjoyed the way its reality matched and elaborated on and twined about the words of the story he was singing, like green vines about a tree.

While he sang, the dishes of the first course were being carried out with a fanfare of trumpets and a shower of preserved violets pelting the guests: the obligatory peacock roasted and dressed again in its own feathers, the famous salt meadow mutton of Gascony, oysters fried in eggs, a boar's head baked in a castle of gilt pastry, capon stewed in a sauce of garlic and dittany. As a conclusion to this course, three men carried out a giant swan made of tinted marchpane, all the feathers very lifelike and the beak and claws gilt, holding in its beak a parchment upon which was inscribed a prayer for the health of the duke and duchess of Aquitaine. The prayer was in the langue d'oc; Eleanor had to translate it into the langue d'oïl for Louis, after which he made a short speech of thanks that she translated into long fluent phrases in her own language. Nobody listened particularly either to the speech or the translation; it was hot, the wine flowed freely, and the swan proved to emit a shower of small gilt trinkets that were distributed among the guests at the high table.

Those who weren't interested in the trinkets had their own thoughts to occupy them during the speechmaking. Cercle-le-Monde sat back and gave his fingers a rest and mentally enumerated the lords who had come to do homage to the young duke and duchess. Auvergne, Parthenay, Lusignan, Châteauroux, Thouars—a goodly turnout. But there were some notable exceptions. Ebles de Mauléon had not come, pleading business in his lands in Brittany. The lord of Angoulême, who'd carried off Emma of Limoges lest Aquitaine acquire too much power in the Limousin, was another conspicuous absence.

And William of Lezay, castellan of Talmont, was not there. Doubtless still sulking in his castle by the sea. Cercle-le-Monde mentally dismissed the impetuous castellan from his thoughts. But the others who had not come, the great lords—he wondered if anybody in the French entourage had noted their absence, or had thought about what it might mean.

He caught Eleanor's eye for a moment. She was a little flushed from the wine and the sun and the heat of her robes; she looked as if the night to come was very much on her mind. But she still had a smile for him. She beckoned him to her side with one finger. Cercle-le-Monde slipped between jovial nobles and their ladies and knelt before her. "Mauléon, my lady, and Angoulême—they have not come to do homage," he murmured.

"We noticed," Eleanor said, so softly that he could barely hear her. "Our seneschal, the count of Vermandois, has the matter in hand."

Young Louis was looking at them, annoyed or impatient—Cercle-le-Monde could not read the boy's sulky face. Eleanor introduced him then, speaking slowly and carefully in the harsh northern dialect, and praising his services to her family.

"Don't praise me too much, my lady," Cercle-le-Monde said quickly. He was not sure why he interrupted; this young prince from the north made him nervous. He turned it into a joke. "I would not have your lord think me a man of importance. He might expect me to take up arms like a knight. Remember that I am only a worthless troubadour!"

Eleanor laughed and looked at him, a swift glancing sidewise glance. "I think I dreamed once that you were more than that."

"Dreams can be deceptive."

"So can truth."

The swift exchange in the soft tongue of the south was annoying Louis; Cercle-le-Monde could see that. He made his excuses and returned to his proper place far down the long table. From there he could just see Eleanor speaking to her new lord, one slender hand on his sleeve, face upturned. A moment later Louis beckoned Raoul de Vermandois to his side.

The subtlety that ended the second course was a fleet of ships painted with silver and bearing marchpane jewels that the servants flung to the crowd. The viscount of Thouars bit down on one of the jewels, cracked a tooth, roared lustily, and ceased his outcry when he realized that the green coating of marchpane had concealed a real emerald.

"Small," criticized his wife.

"Big enough to crack my back molar," Thouars pointed out with a grin. "Have some more marchpane, wife, before the rest of these idiots find out what's being tossed on the grass."

But by then the word was out and the nobles of France and Aquitaine were engaged in an undignified scramble for children's sweetmeats, most of which turned out to contain no more valuable core than a gilt almond or a misshapen pearl. When the last marchpane nut had been consumed, the mock-tourney was already starting: twenty champions in gilded armor, attended by "squires" who juggled swords and danced on their hands. One of the "squires" was a girl—no, by God, they all were! And the champions? The elegant pretense at jousting was dislodging their armor piece by piece, revealing curved limbs slick with sweat and draped with golden nets, glossy coils of hair coming down, full round breasts shielded by the flimsiest of silken tunics.

Between marchpane, emeralds, wine, and bare-breasted "knights," few of the noble guests even noticed when the French at the high table quietly slipped away and moved toward the tents. Fewer still guessed that the line of tents concealed horses and packmules ready to go, that the main contingent of the French army was moving north before the wedding feast was ended, putting as many leagues as possible between them and the lords of Mauléon and Angoulême who had not come to pay homage. The only person near the high table who understood the finality of the departure was not even noble.

"What's the matter, Cercle-le-Monde? Swallow your marchpane nuts before you found out what's inside?" Jaufré Rudel, lord of Blaye, slapped the Gascon on the back and made an obscene suggestion about how he might recover the swallowed jewels. Tomorrow they would be lord and follower again, but today they were two musicians at a feast.

"Aye. I've lost something. I never had it." Cercle-le-Monde jerked his chin toward the line of tents where the French army had been camping. "She's dismissed me from her service."

"I thought you were going with them to Paris."

"So did I. I've been paid off." Cercle-le-Monde tossed a leather purse from hand to hand until a stream of silver pennies cascaded over his knees. "She sent one of the Frenchmen to do it. The seneschal fellow, Raoul de Vermandois. With a message saying, thank you very much for your service, but as queen of the French I prefer to be attended by the French from now on and it would be politically unwise to bring a troupe of raggedy southern hangers-on to my new husband's court."

"Not in those words?"

"No. But that's what he meant."

The lord of Blaye nodded and proffered the only comfort he could. "The seneschal of France, Count Raoul, he's a high-ranking man indeed. She must have meant to do you much honor, to send such a one like a servant with your payment."

Cercle-le-Monde forced a sickly smile and agreed. "And who's to say that I'm not better off? Those northerners are purse-tight patrons. I think I'll visit Ventadour for a while, he was kind enough to praise my lament for the duke, and his young son Bernard had a fancy to learn the art of *trobar*. Or Alfonso of Spain. Marcabru picked up some good songs in Spain; I could learn a lot myself in that court. Have you heard this one?"

Rudel hadn't, but the melody was soft and sweet and easy to pick up, and it was a good melancholy love song for two voices and a fresh skin of Bordeaux wine.

> "I sat in the chapel of Saint Simeon
> and great waves crept around me, came on and on,
> > waiting for my love,
> > waiting for my love!"
>
> "I stood in the chapel, at the altar-side,
> and the waves crept around me, the great sea tide,
> > waiting for my love,
> > waiting for my love!"

"I have no boatman to row for me—
my beauty will die in the boundless sea,
        waiting for my love,
        waiting for my love!"

"I have no boatman, I cannot row—
my beauty will die in the deep sea's flow,
        waiting for my love,
        waiting for my love!"

Chapter Five

The count of Vermandois had charge of the wedding party and of the army that escorted them back to Paris. Dazed with wine and sun and the long ceremonial and the feast, Eleanor passively accepted Raoul de Vermandois's instructions, without worrying about the fact that his care for her safety was separating her from her Poitevins, who were to march in the rear. She and Louis were placed together in the middle of the long procession, surrounded by strange French knights whose rapid, half-mumbled northern dialect was harsh to her ears. The white dust of the roads, stirred up by the riders in the van, was a choking cloud that stung her eyes and left her throat feeling as if she had been drinking muddy water instead of Bordeaux wine.

She was uneasily conscious of eyes upon her: all the French were curious about this southern heiress who would be their next queen. The knights stared, their squires stared, Louis stared, and they all looked away quickly when she saw them at it. The only difference was that Louis sometimes blushed like a girl when she caught his eye, and that difference was enough to gladden and sustain her through the weary march of that first afternoon and evening. *We are married now,* she thought. *In two weeks I've had little enough private discourse with him, and there'll be even less privacy on the road. But we are married. I've done it. No turbulent vassal shall have me against my will; I've got France to protect me and my lands now. France in the person of a strong young man, fair and cleanly made. That's luck most heiresses never hope for. . . .* And then she thought of the night ahead, and she too blushed.

But there was nothing to hope or fear in that night, nor in those that followed. The cavalcade took an inland road, hardly more than a lane for peasants' wagons, turning away from the Château de Fronsac where they might have passed the night in some comfort. Louis, unfamiliar with the land, seemed to notice nothing. Eleanor turned to one of the knights riding close beside them.

"Why are we not going to Fronsac?"

She had to repeat the question twice before he understood her, and then he only shook his head and pointed toward the van, indicating that the choice of roads was not his to make or to question.

"Well, if you don't know, for pity's sake, go and find someone who does!" Eleanor snapped.

He seemed to understand her well enough that time, for he spurred forward, around the other riders who kept to the slow pace of the march. Sometime later, when they came to a crossroads, he was waiting for them—at least Eleanor supposed it was the same man. She had some difficulty in telling apart all these strange knights in half-armor, with chain mail covering their bright feast-day clothes and helmets covering their faces down to the eyebrows and the long nasal bars of the helms bisecting their faces. She had not yet learned the little tricks of style and horsemanship that would enable her to pick out one man from another at any distance.

With him was a squat, tonsured little man sitting on a rather tired-looking palfrey. As they approached, the knight fell back into the group of anonymous men guarding the wedding party, and Abbot Suger kicked his palfrey in the sides to make it amble along beside Louis.

"My lord, I am told you questioned our choice of roads."

"I was the one who questioned it," Eleanor told him. "Why do we not go to Fronsac?"

"Military considerations, my lady." Abbot Suger nodded briskly, as if dismissing a troublesome petitioner, and went on explaining to Louis that the lord of Fronsac was not quite to be trusted in his loyalty: True, he'd sent a son to the feast to swear homage, pleading illness himself, but who was to say whether that illness was genuine?

Eleanor strained her ears to follow the flat vowels and slurred consonants of the langue d'oïl. Fortunately, the abbot seemed rather fond of the sound of his own voice; he managed to repeat every phrase in his brief explanation at least three times, embellishing the long, convoluted sentences with synonyms and elaborate choices of words that turned two sentences of strategy into a prose ballade of politics.

Cercle-le-Monde will love the abbot, Eleanor thought. *I shall have him set these words to music. He will make a lovely parody of it, and these northerners will never understand what he is singing, for none of them trouble to learn our language.*

But this talk of Fronsac's pretending illness was absurd.

"Valéry de Fronsac suffers from the bone ache in his hips," Eleanor interrupted the third elaboration on Suger's basic theme. "Everyone knows that riding is painful for him. There is no need to suspect him of any treachery. I've known him since I was a child."

Abbot Suger gave her a brisk, irritated nod. "Indeed, my lady. But that cannot have been very long, can it now? It is delightful to find a young lady so willing to trust her elders. But in this matter, my children, I beg you will be guided by older and wiser heads. Valéry's son might have thought of winning the duchess's hand; he might still harbor such ambitions. We will rest at Libourne tonight." And he went back to talking with Louis, this time on some point of French politics that Eleanor had neither inclination nor energy to follow.

But she did know that the village of Libourne had no place to shelter even the nobles in the wedding party, much less the knights and men-at-arms and squires and pages who clogged this road before and after them.

Abbot Suger stayed at Louis's side, monopolizing him with talk of the abbey of Saint-Denis and the mill rights of some manor and the need for a larger church at Saint-Denis to hold the increasing crowds of pilgrims, until they were nearly at the village. Then he kicked his palfrey until it trotted ahead, saying something about the need to consult with the count of Vermandois about lodging their party for the night.

"There's not much to consult about," Eleanor said, rather more sourly than she had intended. "There's not much *at* Libourne."

Louis gave her a smile so sweet that all her ill temper melted away at once. "We shall make sure that you and your ladies are well lodged, at least." He drew closer to her and said in an undertone, "I fear, though, there will be little privacy. I shall not insist on . . . I shall . . . You should continue to lie with your ladies, I think, until we reach a place where there can be more of both safety and privacy than we shall find here." He was blushing furiously by the end of this speech.

The tiny, dark nave of the church at Libourne was barely large enough to hold Eleanor's bed—a pile of new-mown hay covered with her scarlet cloak—and the similar piles made for her ladies. Suger and Louis were to sleep in the priest's house. The higher-ranking gentlemen of the French army would evict peasants from their huts; the rest would camp in the meadows outside the village. Raoul de Vermandois said that he would catch a nap when and as he might, among the sentries on guard; Eleanor had the feeling that he meant to stand watch himself most of the night. Petronilla's eyes widened when she said as much, and Eleanor cursed herself for frightening her sister. It was a strange and uneasy feeling to be so much on guard in the center of her own land; it negated the safety she'd thought to achieve with her marriage to Louis.

"Send Cercle-le-Monde to me," she demanded. "I can't sleep without music."

There were whispers, and people hurrying to and fro, and there was no music, only Louis himself coming to her eventually, to explain that Cercle-le-Monde had remained in Bordeaux.

"Why?"

Louis smiled and shook his head. "Who can understand these people? I think he did not want to come to the north; after all, none of us can appreciate his poetry, not speaking the language."

"*I* speak his language," Eleanor pointed out, "and so do all my ladies and my Poitevin knights. And I want—"

She bit her lip. She wanted music. She wanted a proper wedding night, with feasting and wine and horseplay and jokes and a bedding in a fine room with fresh linen sheets. She wanted everything to be as it had been in the time of her father's rule. Well, that was another time, another world; she had left more than a wedding feast behind when she departed Bordeaux.

"It does not matter," she said. "I—am surprised he did not choose to tell me, that is all. Who took my purse to him? Perhaps he said something then."

"Raoul de Vermandois delivered it personally," Louis assured her. "He is busy now, setting guards for your safety. Will you call him from his duty to ask about a *jongleur's* plans?"

The tender laughter in his voice made her understand how silly her concern must seem.

"It is probably just as well the man did not accompany us," Louis added, more severely. "My parents keep a good and pious court. There is little place there for *jongleurs'* tricks and indecent songs."

Dangereuse had not come with them, saying that her old bones were too frail for the long marches with the army. And now Cercle-le-Monde was gone too, without even the courage to tell her that he was leaving her service. Eleanor lay long awake that night, listening to Petronilla's even breathing and the rustling of her ladies as they turned on their pallets of fresh hay, and wondering what else she had left behind in the last few tumultuous weeks.

"Queen of France to be, and I'm sleeping on grass—and alone!" She laughed silently in the darkness, but her eyes stung.

The next few nights followed the same pattern. Their escorting army marched as quickly as an army laden down with followers and baggage, and needing to gather supplies on the way, might do. That meant a long and tiring day for everyone, and a boring day of riding at a walking pace amid clouds of dust for Eleanor. They took obscure roads to avoid any threat that Abbot Suger or Raoul de Vermandois knew or imagined. Neither of them consulted Eleanor about which of her vassals might be trusted.

The peasants in the villages greeted them with respect but with no great joy. Those whom they passed, working in the fields, stopped work and stared after the glittering cavalcade in its perpetual dust cloud without making any sign of greeting or reverence.

From the words dropped grudgingly by Suger, like crumbs from a poor man's table, Eleanor gathered that the army had taken many of these same roads on their way south. No wonder the peasants were not glad to see them again!

"We paid for everything," Sugar said defensively when Eleanor commented on this. "We continue to do so. King Louis is a generous and just monarch. Our people have nothing to complain of in this army."

"If we strip the land bare, gold won't feed them," Eleanor pointed out.

Sugar gave her a half smile, as one tolerating a child's whims. "My lady, the harvest is near; they will eat abundantly soon enough. Peasants are used to an empty belly one day and a feast the next. My lord the king has given strict orders that our army is to do no harm on this march. We pay well, and we take food by force only when the peasants are too dull to understand what we need."

Once at midday they heard whispers and giggling at the side of the road, behind a green tangle of vines. One of the French knights snapped out an order and two men-at-arms went into the wood, swords drawn. Eleanor heard branches breaking, a girl's surprised cry, and the men laughing. Then two half-naked girls and a boy in his teens burst forth from the wood like startled quail.

"Don't look at them, they are indecent!" Louis commanded, but Eleanor had already looked. She saw bared breasts and the flash of a thigh revealed by a torn shift. The boy knelt in the dust of the road, babbling apologies. All three were terrified. They could not know what had occasioned this alarm, why the forest where they played was suddenly the property of armed men speaking a strange tongue.

"Can't understand the villein," one of the men-at-arms grumbled, casually raising his sword. "Spells and devil charms most like. Shall I stop him?"

He glanced at the knight who'd ordered him into the wood, but Eleanor's horse was between them. It almost trampled the man; he took two quick staggering steps back and sat down hard in the ditch, still clutching his sword.

"The boy is apologizing for having disturbed us," Eleanor said in careful French. She spoke to the villein in the tongue they shared, the slow, sweet langue d'oc. "It is we who should apologize for having disturbed you. You and your friends are free to go." She gave the second man-at-arms a cold stare until he released the shaking girls.

Free, the three peasants melted back into the shadows of the forest, brown rags and sunburnt skin, trees and saplings, and then nothing: no path, no sign, only the green leaves shaking where they had passed. Sweat dampened Eleanor's skin under the noonday sun. The forest was cool, and somewhere deep in the shade of the trees there would be a pool, an ancient well rimmed with crumbling stones, a cool fountain spilling over into a glade where all things bloomed and ripened and burned at once. If only she and Louis were churls like those three, to discover one another in the green shade of the forest! They could be together now. Even without Dangereuse or Cercle-le-Monde, Eleanor felt sure that she could find the way. Cercle-le-Monde had promised that she would always find the heart of the forest at need, and love would be her guide.

She glanced at Louis. He was staring at the small round curves of her breasts where her thin dress clung to the skin. He must be feeling as she did. When at last he met her eyes, she smiled, feeling a moment of complicity, but he did not meet her smile. She felt herself rebuked by his severe demeanor.

"It is too hot here in the sun," she said. "Shall we move on?"

When they were on the march again, Louis brought his horse close to hers.

"It is not seemly for a woman to give orders when she has her husband to protect her," he said.

Eleanor bit her lip. "In truth, my lord, I did not think of that. Nor," she added with a smile, "did I stand in any great need of protection! Those poor churls were the ones in danger—and they are my people; your men cannot even understand their speech. Was it not my duty to speak for them?"

"They are my people now," Louis said, "and these are my lands."

That night there was not even a villein's hut to sleep in, much less a church; they camped in a forest clearing. Louis was anxious for Eleanor's comfort, apologizing so many times she thought she would scream. The next day, he explained, they would cross the Charente.

"I do know where we are," Eleanor pointed out.

"Vermandois and Suger will be happier when we are across the river," Louis went on earnestly. "Saintes is still not France, but at least it's the northern part of your domains. We can travel more slowly then. You won't have so many hardships to bear."

He looked so worried that Eleanor decided not to tell him that she found the French army's cumbersome slow march no hardship at all. At least, not in the way he meant. Her father had been used to travel with a far smaller retinue and to make good speed over the best roads in his realm. She found the slow pace of the army tedious but hardly exhausting.

"And tomorrow we will rest at Taillebourg."

"Ah." Eleanor thought that over. Louis kept glancing sidewise at her, as if he expected her to divine some extraordinary meaning from his words. "Count Vermandois trusts Geoffrey de Rancon?"

"Granted, he's a Poitevin, and that's not good," said Louis so innocently that she could not find it in her heart to be annoyed with him, "but at least he has done homage to my father for his lands in the north, and he's visited our court. Abbot Suger thinks he is to be trusted. You will lie in comfort at Taillebourg," he promised her, "and—and there will be more privacy there." His smooth cheeks flushed and he looked away from her.

She knew Louis well enough, by then, to understand his meaning: that by tomorrow night she would know him much better.

Raoul de Vermandois gave his own tent to the ladies for their comfort and privacy—not that there was much of either, with so many of them crowded into one small space. Eleanor was too restless to fall asleep easily in such a crowd. She lay awake late into the night, staring up at the stars that showed through the open flap at the center pole. Petronilla's head rested on her shoulder. On Petronilla's breath she could smell the sweet honey cakes that Raoul gave the child whenever he could find them. Beneath the cloaks that covered their pallets she could smell crushed flowers and fresh-cut grass still warm with summer's heat. Sweet, warm, intimate fragrances. Tomorrow . . .

If she kept thinking of tomorrow, she would never sleep. She watched the stars in their slow dance about the center pole, lying very still with her hands folded under her breasts until it seemed to her that her body was floating upon the earth. Her hair coiled about her like a thicket of vines. The center pole of the tent became a mast, the red and golden walls were sails filled by the warm secret wind that blew from the green forest all around them. She became a ship moving through the earth as through water, sailing to a destination only guessed at from afar. And it was too late to turn back now, even if she had wished to.

> I sat in the chapel of Saint Simeon
> and great waves crept around me, came on and on,
>> waiting for my love,
>> waiting for my love!

There was no feasting at Taillebourg, none of the bawdy revelry and songs and jokes Eleanor had been expecting for their wedding night. If Louis had not already informed her of his plans to consummate the marriage that night, she would hardly have guessed. The only difference from the other nights was that only water, no wine, was served at the ducal table. Eleanor thought she knew why. Louis wanted her to know that he needed no wine to arouse him.

Nor did she. What need of wine and bawdy talk when two healthy young bodies came together? She shivered then, thinking of Louis and the smooth white skin of his arm with the play of muscles under the skin and how once in helping her to dismount on a hot day their bare arms had touched and a tremor of sweet delight ran through her.

usband?" Tentatively.

"Wait." Louis's head was bent in prayer. Under the long gown he wore, Eleanor could see that one part of him, at least, didn't want to wait any longer. She sat up in bed, bent her head, and tried to compose herself to prayer as he did. A woman should follow her man's guidance. Even Dangereuse wouldn't dispute that— although the man she followed had not been her husband. And on that thought, Eleanor remembered her grandfather's song about the two favorite mares he loved to ride—the song everybody thought she didn't know. Eleanor could not imagine the old duke taking time for prayer when there was a practically naked girl warming his bed.

A nervous giggle escaped her.

Louis looked up and she caught a flash of something quite terrifying in those cool blue eyes. But before he could speak there was a tap on the door.

"Cover yourself!" he said, although Eleanor was sure that a moment ago he'd been about to say something quite different. She obeyed, hauling the embroidered coverlet up to her neck, while a serving girl staggered in with two heavy buckets of water.

Eleanor stared at the lines of gold embroidery on the coverlet. The gold twinkled and sparkled most royally in the candlelight. It also pricked her breasts through the thin shift that was all she wore. She had been saving it for her wedding night, a wisp of silk from Constantinople through which the tips of her breasts showed pink.

Audrée de Rancon had meant to honor them with this stiff uncomfortable coverlet, fit for a king's bed. *I could have done with a little less honor.* But the girl was gone now, and Louis was coming toward the bed, face set; she'd think him angry, but for the stiff evidence thrusting his gown out in front. His blood must be dancing like hers. In a moment there would be all the sweetness of that one time when their bare arms brushed, and more, delight to ease the aching between her thighs. In a few minutes she would know all that was known to those bare-breasted peasant girls with their laughing indecent games in the forest.

"You see," Louis said, gesturing behind him to the buckets full of cold water, "I have thought of everything needful."

Eleanor had no time to wonder what this meant; almost immediately he said something stranger yet.

"I suppose we may as well get this over with." And instead of throwing back the

71

heavy, scratchy, gold-embroidered coverlet, he lifted it and the linen sheet by one corner and inserted the length of his body beside hers. Eyes squeezed shut, he took her breast in a fierce grip that made her gasp in surprise and pain. He wriggled, still with eyes shut, until he was lying on top of her. At the same time he pulled up his long gown with quick, impatient jerks. He tried to do the same to hers, but the thin fabric was pinned between Eleanor's body and the mattress by their double weight. The silk tore under his hand and she felt his naked flesh pressing hard against the tangled curls of her body hair, pushing and battering and pulling the little tight curls as if he thought the entrance were there.

"Not there," Eleanor whispered finally. "*There!*" She bent her knee and took Louis in her hand and guided him to the aching soft place between her thighs, as Dangereuse had instructed her. He was in with a tearing rush and the pain made her catch her breath for a moment, but now that he knew his way he gave her no respite, two quick thrusts into the torn flesh, three, and his hand closed grindingly tight on her left breast. He shuddered and then leapt backward like a fish struggling in the net, out of her body and away from her, leaving her with aching at her breast and between her legs and with warm sticky wetness flooding out from between her thighs.

Turning his back to Eleanor, he bent over one of the buckets. She heard water trickling. His gown was strained tight against him, raised up above his long slender white calves, the fabric tight against the long flat lines of thighs and buttocks. Suddenly it came to Eleanor what he must be doing: he had pulled his long gown up in front and was washing himself. All the parts that touched her.

Water spattered out around the rim of the bucket and made a pattern of wet dots on the floor. Eleanor looked at the splashes and tried not to observe, because it seemed disrespectful to her new-wedded lord, that Louis had knobby feet with bones almost poking through the thin blue-veined white skin. She couldn't stop looking at his feet. She stared up at the embroidered canopy over the bed then and counted the figures that winked in and out with the quivering of the candle's flame.

After she had counted the figures of Moses and Absolom and Abraham and told over all their stories to herself, the splashing stopped and she heard Louis padding toward the bed on those long bare feet. She stole a glance. His gown hung decently straight over his body now, a little wet around the hem. And his face was again the face of the young prince she had married, calm and sweet, with golden curls falling to his shoulders and blue eyes fixed on her in a look of love. Not the stern face of the warrior-prince who came into her bed as though she were some distasteful duty. Nothing poking out the front of his gown either.

"I must apologize, wife," he said. "I should have let you go first, but my need was great."

All at once Eleanor—how could she have been so slow!—all at once she grasped what the second bucket of water was there for. Her flesh shivered with anticipatory chill even before she slid out from under the stiff, prickly coverlet. Louis modestly averted his eyes. The long tear in the shift left her with little covering. And it was bloody too. She stepped out of the ruined garment and bent naked over the bucket to wash herself.

The cool water was soothing on her torn parts. *He is my husband,* she thought. *He takes care for me . . . he thought of this beforehand. It will be all right. I do love and honor him. I do.*

Not wishing to seem less cleanly than her husband, Eleanor stood at the bucket for long enough to say six Aves and a Paternoster, splashing and washing until her thighs and belly were chilled as white marble. When she finally clambered back into the high bed, she would have apologized for bringing her chilled wet self between the sheets, but Louis was already asleep. Eleanor blew out the candles and pressed close up against her husband, seeking warmth in the long bony body.

I do love him. I do. The soundless litany went on until she drifted off to sleep on the sighing of a night breeze from the forest that stretched on and on outside Taillebourg, full of secret paths she had not taken.

Louis dreamed:

Images floated through the blackness: a grimacing demon face, a white fleshless skull, *something* under a cowl. Flames leapt up around him. He screamed and the flames died down. Why, they were nothing more than candles, and the faces that looked so monstrous were merely the good brothers of Saint-Denis, going in winter darkness to say Matins. And he was walking with them, a little child holding a crucifix almost as tall as he was.

He had never left the monastery, never grown up and married; *that* had been the dream. Relief washed over and through him, borne on a tide of prayers and holy songs. But before he could enjoy his safety, the voice of Abbot Suger boomed out through the darkness: "The devil is everywhere. Fight the devil! Do not be deceived by illusions! Cast out the evil spirits!"

He swung the crucifix two-handed, like a scythe, and the monks squealed and collapsed around him, their robes billowing and flapping around bodies strangely shrunken—squat little bodies with sharp trotters and blunt snouts, a herd of squealing, writhing pigs trying to run between his ankles and trip him up, but he was too fast for them.

The crucifix became a sword in his hands and he swung it in the rhythm of his arms master's chanting, and *one* and *two* and *turn* and *up*, until his arms trembled with exhaustion. "You handle that sword like a peasant chopping wood!" Raoul exclaimed in disgust. Louis was sorry to have disappointed him. He knew it was a great honor to have the count of Vermandois for his trainer.

One last pig struggled before him, hamstrung and still squealing. Louis took off its head with a downward slash of the blade, burying the sword halfway into the flesh between head and body. He looked up to Raoul for approval, but Saint Denis's tragic carved face met him instead.

The saint's stone face was weeping, and the crucifix he held was stuck in something. He braced his foot and tugged it free and slipped, down into blood and spilled guts and chopped dead flesh, and woke—

Not screaming. But damp with sweat and trembling in every limb. Something snuffled beside him and he started with terror, then remembered all at once who and where he was, and that what lay beside him was not one of the swine of his nightmare but something he'd been taught to regard as even fouler and much more dangerous.

A woman.

His wife, Eleanor, sleeping with one arm thrown back over her head and snoring very lightly on every second or third breath, and her firm young breasts swelling under the coverlet. He laid one hand over the smooth roundness and was suddenly shaken with anger. Through the woman Eve sin came into the world. Why should the woman sleep while he wrestled with night demons?

His woman, he reminded himself.

He woke her all at once, thrusting himself into the softness of her body until a long, shuddering ecstasy possessed him and his hands clenched on her shoulders and the canopied bed shook around them.

Then he cleansed himself and prayed until dawn for forgiveness.

Chapter Six

Poitiers was a golden church on a hill, a river, the dark crypt shrine of Saint Radegonde. Poitiers was the tower her grandfather had built for his mistress Dangereuse of Châtellerault. Poitiers was the scent of linden trees blossoming in summer, the cool waters of the Clain half encircling the town, the white palace that still echoed with her grandfather's songs, her father's shouts, and the crack of his whip at the hunting hounds, the songs her mother had hummed. Poitiers was home.

They were all dead now, all but Dangereuse, who had remained in Bordeaux to safeguard Eleanor's interests there. All gone, and home had been invaded by a crowd of loud, flat-voiced, quick-tongued, sharp-nosed Frenchmen who squirreled into every cranny of the palace. By the right of Eleanor's marriage, these French considered themselves to be the heirs to all the wealth left by William, duke of Aquitaine and count of Poitou. They counted up his rents and lands with greedy eyes and fingers, spoke slightingly of his administration and sternly of his morals. Their clerics made it known that Louis, the new count of Poitou by right of his wife, had no use for minstrels or jongleurs and such lowlifes, little interest in hunting and none whatever in the late William's favorite ladies.

"In God's name, what *does* he care for, then?" inquired Amicie de Périgné, master of the stables, after discovering that the count's stables were to be diminished by two-thirds in the name of economy, and the parks where his breeding mares ran were to be turned into domain farms.

"Louis is a good and pious man who cares most of all for Holy Church," said Odo, the monk of Saint-Denis who had brought this unwelcome news, "and after that, for the good of his realm. And," he added reluctantly, "his wife . . ."

"Well, God bless the marriage bed!" exploded Amicie. "A lot that tells me. I'd like to see the lad of sixteen who wouldn't care to have a pretty, lusty armful like one of the old master's daughters in his bed. I thought my worthless brother Benoît—you know, the one who ran off to be a student in Paris—was as useless as they come, but even he knows what to do with a girl when he can get one; it sounds as if this king is more of a clerk than ever Benoît will be. And as for the rest—well, if he cares so much for the church, he might better have remained a monk. And as for the good of the realm, you can tell him from me that he'll have the devil of a time keeping this realm under control once he's sold off the count's best breeding stock and broken up the herds. Does he think good warhorses can be taken from the peasants' plow teams? Maybe he'd like to use the peasants for his knights, too. Save a deal of silver that way, he would."

"Young Louis is count of Poitou and duke of Aquitaine now," said Odo in frosty tones, "and he intends to be a good Christian monarch and a man of peace, neither having nor making any enemies."

Amicie stomped off, kicking horse dung off his boots and muttering that those fools of Bordelais might have named Louis their duke but as far as he was concerned the boy wasn't count of Poitou yet, nor would be until he'd been crowned in Notre-Dame-la-Grande in sight of all the Poitevins, and there were two weeks yet before the coronation and many a slip between the cup and the lip.

Odo ordered the man watched, and when he reported the conversation to his abbot, Suger took worried council with the count of Vermandois. They agreed to put the coronation forward by a week, regardless of the fact that many noble lords would scarcely arrive in time for the ceremony. And in the days remaining, they would see to it that a quiet watch was kept not only on Amicie de Périgné, but also on any other magnates of Poitou who were suspected of having come to Poitiers only to spread disaffection—which, as Suger sadly said, meant virtually any Poitevin of note who'd arrived so far.

The danger, naturally, came from a completely different and unexpected direction.

Eleanor's head ached abominably. How long had the pain been going on? It seemed like weeks, but that couldn't be true. Less than a week earlier she'd been crowned duchess of Aquitaine at Bordeaux, at the same Mass that had blessed her wedding to Louis. A successful and triumphant conclusion to the dangers that had gathered like shadows around her since Papa's death in Compostela. Next week she and Louis would go through another joint ceremony, this one to crown them as count and countess of Poitou. Then they would travel north to Paris, where the heir to the throne of France must reside. Everything was—should be—most satisfactory.

But Poitiers was stifling in the August heat, crowded beyond bearing by her household and Louis's French escort. Every day half a dozen minor quarrels broke out between French and Poitevins; every day more proud landholders arrived to quarrel over precedence and complain about their lodgings. There was not a private corner anywhere in the ducal palace, even for the mistress of Aquitaine and Poitou; there was not a quiet shadowed place or a cool breath of wind or any ease from the headache that gripped her temples. Petronilla brewed calming tisanes that tasted like boiled grass and did as much good. Radegonde of Maillezais combed out Eleanor's hair daily and anointed it with lotions to calm the dry, flyaway strands. Her ladies whispered in corners when they thought she was not listening: the shock of Duke William's death had been too much for her. There was a strain of madness in the family, almost as bad as the counts of Anjou with their demon grandmother lurking in the roots of the family tree. She'd become a woman too late and married too soon after that, and you knew what *that* did to a girl's health!

And Dangereuse and Cercle-le-Monde had remained in Bordeaux, and in the August heat of the crowded city Eleanor could not even remember the heart of the oldest forest, the clearing wreathed about with green and burning vines, the cool fountain that Cercle-le-Monde had promised she should always find at need. It had been a dream, only a dream.

Now she could not even dream in safety. Her nights were filled with whispering silken shadows, walls of silk behind which danger waited. She flew over a land changed all to harsh silver, with no green and growing thing to rest her eyes. She marched through mud that the winter rains and cold had turned to silver ice, leading an army of skeletons. And she woke not to the comforting crowded big chamber where Dangereuse slept on one side of her and Petronilla on the other and all her ladies snored and murmured on pallets around the curtained bed, but to a narrow stone-walled room that Louis had commanded for the privacy of himself and his wife. She woke to Louis's hands and the quick, punishing assaults on her body that happened two and three times in a night, that she endured in silence, wondering what was wrong with her that she could not enjoy the sweetness of love as the troubadours sang about it.

When the messenger came from Talmont, she was more than ready to hear his words.

By good fortune, Louis was not there to hear the secret insolence of the phrasing in which William of Lezay couched his innocent message. Perhaps, Eleanor thought, it was not exactly good fortune. William was impetuous but not stupid, and the boy who spoke in his name had doubtless been instructed to use quite different words if he spoke before the heir to France.

Before I deliver the falcons, I would see the mistress of the hunt. Come to Talmont and take your legacy from my own hands.

"The castellan of Talmont invites us to come and take the white gyrfalcons that he kept for my father," she told Louis that night, while Radegonde unplaited her long braids and combed out the crackling honey-brown hair. She had thought out her words carefully. Louis cared nothing for the pleasures of the chase. He hunted, he had told her, because it was expected of the king's son, but he had rather have spent his time in prayer or study. It was no use mentioning the game park her father had created near Talmont, the woods where he and his men might find good sport.

"A long way to go for nothing but a few hawks." Louis frowned.

"Gyrfalcons," Eleanor corrected him. "A royal bird, my lord, the only one suitable for the heir to France. I would be proud to give you such a wedding gift."

"Can't he send them here?"

Eleanor thought that William of Lezay had no intention of complying so readily. And she, for her part, had no intention of allowing her father's gyrfalcons to remain as the toys of a minor castellan, when she could be making good use of them wherever she and Louis went! She concentrated on the anger in that thought until she could almost believe that was all her purpose, to recover a valuable part of her father's estate without provoking a quarrel among his vassals.

"We could escape this court ceremonial for a day or two. Talmont is an easy day's ride, and I remember the castle from my father's journeying—it lies by the sea, in cool air." An involuntary sigh escaped her, and Louis bent over her bowed head.

"You wish to go," he said. "Why did you not say so? We shall leave at once."

Eleanor laughed. "In the morning will be soon enough, I think."

"True. In the morning, then. You may leave us," he said in the same breath to Radegonde, and she slipped away without a word, smiling and winking at Eleanor as she passed.

He does love me, Eleanor thought. *He will ride to Talmont only because I wish to be away from the court for a day or two. He does love me.* And she tried to think only of Talmont, of the forest and the pink cliffs and the whispering sea, through the long night that followed.

Talmont: a square sandstone keep at the western edge of the world, mist-enshrouded, with the sharp edges of the native limestone softened by wind and water, the harsh colors of sunlight diluted to soft gold and rose tints upon the native stone. The French knights who were the advance escort on this holiday excursion came riding ahead with jests and laughter that slowly died away as they took in the loneliness of the site. The sea cliffs fell away sharply on either side of the castle, a long, lonely drop to a narrow pebbled strand. Beyond the promontory: waves, mist, more waves, all fading out into gray-blue nothingness.

"End of the world," said Ivo of Soissons. His voice echoed within the iron helm: echoes of the sea, waves crashing upon the shore. "Nothing beyond here."

The Templar, Thierry Galeran, sighed. What ignorance he must live with! He sighed again for the good castles of the order in Outremer, the men living cleanly and by rule, with no women or turbulent birdbrained secular knights to disturb the proper way of things. "Nothing? Perhaps not due west. But to the north, there's England and Wales somewhere out in the mist. And beyond them, Ireland."

Ivo shrugged off the correction. "Nothing," he repeated. "I don't count a couple of islands in the mist where the natives grow tails and barely understand human speech. Only a Norman would think it worth conquering."

Someone else in the party cracked a weak jest about Stephen of Blois, nominal king of England, and the trouble he was having with the old king's daughter, Matilda. Even a woman could try to take England from him.

The knights agreed that England could well be left to women and weaklings. Their lord had Poitou and Aquitaine, and on the old king's death he would have France as well.

"Look sharp," Ivo of Soissons yelled. "Form guard, each side of the road, they're coming!"

Eleanor rode sedately and sidesaddle, as Louis thought befitted a woman, and the slow pace of their little procession had her gritting her teeth and ready to scream with impatience and boredom by the time the lonely castle by the sea came into view. They'd passed the night before at a hunting lodge of her father's, on the edge of his game preserve, a little more than two-thirds of the way from Poitiers. Papa would have made the journey in a single day, with Guilhem de Herbert cursing the speed and praying for time to bring up the wagons of household goods, and she'd have been riding astride with no nonsense about a lady's weakness or anything else that might delay the boisterous, noisy, good-humored progress from one brief stop to the next. Papa—

Eleanor bit down hard on her lip. It was no good thinking about Papa. The big, blond man who'd dominated her childhood was wrapped in a shroud at Compostela. He'd left his lands and people in her care. *Have I done well so far, Papa? Have I? See, I'm married to the king of France's son. There'll be no little wars in this realm while the French army helps me to keep the peace. I've done well, Papa. You would be pleased with me.*

Louis rode patiently at her side, on a gelding so meek and mild it might have been trained as a lady's palfrey. He did not seem to mind the slow pace; he discoursed pleasantly on the Abbot Suger's sermon of last Sunday, about the meekness of Jesus and the need for all earthly rulers to imitate Our Lord in this respect. Eleanor murmured appropriate meaningless responses whenever he paused and strained her eyes for a sight of their destination. Suddenly, between one well-turned religious quotation and the next, the woods opened out to flat salty meadows where the sea wind continually lashed the pale grass into waves. Armor glittered and sparked in the sunshine far ahead of them—the knights of the advance guard, drawn up in two lines on either side of the road before the castle.

William of Lezay greeted his guests with a bluff cheerfulness, as though this were any ordinary visit. He bent his knee to Louis with just the hint of a smile, just enough to say, *See how I humor this sulky boy in his pretensions to being a great lord!* He lifted Eleanor down from her horse with his own hands and made a jest of the small service, saying that he did but stand in place of his liege lord until Louis should grow into his strength. Not lost on anybody, the contrast between Louis's thin frame and William's broad chest and shoulders, the muscles built by years at sword practice or in the tiltyard. Not lost, either, the sly implication that William would happily take his lord's place to fulfill any other duty that Louis might not be man enough for.

William's hands lingered a moment longer than strictly necessary at Eleanor's waist. Just as Louis started forward, the other man swung away with a word of greeting to Ivo of Soissons, leaving Louis awkwardly with one foot up and nowhere to go.

The falcons? Oh, they were in good health enough. They should be brought out after the party had done him the honor of dining at Talmont—just now . . . and William lapsed into technical talk, falconers' talk, meaningless to Louis, and mixed with so many expressions of goodwill and gratification at the honor of this visit that there was no way to interrupt or question him.

He showed them around Talmont with the pride of a freeholder; after eighteen years as castellan, clearly he had no thought of ever being separated from the place and sent to serve his lord elsewhere. They saw the core of Talmont, the little chapel and the old tower, and then they had a lightning tour of the outer defenses. William led them through stair and hall and gate towers and out again between the winding walls of the outer and inner baileys, up and down the uneven levels dictated by building on the edge of the sea cliff. He moved fast and light on his feet for such a big man, with the French knights in their heavy armor clumping behind him, out of breath and unable to keep up. And Louis, for safety's sake, was constrained to stay behind with his men while William of Lezay whisked Eleanor just a few steps ahead. Her fur-trimmed skirt floated out behind her. Louis moved always in a cloud of her passage, the flash of a skirt, the scent of her hair, a laugh or a murmured word from William just too far ahead for him to see clearly.

Eleanor danced lightly up stairs and around passages. She felt free and light as a wisp of silk in the breeze. She had brought only one waiting woman on this excursion, and Radegonde of Maillezais was too stout to take the endless winding stairs of Talmont; she puffed along, well behind the little knot of suspicious Frenchmen, no chaperone at all for Eleanor. They turned a corner and the western world fell away to nothingness at her feet, nothing between her and the sea but a breast-high wall of the native pink-tinged stone.

William of Lezay smiled with delight at her surprise. "A castle can be well defended and also beautiful," he said, "like a virtuous woman."

They stood on a sheltered walkway built out right over the water. The crenellated wall had been constructed to shelter bowmen repelling anyone crazy enough to attack from the sea. Eleanor refused to think about that. All too much of the last months had been spent thinking of nothing but the dangers around her. She could smell salt water and a gentle wind from the west that carried, somehow, a memory of green shores she had never seen. The wind tugged at the heavy silver-gilt sheaths that held her long braids, whipped the extravagant fullness of her sleeves back like long green wings as she laughed with pleasure and raised her arms to the sea.

"This could have been yours," William of Lezay said.

The moment of peace was over. "This is ours," she reminded him. "You hold Talmont by our command, and by my faith and Saint Radegonde, if you forget this again we shall replace you with a worthier vassal!"

Puffing in their weight of armor, Louis's escort caught up to them; the cold Templar knight, Thierry, in the lead as always.

There was a minor stir in the ducal palace at Poitiers. Some commoner was trying to force his way in among the magnates who gathered to do homage to their new lord.

"Name?" demanded the bored page whose duty it was to announce noble visitors.

"Maître André."

"Of?"

"Representing the merchants' guild of Poitiers."

The boy laughed in his face. "You can't come in here, you! We've got seigneurs and nobles sleeping in the halls; there's no place for a fat merchant."

"I have business," Maître André said. He resisted the impulse to tug his gown down, even though he felt sure it had ridden up above his ankles. He wasn't used to walking slowly, like a rich noble who had nowhere in particular to go and nothing to do when he got there.

"What sort of business?"

"A petition from the burghers of Poitiers, asking the lady Eleanor to remit the taxes that her late father imposed for the war on Angoulême. And—"

"Can't see the lady," the page interrupted. "She's gone off to Talmont for a couple of days. That's on the coast," he informed the merchant.

"I do know where Talmont is—"

"Besides, anything like that goes to her husband now. Louis. Not fitting to leave such affairs to a girl," said the page, who was all of twelve years old and very conscious of his masculine superiority.

"Then I'll lay my petition before Louis—"

"He's at Talmont too. On the coast, you know," the page said kindly.

By the dinner hour the white gyrfalcons had been displayed, hooded on their perches in the mews, and William of Lezay had discoursed on their virtues until Louis, bored, broke off the conversation. More as a means of getting away from the talk of falconry than from any other reason, he agreed that they would stay and dine at Talmont before setting out with the falcons. Ivo of Soissons, at twenty-five the oldest man in the ducal party, fretted that they would be late in setting out; it would be close to dark before they returned to the hunting lodge on the Poitiers road. Louis overruled him.

"We do not fear to dine with our loyal castellan," he said, and one of William's men in the background stifled a snigger at this sixteen-year-old pomposity.

All the same, there were far more Poitevins than French dining in the hall. Ivo of Soissons prevailed upon Louis to leave some of his men outside, saddling up and preparing so that the whole party might leave immediately after dinner.

The men who remained in the inner bailey, munching on bread and cold meats, put on their heavy hauberks of chain mail and their conical steel helms after they'd finished the meal. They sweated in the August warmth, even with the sea breeze to cool them, but they would be ready to make a good show for their lord when he departed. Those who dined inside on game pies and hot cheese tarts were bareheaded and unarmed, Poitevins and French alike, except for the little knives they used to cut their meat. Everyone was carefully courteous, even William of Lezay, and the thunder of things unsaid dominated the conversation.

Eleanor and her woman Radegonde were the only gentle females present.

Somehow William managed matters so that Eleanor should share a cup and a trencher with him, so that Louis would seem churlish to object. She challenged him over the cup of thin Loire wine they shared.

"I had heard that you did not live alone in Talmont."

William of Lezay shrugged. "There is a woman; I'm no monk, nor do I live like one. But I would not have insulted you by keeping her. Whenever I marry, she will be sent away."

"Your future wife will doubtless be delighted to hear it," Eleanor said politely.

Louis had been watching them with jealous eyes, but now he was busy arguing some point of theology with his neighbor, showing more enthusiasm for the debate than he'd shown for any of the political maneuverings that occupied Suger and Raoul de Vermandois. "Why did you send such an insolent message?"

William protested. "Insolent? It was only an invitation."

"Yet you refused to send him our gyrfalcons."

"I meant only to invite the two of you here for a pleasant visit." William of Lezay smiled at her and offered the cup of wine, and his fingers brushed hers on the stem. "I wanted . . . to see you again. With *him*." His tone dismissed Louis as a thing of no consequence, save in his possession of Eleanor. "To see if you looked happy, as a new-wedded bride should look, all blushes and smiles."

Eleanor felt her own smile as sharp as the blade of her little knife. "As you see, I am content in my marriage. It is eminently suitable; France is joined to Aquitaine."

"More than lands must be joined in marriage."

"I am content," she repeated. "And you could have seen my lord and me in Poitiers. You could have brought the gyrfalcons there and achieved all your end."

William's voice was low, caressing as the refrain of a love song. "I wanted to see . . . if you would come to me."

Eleanor moved sharply, spilling the golden wine. She could feel the heat rising to her cheeks.

"Do you know how I tame a hawk of the fist? It's a long process. You must live with her and love her and give her all your mind. In the end you must let her fly free; but if she is yours, she will return to your hand at call."

When Louis noticed the spilled wine and the minor commotion of pages wiping up the puddle, William was discoursing with all propriety on the art of falconry, and

Eleanor was toying with the empty wine cup as though it were a dice cup in a gambling game. She could feel the flush that William's teasing had brought to her face. She hoped Louis had not noticed it.

"Enough, Lezay! My wife has no desire to hear you prose on as if you were your own falconer," Louis said, more sharply than Eleanor had yet heard him speak.

William of Lezay laughed—a slow, deep, lazy laugh that reminded Eleanor poignantly of Papa in a good mood. "Ah, but I am my own falconer, my boy. You'll learn that a wise man does not entrust his treasures to other hands. No one can gentle a bird so well as I can."

"Speak with more respect to your liege lord!"

William raised one thick blond brow. "I held my lands of the count direct. I do homage to my lady countess now. Is that not correct?" he appealed to the dry, colorless little man who was his clerk and chamberlain.

"Perfectly correct, my lord," Raoul de Fermont assured his master. "The lady is countess of Poitou and duchess of Aquitaine in her own right, and your homage is due to her."

"And through her, to her husband." Louis leaned across Eleanor to argue the point. His face was splotched with pink and he was breathing hard through his nose.

"Softly, softly, my young lord," William of Lezay advised him. "A falcon gentle cannot be commanded like a beast of the field. She must be coaxed sweetly to your hand." He caressed Eleanor with his eyes; his lazy smile taunted Louis.

"You go too far, you—" Louis leaned farther over the table and aimed a clumsy blow at William of Lezay, who caught the boy's arm in his hand and forced it downward. A thin film of spittle appeared on Louis's lips. He grabbed the little meat knife from his trencher and swung it wildly, point down. William pushed him away, reflexively. Louis slipped on the greasy rushes and went down on one knee, yelling, "Treason! Treason! To me, Franks!"

A tired man in dusty clothes, stinking of his own sweat and his horse's, demanded entrance and an audience with Louis of France.

"Can't," said the captain of the watch.

"I bear news that must be given into his own ears and none other's, and that at once."

"I don't care if you come from the king himself, you can't see young Louis. He's gone off to play at hawking on the coast. Talmont. Be back in a couple of days."

"Then let me talk to Abbot Suger—or better, the lord seneschal, the count of Vermandois."

"In the middle of the night?"

"If I could risk breaking my neck and meeting night demons to ride over the collections of ruts and puddles these Poitevins call a road," the messenger said, "the count can turn out of his warm bed to hear the news. I promise you, keep him waiting until morning for this, and when I leave here I'll be waving good-bye to your ugly head stuck up above the city gates."

In the space of two breaths the dinner had become a melee. Eleanor saw Radegonde, crouched in a corner. Somebody tipped over the table in front of her; somebody else hurled a platter of roast meats. For a mad moment Eleanor wanted to laugh at the Franks and Poitevins scuffling in the hall, big sweating men pushing each other around on the greasy rushes and shouting obscenities in two languages. Then the door burst open and men in chain mail, their faces masked by conical helms with long protruding nasal bars, were all over the hall like ants swarming from a broken hill. *Whose men? We're all going to die here.* For a moment the smallest details that Eleanor saw became very clear and precious and filled with light: the wood-grain pattern of the tabletop, a crumb of gravy-soaked bread that had broken off from the trencher, the white scar on William of Lezay's right hand, reaching for a sword that wasn't there.

Then one of those faceless armed men threw himself half on and half over the table, thrust a sword hilt at Louis, lurched into her and bore her backward off the bench and down into stinking rushes full of the grease and scraps of the last hundred or so meals. Her right shoulder hit the stones of the wall with a sharp crack, and for a moment she knew nothing but pain white as sheet lightning, sickening in the pit of her stomach, making her want to throw up. And the man's weight on top of her, crushing her. Her right arm wouldn't move. She struck up at him with her empty left hand, bruising her knuckles and tearing her nails on his armor. *Stupid.* She hated herself for being so slow and stupid. *Think.* The little knife for cutting her meat, where was it now? Knocked out of her right hand when this man threw himself on her, lying amid the gnawed bones in the rushes, inches away from her useless right arm. *Move. Keep hitting so he doesn't notice what you're doing.* She struck and clawed at the weight of armor and stinking man flesh above her. Each sliding inch gained by her right hand cost her a gasp of pain, but who'd notice with this battle around them? Her fingers touched the haft of the knife, all slippery with grease, just as the man on top of her grabbed her left wrist and squeezed it to grind the bones together. "Stop fighting, you silly bitch," he roared above the din. Something crashed against the stones at the other end of the hall. "I'm here to keep you safe!"

Silence fell on the last words, the shouts of the men around them and the clang of swords pausing as abruptly as if the hand of God had descended on His brawling children.

Slowly, the man on Eleanor moved back. He pushed his helm back with one hand and scratched his long nose. She knew him now: Thierry Galeran of the Templars, one of Louis's trusted knights.

She sat up with a hiss of pain for her injured shoulder and looked at the hall. William of Lezay was backed into a corner, beside a splintered bench. That must have been the crash she heard. Two of Louis's men had their swords at his throat. The other Poitevins stood like children frozen in a game of catch-me-who-can, waiting for the leader's word to break free and run again.

"Move," said Ivo of Soissons with quiet satisfaction, "and your lord dies. Lezay, tell them to yield."

At the hoarse command, the Poitevins threw down what arms they possessed: a few belt knives, planks of wood that they'd been swinging like quarterstaves or holding as shields against the swords of the French knights. There had never been any chance for them. They would not look at William of Lezay. Eleanor saw their hangdog looks and guessed at their shamed relief that the fight had ended so, without requiring them to fight to the death against an armored enemy.

She shared that relief. *What a silly fight over nothing.* Men were idiots, *all* of them. Louis was a fool to have cried treason over a scuffle that he'd started himself; William had been a fool to tease him like that.

Eleanor picked herself up and shook the grimy rushes out of her skirts. She would have gone to Louis, but Thierry Galeran laid his hand on her arm, restraining her so that she could not move forward without fighting him. *There has been more than enough fighting already. Someone has to be sensible.*

Louis jerked his head at Ivo. "Take them outside. We'll settle this now." He was breathing hard, but Eleanor saw no blood on the sword that Thierry had put into his hand.

"My lord, should I bind their hands?"

"That won't be necessary." Louis's smile chilled Eleanor, though she could not say why. "Two of you for each of them, in case anybody forgets his word."

"We have yielded," protested one of the Poitevins, a paunchy middle-aged man with red cheeks above his bushy dark beard. "Our honor—"

"*Outside.*" Louis cut him off with the one word. Belatedly, Eleanor thought that he could not have understood the protest; the Poitevin had spoken in the langue d'oc.

As the shamed Poitevin knights were led out, Louis commanded Ivo to guard William of Lezay with four men. "Let him come with us." His gaze swept the hall. "The women shall stay here. Thierry, you see to it."

When Eleanor tried to follow, the Templar jerked her back by the right arm. She squeezed her eyes shut against the pain that radiated from her shoulder.

"Better sit down," he said, not unkindly, and righted a bench for her from the chaos on the floor. "Won't be long. Here, you," he called to Radegonde, who was weeping quietly in the corner where she'd first taken refuge, "see to your lady. She feels faint."

"What is he going to do?" Eleanor asked the Templar.

He shrugged. "Treason's a killing matter. Could be he'll be merciful, being that he intends to be a meek and Christian monarch."

"Killing—but it wasn't treason! It was a silly scuffle over nothing!"

Outside, there was a dull *chunk* like an ax sinking into wood. A man's groan sounded muffled, as though he'd buried his head in his sleeve. The woodcutting sound was repeated. Again.

Again. This time, a boy's voice sounded in a scream of pain.

Thierry Galeran was cleaning his nails with his belt knife, one foot propped up on the bench, bored and unconcerned. Eleanor chose her moment and ran for the door. He caught up with her at the sharp edge between sunlight and shadow, where she stood frozen, unable to move or breathe.

"He's cutting off their hands." Four men lay against the wall in their own blood; no one had troubled to sear the bleeding stumps or twist a cord around their arms.

No. Three men and a boy no older than Eleanor, somebody's squire. Even as she watched, the fat Poitevin with the black beard was wrestled forward to—it *was* a chopping block. And her husband, gentle, mild Louis, the boy from the monastery who had never wanted to be a prince and make wars, was raising a sword that now was spattered with blood from point to hilt.

Eleanor's knees buckled under her, but Thierry Galeran held her up with hard hands under her arms. "You wanted to see," he growled. "So watch. Know how we Franks deal with traitors. And tell the rest of your treacherous southern vassals to behave, lest they suffer the same fate."

William of Lezay stood in the inner bailey of Talmont with two men gripping his arms and a third holding a knife point against the small of his back, astonished, unbelieving. All his strength and wit and golden songs were useless in this moment. He stared at the blood that puddled in the dust, attracting a buzzing cloud of flies. The sea mists enfolded Talmont, making of it a world apart, enshrouded, protected by walls of rosy stone and a moat of salt waves. It didn't seem possible that the world should end like this, on a quiet misty summer day.

There was no sound in the bailey but the rhythmic chopping sound of the sword coming down on the block and an occasional groan from the dying men who lay on the far side of the block. No one had taken thought to tend their wounds or stop the bleeding; most of them were as good as dead. Better so. To live without a sword hand, half a cripple, it would be a living death. Maybe his woman would bind up those who still lived. After these butchers were gone. He thought he could see the flash of her red gown in the huddle of serving men and women who stood in the shadow of the keep, guarded by one knight.

Talberic of Saintes went to the block, too proud to fight. He knelt of his own will and extended his arm. The burly knight who held the sword now took off Talberic's hand at the wrist in one clean swing. Thank God, at least they weren't letting that French princeling do it now. Not after he took four tries to cut off Sebastien's hand, chopping up the flesh like a butcher mincing meat, and Sebastien screamed, no shame in that. At least what was being done now was quick and clean, and that damned monk-prince who started it all by getting hysterical over a little teasing, he was over by the door with his lady. Sweet Eleanor, a honey morsel too good for that boy who didn't know how to handle her. Well, he'd tried and failed, should have left it at that, shouldn't have enticed her here. Sweet Jesus, Talberic was the last, they were coming for him now, and the boy called out an order—*no*. Not *both* hands. Dear sweet Lord Jesus, no, not that—

"Do you weep for your lover, lady?" Louis asked Eleanor. His eyes were glittering strangely and he seemed to take no notice of the blood that dappled his arms and hands, that crusted thick and black on the quillons of his sword hilt, that ran in sluggish glistening streams down the bright blade.

"William of Lezay was never my lover," Eleanor answered contemptuously. "As you should know. I have known no man but you. *Unfortunately.*" The tears ran down her face unchecked, but she spoke clearly enough.

"But you might be tempted to change that. If he lived . . ." Louis walked forward slowly, deliberately, raising his sword as he went until the tip was level with William's bared throat. The guards stopped trying to force William down to the chopping block and waited for their lord's next order. All sound, all motion ceased in the blood-spattered bailey. High overhead, a gull squawked, invisible in the mist.

William of Lezay stood very still with the point of the sword pressing against his throat, but his eyes moved, searching, until he met Eleanor's steady gaze. She started forward. The Templar's hands held her in the doorway.

"By God, lady, I would have shown you sweet love, if I had lived," William said deliberately, "but now I have only songs to give."

His full-throated, defiant singing voice startled them all for a moment. "*Quant l'aura doussa s'amarzis—*"

The bright blade of Louis's sword sank into his throat, and blood spurted out over Louis and the guards as William tumbled into the dust, blood and dust darkening the yellow head that would make no more jests and borrow no more of other men's songs. And there was a hammering at the gates of Talmont.

"Open in the name of France!"

Louis had been watching William's fall, head bowed, lips moving as if in prayer. Now he lifted his head. "We shall have Masses said for his soul," he said, and in the same breath, "That is my cousin of Vermandois. Let him in!"

Raoul de Vermandois rode into the inner bailey and dismounted before he took in the butcher's shambles that the place had become. His eyes went first to Louis. "My lord! You are wounded?"

"We met with a treacherous welcome here," Louis told him. "All has been resolved now. Your rescue arrived too late."

Raoul glanced to left and right and found a spot somewhat less bloody than the rest. He knelt before Louis. "I did not come to save you, my lord, not knowing there was need. I come with urgent news from the capital."

He raised his head, a tired middle-aged man whose face showed all the lines of worry and fatigue that the long ride from Poitiers had stamped on them, and something else—some fear and concern that Eleanor could not read. "My lord, the king your father is dead. It is needful that you conclude your business in Poitiers and return to Paris with all speed."

"Dead," Louis repeated softly. And then more loudly, "Dead!"

"Yes, sire. Forgive the bearer of such sad news."

But Louis did not seem stricken by grief. He gripped his bloody sword more tightly and stared around the bailey, his eyes lingering on the pale pink outlines of crenellations and towers against the soft misty sky. "Why then," he said aloud, wonderingly, "then we are France." He turned to Eleanor with a gesture that invited her to share in his sudden wealth. "And we have made you a queen."

Chapter Seven

PARIS, 1137

The Île de la Cité was shaped like a ship upon the Seine, with the pointed prow housing the royal palace like a sea captain's castle upon the deck. Behind that castle lay the tangle of narrow streets and old houses, the dark quarter of the Juiverie and the low ninth-century basilica of Notre-Dame. The ship of the île was tethered by two bridges: the Petit Pont, leading to the rowdy student quarters on the Left Bank, and the Grand Pont, leading to the Saint-Denis road on the Right Bank. The stone bridges with their many arches conveyed a sense of permanence; this ship was going absolutely nowhere. And Eleanor, after scarce three months of marriage, and those spent mostly traveling, felt herself sinking deeper into the muddy waters of the Seine the longer she sat at her window there.

She had sat there for many hours when they first reached Paris, staring at the sky and trying not to think of Talmont. War was a fact of life. Men died. *Not bound and helpless, mutilated by a boy who needed someone else to hold them.* Traitors must be executed. *Louis was a fool to cry treason. Her father would have known how to handle William's taunting.* No. It had been necessary. Of course it had been necessary. People whispered that young Louis would never make a king, that a boy snatched from the monastery could never be strong enough to hold France. He had to show them that he could not be taunted. William of Lezay would never have dared tease Papa like that. It was all his fault. He had underrated her husband. The killings at Talmont had been a matter of political necessity, not a boy's savagery bursting out unchecked.

Eleanor told herself all that, not once but many times over. And then she told herself that she was, of course, quite satisfied with her own arrangements. Hadn't she snatched an ending that might have fitted one of Cercle-le-Monde's romances from the disaster of her father's sudden death, arranging for herself to be married to this white and golden prince instead of to the first rude baron who might have forced himself upon her? Hadn't she, by this wedding, made herself queen of France as well as duchess of Aquitaine and countess of Poitou? It was a perfect match, and as soon as she gave her lord a son and heir—something that surely would not be too long in coming—everything else would be perfect as well.

In the meantime, though, she was not ill pleased to share the great curtained bed with Petronilla while her lord went and did whatever martial things were in his head, and which he had not troubled to explain to her before his departure. And on this autumn day, she was conscious of no trouble other than an irritable and increasing boredom. As Radegonde of Maillezais quacked and flapped her arms and yammered on about propriety and patience, irritation got the upper hand of boredom.

"It may not be proper for me to go to the fair myself," Eleanor said, "but by my faith and Saint Radegonde your namesake, it is not right for the queen of France to wait until a band of fat merchants deign to bring their stuffs to her! I want new silks and linen to clothe myself and my ladies. I want the stuffs *now*, not after the *foire des draps* has closed, and I want to select from the best the merchants have brought, and *all* they have brought, rather than waiting for them to choose which picked-over remnants they will show me! It's they, not I, who lack propriety; they should have waited upon me before the fair began, that I might see the best of their goods first."

"The good queen Adelaide never put so much weight on matters of vanity," muttered one of the French waiting women under her breath. Eleanor's quick ears caught the words and understood more than half of them. She had been picking up this slurred, flat-sounding langue d'oïl much faster than the northerners assigned to wait on her were learning her sweet langue d'oc. Of course, she was much cleverer than they were.

"That," she said, sweetly and very clearly, "I could tell from the manner in which she dresses herself—and her ladies!" She smiled brightly at the sensible waiting women who surrounded her. "Now, ladies, understand this: I shall most certainly go to the fair. This is the first day of sunshine I have seen since we crossed the Loire. I have not heard a song or a merry tale or so much as lifted my feet in a dance

94

step since the day of my wedding. The good lady Adelaide's idea of amusement is to spend three weeks creaking over bad roads to visit her cousin in a Norman nunnery, and I've *done* that." She glanced briefly at Faenze, the girl she'd brought back from that nunnery and the excuse for Adelaide's hostility toward her daughter-in-law. No, one could not regret taking Faenze from the convent, no matter what the cost in strained family relations. "And furthermore," Eleanor finished, her voice dulcet with sweet reason, "this palace is drafty, and it leaks. If this is the autumn, what is your northern winter like? I shall die of boredom if I must spend the next six months watching the rain run down the insides of the palace walls!"

"The king's confessor Odo is to preach today to Queen Adelaide on the tempting wickedness of women and its likeness to the poison of an asp," Radegonde pointed out. "You could take this occasion to visit the queen—"

Eleanor's small chin lifted a quarter of an inch and she seemed to grow taller on the spot. "You mean the dowager queen, do you not, Radegonde? Or have you forgotten that *I*, not Adelaide of Maurienne, am now the queen of France? And I have no desire to sit and listen through another of Odo of Deuil's interminable prosings about my inherent sinfulness in having been born a woman! If he dislikes women so much, let him go back to his monastery—and if he fears us so much, let him protect himself against temptation as the Templar Galeran has done! All it takes is a sharp knife and a little resolution."

Faenze giggled; so did the French girl Bertille, going over to the enemy camp. "And small loss to womankind," Bertille whispered, "the ugly old devil that he is!"

"*Most* improper talk!" Radegonde reproved them all. "No, listen to me, girl! You may be queen now, but I know something more about marriage than you, I who've been widowed three times." She went on unchecked while Eleanor glared mutinously at her and Faenze and Bertille whispered and giggled together. It was her duty to help young Eleanor to a right understanding of her own duty. A good and loyal wife, she told Eleanor, endeavored not to be seen or spoken of. She adopted her husband's will as her own. And if the will of young Louis of France was more toward prayer and fasting, and less toward songs and dances, why, such tastes were altogether exemplary in a king—if rather surprising in such a young one—and the sooner Eleanor bent her proud neck to the yoke of marriage, the sooner she would find the true happiness of obedient servitude and the abjuring of her own sinful will.

"Besides," she added as a clinching statement, "I have heard that this fair is not at all a well-conducted one. Besides the merchants who properly belong there, there are all manner of common folk—students and jongleurs and musicians. . . ."

"Last year," Bertille said wistfully, "a Syrian woman danced upon a rope, with two horns fastened to the soles of her feet."

"I have heard," Faenze added, "that there was a Hungarian with a trained bear, and it danced too—the bear, not the Hungarian!" she finished with her usual giggle.

Petronilla, who had been sitting quietly on a footstool, embroidering with tiny painstaking stitches, looked up, her eyes shining.

"*Quite* common," said Radegonde quickly, feeling the thread of her argument slipping away from her. "Not at all the place for ladies of rank."

"Then we shall be common!" Eleanor cried, dragging the gold sheaths from her braids with such violence that a few strands of honey-brown hair came with them. She ran her fingers through the long braids until her hair floated loose about her face, a wanton cloud. "And I shall be the most common of all, and no one will think twice about my presence there, or guess that the queen goes about among them. I will not even buy silks, Radegonde, only mark what I want and send a man later to purchase them—will that content you? And Faenze, will you lend me that vile patched old cloak you had when you came to me? If we hurry, we can be there before Vespers."

Radegonde suppressed a sigh as Faenze hurried to fetch the old gray cloak. One might have hoped that Faenze, of them all, would show some restraint. After all, the girl was Queen Adelaide's own kinswoman, and she had been on the verge of putting on the nun's veil when Eleanor, with that dreadful impulsiveness, took a fancy to the girl and declared that she must come back to Paris with her ladies. Almost at once, and with no show of reluctance, Faenze changed the sober dress of the postulant for a peacock-blue and gold gown of Eleanor's own, for who could gainsay the whims of princes? And now, scarcely two weeks after their return from that visit, Faenze was worse than all the rest put together for giggling and wearing gaudy finery out of Eleanor's chests and making up sly jokes at the expense of King Louis's good and saintly advisers. It was all very regrettable.

Petronilla knelt protectively over her private coffer, digging down to find her good dress from the wedding without letting any of those strange French girls get a good look at what else she kept inside there. There'd been enough trouble the time Radegonde of Maillezais poked into the coffer, and *she* was Poitevin, fat old interfering bitch though she was, and should have known better than to interfere.

Petronilla had carried Dangereuse's little carved box of narwhal horn all the way from Bordeaux, packed safely at the bottom of her coffer under ribbons and veils and a dress that was faded and too tight to wear. It had been Papa's special gift to her on her name day five years ago. The dress had two long narrow panels of purple silk, almost deep colored as if they were the true Byzantine stuff, and when Radegonde suggested the silk might be cut out and worked into something new, Petronilla clasped the crumpled ball of the dress in her two arms and stared unblinking until Radegonde's face flushed in red blotches and she went away without saying another word. Later Petronilla heard her telling one of the French ladies not to cross the queen's little sister because the child had the witch eye like her grandmother.

That story went to the king's cold chaplain Odo, who had Petronilla in to examine her morals and piety, but not for long. Eleanor stormed into the chapel like an avenging angel and hauled them both out to Saint-Denis, where Abbot Suger told Odo that he and Radegonde should both do penance for the sin of heresy. Next thing they would be speaking of witches who rode the night sky and could call down powers that did not come from Our Lord, and if that wasn't heresy, what was?

Radegonde complained that her bones ached more than ever after a week of penitential prayers, and she hinted that it was Petronilla's cold, unchildlike eyes on her putting that ache into her knees, but she did not dare say anything outright for fear of getting another such penance or, worse, being dismissed from the queen's service altogether.

In the sleepy late-afternoon hour before Vespers, the students who'd been tramping muddy roads to come to the fair were bored and disappointed. It was too early for the entertainers to be out, the jongleurs and the ropedancers and the singers and the pretty girls who sold their wares in the shadows of the bushes at the edge of the fair site. The sober drapers and the money changers haggled over bolts of felted wool and linen, nothing worth taking a holiday to see. There was one length of silk in the colors of a new peach amid new green leaves, but the heathen Greek who displayed it said it was not for the ink-stained fingers of barbarian clerks to touch. One tight-packed knot of girls drifted through the drapers' hall, but they stuck close together and kept the hoods of their dingy old cloaks pulled down to shadow their faces. Clearly they were not yet open for business, though there might be some sport later, when they deigned to show off their finery. Benoît noticed one girl in particular, a slender one with the ring of the warm south in her clear voice, whose scarlet gown blazed like a sunset sky under the gray cloud of her cloak.

"Why did we come now, instead of waiting until the fun starts?" complained Benoît as they wandered out of the drapers' hall to look disconsolately at the muddy expanse where a double row of stalls showed the wares whose sale was not regulated by the marshals. Apart from a few bright, glittering baubles at the goldsmith's booth, even these displays were depressingly practical: waxed thread, hanks of linen ready for weaving, copper and bronze pails, candles of wax and tallow. "I might have stayed at home to finish the copying of that portion of Master Abelard's book; I had only two columns of the sixteen to complete."

"A d-dangerous book to copy," warned the tall, slender boy who stood beside him. He brushed a sheaf of black hair back from his face, revealing a high forehead and a beaked Norman nose. "You know what the bishop says about Master Abelard's work—it comes d-desperately close to heresy." He spoke so quickly that his slight stammer was hardly noticeable. "For myself, I'll stay away from the Mont-Sainte-Geneviève. Anybody can set up a classroom there; even *you*, I suppose, if you could get anyone to listen to you! At the cathedral school of Our Lady one hears good sound d-doctrine and no heretical side paths."

"Suitable," Benoît said calmly, "for a good sound merchant like you, Thomas, with a good sound future ahead of you in your father's countinghouse—ah, no you don't!" He dodged the mock blow Thomas aimed at him, stepped back onto the trailing hem of his torn black gown, and saved himself from a mud puddle by grasping at the shaky poles holding up a money changer's booth. The proprietor shrieked curses at him and threw himself protectively over the leather bags of bezants and deniers, coins of Provins and Italy and ingots from the far north.

"*Now* I remember," Benoît gasped, when he'd recovered his balance, "why you wanted to come out here before the *foire des draps* closed for the day. It's a chance to visit your old friends. You miss the stink of the wool bales; you want to get your hands greasy with lanolin and reckon up deniers owed to some merchant. Returning to your natural habitat."

"At least," said Thomas with a sunny smile, "my natural habitat feeds and shelters me well enough, unlike your one-thirty-second share in a tumbledown castle on top of a barren rock! The way you Poitevins split up your inheritances and your lineage, in a few generations every serf among you will be able to claim nobility."

"Compared to a drunken Englishman with his tail tucked into his braies," Benoît countered, "even a serf from Poitou *is* noble."

Thomas only grinned. "What a lousy crew I've fallen among, you students. Poitevins are traitors, Germans gluttons, Burgundians are all d-dumber than rocks, Lombards are as avaricious as Jews, and Flemings are too lazy to come to the masters' lectures. Nice of my father to send some d-drunken English money by way of his old friends in Rouen. When I've collected my allowance, I'll buy you a d-drink with it."

He disappeared into the hall of the drapers, presumably to look for the Rouennais wool merchant who was bringing his allowance from London, and a mud-splashed, square fellow who'd helped to prop up the money changer's stand edged closer to Benoît.

"You're from Poitou," he stated.

"Want to make something of it?"

"Na, na," the fellow said peaceably, pointing to the cockle-shell badges sewn all over his leather purse. "I'm just a poor pilgrim, lately passed through your lands." He spoke the langue d'oïl with such a heavy Flemish accent that Benoît could hardly understand him. "Terrible things going on there these days. I was in Compostela when your Duke William died—saw him on his last day, in fact. How he suffered!"

"That was six months gone." Benoît considered making some remark about how only a Fleming would be slothful enough to stretch out the journey from Santiago de Compostela to Paris for six long months, then thought better of it. The man meant no harm, he only wanted to unload his gossip on somebody. And there'd been precious little news from home lately. For some reason, none of the chief merchants of Poitiers had even sent men to this fair. There'd been talk of a petition to the duchess, of granting the city certain rights, but that shouldn't have stopped trade.

The Fleming sighed. "Aye, and a weary six months it's been, too. I was seized with the same bloody flux that carried away your late duke. My companions left me there, despairing of my life. But I lived," he announced proudly.

"So much I'd gathered."

"But the pain, aiee, I tell you it was awful, like having burning spears thrust into my gut. They said your duke died of eating bad fish, but let me tell you, I ate nothing but bread and beans down there, and drank nothing but water out of the streams, and I had the same ailment. Exactly the same as your duke. God strikes gentle and simple alike; we're all equal in the sight of God."

"Amen to that," said one of the students who'd come closer to hear the gossip. Benoît recognized him, one of the French students who'd lost the prize to him in the public disputation last Sunday. From the boy's hard unfriendly look, he recognized Benoît too.

"Bad times since then for you Poitevins, eh?" the Fleming said sympathetically.

"Oh, come now," Benoît said, startled, "not so bad as all that. My brother Amicie, God rot him, did write there was some fear when the news began to get out about Duke William's death, but that was all settled right enough when the old king sent his son down to wed our duchess. Claimed he couldn't send me any money because it all went to extra taxes to help pay for the wedding."

"Could be," said the Fleming, nodding sagely, "and a fine wedding it was, by all accounts! I missed it, you understand, being still laid down with the bloody flux in Santiago de Compostela. I tell you, anything I ate went right through me like an impaling stake, a rough splintery one at that. And the stench, you wouldn't believe how I stank."

"Yes, I would," Benoît said. "You're not so fragrant now."

The Fleming shrugged. "Fine thanks I get for riding through mud as deep as a monk's drinking horn, just to bring you news of the terrible happenings in Poitou. What about the rest of you students? Who'll pay to hear why none of the Poitiers merchants have come up to this fair?"

He looked around the growing crowd of black-garbed students and repeated his question, a bit louder. There was an uneasy rustle. Two or three of the French came up with a handful of coppers. Behind the crowd, the money changer whom Benoît had nearly overturned quietly set his leather bags of coins into an iron-banded strongbox and dropped the tattered awning over the open top of his stall.

When the Fleming was sure he had everyone's attention, he began like a natural storyteller, speaking first of the unrest among the merchants of Poitiers, their desire for relief from the war tax that should have ended when Duke William died and the war ended, their anger at the new imposts and tolls levied by the French as soon as Aquitaine and Poitou were legally joined to the French realm.

"They've announced a commune," he said finally with a grand sweep of his square hand.

There was a hiss of indrawn breath from the back of the crowd. "Laon," someone blurted out.

Twenty-five years earlier, the burghers of Laon had formed a commune that was promptly dissolved when their bishop paid the king to ignore the matter. The citizens stormed the palace and found Bishop Gaudry hiding in a wine barrel in the cellar; they dragged him into the cloister, shattered his head and chopped off his limbs. The dismembered, bleeding corpse was the standard for a general rebellion. Nobles and their families were massacred, the palace and the cathedral burned. The burghers who'd started the revolt fled the city, and peasants from the surrounding countryside looted what remained of Laon.

The Fleming shook his head firmly. "*Not* like Laon. Your king will stop this before it goes so far. As I was leaving the city, he and his troops had just arrived. They were herding the burghers' children into the town square."

"What for?"

The pilgrim shrugged. "Some said to cut them down. The next generation won't have such grand ideas if there is no next generation. But I heard the young king is merciful; he'll execute only the children of the ringleaders first, then the leaders themselves. The rest of the children are to be sent north as hostages. I hope he's got a castle big enough to hold all of them," he added cheerfully, "and servants tough enough to take it. He collected all sizes, from babes at suck to young men and women about to be 'prenticed in their parents' trades."

The clear blue sky and gaudy painted stalls of the fairgrounds wavered about Benoît as if he stood on a ship's deck, instead of solid ground.

"Not *all* the children," he heard himself saying.

"No, only the bourgeois."

Benoit remembered Maître André, master of the wine traders' guild, who'd always had a cup of wine and a bite of bread for a hungry boy growing up half wild in a family too large to feed him and too noble to work for bread. André and his wife had a late-born child, a baby girl when Benoît left the south for the learning of Paris. Little frail Jeanette, the treasure of the house; where was she today?

"You're wrong," he said with new conviction. "Louis won't kill children, or seize them out of their parents' hands."

One of the French students looked at him coldly. "You think our king has no stomach for war, because he was raised as a monk? I tell you, *you're* wrong. And he's out to prove it."

"The queen won't let him," Benoît insisted. "Our own young duchess is his queen now, have you forgotten? She wouldn't let him wreak such savagery on her own people, people who are only asking for fair treatment."

The French boy laughed, too loudly, and Benoît could smell the gusty fumes of strong wine on his breath. "You Poitevins, all you're good for is making pretty songs and letting a woman lead you around by your undersized balls. Our king's a real man. He doesn't ask some stupid cunt's permission before he settles the matter of traitors. Look what he did to the castellan of Talmont and all his men, and ask if Louis is the sort of man to go soft on a bunch of Poitevin traitors. With any luck he'll kill off the whole race and we'll no longer be troubled with you scummy rats. As for that slut he married—"

"You are talking about *our duchess*," Benoît said between his teeth, "and I won't hear such lies spread about her, that she'd let her people be treated so!"

"I tell you, I heard what I heard, and who the devil are you to call me a liar?" The Fleming swung a meaty fist at Benoît, who jumped back and let the blow go past him to strike a Norman clerk. Benoît's move backward knocked over a German who took exception to being pushed down into the mud; he rose, growling inarticulately, and hurled Benoît bodily at the French student whose jeers had started the fight.

"*S'arretez! Halten Sie!* Stop!" someone was yelling from outside the milling crowd, making a valiant attempt to cover all the diverse languages of the fair. "*Fermez la foire!*"

"What's that about?" asked the Fleming, who had prudently backed out of the swinging, cursing mob of students after his first unconsidered blow.

"We're closing the fair," panted the marshal of the guards. "Only way to cut off one of these riots—before it gets going." He surveyed the mass of black robes and bare arms and legs and tonsured heads. "Students," he said in a voice that made an obscenity of the word, and then raised his voice to call the guards of the fair. "*Au secours, à moi, mes hommes!*"

"*Haro! Haro!*" the Fleming shouted in a deep voice that carried over the shouts of the students and even checked a few of the Germans for a moment. Then, having done what he could by contributing his own country's signal for the closing of the fair, he helped a goldsmith pack up his goods and depart for the safety of the Paris road. As he left, he glanced over his shoulder and saw that the roiling mass of students had spilled into the hall of the drapers and out the other end, trampling lengths of good Norman wool and Flemish linen and silks from Troyes and Constantinople into the mud of the fairgrounds while the merchants yelled curses at them. The guards of the fair were doing little but watch the riot that now raged unchecked among overturned stalls and screaming stall holders. A monkey leaped to the top of one stall and gibbered abuse at the combatants. A girl screamed as somebody tore her dingy gray cloak half off her body, revealing a flame-red gown that clung to her like silk. The ragged Poitevin clerk who'd been so quick to deny his news popped briefly to the top, like a cork out of water, and shouted something incomprehensible about the queen. One of his eyes was swelling shut and a blow to the nose had given his voice a quacking timbre.

The Fleming sighed and plodded on. He'd not intended to go back to Paris that night—his road lay north—but perhaps the goldsmith would give him shelter and a meal for his services as a pack animal.

Eleanor was in the hall of the drapers, fingering a pleasantly dyed peach and green silk and listening to the lies of the Greek merchant who'd brought it, when the riot erupted outside.

"What *do* you suppose they're doing out there?"

The answer surged into the hall on an angry tide of shouting young men, most of them tonsured like clerics and gowned in flapping black robes. The wave of riot broke over her head and tumbled the silk merchant's wares upon the floor of the hall. Petronilla screamed and Eleanor grabbed for her hand. "Stay with me!" she shouted over the tonsured heads of the mob to Faenze and Bertille, but it was no use. The two waiting women were being carried away even as she spoke, forced back against the far end of the hall. A fist swung under Eleanor's nose and she threw her head back, stumbled, almost went down in the mass of fighting humanity. Her left hand ached from Petronilla's frantic grip. She tried to smile at Petronilla, to reassure her, but the younger girl was not looking at her. Merely holding on to her hand with fingers tight as death.

We have to get out of this. She couldn't voice the thought above the roar of insults in a dozen languages, nor could she move. But the wave of students carried them out of the hall, into the muddy open spaces where a moment earlier the tables of the money changers had been set up. Now there was nothing but a trampled field between two rows of shuttered stalls. For a moment Eleanor breathed easier, just to see the sky above her, then the crowd closed in, jostling her and Petronilla this way and that, and they were even more closely hemmed in than they'd been within the hall. A boy's elbow slammed into her ribs and she staggered, catching her breath against the sudden pain. Something dragged at her cloak. She screeched at the beggar who had his hand on her hood and snatched the cloak back, hanging on to it with one hand while with the other she kept safe hold of Petronilla.

The turbulent ebb and flow of the mob began to take on direction, helped by shouting students who perched on the tops of the closed stalls. Eleanor stared up at one of them, swaying atop the rickety structure like an ungainly crow on a cornstalk too slender to bear his weight. He was shouting something in French; with the noise of the brawling crowd all around them she could not make out the words. All the students on the fringes of the mob seemed to be northerners, French or Normans. She pushed toward the stalls but could not reach them.

"Let me out!" she screamed, knowing as she did so that no one could hear her. "Let me pass! I am the queen!"

A tall student beside her chuckled. "Aye, and I'm the count of Vermandois," he teased in her own language, so warm and kindly after these weeks of striving to accustom herself to the French tongue. He had the beginnings of a fine black eye already, but it didn't seem to have harmed his temper. "Don't draw their attention, my love," he advised her. "It's turning into a fight between north and south. If you can't keep the langue d'oc from your tongue, then keep your mouth shut and pray."

The French students linked hands and made a barrier wherever there might be a space to get away between two stalls. They were being forced, all of them, into the narrowing space where the two lines of stalls converged, with yelling students in their flapping black robes everywhere, inside the mob and atop the stalls and waiting at the single exit of the funnel. All the decent citizens seemed to have vanished. Eleanor was wedged in between the clerk who'd advised her to keep silent and a one-legged beggar in tatters who stank like the Seine at low tide. He hopped dexterously along, using one crutch for balance and the other to strike out at the people around him, and shouting the same two or three words in a monotonous cracked voice like the clang of an ill-cast bell. Gradually Eleanor began to understand the sense of them.

"Down with the Poitevin traitors!"

"What is he talking about?" she demanded. "Why does he name us traitors?"

But the man who'd spoken to her was gone, with his reassuring deep chuckle, and his place had been taken by an enormously fat woman whose breasts heaved out of her bodice like fat white piglets. The woman's bulk was between her and Petronilla. Eleanor's fingers were almost numb with the strength of Petronilla's grip, but at least the pain reassured her that her sister was still there. So small and frail, if she fell, Petronilla could be trampled by the crowd. . . . Somewhere up ahead, Faenze's bright curly head bobbed over the crowd; she'd found a burly man to take her on his shoulder. If only someone would lift up Petronilla like that! Eleanor couldn't even take a deep breath to shout to Faenze. She shoved at the woman whose gross bulk forced her against the beggar. It was like pummeling a mattress of goose down, vast and resilient, but at least she could breathe for a moment.

"A moi, Faenze, Bertille!" she screamed at the top of her lungs. The noise of the crowd swallowed up her voice as Jonah was swallowed into the belly of the whale. Only the fat woman heard her. She turned her head and gave Eleanor a vast, good-natured grin full of blackened tooth stumps. "Leave over shouting, dearie," she advised in puffs of garlic-scented breath. The inexorable pressure of the crowd nudged and jerked them nearer to the mouth of the funnel where three students bearing sticks stood like a guard, questioning all who passed. "The boys'll do no harm to a pretty piece like you, for all you talk like a southerner. See you, they're just knocking the Poitevin lads about a bit to teach them some manners."

Now they were so close that Eleanor could see the set faces on the shaven-headed student clerks who blocked the narrow exit. Each person who reached them was asked a question that she could not hear. She could not hear the answers, either, but she saw two commoners and a student pass free after speaking for a moment. The next man was the tall clerk with the beaky nose who'd chuckled at her claim to be queen of France. They didn't question him; one of the French clerks gave a yell of triumph at the sight of him and all three set on him with their sticks until he crumpled out of sight.

"Couldn't say 'oui,' like a proper Frenchman," the fat woman commented. "Now don't be so scared, pretty, they'll not hurt you or your friend. You may get a rough tumble on the grass and have to give away what you came here to sell, but be nice and obliging and you'll get off no worse for wear."

Petronilla was crying, soundlessly, white streaks of tears running down the grime on her face. Eleanor dropped to her knees and wrapped her arms around her sister while the crowd surged past. A shove brought them both down in the mud, and she saw their death in the trampling feet, then something yanked her backward and hauled her unceremoniously out of the crowd's path, right under the split logs that held up one of the shuttered stalls. She felt Faenze's old patched gray cloak ripping under her, rolled out of it with Petronilla in her arms, and found herself lying on the damp ground, in the eighteen inches between mud and stall floor, facing the man she'd last seen going down under the sticks and fists of the French clerks. One eye was closed and puffing up, there was blood at the corner of his mouth, and his black gown was rent like a scarecrow's rags, but he beamed upon her with undiminished good cheer.

"Can't let those scabs of French get their dirty hands on a countrywoman," he explained out of the smiling, unbruised side of his mouth. "Knew as soon as you spoke, there in the crowd, you come from Poitou like me. Sorry I couldn't get you out of there sooner, but—they know me, you see."

"Friends of yours?" said Eleanor dryly.

"Hardly. But they know me! *Everybody* knows Benoît de Périgné. Master Abelard says I've the best brain he ever—well, that can wait. Those Frenchmen have had a grudge against me ever since I tripped up their master in a public disputation. This fight was a convenient excuse. If I'd ducked out of sight before they had a chance at me, they'd have been quartering the fair after me. Now—"

He broke off, listening to the shrieks and cries of the crowd. Something had changed; now the French were as alarmed as the southerners.

"Perhaps," he said, "we'd better be getting out of here. If your majesty would condescend to roll this way, after me, and slide through *here*—ah, good girl!" As Eleanor emerged flushed and muddy on the far side of the stall, he slipped his arm around her and kissed her full on the mouth. Then, before she could react, he grabbed her hand, put his free arm around Petronilla, and urged them both forward. They scurried from stall to tent to fence without being caught by the French students who were all watching the fight in the center of the fairgrounds, but at the last fence the student ducked back with a groan.

"Knights and men-at-arms," he explained. "King's men, I think. Damnation! How did the fair marshals send word so quickly?"

"You should be glad to see them," Eleanor said. "They'll stop the fight. And not above time!" Her gown might be old, but until now it hadn't been past praying for. Her side ached from the elbow she'd caught in the ribs. And Petronilla was shaking from head to foot.

"Ah, you don't understand. They'll stop it, to be sure, but they won't care who they take up and throw in the Grand Châtelet—and I haven't a clipped denier to pay my fine. Besides, it was a *good* fight, only a slight miscalculation on my part," Benoît said with an apologetic bow, "taking on the French when there were so few good Poitevins and Gascons to back me up. Still, what could I do? If you'd heard what they were saying about our queen—and after all, Eleanor is a countrywoman of ours, you know—you'd have agreed I had to beat them."

Eleanor peeped around the fence and drew back hastily. She knew half the men-at-arms who were riding down the fairgoers. And there was Raoul de Vermandois, dwarfed by his massive white destrier, shouting orders while his soldiers rounded up turbulent students and plowed through the silenced crowd.

She felt marginally safer. Raoul, at least, wouldn't offer her violence. On the other hand, she had no great eagerness to be discovered by him in this condition. Perhaps if she and Petronilla just waited here for a few minutes everything would calm down. "It looks to me rather as if they had beaten you! What *were* they saying about the queen?"

"Filthy lies, not fit for a pretty girl like you to hear, or a cleric like me to repeat," said the student. "It all started when some Flemish pilgrim spread tales of the trouble at home." In a few quick sentences he told her of the rumors attending Louis's march south, the tales that he meant to kill or take hostage the children of Poitiers in reparation for their parents' revolt. "Mind you, I'm not personally acquainted with Queen Eleanor, God save her," said the student, "but isn't she the get of old Duke William himself, and can you believe any of that line would see a bunch of Frenchmen and priests mistreating their own people so?"

Petronilla cried out in pain, and Eleanor realized that she'd clenched her hand on her sister's so hard that the child's fingers were hurting. Muscle by muscle, she relaxed her grip. "I cannot," she said clearly, "and I *will* not countenance it—you have my word on that, sir!"

"Oh, *much* obliged, your majesty," the clerk said, and he gave her another impudent kiss that landed on her muddy cheek as she turned her head away. A destrier's heavy tread shook the ground behind him.

"Majesty." Count Raoul de Vermandois, impassive as ever in half-armor, sitting astride a horse almost too much for even his whipcord strength to control, invested the word with all its meaning and twice the irony that the student had given it. "Your woman Radegonde told me that you had come here with insufficient escort to protect you. I see," he commented with a glance at the student, "that she was correct."

Petronilla burst into tears before Eleanor could say anything. "I was so scared," she wept, and then, angrily and unfairly, "Where *were* you? Why were you so long coming to get us?"

Raoul de Vermandois leaned down and reached out his hands to Petronilla. "Come, *petite*, mount before me, and do not be afraid," he said, more gently than Eleanor had ever heard him speak. Petronilla hung back, clasping Eleanor's hand and looking uncertainly at her.

"The lady queen will ride with one of my men," Raoul said. "Soissons!"

A young, black-haired man spurred his horse forward and took up Eleanor. She recognized him: Ivo, son of the count of Soissons, one of the few Frenchmen who had not made her feel unwelcome at court with muttered asides about Poitevin manners and Aquitanian laxity.

Petronilla was sitting very straight before the count of Vermandois, looking slighter and more like a child than ever atop the destrier.

"Your other ladies have already been seen to," Raoul said with a backward nod of his head toward Eleanor.

Benoît de Périgné had disappeared into the tangle of stalls and small trees and tents and carts that lined the fringes of the fair. There was, Eleanor supposed, nothing to stay for.

The ride back to the Île de la Cité seemed twice as long as the gay ride out had been. Ivo of Soissons scarcely spoke, except to apologize whenever his horse stepped out too quickly or shied at a falling leaf. Before them, Raoul de Vermandois rode with his back straight, murmuring something to Petronilla. Eleanor could not catch the words, but at least he must not have been scolding her, for Petronilla's sobs had died down into a mournful snuffle.

At the inn of Saint-Lazare they retrieved their own mounts. Eleanor rode between Faenze and Bertille, both of whom were unnaturally subdued; Petronilla stayed with the count of Vermandois, saying she was too tired to make the ride back on her own. Eleanor rode as straight as the count himself, her spine stiffened by indignation, but it seemed a long way back to the city, and before they had covered half the distance the clouds had returned and a soft gray drizzle dampened them all, and even the autumn leaves and the harvested fields seemed gray and cold and dreary.

Radegonde of Maillezais was waiting for them with many a clucking word of I-told-you-so and what-were-you-thinking-of and I-never-heard-the-like. Eleanor kept silent while Radegonde scurried and lectured and brewed a hot posset for Petronilla and predicted that the child would be abed with another of her chest colds as a result of this day's folly.

"And lucky you'll be, my lady, if that's the worst of it," she advised Eleanor. "We must hope that nobody ever hears of it."

"On the contrary," said Eleanor, bright-eyed and thin-lipped. "On the contrary, Radegonde, a great many other people are going to hear of it."

Chapter Eight

Eleanor paced with quick, nervous steps through the solar, emptied of waiting women (save for Radegonde, for propriety's sake) during this stormy interview with the constable of France. The crumpled hem of her red dress brushed across the litter of trinkets that lay scattered across chests and stools and window ledges: sharp-pointed scissors for embroidery, skeins of gold thread and twisted silk cords, a needle case of worked ivory, a chessboard of ivory and ebony on a stand that rocked in the wake of the queen's passage, two tall enameled candlesticks in red and blue patterns with silver wires, a Psalter in a cover of beaten silver, embroidered herb pillows of lavender and rosemary to drive away fleas and evil spirits, discarded girdles and braid sheaths, an ivory comb whose teeth were the claws of a snarling lion, a mirror of polished bronze whose handle was a serpent coiling to meet the hand. Raoul de Vermandois stood with his legs slightly apart, feet planted solidly amid the sea of expensive baubles, receiving the words Eleanor flung at him as if they were arrows thudding against his shield.

"He usurps my right of justice over my vassals!"

"His majesty usurps nothing," Raoul de Vermandois explained for perhaps the tenth time, holding on to his patience as he would hold the bridle of an angry destrier. "He is your king and your husband, madame, and you owe him obedience on both counts. If he has gone himself to quell a little disturbance in Poitou, without troubling you over the matter, then you ought to be grateful rather than angered.

Was it not for this that you wed—to have a man's strong arm to defend your lands?"

"I thought to have married a man who would defend me against my enemies, not one who would destroy the heart of my realm!" The long flame-red skirt swished around Eleanor's ankles with every step. Somehow she threaded her way through the appalling clutter of the room without looking where she stepped and without disaster. A gaudy brocaded cape hanging on one of the tiring poles swayed with her passage, the chessmen set out on the board trembled under the light brushing touch of her long sleeves. At each turn her light eyes were fixed on Raoul, snapping out sparks of brilliant fury, demanding that he do *something.*

"I think you do not approve his actions," she said suddenly, "or why are you not at his side now?"

A home blow. Raoul de Vermandois and Thibaut of Champagne, the two lords most powerful in Louis's realm, had both advised against his striking thus at Poitiers. What had begun as an innocent association of merchants could end as a full-scale rebellion like that in Laon if the king acted with the hysterical anger he'd displayed on receipt of the news. So Louis had gone almost alone, with a hastily raised private army of two hundred men—not enough to fight a war, but more than enough to put down an organization of sheltered merchants.

Raoul de Vermandois shifted uneasily under Eleanor's penetrating glare. His muddy boot encountered something yielding; he looked down and hastily stepped away from the coil of gilt ribbons that spilled over the floor like a shining snake. He hated being here, cramped among these women's things, returning patient answers to this girl in her teens. If this child queen had been his daughter he'd have beaten her soundly for her escapade at the fair, and she'd be on her knees now praying for mercy instead of scolding at him in her broken French. What was she going on about now? God save us, she presumed to explain feudal rights and obligations to him—to the high constable of France!

"Aquitaine and Poitou are no part of France's feudal domains," Eleanor lectured him. "I hold title to those realms in my own right, by the will of my father Duke William of blessed memory"—at least she stopped there long enough to gulp down an angry sob and cross herself—"and I hold the right of justice over my vassals, who owe no liegeance to any Frenchman."

"Through your marriage, the overlordship passes to your husband," Raoul explained yet again, "for the man is the head of the house, as the king is the head of the land, and so—"

"Without me," Eleanor burst in on his patient explanation, "your Louis would be king of no more than this patch of mud in the Seine and the quarrelsome barons who live around it!"

Raoul de Vermandois permitted himself a small smile. "The barons of Poitou and Aquitaine are also not known for their meekness, your majesty. Else why would this marriage have been put forward in such haste?"

She did not acknowledge his point but went on with her quick, nervous pacing, up and down, down and up the length of the solar, long fingers tapping at her sides, each quick turn sending skirts and sleeves flying to place a hodgepodge of scent bottles and crystal vases and ivory combs and unstrung lutes in jeopardy. The soft cloudy light of a Paris autumn evening filled the slits of windows behind her and illuminated her flying cloud of unbound hair like an angel's halo about a face distinctly unangelic. *A cat in heat*, Raoul thought. What had that boy of old Louis's been doing in all those nights since the wedding? This girl should have been swelling with an heir for France by now, something to keep her fat and contented in the bower where she belonged.

The wine shop of the Cat and Bones was a single smoky, low-ceilinged room opening out onto the muddy ruts of the rue de la Bûcherie. It was thus well situated between the road to the Mont-Sainte-Geneviève, where Master Peter Abelard cut theological knots by the sharp edge of reason, and the rue du Fouarre, where more conventionally inclined clerks discoursed on the works of Priscian and Aristotle to students sitting on the straw for which the street was named. In theory, the Cat and Bones should have attracted the custom of students from both centers of learning, and the proprietor's special wine cup (mixed from a secret recipe known only to himself and his wife) should have been the talk of Paris. In practice, a group of beggarly Poitevin students had claimed the place as their own, effectively driving away the better-paying trade of the French and English. And the wine was usually sour.

That evening the fine drizzle that had grayed the afternoon died away, and the aftermath of the riot at Saint-Denis spilled knots of students into the narrow streets of the Left Bank, wrangling, energetic, ready for a brawl or a song or a woman. Maître Clement shouted to his wife to unbar the door before they lost their trade to the Saint's Head down the street.

"We'll lose it anyway, do they taste the wine," grumbled Madame from the hot little cooking shed attached to the back of the drinking room. "This new cask's turned like the last, and nought I can do will sweeten it. I've tried the powdered elder and the grain of paradise powders, and hung egg whites in their shells inside the cask, and the broken pot—"

"Here, you've never broken a good pot just to clear muddy wine?" Maître Clement exclaimed.

"Nay, but remember that pitcher our Moll dropped in the midden? Been saving the pieces, I have, until need arose. But I've stirred 'em all in, and still the wine's as bitter as an Englishman's piss. Go unbar the door yourself. I've to tend my pigs, and then I'll try if some of the barley soup boiled won't sweeten the cask."

To supplement the income of the wine shop, Madame sold cooked stews, in direct contravention of the regulations of the wine sellers' and cook shops' guilds. Even more illegally, she raised pigs that got their nourishment from foraging in the street just outside. She pointed to the pigs as proof of the superior ingredients and nourishing content of her stews; student lore had it that nothing more nourishing than the pig's squeal ever made it as far as Madame's cook pot. She was too canny to waste good pork on students when right there in the rue de la Bûcherie were butchers who'd pay down good coins for a nice fat pig, and slaughter it themselves.

Before Clement bestirred himself to open the door, a long, bony arm wrapped in rusty black rags reached through the open half of the window shutter and undid the fastening on the other half. A shaggy yellow head crowned by a tonsure no bigger than a clipped denier came through the square-cut hole in the wall that served as a window, followed by sections of a lanky body in a sadly torn and stained black gown.

"Try a basket of holly leaves," he advised.

Madame Clement snorted contempt. "That's to clear the red tinge out of white wine, thou fool, and where am I to get holly leaves in the middle of Paris?" She came out of the cooking shed, arms akimbo, and looked the clerk up and down. "Benoît, you've been fighting again."

"Who hasn't?" Benoît said in a voice rendered slightly nasal by the swelling and sidewise slant of his nose.

"Bide there," Madame told him, pushing him down onto a bench, "and I'll make a poultice for that eye. And—"

Maître Clement lifted the heavy bar on the door, and half a dozen southern clerks rushed in at once, interrupting Madame's plans. "Benoît, you idiot, why didn't you wait for us?" exclaimed a short boy with a sunburnt face. "You should have known better than to let those cheating French get you surrounded."

"Couldn't wait," Benoît apologized. "They were slandering the queen. Said she didn't know or didn't care what happened to our folk in Poitiers, that she'd left us to the mercy of the king and—oh, but did you hear about the commune? And the hostages?"

He summarized the story for them while the short boy who'd first spoken banged on the table and called for wine to wash down the bitter tale.

"Pah, sour as your story," he remarked on first tasting the cup. "Clement, tell Madame to cast in a quarter of pounded alum and two silver pennies before she draws the next cup."

"No, she should pour a little on the ground to appease the earth demons, and then say a Paternoster to keep the demons from getting her soul," another student suggested. "That's what my mother always does, and she brews the best ale in Gascony."

"Oh, *ale*," said the first boy, "that's different, only fit for Englishmen to drink— and here's one now, speak of the devil!"

"Should I take exception to that remark?" Benoît's friend Thomas strolled in the open door, neat as a black cat from his smooth dark hair to the hem of his immaculate gown, and took his place on the bench beside Benoît. Most Norman and English students would not have been welcome in this gathering of southern exiles, but Thomas, like the cat he resembled, went where he pleased, and such was his charm of manner that no one objected, whatever company he chose to keep.

"Benoît was just telling us the news from Poitiers," said Guibert, the boy whose mother brewed the best ale in Gascony. All the brightness died away from his face as he repeated the tale for Thomas's benefit.

"Children taken? Not one or two from noble families," Thomas said slowly, "but *all* the children? He can't d-do that."

"He can if he wants to," said one of the Poitevins. "That's what we get for this joining of the realms: France's boot heel to crush us!"

"Damn this Eleanor," another one cursed. "This would never have come to pass in the old duke's time!"

"No, don't blame her," Benoît said too quickly, before he thought about the effect of his words tumbling out. "She knew nothing of the matter till today, I'll swear that. And now she does know, she'll put a stop to it. I have her word on that."

The somberness of the meeting dissolved in laughter at this absurdity. "Oh, you've been flirting with the queen now, have you, Benoît? What do you say to that, Thomas à Becket? Did you see any noble ladies in the wool merchants' booths?"

"No," Thomas acknowledged with a smile, "but then, I missed the riot. It didn't look like much fun—"

"So you strolled away, quiet as a cat, and reappeared when all the fun was over," Benoît said without malice. Thomas à Becket was a charmer, a quick-witted disputant and a fine drinking companion, but not the man one would choose to stand at one's shoulder in a fight. Benoît knew that and tolerated him anyway, so he had no business taking offense now.

The other students wouldn't let him pass so quickly over his hasty words about the queen.

"So maybe her majesty was down in the mud, fighting like Benoît for the honor of our race?" proposed Guibert.

"And they became comrades-in-arms on the spot—"

"—And she was so mightily impressed by his prowess, she invited him up to the palace to continue the argument—"

"In private, no doubt. The king's away and our Benoît's a handsome man, or was before he got that black eye and broken nose to spoil his pretty face—"

"And I hear the queen has an eye for a pretty man. Didn't Louis have to kill William of Talmont for his honor, and the marriage not three weeks old then?"

Benoît's shoulders tensed under the flow of innuendo, and his big, bruised hands gripped the edge of the table, ready to heave it over his friends. Thomas, sitting beside him, had taken no part in the good-natured teasing. Now he laid one hand on Benoît's shoulder. "Softly, softly! They're only playing. Let it alone, and they'll be on to something new in a moment."

And so they were. Benoît looked gratefully at his friend as the students went on to boast of the ladies they served, each one, to hear them tell it, fairer and better endowed than Eleanor of Aquitaine. Paien declaimed a song to his fair Alis in Bordeaux, and Benoît sat back in the shadows and tried to think of some way to finish the song he'd begun scribbling in the margin of Master Abelard's book.

Stetit puella rufa tunica . . .

There was a girl in a red dress . . .

Guibert, the flesh on his solid frame still shaking with laughter, proclaimed that he loved Fat Annie of the Cat and Bones better than any nobly born lady, and to prove it, he hauled her into his lap and gave her a smacking kiss. Their combined weight brought down the bench, and all the students on that side slid down into a wine-splashed heap from which they arose with the demand that Benoît and Thomas should take their turns at praising their ladies and at paying for a round of wine to pledge them.

"For the queen's sake you ought to drink to her in the best malmsey!" Guibert shouted.

> *Stetit puella rufa tunica*
> *siquis eam tetigit*
> *tunica crepuit.*
> *Eia!*

> There was a girl in a red dress
> the silk rustled when you touched her.
> Eia!

"I never said I would dare to serve the queen," Benoît protested, forcing a crooked smile. He'd said too much already. Belike she'd forgotten him before she reached Paris again. Better so; it wouldn't do to be remembered as the impudent clerk who'd stolen a kiss from her majesty.

Two kisses.

Guibert kept pressing him, so he said what was no more than the truth. "There is this girl . . . I met her at the fair. But I don't know if I'll see her again. She was . . . she had a red dress; she looked like a rose in bloom."

Stetit puella tanquam rosula . . .

There was a girl like a rose . . .

They left him alone with his memories and descended on the Englishman.

"What about you, Thomas, haven't you found a lady yet?"

"Nay, don't you know about the English vice? They only serve each other."

"Don't their tails get in the way?"

Thomas folded his hands and gave them a seraphic smile, catching the eye of each one in turn until they fell silent. "For myself," he said when all was quiet, "my lady is more gracious and lovely than any of yours, for I serve the Blessed Virgin, Queen of Heaven."

That damped the spirits of the party, reminding the students of their minute tonsures and of a future, adult life in which they would have to be respectable, chaste men of the church.

Thomas took his leave soon after that dampening statement, much to the relief of the Poitevins. "I know he's a friend of yours, Benoît," one of them said after the English student was gone, "but by God's bones, he has the *worst* effect on a good party!"

"And it wasn't even true. About serving the Blessed Virgin," said Guibert.

"What, you're not going to tell me old Chastity Bones has a girl hidden away somewhere?"

"No," said Guibert with unaccustomed solemnity, watching the door through which the English student had disappeared. "I meant that I seriously doubt whether Thomas à Becket has ever served anyone other than Thomas à Becket—or ever will."

Benoît paid them no heed. He was lost in the last words of his song fragment in praise of the lady he served for life and whom he never expected to see again.

> *Stetit puella rufa tunica*
> *siquis eam tetigit*
> *tunica crepuit.*
> *Eia!*
> *Stetit puella tanquam rosula*

facie splenduit,
et os eius floruit.
Eia!

There was a girl in a red dress
the silk rustled when you touched her.
Eia!
There was a girl like a rose
her face a flower,
and her eyes blooming.
Eia!

The clouds that passed over Paris brought a chill autumn rain, unseasonably early, to Poitiers. The hostages in the open square before the church huddled together for warmth and comfort. Children and youths of all ages were gathered there, from toddlers barely able to lisp their names to strapping young men and girls in their teens. The king's orders had stopped short at taking the babies still suckling at their mothers' breasts.

For a day and a night, the children had been gathered there, shivering in the fine drizzling rain while the king debated what to do with them. The older ones did what they could to comfort the little ones, sharing out the cloaks and bits of bread they'd managed to snatch when the kings' men bundled them out of their homes. Melaine, the baker's daughter, who was a big girl and nearly of an age to be married, collected some of the little children around her and told them stories: of the Green Man in the forest, and the three ladies who brought fairy gifts to every child's christening, and the jeweled towers of Constantinople where wizards made singing birds out of gold and precious stones. But there was always a child somewhere in the crowd who cried for its mother and would not be comforted by songs and tales; and there was always the line of armed men, faceless behind their iron helms, standing between the children and their parents who wept and prayed for the king's mercy; and by now, at noon of the second day, they were all cold and hungry and most of the babies were crying for bread. Jeanette, who had at first disdained to join the crowd of little ones clinging to Melaine's skirts, now drifted closer and closer to that circle. Her two middle fingers kept creeping toward her mouth; that was babyish too, unfitting a big girl of nearly six, but sucking on them seemed somewhat to ease the gnawing ache of emptiness inside her.

"So the good midwife mounted behind the stranger on his horse, and they rode as fast as the wind until they came to a great hill all of glass," Melaine told the children. Her voice was tired and husky by now; Jeanette had to stand right by her shoulder to hear the words.

And even listening to Melaine's stories didn't help, not anymore. What good was it to hear about the rich feast spread for the midwife inside the fairy mountain, the silk sheets she slept on and the crackling fire that roared day and night, when they were all cold and wet and hungry and these bad men wouldn't let them go home again? Jeanette's lower lip trembled and she swallowed hard over the sob that wanted to come out.

The old abbey church of Saint-Denis, with its narrow west door and its antiquated wooden roof laid down by the carpenters of Charlemagne's day, resembled nothing so much as a shell half pulled to pieces by the inquisitive fingers of a giant child. While the roof and supporting walls remained in place, the western entrance had been brutally enlarged, with doors triple the size of the old ones, far too wide and high for the proportions of the existing church. The abbot had plans to change those proportions as well. The nave, with its gaily painted images, had been opened in five places through which master masons extended lines to show the planned thirty-foot extension of this section. The old walls shuddered under the onslaught of hammers and stonecutters' chisels. A workman covered from head to foot in stone dust, his eyes and mouth black holes in the white coating, trundled his barrow of dressed stones right across Eleanor's path with a shout of warning. Behind her, somebody dropped something heavy that crashed upon the other stones like the call to judgment, and someone else cursed the clumsy fool in words that should have made painted Moses tremble with rage.

If you can't win by one path, take another one, Eleanor's father had once said cheerfully when Ebles de Mauléon walled himself up in his impregnable castle by the sea, and all the arts of siegecraft couldn't bring him down. Three nights after Duke William's army departed, with great noise and fanfare, a much smaller force paid the Breton fishermen to bring them in along the rocky coast, and in the morning, the knights

Ebles de Mauléon had refused to send for their due term of service were dangling from the battlements by their necks, and Ebles, allowed to live, found that his lands in Poitou would in future cost him considerably more than they had before.

Raoul de Vermandois had been an impregnable fortress wall. Could Abbot Suger, that bustling, self-important little man in the midst of all this chaos, be a postern gate by the seawall? In any case, a change in tactics was required. . . .

"My lord abbot, it is gracious of you to receive me." Before he had quite registered her approach, Eleanor sank to her knees before the disconcerted abbot. When he put out one stubby, beringed hand to raise her, she looked up and let him see the glitter of tears on her lashes.

"I come as a supplicant," she announced, "and I shall not rise until you grant my prayer!"

"Our Lord Christ Jesus grants prayers," said the abbot. "My powers are somewhat more restricted. Don't you think you would be more comfortable, your majesty, if you walked around the building site with me while we discussed your desire, rather than kneeling in all this dust and trash?"

Eleanor shook her head.

"Well, I would be," Suger said. "In this world, queens do not kneel to clerks, save in the confessional—and I think you are not here to make confession?"

Eleanor dropped her eyes. "Perhaps later," she murmured. "This is more urgent."

"It's always so," said the abbot with a chuckle. "We are greedy children at our Lord's feet, stretching out our hands to catch His robe, demanding proof of His love before we will give Him ours. 'First give me what I want, and then I will do Your will.'"

"It is the way of the world," Eleanor acknowledged.

"Then," Suger told her, "we shall be worldly. You will give me what I want, and perhaps I may be able to do the same for you. No, no—" He stopped her with a gesture, "I do not wish to usurp the place of your confessor! Just walk with me a little and let me show you what we have accomplished with the work here, as I have so often prayed the king to come and see for himself the difficulties under which we labor."

The largest gap in the wall of the nave had destroyed a part of the Expulsion from Eden. On the right, the angel raised his flaming sword; on the left, Adam departed, head bowed in shame, clutching a disembodied hand. Eve had been sacrificed to the plans for expansion.

"These paintings were well enough in their time," Suger said, briskly dismissing the very work he had commissioned not five years earlier, "but before they were finished it became evident to me that we had not understood the true needs of the church. Such a rustic little church as this may have sufficed for the needs of his majesty's ancestors, but it is altogether inadequate for the glorious reign of your husband. On feast days the worshippers could barely get in at the narrow door in the west porch. Our first concern was the enlargement of the doors. Did you observe the new doors? They represent the Passion of the Savior and his Ascension."

"I saw them," Eleanor agreed.

"A mistake," Suger announced, "to enlarge the entrance without providing adequate passage for the throngs of the faithful who enter on feast days to seek the intercession of the saints—" He sighed. "The early arrivals enter, fill the church, and then seek to leave, but the press of the latecomers forces them back. On the feast of our own Saint Denis, just past, there were women all but crushed to death in the crowd, crying out as if in labor, fearing to be trodden underfoot."

Eleanor remembered the rioting mob at the fair, pressing her and Petronilla so close.

"They might have perished in the holy church itself, save that certain pious men lifted them above the heads of the crowd, and they ran forward then as though upon a pavement, so closely packed were the worshippers. My lady, we *must* enlarge the church. As you see, I have already drawn up plans and set the masons to work on this extension of the nave."

Eleanor paused between the painted Adam and the avenging angel, looking doubtfully at the chaos of builders' lines and dressed stone and barrows of rubble that lay before her.

"An admirable project," she said.

"I had hoped to have it completed in time for the christening of your first son," the abbot confessed.

Eleanor's heart warmed to the little man, who had spoken with such certainty of what she began to doubt would ever come to pass. Three months married, and she had not yet quickened!

"I think you will have no difficulty in doing that," she said.

"Alas," the abbot sighed, "the work is all but halted, as you see here. The new nave will require fine stone columns, and the local stone that we have been using for building is too soft to support the weight that these columns will bear. I had considered bringing marble columns from Rome by water, but the dangers and expenses of the journey deter me."

"Yes . . . ," Eleanor said slowly. She knew now why the abbot had insisted on receiving her here, among the noise and clutter of the half-rebuilt church. "Yes, that would be a problem. But at least you have some time to solve it, Abbot Suger. Mine is more urgent." Too urgent to delay any longer while Suger hinted around his needs. "You know of my lord's journey to Poitiers?"

Suger blinked twice. He had known, clearly, but he had not expected her to. "I advised against—that is, the handling of his realm is in my lord's hands—"

"Neither the count of Vermandois nor the count of Champagne was willing to accompany him on such an errand," Eleanor pointed out. "I am only a weak woman, Abbot Suger, incapable of understanding the complexities of politics or the necessities of war. I am grateful to Louis for seeking to shield me from this trouble, but I fear that his righteous anger may lead him into actions that he will later repent."

Suger raised one hand, fingers outspread, and studied the flash of rings in the morning sun. "Such fears are not unfounded," he agreed without looking at Eleanor. "But it would be a bold man who questioned the decisions of the king."

"By remaining in Paris, it seems to me that both you and the counts of Vermandois and Champagne have already shown your doubts." Eleanor forgot to be careful. "Abbot Suger, someone must stop him. My people will hate him forever if he takes away the children. I myself—"

No. She could not say that she would hate him forever, not her golden husband who had saved her from being the prize of a barons' war. Their marriage *was* a success, she *was* happy, and as soon as she had given him a son all would be well. Talmont had been a long time ago. He'd meant well; she would not think again about William of Lezay's bared throat in the sunlight. But this—how could she meet Louis again, if he returned to Paris with this act between them? Eleanor fell silent and bit down on her lower lip.

"You have not seen the new windows in the choir," Abbot Suger commented as though she had not spoken. "This was one of my earlier efforts. I hope the glass can be saved when we enlarge this part of the building."

The morning sun passed through the stained glass and was transmuted into essence of color and light. The first window showed Moses as a child in the bushes, and then in a second panel showed the Lord appearing to him in the burning bush; from the arched top of the window, the Virgin smiled down on her children, her blue robe outspread to catch the stars and the moon of heaven.

Eleanor passed through the fiery light of the burning bush and stood in the radiant shadows of the upper window. She was bathed in the blue of heaven, the blue of the Virgin's robe enfolding God's creation, the cool blue-green of the stone Cercle-le-Monde called *patteraenu*, blessed by the spirits of earth and stone and sea. Clouds passed behind the window and dimmed the blue light to a stormy gray, but the gold of the Virgin's crown caught a straying sunbeam to dazzle her eyes and light a flame of hope in her heart. When at last she looked away from the glory of the window, she was almost surprised to see the gilt and painted walls of the church rather than the green and flowering vine and the rising oaks of the secret forest. For a moment her eyes met Suger's and they shared an unspoken worship of the beauty he had created here, and she spoke to him as she would have done to Cercle-le-Monde.

"This madness in Poitiers must be stopped, Abbot Suger. And who but you can persuade my lord to abandon his plans?"

Suger shook his head slightly. "I have a duty to my monks of Saint-Denis and to our work here for the glory of the Lord."

Eleanor looked back at the window and read the inscription beneath the infant Moses: *Est in fiscella Moyses Puer ille, puella / Regia mente pia quem fovet Ecclesia.*

"It means," said Suger helpfully, "Moses in the ark is that child whom the royal maiden, the church, fosters with pious mind."

Eleanor refrained from telling him that she had enough Latin to read not only that but all the self-congratulatory inscriptions she had observed wherever a piece of work was finished: "Suger, abbot of Saint-Denis, caused this to be done.... This work was ordered by Suger of Saint-Denis.... Abbot Suger has set up these altar panels...." Instead she only remarked pensively that good intentions of all sorts seemed to have gone astray. The church cherished Moses but forgot to take care for the living children in Poitiers; the royal house of France, occupied with war, forgot to take proper care of the needs of that same church.

"There is a quarry in Pontoise," she said, "where you may find stone of the necessary hardness. We have better stone in the south, but the cost of transporting it might be too great. I do not think the king will object if I grant this abbey the right to cut columns out of that quarry."

"Now he might not," said Suger frankly, "but if I go south and argue with him about his set plans—"

"Even less then," Eleanor predicted. "He will be grateful to you for saving his soul from such a black deed. Only make sure that he sees the matter in its proper light—which I am sure, my lord abbot, you with your great eloquence will be able to do." She added that her own personal funds were more than sufficient to pay for the bringing of stonemasons from the south, artisans of Toulouse and Moissac who were experienced in working this hard stone and who would be able not only to shape the columns but also to decorate the church with stone carvings in the style of Saint-Étienne of Toulouse or Saint-Martial of Limoges.

To Eleanor, beloved wife and consort of the glorious Louis, by the grace of God king of the Franks and duke of the Aquitainians, and our dearest lord. Suger abbot of Saint-Denis sends devoted greetings and faithful service.

Upon our arrival in Poitiers, the citizens ran to meet us in groups and threw themselves beneath the feet of our horses, wailing and most bitterly begging that we should piously intercede for the redemption of their children with the lord king. Since I was hardly able to bear the sighs and groans of the mothers and boys and girls, as if they saw themselves and their children being tortured before their very eyes, I met with the lord king, rejoicing in our arrival, and privately and in a friendly fashion I pointed out to him the cause of the sorrow and misery that I had heard. Who, such was the great nobility and clemency of the young man, teachable that the power of the imperial majesty is born of piety, although he had pronounced sentence on many appropriate and widespread cases with so much harshness, which he by no means believed to be harshness, all, however, he submitted to our council and arbitration whatever I thought right to do.

On the next day, when we knew that the hearts of the miserable citizens were not impenitent, he ordered early in the morning that carts, packhorses, wagons, and asses (prepared by the parents to carry the boys and girls to diverse and remote regions of the earth) be convened in the place before the palace, where a desperate clamor arose as if they were going to their own funerals. The din of this terrible clamor mounted almost all the way to the sky, sparing neither the ears of the king nor ours nor the nobles; thither assembling at the windows of the palace we heard such grief, weeping, beating of the breast that we believed them to be in hellish misery. And so the gentle king leading us that way, he asked anxiously what he should do. He was distressed on both sides. If he should release them he might thereby injure his authority, if he should have them carried off as arranged he would be acting too harshly.

Wherefore, when all were equally perplexed in discussion of this in council, we brought forth audaciously in the midst of all: "Lord," said I, "the king of kings and lord of lords guiding you and your kingdom, if you will condescend to relieve such unexpected torments of such distresses, he will compassionately preserve your person and the merciful Lord will subjugate these and other contemptible cities of Aquitaine. Be thou secure, since indeed by however much less harshness you shall have allowed, by so much the divine power will amplify the honor of the king."

Who instantly, led by divine instinct, said to me, "Come to the window and publish the remission of the injury of the commune by the gift of the king's generosity, the return of the children free and quiet to all, and if they do not offend in such a way thereafter, no worse may happen to them."

Which being heard, wonderful to relate, great sadness was changed to joy, mourning to exultation, intolerable sorrow to rejoicing, the grief of death to the glory of life. Which being done by the mercy of a king as pious as noble, has bound all of Poitou in his love and service.

Chapter Nine

1142

The next few years of Louis's reign were peaceful enough in France. The barons of France saw him crowned at Bourges; the men of the Aquitaine and Poitou accepted his authority without overt rebellion.

Eleanor prayed daily for a son, took every bitter medicine Petronilla's herb craft recommended, and made pilgrimage twice to kiss the girdle of the Virgin at Chartres—all to no avail. The palace on the Île de la Cité sat cold and barren and untouched while the winds of change swept past it.

Geoffrey Plantagenet, the count of Anjou, claimed Normandy in the name of his wife Matilda, who was at the time busy claiming England. Geoffrey was more successful than his wife. Year by year he conquered more of the rich Norman castles and cities. Raoul de Vermandois advised Louis to stop this upstart before he combined Anjou and Normandy into one powerful realm with France caught between them. Louis responded that for his soul's sake, he dared not interfere in a war that was none of France's concern. Instead he mounted a siege against Toulouse in Eleanor's name, from which his army returned hastily without honor, and he interfered with a papal election in Bourges, for which he was excommunicated.

Meanwhile, in England, the ongoing civil war between Stephen of Blois and Geoffrey's wife Matilda devastated the country without bringing a definite advantage to either side. In the summer of 1142, Matilda was in so much difficulty that she sent her half brother Robert of Gloucester to Normandy with a plea for aid from

Geoffrey. Geoffrey promised to come to his wife's aid as soon as the summer campaign in Normandy was over and persuaded Robert to stay and help him with the
conquest of Caen and Bayeux.

The king of France and his court went south for the summer.

Paris had been hot and dusty and noisy: Poitiers was hot and wet and green and
noisy, and it seemed to Eleanor that the townspeople were not uniformly welcoming toward her. She wondered what they had thought about Louis and his treatment of the commune. Were they grateful to him for clemency, or angry that this
northern prince had taken the right of justice over them? What had they seen? Her
husband in the town square, a young king shouting orders in his queer flat northern
tongue, directing the northern knights who fought their way through the town and
took their children and beat or killed anyone who interfered, ordering the northern
men-at-arms to form a wall of living steel between them and their weeping children. And then they'd seen another man of the north, that little peasant-abbot with
his flashy jewels, kneeling in the mud and begging Louis for mercy.

They might not know what it had cost her to persuade Suger to intervene. All
they would know was that she had married a foreigner who thought they were his
cattle. What would Dangereuse have advised? Eleanor wished passionately that they
had made this visit to the south earlier, before a bad winter and the lung sickness
carried off her grandmother.

The bishop of Poitiers himself preached the sermon on the day that Eleanor
and her sister and her northern waiting women and her northern knights filled the
front of the church. Louis, being excommunicated, chose to hear a private Mass in
the palace rather than embarrass the bishop with his presence. The bishop repaid his
kindness with a sermon so outspoken that it verged on treason, except that all the
treasonous parts were only implied, not said outright. He spoke on Saint Radegonde of blessed memory, who (like Eleanor, but this went unsaid) had been a
woman of Poitou, and who (like Eleanor, it went without saying) had been constrained to marry a murdering warrior-king from the north. But Radegonde (unlike, the unspoken accusation went, Eleanor) had fled King Clovis for Poitiers. And
though it was February when she fled, just past the Feast of Lights, when peasants
were sowing the bare fields, when the king's men caught up with Radegonde just

outside Poitiers, and she was in need of a hiding place, the grain grew up all in a moment to make a green curtain about her. And when the king's men asked after her, the peasant who worked the land told them truthfully that he had seen no woman pass this way since he sowed his grain. And the knights rode away, and Radegonde was free to enter the cloister where she was safe from lust and war, and where she put aside her vainglory of queenship and labored humbly to do good works with her own hands until by the time of her death she had expunged the sin of Eve's daughters and was raised into heaven to join the blessed saints, leaving behind only her holy and incorruptible bones. Alas for the land that in these degenerate days there were so few to follow the saintly queen's example!

"Do they hate me so?" Eleanor whispered to Petronilla during the long chanting that followed.

"They're not fond of Louis."

"By my faith and Saint Radegonde," Eleanor snapped, "I spared them his vengeance, and they'd do well to remember it! Do they imagine this land would be safe from wars, if I donned the veil and thought only of my soul? Do they think—"

The chanting stopped, and the bishop looked reproachfully at Eleanor. "Woman, keep silence and hear the word of God. Remember that thou art Eve; for thy sin man had to die."

Eleanor stood, shaking out her long brocaded cloak about her; the candles in the church and the colored light that fell about her head picked up the flicker of gold threads in the brocade and clothed her for a moment in sparks of fire. "And was not Saint Radegonde also a woman?"

"Silence! Remember where you are!"

"You, priest, remember what my grandfather did to an insolent bishop of Poitiers, and think not that I will shrink from doing the same to you!"

Eleanor turned on the last word and marched from the church. Radegonde of Maillezais gave a long-suffering sigh and rolled her eyes to the painted ceiling of the church, as if saying, "See what I must bear from this headstrong young queen!" But with her next glance she gathered Eleanor's ladies about her and led them to follow their mistress. The knights of her escort came last, a mixed group of French and Poitevins. Some of the bourgeois in the back of the church were grinning as they left. The bishop was not universally loved in Poitiers, and Eleanor, whatever they thought of this unfortunate marriage, was still one of their own.

Poitevin to the soul," Maître André declared afterward when his wife told him of the shocking scene. "There's some of the old lord's blood there, right enough!"

"Papa, what did the old lord do to a bishop, and why?" Jeanette interrupted with the freedom of a favored child.

"Hmm? Oh—well!" Maître André laughed, a deep rumbling from his contented belly. "Nothing so very much. You know the lady Dangereuse was not his wife, and it was very wrong and very wicked of him to carry her away from her lawful lord—not that she ever seemed so unhappy about it, mind you, and I never heard that Aimery of Châtellerault said aught but that he was well rid of her—still, it was a wrong thing for William to do, even if everybody was happier as a result."

"I know," Jeanette nodded cheerfully. "The lady Eleanor's grandfather was *very* wicked, wasn't he? I heard one song that he made—"

"Well, don't sing it in this house!" Maître André said hastily. His wife was always on at him as it was, saying he told Jeanette things a girl didn't need to know and encouraged her to act above her station. "Anyway, Bishop Peter excommunicated him for it, and William wasn't pleased."

"King Louis has been excommunicated too," Jeanette added. "Melaine said that was why he couldn't come to church with the lady Eleanor. Whose wife did he carry off?"

"Melaine," said Maître André, "should have been married off five years ago, and King Louis didn't carry off anybody's wife, not him, and if you interrupt again I won't tell you the story!"

Jeanette curled up on her favorite cushion in the coolest corner of the big room, tucked her pointed slippers neatly under her skirt, and nodded. "All right, Papa. Do go on, please."

"Well, the old duke caught Bishop Peter coming out of church one day, and he was wearing his sword, and he threatened to behead him then and there unless Peter lifted the excommunication.

"'Go right ahead,' says the bishop, sticking out his scrawny neck. 'You kill me in my own church porch, and you'll never get this excommunication lifted. And me,

I'll be with the blessed martyrs above, and happy to be through with the task of guiding you lot of heathens to the Lord.'

"Well, William knew when he'd been bested. But he was a troubadour as well as a fighting man—no, *don't* mention that song of his, forget you ever heard it—and quick-witted enough to turn the whole affair into a joke. So he sheathes his sword and gives a great rolling laugh that has half the people in the church laughing with him, even though they don't know what it's about yet.

" 'Not a chance, priest,' says he. 'I don't love you enough to send you to paradise to-day! You'll just have to keep working on saving my soul. And so you can have more opportunity to do so, I'll let you stay in the palace from now on, as my honored guest.'

"If Bishop Peter had been as clever as our lord, he'd have thrown himself across his own altar and claimed sanctuary then and there. But no, the bird-witted priest was so flattered to be old William's guest, he trotted up to the palace with him, willing as a dog following a bone. And there he stayed, treated decently by all accounts, but locked up tight and never set free to preach again, until he died and William installed a more obliging bishop in his place."

"Not," said Jeanette primly, "a very edifying story, Papa." But she spoiled the effect by grinning.

"Depends on whether you trust lords or bishops more, I suppose," Maître André said. He looked appreciatively at his daughter. Almost a woman now, at eleven, and as pretty as the duchess herself, with her slender waist and neat little feet and her hair falling down in long fair plaits. Well mannered, too—look how she'd forborne interrupting him—and clever. As fit as any of those giggling noble ladies in church to grace a queen's court.

"Come on," Maître André said suddenly, heaving himself off the padded stool where he liked to sit and take his ease after dinner. "No, go to your mother first. Tell her to put you in your best dress—the one with the trimming of real green silk ribbons from Outremer—and comb your hair again. And wear your silver chain."

"Why? Where are we going?"

Maître André smiled. "I think the lady Eleanor might be wanting to know, about now, that some of us know what she did for us five years ago. And appreciate it." And if this worked, then next time there was need—God forbid there should be such a next time—he'd have a way to the queen's ear, good as any noble at court.

Eleanor knelt in the crypt beneath the little church of Saint-Radegonde. The darkness enclosed her, comforting and close; the curved arches of stone grew up around her like living trees. Candles flickered around the small shrine of the Virgin of the Woods, the black image that had been miraculously discovered in the forest outside Poitiers in her grandfather's time. For a while she had been given a place of honor in the upper, daylight levels of the church, but the bishop had been heard to make comments about pagan images masquerading as saints, and to cast doubts on the miraculous nature of the Virgin's appearance in the forest. And so the Dark Virgin's shrine had been quietly moved to this underground crypt, where some worshippers found a comfort that they could not find in the newly painted and gilded smiling Virgin of the daylight church.

Dangereuse had always paid her respects to the Dark Virgin. Dangereuse was dead now, carried away three years ago by a sudden chill, but Eleanor still followed her grandmother's tradition and paid a visit to this stubby wooden image whenever she was in Poitiers.

"Blessed Virgin, forgive me my sin in quarreling with the bishop," she whispered between her fingers. She paused and thought for a moment. "And forgive me that I would probably do it again, if he put such affront on me and my husband. He doesn't understand Louis."

Do you?

The question echoed within her head.

"Better than anyone else." The knowledge had been dearly bought, but after five years, she knew Louis and she was ready to fight for him. To fight for his soul—but she shrank from putting it that way. Louis stood between Suger and Raoul de Vermandois, church and war, both pulling at him until he could serve neither properly. Abbot Suger would have said that he was fighting for Louis's soul. All Eleanor wanted was to see him free of both men, free of the vicious cycle that kept him swinging back and forth between the worst cruelties of war and passionate repentance. Trapped between those two, he was neither a good man nor a good warrior.

If she could give him a son, she would have some power in this endless struggle, perhaps enough power to draw him away from both men and what they stood for. Perhaps he would then be a true king, sure of himself and acting from his own conscience.

"Blessed Mother, give us a son," she prayed. "Unlock my barren womb."

The image of the Virgin was of wood, a cylinder roughly hacked into an approximation of human shape, with nothing more than deeply scored lines to separate head from torso, arms from body. The face was expressionless, hardly more than a few gouges in the wood suggesting features. The wood itself was black, as if it had been sitting in the smoke of the candles for hundreds of years—a sooty black that absorbed light, a stillness that absorbed movement, a silence that swallowed sound. All around the wood, the wax tapers Eleanor had brought burned like stars in the night sky.

She had fasted since the previous night. Now she knelt on the stone floor, ignoring the ache in her knees and the trembling in her thighs, willing the Dark Virgin to answer. She remembered the Black Virgin of Le Puy, an image glossy with black paint, glittering with a crown and jeweled robes, holding a crystal-tipped scepter in one carved and painted hand.

"Do you want jewels?" she whispered. "Wax tapers to burn every day of the year, a robe of silk from Constantinople? Only give us a son, Lady—"

The ring of candles danced before her eyes. Dizziness spun through Eleanor's head like a wave, advancing and receding, tumbling her until she could no longer tell the solid stone from the vision of lights that spun before her. A crown of silvery light rose from the Dark Virgin's forehead, illuminating all the symbols of her power: grain growing high beneath her outstretched hand, serpents writhing beneath her heel. The stubby cylinder of wood was larger than the crypt now, a cloak of midnight within which the stars moved along their ordered courses.

What gifts could add glory to her? She was all that she wished to be; she encompassed the sky and the sea and the earth.

"Then what can I do?" Eleanor cried aloud. "What can *I* do?" Her numbed legs would no longer support her. She fell into black night, striking her head on something sharp, falling through stars and moons of rainbow light into the infinite blackness of the Virgin's midnight cloak.

Radegonde of Maillezais had some sharp things to say about foolish girls who fasted and prayed until they fainted. "That's no way to get a baby!" she told Eleanor. As she scolded, she took pounded herbs from a mortar and mixed them into a small pot of grease that stank of garlic and rancid fats. "Do you want to be like the holy lady Mathilde in Fontevrault, who lived on nothing but a sip of water and a spoonful of boiled nettles each day? Here, put this on your head." She plastered the smelly mixture liberally onto a white linen cloth and rolled it into a soft, squishy bundle.

"She could work miracles," Eleanor said. Every word made her head ache again, and the smell of the beef tallow mixed with rue and willow bark made her feel sick at her stomach. "It's been five years. I think we need a miracle, Louis and I."

Radegonde of Maillezais sniffed. "Maybe she could work miracles for others, but I promise you she couldn't have had a child. They said her courses stopped and she grew a pelt of hair all over her arms and legs, and her arms like two dry sticks. No man would have come near her long enough to get her with child. Do you want to be like that? Do you? Eat your soup, it's good for you. You, girl, stay with this stubborn queen and feed her. I have to oversee those idiots of waiting women in the packing."

Eleanor sat up. White pain lanced through her head. "Packing? But we just came to Poitiers! I thought we were to stay until the heat broke in Paris."

"We are," Radegonde confirmed, "but not in the palace. Moving to your father's old hunting lodge in the forest, and how we're to house a crowd of French nobles like locusts, let alone bring food for them all, is beyond me. Your husband finds this city too hot for him." She sniffed once more, eloquently. "Lie down and rest. Drink your soup. Think what we're to pack."

"I can't do all three at once," Eleanor grumbled under her breath as Radegonde sailed out. The little girl who'd brought the tray giggled once, then covered her mouth with her hand. "And who might you be?" Eleanor demanded.

"M-My father is Maître André, the wine merchant," the girl stammered. "He brought me here to wait on you while you were in the city. Only you were away, and that lady"—she jerked her chin toward the curtain over the door, still swaying from Radegonde's exit—"said you had nobly born ladies enough waiting on you and no need to cumber your household with a merchant's brat. Then when they brought you back and said you'd hurt your head, I ran to Mère Hébert in the rue des Valles and got some ivy berries and hazel for the head salve, and the lady said I might as well stay and make myself useful because——" She stopped and covered her mouth again.

"Because you seem to have more sense than the rest of these silly, giggling creatures who don't know any better than to run around and shriek and burn feathers under the queen's nose, when anybody knows that a foul odor drives the soul away and a sweet one brings it back," Eleanor finished.

The child gasped. "Oh—you heard that?"

"I have known Radegonde for quite some time," said Eleanor, "and I can still smell the burnt feathers." She smiled at the girl. "What is your name, then?"

"Jeanette. My lady. And my father sent me here because he said—you should know that some of us don't forget what you did for us at the time of the commune." Jeanette gasped and put her fingers over her mouth as if to stop the last word that had slipped out.

"It's all right," Eleanor said. "I don't bite at the sound of the word. You have a pretty voice, Jeanette. Most of my ladies have begun to forget the langue d'oc. It's good to hear it again, and with a Poitevin twang, too." Her head still ached abominably; she lay back for a moment against the pillows. Jeanette's little fingers moved in feathery circles over her temples, easing the pain. "I thought everyone here hated me for what Louis did. Were you one of the children he would have taken?"

"Yes . . . The soldiers killed my cat Miaou-Miaou. They made us all stand in the square for three days and nights. I was so scared," Jeanette murmured. "But you sent the good abbot to save us."

"I was afraid like that," Eleanor said, "when my father died, and the men around me thought to marry me to the first baron who came with an army big enough to take me. It's the lot of women to be afraid, Jeanette. We have to make up for it by being very clever."

"And by prayer and obedience, my mama says."

"That too," Eleanor conceded, "but it also helps to think quickly and get as much advantage as possible on your side. I can't give you back your kitten, Jeanette, but I can keep you with me and teach you how to act like a lady of the court. And in time, perhaps, we shall find you an important husband who will not let anybody hurt or frighten you."

Her eyes closed again and she seemed to be sleeping, but Jeanette heard her murmur, half conscious, "What I can't do for myself, Lady, let me do for this innocent. . . ."

135

The countryside outside Poitiers was lush and rich with the steamy growing heat of a wet spring and summer. The trees grew closer to the hunting lodge than Eleanor remembered them from her father's day, and long green vines tangled among the trees and put forth flowers she could not name, and the earth smelled of water and rich darkness and things bursting forth in fruitfulness. Each morning the shade of the vines turned her windowed chamber into a green-shadowed forest glade, and each day it seemed to her that the trees and the rampant vines encroached a little more on the clear space between the forest and the walls of the lodge.

She sent servants out with cleavers and axes to chop back the lush new growth, but the lazy churls left the overhanging, swinging vines alone and contented themselves with hacking off the tender shoots that struggled upward from the earth.

"The poor leaves do no harm," advised Cercle-le-Monde. He had appeared from nowhere a year earlier, when Louis was off making war on Toulouse, with a song of mourning for Duke William as his entrée. Eleanor never asked him why he had deserted her, and he never spoke of his wandering years, save when he offered her some exotic flower of song plucked on his travels.

Now he sprawled half on and half off a garden bench, advising Eleanor to let the wild growth of the forest alone, swinging his long legs in their fantastic patched and embroidered hose and strumming idly at a five-stringed harp with carved dragons' heads, a souvenir of his travels in Ireland.

"My father would never have allowed the forest to encroach so near to our walls," Eleanor said. "It provides cover for an enemy in case of war."

"But your good king has no enemies, and we are not at war. Or have I missed something?" A ripple of lazy, dancing notes hung between them, expanding the question into something Eleanor dared not think about.

"One never knows what may happen," Eleanor said finally. She sent out the men-at-arms, with pikes to pull down the long trailing vines and swords to chop through them. They made a great show of sweaty labor under the hot sun, with a din of shouted commands and clashing metal that made her ears ring, but in the cool of the evening what progress they had made against the forest was barely perceptible, and Cercle-le-Monde sat at her feet in the twilight-blue grass and sang a heathen song of love and longing that he had picked up from some Moor at the court of King Roger in Sicily:

"Que farayu, o que serad de mibi, habibi?
Non te tolgas de mibi!"

"All I want is a little peace," Eleanor said fretfully. "I cannot even sleep at night!" But how could she find peace, when the hunting lodge was crammed full to bursting, with ladies laid out to sleep like rows of herring in her chamber, tents pitched outside for the knights and soldiers who guarded the royal couple, nobles quarreling over the wall chambers, half her personal servants spilling over into the village and dispossessing peasants of their smoky huts? Raoul de Vermandois had flatly refused to let his king and queen go off to the hunting lodge in the forest with as little ceremony as Eleanor's father had used. He was there to watch over them personally, with his own personal guard and servants to add to the confusion, and the king's young brother Robert, strutting like a man in his sixteen-year-old pride, had insisted on coming too—with all the men and servants suitable to *his* state. In the little country manor where Eleanor had thought that she and Louis might find peace and privacy, she had found only crowding and quarrels over precedence and people sleeping where they didn't belong and couples whispering in corners. A fever of excitement and temptation passed through the rooms like a warm wind from the south. Cercle-le-Monde sang his songs of love, and the ladies sitting around Eleanor sighed and smiled and drifted away without permission. There wasn't a one of them who hadn't some follower or flirtation—save perhaps Radegonde of Maillezais. Even Petronilla had succumbed to the prevailing wind; her cheeks were flushed, and she sang to herself and disappeared at odd moments. Perhaps, Eleanor speculated, her little sister had been the attraction that inspired the king's young brother to follow them here. She was not entirely happy about the match. Robert, count of Dreux, had a bullying, swaggering manner about him that she would have thought would frighten a shy girl like her sister. But Petronilla was eighteen now. Time she was wed. And the king's brother, for all he was two years younger, would be an entirely suitable match.

She lay awake at night, thinking about these things, trying to control the love fever all around her with sensible thoughts about marriage portions and dower rights, hot and confined in the curtained bed that shut off any cooling breeze. The rustling of the wind in the trees was a constant intrusion; she could not shut off knowledge of the rich, fruitful, green forest all around them, nor could she say why it annoyed her so. Perhaps it was the contrast with her own barrenness. Louis lay stiff and rigid as a statue beside her, careful not to touch her while her ladies whispered and giggled around her. Later, in the dark hours before morning, when everyone slept soundly, he would awaken her and use her, silently, fiercely, as if he hated himself and her for the useless union that never produced fruit.

"This year I shall take Toulouse for you," he told her one July morning. They were walking in the narrow pleasaunce between the manor's southern wall and the encroaching forest. Eleanor's ladies kept a discreet distance at one end of the pleasaunce; at the other, a pacing guard in armor could be seen at intervals. It was as much privacy as they could expect.

Eleanor looked away, unwilling to meet his eyes. Toulouse should be part of her lands by right. It was a noble desire in Louis to win it back for her. But after last summer's brief inglorious siege and sudden return, she doubted that he could raise enough support among the nobles to revive the war.

"Will Raoul de Vermandois go with you?"

Louis flushed and bit his lip. "He—is unwilling. I don't know what keeps him here; he is a man of war, not a poet or a student to spend all day sighing at a lady's skirts."

Eleanor considered each word carefully before she spoke again. Her father would not have tolerated a seneschal who refused to follow him into battle. Twice now both Raoul de Vermandois and Thibaut of Champagne, the magnates of Louis's realm, had turned away from his desire for war. The old rivals, kept in an uneasy truce only by Louis's father's insistence that Champagne should marry his niece to Vermandois, were united only in this. Such disobedience was despicable.

On the other hand, neither war had been a good undertaking. Five years ago, when Louis marched south to break the commune of Poitiers, the land would have been devastated if he'd gone with the backing of Raoul and Thibaut. As for Toulouse, both counts had supported Louis's initial bid for that territory. He was the one who'd retreated from the realities of a long, sweaty siege and the danger of being encircled by Toulousan reinforcements. She could hardly blame the counts for their reluctance to begin the war again.

She seated herself on a bench, spreading out her skirts carefully, pleating the fine material between her fingers rather than look at Louis. He was watching her as if he expected her to give him something—what? What did she have for him? She couldn't even make a son for him. "Can you take the city with no more than your private forces?"

She knew he could not. Toulouse was rich and powerful, and the count of Toulouse had the dishonorable habit of hiring mercenaries. If Louis had not taken the city last year, with the advantage of surprise and with the weight of Raoul and Thibaut behind him, how could he succeed now?

Louis dropped to his knees beside her, awkward and hasty, laying his head on her lap. "I want to give you Toulouse," he said. "I love you more than life."

"You have made me queen," Eleanor said. "You have kept peace in my lands." His head was hot and heavy on her thigh. She could feel sweat starting where he lay against her, arms thrown about her hips.

"You don't love me." His voice was high, petulant, like a child being denied a sweet. "You want a brave knight like your father, a man who'll conquer the world and lay it at your feet. I would do that."

Eleanor wished he would stand up. She could sense the eyes of her ladies watching them.

"You are my lord," she said at last. "In time, God willing, I shall give you a son to rule after you. Is that not worth more than making a war we cannot win?"

Louis's face brightened. "Do you think—?"

"I don't know yet." It was not quite a lie. She did not expect her courses for another week; how could she tell? She might even now be with child.

There were tears in Louis's blue eyes. He buried his face in her lap. "I need you more than life," he repeated. "Never leave me."

"Do you think I would betray the vows we made?"

"Say it. Say that you will never leave me."

"I will never leave you," Eleanor repeated. The words sounded dull, heavy syllables with no meaning. The sun bore down on her head, brassy as a beaten gong. Between the manor walls and the tangled darkness of the impenetrable forest there was no shelter, no shade for her. She stroked Louis's blond head and wished he would stand up.

Petronilla knelt beside the man she loved while the priest gabbled questions and rushed them through the responses. In this midday hour the little village church was empty, dark with cool shadows that were a welcome relief from the glare of the noonday sun. She felt sleepy and satisfied, hardly able to keep her heavy eyelids open. The priest said Mass over them in such desperate haste that all the Latin syllables rolled together into one long wave of sound that carried her away into a dreamland where it was always golden summer.

"It's not what I wanted for you, little queen of my heart," her new-made husband whispered, shifting from one knee to the other with a creaking of leather that made the priest stammer and lose his place for a moment.

"You are all I want," Petronilla whispered back, and in that moment she meant it. She didn't need a chapel crammed full of overdressed nobles; she had no desire to be a showpiece in red satin for the crowds to gawk at. Eleanor was welcome to all that, just as she was welcome to the heavy inheritance of Aquitaine and Poitou that constrained her marriage and all her future life. Petronilla was used to being in the shadows, half unseen and seldom considered. On the whole, she thought, she preferred it that way. At least she had her choice of a man, and the man she wanted had seen her at once, shadows or no shadows. In his eyes she saw herself reflected, a beauty for once in her life, the heroine of her own story: their secret love, their desperate longing, and this final happy ending were as wonderful as any romance sung by Eleanor's pet musicians.

The priest came to the end of his prayers with a rush of words that stopped suddenly, like a wave breaking on solid rock. He closed his book and bowed to the couple who knelt before him.

"It is done, my lord."

"Good." Petronilla's husband stood, rather stiffly, and Petronilla rose beside him with a rustle of silk.

"And—your promise?"

"No one will punish you for this day's work. Do you think the king would permit it?"

The priest thought to himself that the king wasn't the one who'd just been married in such haste, and that one could not always be sure of one's kinfolks' reaction to a surprise. But he kept his mouth shut. It was not for a village priest to question what three bishops had ratified.

Outside, the sun dazzled through green leaves and trailing vines, creating a mosaic of light and green shadow against the blue of the summer sky. Petronilla saw rings of light around everything she looked at; she blinked against the strength of the sun and leaned on her new husband's arm, letting him guide her to their horses. The short ride to the manor gave her time to grow used to the light again. She left him to do whatever it was men did, seeing to horses and soldiers and investigating the guard shifts, and hurried to tell her sister all her wonderful news.

Eleanor's brows drew together sharply when Petronilla burst into the solar, and after the first happy words she dismissed her women. "You too, Radegonde, if you please!" she said when the old lady lingered at the door.

"Now, Petronilla, what is this?" she demanded when they were alone.

Petronilla blinked back tears. "I thought you would be happy for me."

"I—I am surprised," Eleanor said. "Married in secret, and in such haste? Why did you not speak to me?" She opened her arms to Petronilla then, but Petronilla hung back. She was not ready for an embrace that came with so much implied criticism.

"I am eighteen," she pointed out. "Three years older than you were when you married Louis!"

"Why, yes, and it's time you were settled," Eleanor agreed at once, "only I thought you would have discussed it with me first."

"I was afraid you'd disapprove," Petronilla confessed.

"Because of the age difference?"

"Well, that, and—"

"He is a little young for you, but—"

"*Young?*"

Eleanor's lips parted, but she did not speak. Petronilla felt a sinking in the pit of her stomach. Something was wrong; Eleanor's initial acceptance of the situation had been too easy. She turned aside and reached for a box of sweet honeyed fruits that sat open beside Radegonde's tapestry stand. She bit into one; the sticky sweetness soothed and sickened her at the same time.

"Perhaps," said her sister behind her, speaking very slowly and carefully, "perhaps I have misunderstood something. My lord's young brother has been very fond of our company this summer. I thought he might be courting you."

Petronilla would have laughed, but the honey was sticky on her lips and fingers, and the sweet preserved fruit caught in her throat. "Robert of Dreux? He's a child. I've married a *man*."

She waited for the next question. A fly buzzed through the room, circled the box of fruits, and settled on a slice of quince. Finally Petronilla swallowed the last cloyingly sweet bite of her own fruit and turned to face her sister. Eleanor was sitting straight-backed and tense in her high carved chair, hands folded before her. "I think," she said, "you had better tell me all about it."

Petronilla shrugged. She felt awkward and young and plain again. "What is there to tell?" She winced at the sound of her own voice, too shrill. "Raoul loves me. I love him. We were married this noon, in the village church, and no one can put us apart now."

"*Raoul?*" Eleanor's fine arched brows rose. "Vermandois? But he's—"

"He's not too old for me," Petronilla said. "He's not fifty yet. He is strong and—" Her lips curved in a soft smile. "He's not too old for me," she repeated.

"Our father would have been much of an age with him, if he had lived," said Eleanor dryly. "But I was about to point out that he is married already."

"Not anymore. Why do you think he asked Louis for a leave of absence?"

"To visit his brother, or so he said—oh." Eleanor sighed. "His brother, the bishop of Senlis. I think I begin to see. He went to get an annulment?"

Petronilla shrugged. "He and Leonora were kin within the forbidden degrees. I forget how it works out, but I think his great-aunt married in Champagne."

"I'm sure they were," Eleanor agreed. "Everybody can find some such relationship, if they're willing to look far enough back. Even Louis and I have some connection, but that was never raised as a serious bar to our marriage." She sighed again. "Petronilla. Little sister. I do love you. I will do my best to smooth it over. But I wish you realized just what you've done. The only thing keeping Thibaut of Champagne and Raoul de Vermandois from one another's throats has been that marriage alliance."

"What can Thibaut do?" Petronilla demanded. "Everything was perfectly legal. The church assented to Raoul's annulment. The church has blessed our marriage. This sort of thing happens all the time. It's not as if they had children . . ."

Eleanor's lips compressed for a moment, and Petronilla took an uncertain step backward. "No," her sister agreed in an even voice, "it's not as if they had children. That is perfectly true. Some unions are—more blessed than others. Do I begin to understand the reason for this unseemly haste?"

"I thought," Petronilla said uncertainly, "I thought you would wish me to be happy." Her lower lip was shaking.

This time she did not evade her sister's embrace. She leaned her head on Eleanor's shoulder and cried softly while Eleanor rocked her like a child. The sweet scents of rose water and jasmine enveloped her; the warmth of Eleanor's flesh comforted her. "We used to lie together in one bed when Papa was away," she said when the tears stopped. "Remember? I would be frightened to lie alone, and you comforted me."

"And after he died," Eleanor said, "you were so frail, I was worried for you." She drew back, hands on her sister's shoulders, and smiled at Petronilla. "You're not a fragile little girl any longer, are you, my love? You're a woman, and—and bearing your husband's child, and yes, I am happy for you. Come now, let me see what I can find for your wedding gifts, since you've taken us all by surprise like this!"

She went down on her knees before a carved chest and spent the next hour going through folded lengths of emerald silk and scarlet samite and brocaded trims and supple furs and girdles of linked silver snakes, pressing gifts on Petronilla and carefully not talking of the things that Petronilla knew she must be worrying about: how to tell Louis, what to do about the rivalry between Thibaut and Raoul, whether this move would cause more tensions between Louis and the pope. All the things Petronilla had refused to think about until now.

"You are too good to me," Petronilla said, blinking very fast so as not to drop a salt tear on the length of blue samite that Eleanor was draping over her. "I wish— I wish you could have been free to choose, as I am."

"Louis is very good to me," Eleanor said lightly, but she bent her head for a moment and made herself very busy folding the discarded fabrics that were too strong of hue for Petronilla. "And he loves me. I have nothing to complain of."

"Truly?" It seemed terrible, unbearable, that Eleanor should never know the glowing sweetness Petronilla had found with Raoul de Vermandois, should never know a man who worshipped her and delighted in her and gave her pleasure. And Petronilla had never seen much chance for pleasure in Eleanor's pale, reserved husband.

"Truly," Eleanor affirmed with a smile just too bright to be convincing. "Why, silly girl, I am queen of France; one can hardly marry much better than that. One day I shall give Louis an heir, and then everything will be perfect. It was—it is a good marriage, the best I could have made."

And Petronilla felt years older, hearing what her sister didn't say: the *only* marriage she could have made. Who else could have held Aquitaine and Poitou for her?

By September of that year, Geoffrey Plantagenet and his wife's bastard half-brother had conquered another significant portion of Normandy. Starting from Robert's hometown of Caen, they first took Bastebourg above the river ford, then moved southwest through Bayeux and up the left bank of the Orne. Then Geoffrey began his methodical sweep to the west, taking all of the county of Mortain between the river and the sea. Tinchebrai, Mortain itself, Le Teilleul, and Saint-Hilaire fell or surrendered to him. The victorious push westward advanced like a wave until it met the sea at Pontorson, a castle at the bottom of a sandy bay guarded by Mont-Saint-Michel. The castellan of Pontorson was loyal to Stephen; more to the point, he was well supplied, had a strong position impregnable from three sides, and expected his lord to send more supplies from England. Geoffrey paused there, briefly, to consider the problem of Pontorson and to make certain other arrangements connected with his promises to his wife Matilda and her brother Robert.

In connection with these plans, he sent for Robert at dawn one morning, while his siege engineers studied the rocks and sand around Pontorson and tried to come up with a plan of attack.

"I've sent for the boy," Geoffrey said as soon as Robert entered his tent. "He's to go back with you. He doesn't know yet."

He was wearing a long robe, a scholar's gown, and he had been writing on a roll of parchment like a common scribe. His beard, once all golden, flashed with lines of silver in the pale morning light that spilled in through the opened tent flaps and puddled in the folds of his robe like melting snow. There were blotches of ink on his broad fingers. When he pushed back the sleeve of his robe to keep it out of the way of the inkpot, a long silver scar gleamed slanting along the underside of his right arm, memento of some long-forgotten battle.

"I had rather hoped," Robert said slowly, "that you would accompany me back to England yourself."

"I have business here," Geoffrey pointed out.

"Once Pontorson has fallen?" It would not be tactful, Robert supposed, to ask if Geoffrey had any idea how he meant to take a castle surrounded by the unpredictable tides of the Breton coast. But some of his skepticism must have showed, for Geoffrey looked up and gave him a brief smile.

"They'll come over to me," he said cheerfully. "It's only a matter of waiting until that nit Roger de Pontorson figures out that he can't count on Stephen to supply him. Nobody can count on Stephen. In time, that'll settle Matilda's problem too; the English are slow, but they aren't stupid. If she'll just keep from alienating them, they'll give up on Stephen and turn to her in time."

That might be true, Robert supposed. Certainly it had been true of him. He'd gone over to Matilda's side not from blind family loyalty, but from a deep conviction that Stephen of Blois would never hold to one course of action or prove faithful to one party for longer than it took the wind to shift—or a new adviser to whisper in his ear. In time, perhaps, the rest of Stephen's English supporters would come to that same conclusion. But would they turn to Matilda, or would they look to one of their own to take the throne? Too many barons would never swear to a woman. If Geoffrey himself had been there, to rule by right of marriage to Matilda, they might be able to generate the loyalty they needed.

"I'd hoped you would come," he repeated without much hope of swaying the big, blond man who sat trimming his quill over a stack of parchment. "You promised your help after this summer's campaign."

"And help you shall have. Young Henry is just what you need. Matilda's son, heir after her. Let the people see him. Trust me, it'll all work out."

The pieces don't fit, Robert thought. *It's not autumn yet, and I'm so cold my bones ache in this tent that's open on two sides for the wind to whistle through. I've been fighting beside this man all summer, I know him for a soldier and a good one at that, yet in his leisure time he dresses like a clerk and wastes his time writing letters and reading books like one of those useless scholars at Paris. I came here to ask him for help to defend Matilda's crown in England, and he promised me help if I'd stay and see him through this summer's campaign. Now he's talking about sending back a child of nine when what I need is a good troop of heavy cavalry with Geoffrey himself to lead them.*

"He should be here in two, three days at the most. Even riding easy, it won't take him that long to come up from Angers." Geoffrey squinted at a blurred line on the parchment before him, held it up to the light, and scratched a correction. A dog yipped outside the tent, something clanged like armor. Robert's hand went to his empty belt. "Squire!" he yelled. There wouldn't be time to arm himself. What the devil had the guards been thinking of?

A man's outraged shout and a boy's high piping voice jousted unintelligibly over the waves of sound. Geoffrey Plantagenet laid down his quill, covered the inkpot, and rose leisurely to his feet. He appeared remarkably calm. Robert reckoned that only a man who knew him well, say a man who'd been fighting beside him in Normandy all summer, would have recognized the eagerness that possessed him under that controlled surface. "That'll be the young hellion now. Only, what the devil does he mean by arriving at this hour?"

Two boys, one in a miniature suit of half-armor, the other in a leather corselet that gapped at neck and waist, burst into the tent like a summer storm. Accompanying them were half a dozen dogs and a harried, apologetic man-at-arms.

"Begging your pardon, Count Geoffrey, but I couldn't keep up there—"

"Nobody can," panted the boy in half-armor, a tall, fair-haired lad whom Robert took to be the expected heir. "*Down, Sable!*" He swatted ineffectually at the nearest hound, which was competing for the bread and meat clutched in his hand.

The other boy was down on the ground with the dogs, laughing and egging them on to snatch the meat. "Go on, Sable, *beau, beau,* Courant, take the food, he eats too much anyway!"

"Do not!" retorted the tall boy.

"Always thinking of your stomach!" taunted the redhead, deftly hooking the other boy's legs out from under him and bringing him down amid the yapping dogs.

"Somebody must, when you travel, or we'd all starve." Sable wolfed down the disputed meat and panted approval at the boy's words.

Geoffrey took two steps forward and grabbed the freckle-faced brat in the leather corselet, hauling him upright by a handful of his sandy-red hair. "It's so gratifying to see how your manners have improved," he said between his teeth. "I shall instruct your new tutor to beat you twice a day."

Robert's mouth sagged. So did his spirits. *This* was the heir to Anjou and—if Matilda had her way—England? This freckled, snub-nosed, slightly bruised, and very dirty infant? God help them all. At least the other boy had some presence, and dressed decently. But what could they do with *this*?

"What new tutor? I like Master Peter," the child Henry protested.

"Your likes and dislikes are of no great concern to me," his father said, seating himself again. "Get those dogs out of here!"

The man-at-arms collected Sable and Courant by the scruffs of their necks, kicked another dog, and flicked a whip at two others. Suddenly the tent seemed almost empty, and very quiet.

"Am I to stay and help you here?"

"*No*. You're going to Bristol with your uncle Robert, to be taught letters and gentle deportment."

"Now, just a minute—" Robert started to say. He hadn't agreed to take on this—what was it Geoffrey had called him?—this young hellion. Damn it, he had a war to fight; he didn't have time to be a nursemaid or tutor!

"I could help you, you know, Father. I've been studying Vegetius on the art of war."

Geoffrey smiled. "Have you now! And what have you learned?" He seemed genuinely interested in the question. "Have you read what Vegetius says on the employment of mercenaries?"

"He says that princes should teach their own knights the noble profession of arms rather than to take foreigners and common men into their pay."

"And do you agree? Should I try to take Pontorson with my own men, or pay mercenaries to besiege the castle?" It was a loaded question; more than half Geoffrey's sieges in Normandy had been aided by mercenaries to supplement his Angevin knights.

"Neither," Henry answered. Geoffrey's golden brows went up.

"Vegetius also teaches that one should study one's enemy in detail," the boy went on, confident and cocky as a Paris master dilating on the art of logic. He nodded toward the boy in princely armor who'd come in with him. "My friend Yves comes from Dol, just across the river. He knows a lot about Roger of Pontorson. For instance, did you know that Roger has a very good friend in Dol? A widow?"

Geoffrey frowned. "If you're thinking that we should threaten her, boy, that's unknightly. Besides, it wouldn't work. Pontorson isn't fool enough to surrender a castle for the sake of some woman he isn't even married to."

"Not for her sake," said Henry cheerfully, "for his own. He slipped out of the castle and visited her last night—or meant to. Yves and I, um, interfered with his plans. You see, that's why the rest of my escort isn't with me. I told them to stay in Dol, guarding Roger. You might want to hurry to get him," he added. "We tied him up, of course, but he was not very happy about being captured by a couple of boys and their servants. If he does get loose, I'm afraid he won't be in a very good—"

Geoffrey was on his feet, shouting orders in all directions. In less time than he'd taken to sharpen one quill, he had dispatched a troop of knights to Dol, to take possession of Roger of Pontorson, with Yves as their guide. Henry, under protest, he sent to bathe and pack. When the tent was empty, he sat down again, rested his golden forearms on his knees, breathed in once, and looked up at Robert.

"Well," he said quietly. "You see what I mean. Boy's a natural leader."

Robert made a noncommittal grumble.

"You'll take him?"

Robert remained silent.

"*Please,*" Geoffrey added. "My nerves aren't up to it. Beat some sense into him. Hire tutors. Let Matilda work on him for a while, she's not doing anything else useful while she's in England." He sighed deeply. "You know, if I'd been Fulk's second son instead of his first, I could have gone into a monastery. Sometimes I think about that. I'd have been a good scribe, I think, maybe even something of a scholar. A quiet life. Peaceful. Not without its attractions . . ."

Pontorson castle surrendered that afternoon. Two days later, Robert of Gloucester and Henry Plantagenet set sail for England.

Chapter Ten

At Lagny-sur-Marne, in the territory of the count of Champagne, the papal legate held a church council that reversed the divorce of Raoul and Leonora. The three bishops who had agreed to the annulment were excommunicated, as were Raoul and Petronilla.

This time Raoul de Vermandois did not persuade his lord to caution. The decree of excommunication was followed by a brief and savage winter war. Just after Christmas, Louis and Raoul together led the French armies into Champagne. At Thibaut's castle of Vitry-sur-Marne, not far from the site of the church council that had incited Louis to war, they were briefly opposed by a handful of knights from Thibaut's army. Raoul's archers sent fire arrows into the castle and the surrounding village of wooden huts. By the time the castle surrendered, the village was ablaze, and men, women, and children had taken refuge in the imposing church of Vitry while Louis's soldiers ransacked the town.

In Paris that winter there was ice on the Seine. Wolves were reported in the forests outside the walls, and citizens were warned to keep close watch on their children. The vendors of roasted chestnuts moved their charcoal braziers out onto the ice-topped river, and boys skated across the ice with the blade bone of a sheep strapped to each shoe.

Under the glowing braziers, under the swiftly passing sharp bones that scored the ice and threw up drifts of crystalline powder, under the arches of the Grand Pont and the Petit Pont, the Seine still ran beneath the ice, a deep green current through the heart of the city. The Île de la Cité was a ship trapped in the ice; the royal palace was a castle surrounded by a glassy plain. Eleanor sat within the damp stone walls of the palace and thought about the strong currents flowing out of sight.

At thin places where the river ran too swift for the ice to take good hold, she could still hear the water rushing past, imagine the strength of the current like a beating heart, shiver and envision what would happen if the ice cracked beneath her feet, if she slid into the black gap and down, down into the jealous turbulent embrace of the river, a lover who would tumble her under the ice and, eventually, into the green waters of the salt and unfrozen sea, unless her body caught by sleeve or tunic on one of the wooden timbers that stood beneath the water and danced there, grinning fleshless in the rushing water, until with the coming of spring, the ice dissolved to set her free.

The castle should have been protection enough from such wayward fancies. Tapestries covered the cold hard stones, windows were shuttered against the cold, candles and torches and the glow of burning charcoal lit her rooms, and the air was thick as nightmare with the smell of too many noble bodies kept together for too many weeks. At either end of great hall, the nobles of the royal court clustered around the fires, playing at tables and singing and flirting and hearing sermons and telling lies about their hunting expeditions and sharing rumors about the war in Champagne. The fires roared up as if to consume them all. Eleanor looked into the heart of the flames and looked away, eyes burning. A vague fear oppressed her. She left the hall without signaling to her waiting women.

Benoît de Périgné, reading heretical works and scribbling dangerous marginal notes by the light seeping through a cracked shutter in a window niche, was evicted from his corner by a giggling young couple whose noisy flirtation shattered all hope of concentration. He observed them sourly: the king's young brother Robert, well on the way to being a libertine at the age of seventeen, Eleanor's waiting woman Faenze. If he'd been charged with choosing his lady's servants, he'd not have tolerated that giggling bit of fluff, but he was no one here, a poor clerk who'd never even attained the coveted status of magister. He never would, now that Master Abelard had been driven to his death by charges of heresy. He could not lower himself to study under one of the canting jackdaw clerics who'd hopped into Paris to take the great man's place.

The queen's gratitude, the purse she sent and the offer of employment, had come in a good hour, shortly after she saw him at Master Abelard's hearing at Sens. At the time he'd been only too happy to leave the strife-torn academic world to serve the lady of his dreams, even if she never alluded by word or look to the autumn day when he'd taken liberties in his ignorance.

Sometimes, though, in winter, he wondered if he'd made the right decision. Winter and a palace full of boneheaded nobles were a poor combination for a scholar seeking quiet; he could almost regret his bare attic room above the Cat and Bones, with his writing stand and his hoard of tallow candle stubs and the wind biting through every crack in the ancient walls like a master archer shooting through the arrow slits into a castle. Almost.

Faenze's high hysterical laughter blended in with the shriek of the winter wind and the noisy games in the great hall. Benoît slipped his book inside the loose front of his gown and warmed fingers as numb as icicles before the fire, or as close to it as he could get in a room where nearly everyone outranked him. He stared into the fire over the shoulders of two barons from the Loire who spoke of their hawks as students boast of their ladies, but he did not see in the flames the visions that had sent Eleanor away.

She left the fires and the warmth and the company of the great hall behind her, like a fur-lined cloak dropped carelessly on the floor, and mounted by a small private stair to a turret that was not part of her suite of rooms and hence was not infested by her own women. The stone stairs turned sunwise and sunwise up the tower, striking cold through her feet and deep into her bones. At the top there was only a bare small chamber once used to shelter guards.

There were no guards posted here now. It had been many a year since the Seine brought raiders out of the far north to burn and raid into the heart of France. The Northmen were tamed now; they were dukes and barons and knights in Normandy and England and Sicily. The wild Northmen who had burned Paris and Chartres two hundred years ago would not come again. But the tower remained. And somewhere the fires of war still burned.

Eleanor flung open the shutters to winter air that bit her naked hands. She felt stiff and cold as a stone column in the church porch, with her mirror of polished bronze cold in her hand and her eyes fixed upon the mirror. It was nearly night; only a glimmer of light fought through the clouds to dance on the mirror's face. The flickers of reflected light from the dying sun made the serpent handle of the mirror seem to turn against her wrists. Somewhere outside the city walls, a wolf howled.

Flames danced over the bronze surface of the mirror. The Seine ran full and strong beneath the ice. Air froze around her, crystalline, sharper than a blade of Damascus steel. The stone floor was frozen earth beneath her feet; the walls were the black bare limbs of winter trees, interlaced with dead thorny vines and snowflakes big and soft as white flowers. Fire spilled out of the mirror, a blazing fountain that ran over her hands without burning her. Within the fountain of fire a village burned, a church stood as a black shell against glowing coals, a bell rang, men and women and children screamed for a mercy that was denied.

Outside, the wolves howled and the river ran deep and strong to the sea.

The king's messengers were in the great hall when she returned, gabbling their news to all who wished to hear it. Eleanor paused on the stairs. She had no desire to hear it confirmed. But after a moment's shrinking, she came on down and entered the hall. She was a king's consort and a sovereign in her own right; it was not for her to disavow or disallow what Louis might have done.

What he has done for my sister's good name, and hence for me.

It was Ivo, the young count of Soissons, who'd returned to Paris with the news. The war was over for the time being. Something had happened at a village called Vitry-sur-Marne, something that had made the king withdraw his armies.

"Not a defeat, no," he answered a baron who questioned him. "We—we took the castle. But . . ." His eyes glanced around the circle, meeting no man's face directly. He looked at Eleanor and looked away quickly, and spoke of a castle taken, a village looted and burnt, of peasants and wounded men and children taking refuge within the church that had been one of the jewels of Champagne.

"Had been?" another courtier caught the words from Ivo's mouth.

And Eleanor understood the vision of the tower room. "He burned the church," she said. "Didn't he? He burned the church and all the people in it. And now, for his soul's sake, he has given up the war." She laughed into the silence that fell over the crowded room. "For his soul's sake . . . I'm sure that will vastly comfort the villagers of Vitry."

They drew aside from her then, whispering among themselves and glancing sidewise at the king's barren wife from the south, who dared to laugh at death and fire, who had known the details of the tragedy before Count Ivo spoke.

April 1143

That spring an emperor of Byzantium died, and a new emperor ascended the throne. John Comnenus had been hunting with his youngest son, Manuel, when a scratch on his hand became infected. He died without returning to the city. Upon his death, Manuel proclaimed that his father's dying wish had been for his youngest son to succeed him.

John's two older sons, Alexios and Andronikos, were already dead. Manuel sent John Axuch, the grand domestic, to prepare for a smooth transfer of power. The principal preparations consisted of seeing that Manuel's last surviving older brother, Isaakios, was arrested before he learned of their father's death.

The arrest was made without violence; Isaakios was kept in the Pantokrator monastery while John Axuch completed his preparations. After arranging for the citizens of Byzantium to proclaim Manuel emperor, he made his private arrangements with the clergy who might have opposed Manuel's impious seizure of the throne. A letter written in imperial red letters and secured by a gold seal and silken cords announced that Manuel conferred on the church two hundred pounds of silver annually.

The patriarch and his clergy acclaimed the wise and just and generous and pious emperor of Byzantium, Manuel Comnenus, and John Axuch put away, for return to his master, the second letter, which increased the bribe to two hundred pounds of gold.

In July 1143, the young emperor entered Byzantium in state. The citizens acclaimed him with the proper degree of jubilation and respect; John Axuch was thorough in his preparations. Some at least of the celebration was heartfelt; women were pleased to see this handsome young man becoming emperor, and the prettiest girls in the city pushed their way forward to throw flowers, which Manuel returned with a smile that won many a heart. Only one minor omen marred the day's celebrations: as Manuel reached the Emperors' Gate to the Imperial Palace, his horse reared, neighed, whirled about, and nearly brained two spectators before Manuel brought it under control and passed through the gate. John Axuch immediately arranged for the correct interpretation of the prophecy. Before the day was out, soothsayers proclaimed that the episode was propitious and that the pattern of the horse's movements foretold long life and a successful reign for the emperor.

DECEMBER 1143

The royal chaplain, the king's confessor, stalked the halls of the palace like a lean bird of prey stooping over his victims. Faenze saw him coming and tried to slip away, but he was too quick for her. In a corner shielded by tapestries, he interrogated her about the queen's movements and habits.

"I know nothing, nothing!" Faenze insisted tearfully. "Let me carry this bowl to her before the water cools, I pray you, sir!"

Odo of Deuil poked at the dried leaves and flowers floating on the surface of the steaming water. "Some pagan practice, no doubt. She divines the future through observing the patterns of these herbs. Did you gather them at midnight, under a crescent moon, using a blade of pure metals to cut the flowers?"

"It's rosemary and dried lavender petals," Faenze said. "A wash to clear the skin and brighten the eyes. *Please*, sir—"

"No doubt she sees her visions by aid of the sorcerous enchantments in the water."

"She sees no visions!" Faenze cried. "She is purer than any of you!"

"Certainly more so than *you*," purred Odo, "who risk your soul daily by going in lascivious embraces with the king's young brother. If the queen is so pure, why does she permit such lustful goings-on from her women?"

"She knows nothing," Faenze said. "Please, you won't tell her—"

"Not if you tell me what I need to know."

"There is nothing to tell."

"I will be the judge of that. The screech of an owl and the scream of a black cat were heard at midnight in her rooms, and flames burned as if she raised demons from hell. . . ."

Faenze laughed in the monk's face and set down the cooling bowl of herbal waters. "Oh, that, that's nothing. Let me explain to you . . ."

When at last Odo reluctantly let her go, she slipped between two tapestries and reached a corner stair, only to come up with a sudden stop against a second black-clad, grim-faced figure.

"Telling stories against the queen, are you?"

"I'd rather die," Faenze said, "and it's none of your business, Master Clerk, so let me pass!"

"When one of the queen's waiting women makes secret trysts with the chaplain who hates her, it *is* my business," said Benoît de Périgné. "I serve the lady with my life. If you are slipping away to tell tales on her to that monk of ill omen—" His big hands tightened convulsively, like those of a man wringing the neck of a trapped coney.

"There are no tales to tell," said Faenze. "The queen is troubled by bad dreams, that's all, and sometimes she cries out in her sleep. Odo was trying to make some brew of witchcraft out of the rumors of noises from her chambers, so I told him the truth." She sat down on the lowest step of the stone stairs and glowered up at Benoît. "Look. I know you hate me, but you know the truth as well as I do. The queen is virtuous, she does her duty to her husband. She may not enjoy it overmuch, but what woman does?"

"I should think you'd know the answer to that," Benoît sneered.

"Oh. My lord Robert." Faenze leaned her chin in her hands and gazed at the cold stones beneath her feet. "You *would* think so. You clerks never understand anything. Robert is count of Dreux. He is the second man in the kingdom after the king himself. I'm just a little nobody out of a Norman farm, even if my family is related to the king's mother in the sixth degree. If I'm nice to Robert of Dreux, he gives me pretty things to wear and perfumes from Arabia and—oh, all sorts of nice things. If I make him angry, I could be sent back to Normandy. And I'd rather die. If the choice were between having a little fun with the king's brother, and jumping out this tower window into the snow and smashing both your legs, what would *you* do, Master Holy-Virtue-and-Righteousness?"

"Do you really think he'd throw you out the window?"

"No," Faenze said calmly, "I'd throw myself."

"You love court life so much?"

"Actually," Faenze said, "I do. And that's not a crime. It's not even a sin, so don't glower at me that way. I like bright-colored clothes and gaiety, feasts and fairs and jongleurs walking on their hands, sweet cakes sticky with honey, tourneys and pennons flying from lances and knights crashing together in the melee for the honor of their ladies. And if any of those knights should ask to wear my favor and another dispute him for it, or if the jongleur wants to shout out a *fabliau* about cheating, fornicating priests, I wouldn't mind that either. You don't understand, you can't possibly understand, so why don't you just go away and leave me alone!" Her eyes were bright with tears.

"I'd rather listen," Benoît said quietly, "and try to understand."

"All right, then! Listen, this is how it was: you'd crave noise and gaiety and color and fun too, if you'd been brought up as I was, in a stone-cold manor house where the river damp got into the walls and the rushes every winter, with nothing but our pride and our piety to keep us warm." She rubbed her fingers together. "Oh, how my hands were sore from peeling wet rushes every winter to make rushlights. If I never *see* another rush again—and I won't have to, as long as I'm here. In the queen's chambers I can call for a branch of wax tapers whenever I want, and a cup of hot mulled wine with it to take the chill from my bones."

She glared at Benoît. "Sound like an old woman, don't I? I tell you, sometimes I felt as if I'd never be warm again. God bless Queen Eleanor for bringing me where I have dances and compliments on my pretty hands and feet to warm me from the inside out. Why shouldn't I enjoy those things? A little game in the corner with Robert of Dreux isn't going to spoil me for marriage; oh, no, my brothers already took care of that. They used to get drunk on the long winter nights and then . . ."

She clasped her hands together and stared into the stones as if she could see nightmares moving there. "I ran away to Aunt Gunhilde at the convent and begged her to let me stay there. It was just as cold and just as much work, but my brothers couldn't get at me. But I hadn't the dowry they wanted, and Father insisted I come back because my running away had made a scandal and the neighbors were whispering, and too much of the abbey's income was tied up with our land. And that was how things stood when the king's mother and Queen Eleanor came to visit. Aunt Gunhilde told them about me and said, 'I can't prevent a father taking his daughter back, and if I try he'll ruin our abbey.'

"'Well, I can,' said Queen Eleanor. 'He'll not refuse a queen, and I've need of another girl to wait on me,' which was a lie, for she had such a train of attendants she didn't know half their names, and that not even counting the ones she'd left in Paris. But she took me back with her, and Father didn't dare speak a word against it, just as she'd said."

Faenze dropped her head and gazed into the floating herbs on the surface of the bowl. "So you see now," she said, almost inaudibly, "why it doesn't matter if Robert of Dreux takes a fancy to me. There's nothing he can do that hasn't been done before, and worse, and he doesn't hurt me when he's doing it. But I'd die before I said anything against the queen.

"And if you tell that black bird of ill omen, the king's chaplain, he'll have me sent away for being a sinful bad influence," she added after a little while.

"Well? What do you think?"

Very gently and slowly, Benoît leaned forward and picked up the bowl of herbs and water, cradling it between his big-knuckled hands as tenderly as if it were a rare Arabian manuscript.

"I think," he said, "we'd better get this water heated up again before you take it to the queen."

Louis knelt before his confessor.

"Bless me, Father, for I have sinned."

The silence ached with cold. The stone saints around them wept (the palace was damp in winter), the carved devils around the chapel door writhed and shouted in silent glee, and the golden Loire stone turned to black shadows and living gold in the flickering of the candles.

The king of France sweated in that chill silence until his confessor spoke. Odo, monk of Saint-Denis, had been Louis's teacher once. Now he had risen to the post of royal chaplain, an adviser more powerful even than Abbot Suger. In his eyes,

Louis saw himself always as an ignorant boy, not worthy to stay among the monks, unable to live according to their pure rule.

"I have lain with a woman—" Louis's whisper was harsh in the darkness.

"Marriage is a sacrament," observed the calm monk, standing like a pillar of stone to hear his king's confession, "and it is the duty of a monarch to beget an heir. Having chosen the way of the world, you must not repent the sacrifices that are called for."

"I did not *choose* this," Louis cried in protest. "You know it was forced upon me when Philippe died! I never wanted anything more than to live in the monastery."

"Where there is no desire," counseled Odo, "there is no sin."

"I have done more than lie with her."

"Have you been guilty of perversities?" The monk's tone sharpened. "Have you polluted yourself through the violence of your imagination? By your own hand? By the aid of others?"

Louis shook his head violently at each question. Odo sighed but continued the inquisition.

"Then have you lain with the woman when she was unclean? Have you enjoyed her after the unnatural manner? Have you washed yourself in a bath with her?" Odo's voice lowered. "Do not fear to confess the details to me, my son. Cleanse your heart of this burden."

"God preserve us," Louis muttered, "such foulness never entered my mind. But . . . I have taken pleasure in that which ought to be my duty. I have taken excessive pleasure, Father. At night I cannot sleep for thinking of her. Her skin is so soft and white, and she bathes in water of roses. Her hair is silk and her little breasts just fit in my hands. Sometimes I lie with her twice and thrice in one night, and all for the pleasure that I have of her. I have even taken her to me at forbidden times—on days of fasting, and during the forty days before Easter, and on Sundays."

"The woman tempts you with lascivious words and sights," stated his confessor. "She is flesh and earth and the sin of Eve; her lusts drag you into sin. She displays herself to you, no doubt. She opens up her shameful parts and beckons you to enter. With hands and tongue she tries your continence in perverse ways—"

"No!" The king's cry of protest interrupted the catalog of female frailties. "No, Father. She covers herself modestly. She hardly moves when I possess her. Nor does she speak—except," he added with boyish, incurable honesty, "when she complains that I hurt her through the excess of my desire."

"See the vile deceit and trickery of women in this. She pretends to be pure and modest, knowing that the love of her modesty will inflame you, a virtuous monarch. For there is manifestly no purity in women. Is not her body itself an occasion of sin for you?"

The king bowed his head and nodded.

"You must be strong against this temptation," the confessor advised. "You must not allow the woman to destroy your virtuous soul. If you go to her in desire, remind yourself of her as she will be on the last day: a bundle of bones wrapped in her shroud. Go to her in decency and without lust, and God will reward you as you deserve."

"An heir?"

"If it be God's will. I cannot promise. But surely God will not look with favor on one who is led by his wife, instead of leading and controlling her. Conquer impurity. And if prayer and meditation do not serve, then drive out the devil as you were taught in boyhood."

From the folds of his robe he drew out a short whip of knotted cords. The king's face shone and he took this gift in both hands. He bent his head and kissed the stiff cords.

Odo of Deuil left the king's private chapel and fell into step beside the man who waited outside the room. From within, they could hear the murmur of prayers, interrupted after each line by a whistling sound and a sharp crack.

"The woman is most assuredly a heretic and a witch," stated Thierry Galeran, knight of the Order of Templars.

Odo made the sign of the cross. "God forbid. You speak of our queen. It is true her influence over the king is too strong, but you should be careful of making such accusations."

"She knew about Vitry before the messenger came. Her sister bewitched a decent man to make him put aside his wife. They both practice divination and evil arts."

"Even if you could prove what you say," replied Odo, "you would be unwise to say it. Our king is devoted to her. And as for your accusations—" He shrugged. "I do not condone Raoul of Vermandois in the matter of the divorce. He brought his own punishment upon himself; the excommunication was right and just. But he is not the first old man to ruin himself for a pretty face."

"He is not ruined," Thierry Galeran said sharply. "He sits at the right hand of the king, and the woman sits at his left hand, and together they lead him into sin."

"Be careful what you say," Odo repeated. "The king's mind is much disturbed. I would not be the one who crosses him."

"He suffers over Vitry?" Thierry hazarded. "But that was not his fault. It was Raoul and that woman between them who persuaded him into war, who should bear the blame."

Odo's laugh was harsh. "Vitry? He has never mentioned the matter to me. I think the deaths of those innocents have slipped from his conscience as easily as water flies from an oiled skin. No, he is troubled over his little lusts and private sins."

"All the same thing."

"Perhaps," Odo agreed. "Perhaps . . . But I have spoken with one of the queen's waiting women. She says that they are waked almost nightly by shrieking of fire and death, that no candle may be left burning in the royal bedchamber."

"Vitry does trouble him, then."

"Not the king," Odo corrected. "He sleeps as sweetly as a new-baptized babe. The queen, my friend. It is the queen who dreams of Vitry."

JUNE 1144

Abbot Suger admired his new-built church on the eve of the consecration ceremony. How different it looked from the squat little building he'd inherited from his predecessor! The old church was all but gone now, removed piece by piece as Suger's enlargements and additions in the new Gothic style replaced antiquated narrow doors and crumbling walls. Even the murals that he himself had commissioned as a first gesture toward renovation were gone, the walls that held them removed to open up the nave with its soaring columns and jeweled windows. Living light of emerald and sapphire, ruby and topaz played over the interior of the church. The twenty new altars awaited consecration—a pity, Suger thought, that he could find only nineteen bishops to attend the ceremony. The bishop of Meaux would have to officiate at two altars at once. Should he have delayed the consecration once again?

But no—such an opportunity as this would not come again. The king and queen would attend as a matter of course, but this month he could also count on the presence of Geoffrey Plantagenet, count of Anjou, who had come to Paris that Louis might accept his homage for Normandy. By that act Louis had recognized Geoffrey's suzerainty over Normandy. Stephen of Blois could no longer call himself duke of Normandy. He was only king of the English, and that for how long?

Suger shook his head. Praise God that France was not torn by such strife as the war that raged between Geoffrey's wife and Stephen of Blois! Well, it could make no difference to him or to his lord who won that battle. All Geoffrey's victory in Normandy meant for Suger was that the Plantagenet had brought himself and his oldest son and a crowd of Norman magnates and bishops to swell the throng of distinguished guests. And at the same time, by great good fortune, the heads of the Cluniac and Cistercian houses were in Paris to see Suger's triumph.

That thought brought a slight frown to the abbot's round face. Bernard of Clairvaux was likely to disapprove of the planned ceremony. Louis was still excommunicate for his interference in church elections, and now he had as well the sin of the war in Champagne and the burning of Vitry to atone for. At least the other excommunicated couple, Raoul de Vermandois and the queen's sister, had the good taste to stay away from the morrow's ceremony. Petronilla had been delivered of a son, shamefully soon after the marriage that was no marriage. Bernard would scarcely have missed the opportunity to dilate on the irony of a son's being born to this sinful couple while the king and queen of France were yet childless.

Suger might have saved his worry. The saintly Bernard was offended by so many aspects of the ceremony and the guests, one more would hardly have added to the strength of his fulminations. Noble guests had been arriving at the abbey all week. Most of them avoided Bernard and his strictures against every worldly pleasure, but Louis and his young queen begged for an audience with the ascetic abbot. Even as Suger admired the dull gleam of the golden cross over his high altar, and worried about what Bernard would say about the display of costly jewels, the abbot of Clairvaux was haranguing Louis and Eleanor about the sinful worldliness of Saint-Denis, the court, and everything remotely connected with this occasion.

"What good to the soul are these ridiculous forms of decoration?" he demanded rhetorically, pointing at the carved doorway where Louis had knelt for his blessing. "Deformed figures and disfigured forms, monstrosities with the head of a fish and the body of a horse, the tail of a serpent conjoined with the form of a woman? These are vanities to distract the eye, as worthless as the mincing gait of a daughter of Belial who walks with head high in sinful pride, adorned like a temple of Baal in precious raiment, with jewels heavy enough to weigh down her soul to eternal perdition."

Louis bowed his head beneath the stinging onslaught of the monk's words. Eleanor, kneeling beside him, looked straight ahead, staring at one of the carved monstrosities Bernard disparaged. Two spots of red burned on her cheeks.

"But enough of this, my son," Bernard said, abruptly bringing his peroration to a halt. "I can see from your meek and contrite demeanor that you truly regret the evil you have done. Indeed, I am certain that your actions sprang not from an evil heart, but rather from the bad advice and worldly folly of those who surround you. You must not give way to despair; this too is a sin. You can be saved; God's mercy is infinite. Only make amends for your sins, and all shall be well."

Louis bowed his head again and murmured agreement as Bernard listed what he considered necessary conditions for the king to make his peace with God and the church. He must give up the lands he had captured in Champagne, renounce his oath to see Cadurc made bishop of Bourges, and admit Pierre de la Chatre, the church's chosen candidate, to that position. These things being done, and the king displaying his penitence on the morrow by wearing a monk's gray robes and sandals instead of his royal garb, Bernard promised that he would personally intercede with the pope to see that Louis's excommunication was lifted.

At this Eleanor spoke. "And what of my sister and her husband?"

"Raoul de Vermandois and his paramour remain in a state of sin," Bernard pronounced, "and God has not forgiven them."

"God has given Petronilla a fair boy, and I remain barren!"

"Woman," said Bernard, "cease meddling in affairs of state, and God will bless you with a son within the year. And do not think your sister's bastard a sign of God's grace, for all has not been shown unto you yet."

Eleanor drew in a sharp, angry breath. Louis's hand closed about her wrist, so tight that she gasped again with sudden pain. He glared at her; the set face was the one she'd seen holding a sword at William of Lezay's throat. She bowed her head while the abbot of Clairvaux pronounced a blessing over them.

When they left the private rooms that had been set aside for Bernard's use, other noble visitors were waiting for an audience. Eleanor blinked away tears and scarcely saw the people who moved aside for her.

Foremost in the group was a tall blond man whose eyes followed Eleanor with frank admiration. The tousle-headed boy who stood beside him also watched. His head was still turned when a monk beckoned them forward.

"Get on with you," his father muttered, shoving the boy in the small of the back. "I didn't bring you back from England to chase after the first skirt you notice. And you can't have that one, anyway; she belongs to Louis. Try to look intelligent. You're here so that Louis and his friends can see that I've got a good strong son to hold Normandy and Anjou after me. And as long as we're here, you may as well get a saint's blessing."

Henry Plantagenet shook off his father's hand and strode forward into the abbot's private chambers. As he knelt, his mind was full of most unsaintly thoughts. His father had been wrong. Not that he didn't like girls; they were sweetly scented, soft things, given to giggling and dropping scarves in his path. At eleven he had not yet developed much personal interest in them, but he understood from older squires that they could be remarkably pleasant playthings when one was grown. But what he'd just seen had been no soft plaything for a man's entertainment. She stood out among the others like a fine sword among butchers' tools and kitchen cleavers, a woman like a Damascus blade, he thought, bright and flashing and dangerous, and with tears in her eyes. When he became a man, if ever he got a woman like that, he wouldn't be such a fool as to make her cry.

And after all, the abbot of Clairvaux didn't bless them. He dropped one hand on Henry's red head and lifted it hastily as if he'd touched red-hot coals.

"From the devil he comes, and to the devil he'll go," he muttered, and crossing himself, motioned to the monk in attendance to shoo the duke of Normandy and his son out like a pair of peasants. Geoffrey was mightily displeased and inclined to blame his son's cloddish manners.

"Why couldn't you have said something intelligent to show the abbot how clever you are? God knows it's hard enough to keep you silent any other time."

"I was thinking." Henry avoided his father's cuff with an automatic ducking movement. "Does it matter? You've got Normandy. Even Louis isn't giving you any argument about that now."

"Argument, ha! That shows what you know about it. I had to cede the Vexin to him in return for his recognition."

"You'll get it back." Henry said cheerfully. "Louis isn't man enough to hold on to anything a Plantagenet wants."

Chapter Eleven

News traveled slowly from Outremer to the damp cold cities on the western edge of the world. Fulk of Anjou, king of Jerusalem, had been in his grave more than a year before his son in Normandy heard of the death.

"Died chasing a rabbit, so they tell me," Geoffrey informed his sons at Rouen. "Horse stepped in a hole, Fulk fell off and got hit on the head with his own saddle. Your grandfather never did have the sense to look where he was going. The rabbit probably outsmarted him. God rest his soul," he added hastily, and took a long draft of his hot spiced wine.

Young Geoff, his second son, looked up with bright, speculative eyes. Well, one couldn't expect them to mourn the grandfather they'd never met. Geoffrey was surprised at his own hollow feeling; he hadn't seen Fulk since he was a boy. "Will you be king of Jerusalem now?"

"Don't be unnecessarily stupid, Geoff," said Henry from the superiority of his extra year in age. "Grandfather was king of Jerusalem only because he married Melisende. Her son will take over the throne. We don't come into the picture."

"Is that true?" Geoff demanded.

"More or less. Baldwin's too young to rule alone—I think he's about your age, Henry. The man said Melisende had herself crowned together with Baldwin, double ceremony, last Christmas. So if you were thinking I'd conveniently take off for Jerusalem, leaving you two to squabble over Normandy and Anjou, you can forget it." They *had* been thinking it, too, at least Geoff had, and the boy wasn't ten yet. Well, they were a proper pair of Angevin whelps, snarling and scuffling from their cradles. At least Henry had the brains to think out the lines of inheritance, to realize before he spoke that he'd gain nothing from Fulk's death.

"Don't know that I'd want Jerusalem, even if I had some claim on it," Geoffrey went on, more to himself than to his sons. "By all accounts, they're in for a rough time of it. Well, Fulk never was much of a hand at keeping his barons in line, and now—who's going to pay attention to a woman and a small boy? Antioch and Edessa are already squabbling, and the messenger thinks Joscelin of Edessa has made a secret pact with Kara Arslan. If that's true, Antioch's in trouble—and if Antioch falls, there goes the rest of the kingdom."

"A pact with an *infidel*?" That was Geoff, squeaking in amazement. God help us, the boy must have inherited old Fulk's thick head. Probably be outsmarted by a rabbit himself someday, if young Henry didn't cheat him out of his inheritance first. Have to do something to make sure Geoff got his proper share. Later, Geoffrey told himself. *Much* later. He was by no means an old man yet; it was just the wind of mortality blowing from his father's distant grave that made him think such morbid thoughts.

"You don't understand Outremer," Geoffrey told his younger son. "If our Christian lords there couldn't make truces with some of the Saracens, some of the time, they'd all be swept into the sea and Jerusalem would fall back into the hands of the heathen. No shame in making friends where they can. But Joscelin shouldn't be bringing in Saracens to help him tear down another Christian city. If these French of Outremer don't stick together, they'll tear the kingdom apart with their quarrels, and there'll be Saracens ready and waiting to pick up the pieces. Antioch's in trouble now, and after Antioch goes, who knows how long Jerusalem will last?"

As Geoffrey had predicted, the strife between Antioch and Edessa drew Saracen attention. But it was Edessa that fell first, not Antioch. In the same month that brought the news of Fulk's death to Normandy, the consequences of that death were pressing hard on the Christian citizens of Edessa.

Secure in the belief that the queen and her child would never be able to lead an army against him, Joscelin of Edessa maneuvered to get control of the entire northern half of the kingdom of Jerusalem. The truce with Kara Arslan was followed by a pact of peace with Sawar, the governor of Aleppo. With Saracen allies on all sides, Joscelin was ready to move on Antioch when a third Saracen spoiled his plans.

Imad-ad-Din Zengi, the master of Syria, was said to be half Frankish himself: son of the margravine Ida of Austria, who had disappeared during the First Crusade and was rumored to have ended her days in a heathen harem. If the rumors were true, they did not soften Zengi's attitude toward the invaders; he considered himself chosen by God to uphold Islam against the Christians. In the fall of 1144, he drew Joscelin of Edessa out of his city by an attack on his ally Kara Arslan. When Edessa was empty of defenders, Zengi struck there. For four weeks the tradesmen and commoners of Edessa defended its walls, led by their bishop, while Joscelin with his knights retired to Turbessel, well out of the way of the fighting. He explained to anyone who was interested that his army was not nearly strong enough to defeat Zengi's, and he had every confidence that the fortifications of Edessa would keep the Saracen out without his intervention.

All through the holy season of Advent, Zengi's siege engines battered the walls of Edessa. For four weeks the women and children in the town carried stones to rebuild the walls and brought water to the men who labored under the rain of missiles from the siege engines. Silk weavers and merchants, priests and cobblers worked side by side, grimy, exhausted, blistered. Their best efforts were not enough to keep the walls in place; little by little the fortifications of Edessa crumbled.

On December 23, Abu Ali of Zafaran led a group of men right up to the battered north wall of the city, where miners had destroyed the foundations of the wall. Under the tottering stones, Abu Ali's men stuffed beams of wood; the spaces between the beams were filled with a lethal mixture of naphtha, oil, and sulphur.

The fire burned through the night, aided by a north wind that blew the smoke and flames into the faces of the defenders. Zengi sent more men to pour oil on the flames. At dawn a large section of the wall swayed and fell into the burning pit, and Abu Ali's men sprang into the gap.

If the town had surrendered, there might have been some mercy for the inhabitants; since it had resisted to the end, death was the best they could hope for. The shopkeepers and tradesmen and clerics of Edessa fought from dawn until evening in the open gap, choosing to find their death there at the swords of the infidels rather than waiting to be tortured or enslaved. At dusk on Christmas Eve, the Turkish forces surged through the gap and the few remaining defenders flung down their spades and cleavers and fled after their women and children to the safety of the citadel.

The gate of the citadel was closed and barred. The terrified Christians threw themselves against the walls, begging for sanctuary.

"We're not to open for any but the bishop himself," shouted one of the priests who had already taken refuge there.

The bishop of Edessa was dead, cut down by a Turkish ax on the road to the citadel. Two days later his mutilated body would be found and buried. But now, the gate remained locked. The Christians surged against the walls, pressing in blind terror of the Turks, until those closest to the citadel were crushed to death. The weakest among them slipped to the ground, suffocated by their own friends and neighbors, and still the waves of panic-stricken people pressed onward.

More citizens of Edessa died in that hour of panic before the citadel than Zengi had killed in four weeks of siege. The survivors were roped together and sent into slavery, and then, when it was too late to save anyone, the defenders of the citadel opened the gates and surrendered themselves.

The fall of Edessa was the first crack in the unstable structure of the Frankish kingdom of Jerusalem. Its consequences would not be felt in the West for another year, but the ripples of that fall spread out, touching first Jerusalem and Damascus, then Byzantium and Sicily, until by the next Christmas they had reached the court of France.

By that winter of 1144, when Geoffrey Plantagenet was telling his sons of a death in Outremer, Eleanor had happier news to give to her lord: a tale of a birth to balance the many deaths of the past years. The implied promise made by the monk of Clairvaux had been fulfilled: she was with child.

She spent that spring in Paris, sitting with needlework or listening to Cercle-le-Monde's songs or letting Benoît the clerk read to her from his stock of learned works. Louis had forbidden her to endanger the coming heir by joining in the hawking parties that amused the nobles of the court with the coming of spring, and there had never been any place for a woman among Louis's grave counselors. There was nothing for her to do but stitch, and listen to songs and stories, and sleep. And for once she did not object to the enforced inactivity. A dreamy lassitude possessed her in which she could spend hours at a time contemplating the creamy petals of a flower or the coiled gilt serpents of her couch-work embroidery.

"I felt like that when I was carrying our little Raoul," Petronilla said with a wistful sigh. "The world was very far away, and nothing seemed to matter, not even—" Her hands clenched on the silk she worked, marring the glossy fabric with creases. The last two years had seen two new popes in succession. The old man who became Celestine II was indebted to the French court, and he had been willing to lift the ban on Raoul and Petronilla, but within the year he had been succeeded by Eugenius III, formerly a monk of Clairvaux. The fiery, dogmatic personality of Bernard of Clairvaux dominated Pope Eugenius. Men jested that he did not use his chamber pot without writing for Bernard's advice. But to Petronilla it was no jest. Bernard was uncompromising in his view of her marriage: it was no marriage. The lady Leonora was Raoul de Vermandois's lawful wife, and Petronilla and Raoul lived in a state of sin and should not find grace until they separated.

The excommunication remained in force.

Eleanor was brought to bed on a hot summer day. No rain had fallen for a month, and the city of Paris stank more than usual. The river was low and the exposed muddy banks were draped with rotting weeds, and no water had carried away the heaps of refuse in the streets for weeks. Ever after her memories of that first childbirth would be mingled with the hot, still air, the stench of rotting things in her nostrils when she gasped for breath, the pains that shot through her until the heat and the smells were unimportant. Afterward her ladies said that it had been an easy birth, for a first time: only one day in labor, and a fine strong baby to show for it! She had been fortunate indeed.

"God preserve me from any more such good fortune," Eleanor said weakly. Her hair was matted about her face, and the room smelled of blood.

Radegonde of Maillezais made the sign of the cross to avert any ill luck from Eleanor's blasphemous words. "You'll be lucky if it goes so easily next time, you ungrateful girl!"

"Never mind that." Radegonde's face seemed to be moving back and forth, very close and then very far away. It made Eleanor dizzy to watch, but she felt too weak to bother with a complaint. "Where is my son?"

The ladies fell silent then, and Eleanor knew that something was very wrong. God had cursed her after all. Petronilla's baby was still weak and sickly, and Petronilla had not sinned so greatly. What price had God extracted for the thousand souls burned at Vitry? She imagined a baby armless and legless, or coming dead from her womb— no, not that; she'd heard the child crying. She thought she had heard it. Marked by fire, then, or a leper. Dear God, the possibilities were endless, and she had been so foolishly confident all this time!

"What's *wrong*?"

"Nothing," Radegonde told her. "Nothing. You, fool," she snapped over her shoulder at someone Eleanor could not quite see, "tell the wet nurse to bring the child, that her majesty may see for herself all is well! *Nothing* is wrong," Radegonde repeated with a fierceness that convinced Eleanor of the opposite. "You see?" She turned and took a tiny bundle from someone's arms. "You have a perfect baby, my dear. A beautiful little girl."

A girl. For one moment Eleanor felt the sting of failure, then the swaddled bundle was in her arms, and she drew in her breath with shock and delight. Tiny eyelashes, each one a wonder of God's work, a wrinkled rosebud of a mouth, just opening to wail at the cold world into which the infant had been cast so rudely.

"Don't cry, don't cry," Eleanor murmured, "you're here now, it's all right, everything will be all right soon."

Louis was disappointed.

"The midwife swore it would be a boy," he kept saying. "What have I done wrong? Oh God, why have You deserted me?" He fell to his knees beside the bed and wept over his clasped hands. Eleanor looked at the long white fingers and thought about those hands on her body, always demanding, prying, and then pushing her away.

"Never you mind, dear," Radegonde of Maillezais said when Louis was gone again. "Men are always like that, all they can think of is sons to come after them. It's for us women to suffer, and bear, and love our daughters."

Eleanor propped herself up in bed, carefully, with many pillows. It hurt to sit up, but she had been weak long enough. She would need strength for herself and her daughter. "How would *you* know?" she said to Radegonde, and in the next breath regretted her cruelty. But at least the old woman kept silent after that.

"Next time," she said, "I will have a son. Bring me the baby."

But the small niggling pain that had begun when she sat up was growing like a green vine about her, thrusting inside her and tearing her apart so that the last word came out on a gasp. She felt something liquid rushing, and smelled blood again, and fell back against the pillows, wondering why everything was so far away suddenly.

Six weeks later she sat up for the second time, against the advice of the midwife who examined her daily and the surgeon to whom the midwife reported her findings. In all that time Louis had not returned to her chambers.

Speaking from behind the red curtain that separated her woman's body from his man's knowledge, the surgeon sonorously advised her that if her husband were absent, it was on the best medical advice. She had been torn by the hard, sudden birth; her healing had been slow, and she would be well advised to abstain from marital relations for some months yet.

"He could have come to see me," Eleanor said. "And the baby."

He had not even attended the baby's christening in the royal chapel; Faenze had admitted as much when the other ladies evaded her questions.

She called Faenze and Bertille to open her chests and lift out garments for her to try on. Silks and brocades and fur-lined cloaks spilled across the bed; sinuous links of beaten silver coiled serpentlike over the clothes. While her ladies lifted down cloaks and gowns from their hanging poles, Eleanor washed her face in a decoction of rosemary boiled in wine and set the little maid Jeanette to pounding cochineal. Mixed in a base of scented creams, the red powder added life to Eleanor's pale cheeks until she bloomed to match the flamboyance of the garments she selected.

Faenze sighed and rolled her eyes when Eleanor insisted on lacing a grass-green silk gown over a crimson shift. "*Both* colors are too bright for you," she said.

"You're right. Give me the box of colors again." Eleanor rubbed more crimson cream into her lips and outlined her eyes with dark smudges from a charcoal wand. "There, that's better. Now the silver double girdle, please, and the matching sheaths for my braids, the ones with the serpents entwined."

The double girdle emphasized the slender waist she had regained and drew both silken gowns close against the new fullness of her breasts. Her hair was almost concealed beneath a veil of silver gauze and the heavy silver braid sheaths. Her face was artificially bright, and the eyes outlined in dark colors that made them seem unnaturally large and sparkling. Faenze gave a little sigh of impatience and frustration even as she admired the results. She could have chosen soft shades to flatter Eleanor's coloring and bring out her fine-boned beauty. In these brilliant, formal garments Eleanor was not beautiful. But she was striking, a jeweled icon impossible to ignore. And when she made her grand entrance to the great hall, followed by her Gascon troubadour and her Poitevin clerk in new finery, and all her ladies decked out to match her, Faenze began to understand what was going on.

Impossible though it might have been, Louis managed to ignore the gaudy procession after one amazed flicker of his eyelids. Eleanor swept a deep curtsey to her lord and retired to the side of the hall farthest from him. "Sing, Cercle-le-Monde!" she commanded. "And you, my ladies, sing and dance with him! I am tired of prayers and sickrooms; I want some gaiety!"

Cercle-le-Monde raised his clear tenor voice in an old dance song, a lively stamping dance of spring that was quite out of place in this autumnal room.

> *"A l'entrada del tens clar, eya,*
> *Per joia recomencar, eya,*
> *E per jelos irritar, eya*
> *Vol la regina mostrar*
> *Qui es si amoroza."*

It was the kind of dance tune the priests preached against, a wild dance to crown the summer queen who brought the sun back after winter's darkness. It was a dance of the south, with the light and music and magic of Poitou in every word.

Faenze looked at Petronilla. They stood up and joined hands and began to circle to the music.

> *"A la vi', a la via, jelos!*
> *Laissaz nos, laissaz nos*
> *ballar entre nos, entre nos!"*

Bertille joined them. Benoît, tall and awkward, broke into the circle between Faenze and Bertille. The rest of the queen's ladies came forward, one after another, until only Eleanor and Radegonde of Maillezais remained seated. The baby Marie, in her nurse's arms, gurgled with pleasure and waved her tiny fists as if she were trying to keep time to the music.

> *"Lo reis i ven d'autra part, eya,*
> *per la dansa destorbar, eya,*

que el es en cremetar, eya,
que om no li voill' emblar
la regin' avrilloza."

Louis frowned at the dancing group. Saying a few words in an undertone to his chaplain, he turned on his heel and left the hall without ever having greeted his wife. Odo of Deuil and the Templar Thierry, his constant companions of late, were close behind him. After a long awkward moment, most of the French nobles followed Louis. Eleanor and her ladies remained in possession of the hall.

"A la vi', a la via, jelos!
Laissaz nos, laissaz nos
ballar entre nos, entre nos!"

By Christmas, it was well established that there were two courts in Paris. The king's court was virtuous, sober, and deadly dull; the queen's court was gay and vivacious and full of sound and music, with visiting physicians from Salerno, astrologers from Moorish Spain, mountebanks from Sicily, poets and musicians a dozen for a clipped sou. But apart from Raoul de Vermandois, who kept unsmiling attendance on his young wife and their sickly son, none of the powerful men of the kingdom were to be found at the queen's court.

More and more, power was concentrated in the hands of a few men with a single stamp of mind. Little Abbot Suger was still influential in the king's court, but he was aging and more interested in his great building projects than in politics. Younger men, more strictly virtuous (according to their friends) or more narrow-minded and provincial (according to their detractors), had the king's ear and guarded his conscience. Chief among them was Odo of Deuil, once a monk of Saint-Denis, and behind Odo, the shadowy figure of Bernard, abbot of Clairvaux, who searched every man's conscience and knew everyone's secret sins.

When news of the fall of Edessa reached the West, Bernard knew exactly what must be done. It was time for a second Crusade, an army of Christians to salvage the crumbling kingdoms of Outremer and to purify the hearts of those Latins in the East who had become half Saracen themselves. Bernard spoke fiercely and persuasively to Pope Eugenius, who had once been a simple monk of Clairvaux, and the pope issued letters calling all of Christendom to fight the heathen and recapture Edessa.

One of those letters came to Bourges, where Louis and Eleanor were holding their dual courts at Christmastime.

"It is a great opportunity for you and for all Christendom," said Odo of Deuil. "You will be a famous warrior—but for good, not for personal gain."

Louis glanced at the far side of the hall, where Eleanor sat on a low cushioned stool with her people around her. The tinkling notes of the Gascon's lute were a subtle undercurrent to their laughing, quick repartee. He had never learned to follow the langue d'oc.

"Truly," he said, musing, "I believe God has called us to this mission." His pleasure in the idea of a crusade grew as he examined it. He imagined himself in the white surcoat of a Templar, in the forefront of battle, swinging his sword with both hands and hewing down infidels. Their blood splashed over his feet; they howled and bowed down in submission, but he was merciless. Somewhere in the background, Raoul de Vermandois was watching Louis and saying, "The boy has used well all the craft of arms that I taught him." And somewhere beyond that, a choir of angels sang thanks to the godly man who had rescued Jerusalem.

"Let it be announced to our court," he commanded Odo. "We shall take the Cross and lead an army to Jerusalem."

"Edessa," Odo corrected in a deferential murmur.

Louis waved one hand to dismiss the correction. "It is all part of the Holy Land."

That night, for the first time in some months, he visited Eleanor's apartments. The noise and clutter and smells struck him like blows, so used was he to the monastic simplicity of his own rooms. Here there were gaily bedizened Gascons and Poitevins as bright as fairground dancers, girls giggling in corners, three different songs competing for auditors, and—was that a *monkey* scuttling across the floor? The shadowy little figure slipped behind a curtain of white samite before he could be sure that he had seen anything at all. It might have been a demon.

In the farthest apartment, a narrow room overlooking the inner courtyard, his wife lounged on cushions while a big yellow-haired fellow bent his head and murmured confidentially in her ear. Louis advanced as far as the doorway before either of them noticed his presence.

"Wife," he said, "I would speak with you. In private," he added irritably when she did not at once order her followers away. He glared at the blond man: one of her Poitevin beggars, he thought. Bernard or Berengar or some such. Louis had his opinion of these so-called clerics whose tonsures could barely be discerned, who spent their lives in composing bawdy songs or drinking in a tavern.

"Get out," he ordered the clerk. "Out! All of you!"

Finally they were gone, with much clattering of tongues and instruments, leaving the suite of rooms occupied only by the trailing ghosts of a silk robe hanging from a pole, a wisp of perfumed air, and a tray of half-eaten sweetmeats. Eleanor stretched, provocative and languid as a cat, and looked up at him coldly. "Was it necessary to tell all the world that you intend to exercise your marital rights?"

"How else should I have a moment alone with you?"

Eleanor shrugged. "You could always demonstrate some desire for my company."

Louis let out a jerky sigh. "If you wished *my* company, you would not surround yourself with this sort of people. And I did not come for—for the purpose you are thinking of."

She lay back on the cushions and stared at him with those strange light eyes, and despite his virtuous resolves he felt his loins stir with remembered desire. *Not now.* Not when, as she said, all the members of her entourage would be thinking about them. He had some control. Didn't he? He remembered his confessor's voice. "The woman tempts you . . . she opens up her private parts and beckons you . . . she confuses you with a pretense of modesty, when we all know there is no modesty or decency in women. . . ."

"What is his name?" he demanded.

"Who?"

"That fellow who was whispering love words into your ear when I came in."

Eleanor laughed. "Master Benoît is a clerk, and he was teaching me some words of the Greek tongue."

"Why?"

She looked up at him with such a clear and innocent gaze that he almost doubted the evidence of his own eyes. "Did you not announce that you meant to take the Cross? And will you not be marching through Constantinople? I would learn something of the lands where you will be traveling, that my thoughts may accompany you on your arduous journey."

She was mocking him. Or was she? He could never be sure. "Then you would do better to learn words of Holy Writ," he told her, "for my heart and my soul are fixed only on Jerusalem."

"Edessa," Eleanor murmured.

"We will discuss it later." Why had he thought to tell her of his glorious plan, his certainty that God had always meant him to lead a Crusade? It all fit so perfectly. His years in the monastery had made him a man of peace, loving virtue. His training as the king's heir had taught him the arts of war. He had never yet been able to satisfy both masters at once. When he made war at Vitry, Abbot Suger preached to him of widows and orphans and men maimed for his pride. When he kept peace with the Plantagenet over Normandy, his constable Vermandois ranted at him that he was neglecting his kingdom's temporal needs for his own spiritual vainglory.

The Crusade was the perfect solution. He would make war—but for God; he would do right—but with a sword in his hand. He had wanted to explain it all to Eleanor, to make her see the shining perfection of his vision. But women could not understand these higher things. They had to worry about details like the name of this city that had fallen to some Saracens.

Louis left. Somewhere in Bourges there must be a map of Outremer.

The nobles of France and Aquitaine were not unanimously enthusiastic about Louis's call for a holy war. Instead of the outpouring of support Louis had envisaged, his proclamation was met with averted eyes and mutters about the high cost of the war in Champagne, still not fully paid for. Raoul de Vermandois dared to speak out in open council against the Crusade, and Abbot Suger murmured privately that he feared the time was ill chosen.

Louis retired to Paris in chagrin, and for a time no more was said of the sufferings of the Christians in Edessa. Then Bernard of Clairvaux took up their cause. All the energy and eloquence he had once used to bring down that heretic Abelard were now turned on the laggard nobles of France. Letter after letter poured from his pen, urging Pope Eugenius to issue a second bull in favor of the Crusade, reproaching the laggards who thought of their own lands and purses when there were Christians in need of rescue.

In the queen's apartments, the gaiety of the Poitevins took on a forced tone.

Everywhere there was talk of war, penitence, and Crusade. Eleanor felt her life slipping away from her like grains of sand through the narrow neck of an hourglass: one, two, three, a hundred, two hundred, and each one gone forever. She tried to shut out the cold winds and the knowledge of time passing, to live inside a golden bubble of songs and memories of the south. But the moments slipped through the fingers of her cupped hands like water pouring away. Louis seldom visited her bed now, and she had not conceived again. Their daughter grew fat and happy under her nurse's care, but to Louis and the cold gray men who surrounded them Marie might never have been born; they spoke of Eleanor as the barren queen. She felt dry and old. Louis would go on Crusade and she would wither away without ever having truly lived. "Closer to heaven," the priests would say, but Eleanor did not want heaven, not yet; she wanted to live on this earth. This was her time, and it was slipping away from her in words and prayer and pious platitudes: a barren queen, a cursed lineage, a hateful marriage.

She was twenty-four years old.

"There are still some who oppose this holy war," Thierry Galeran reported in private to the king.

"Who?"

"The count of Vermandois you know about."

"Yes. Yes. But he was my father's good adviser. We cannot deny our uncle of Vermandois his right to speak." Louis put the fingers of one hand to his mouth and nibbled fretfully upon the nails. "Very well. If he does not wish to accompany us, then let him remain behind with Abbot Suger. They shall be coregents in my absence: the man of war, the man of peace. Who else opposes us?"

Thierry looked down and murmured words that Louis could barely hear, halting disjointed phrases. There was disaffection in the court. Some of those who were very close to the king were not truly French. It might be that Raoul de Vermandois's opposition came from that source. . . . Not the queen, Thierry hastened to say, seeing Louis's face set in obstinate lines. He had no word to say against the queen. But she was young and frivolous, and easily persuaded . . . Delicately, without speaking a word of accusation, he reminded Louis of those things that he had tried not to remember. The way Eleanor chattered with her ladies and musicians in that southern dialect, looking sidewise at him and laughing. The way that clerk bent over her. He could not leave her here among these corrupt southerners. He would dismiss them all before he left. But how could he be sure they would not come back? That Gascon musician: he'd been sent away once, and now somehow he was back among Eleanor's hangers-on.

The solution came into his mind, so clear and beautiful that he wondered he had not thought of it before. He cut short the Templar's whisperings with a gesture and hastened to inform Eleanor of his decision.

She would accompany him on the Crusade, thus neatly and simultaneously cleansing her soul and separating her from the bad influence of her southern followers. After so striking a double pilgrimage, culminating in his heroic defense of the Holy Land from the infidels, surely God would grant them a son.

It could not fail.

And for once, by God, the world would see his queen submissive to her husband's will, following meekly behind him, sharing in his tribulations and humbly making this holy pilgrimage with a contrite heart.

On Palm Sunday, at Vézelay, Bernard of Clairvaux was to preach the new Crusade. For months his letters had been circulating in all the Christian countries of Europe: he had written to the English people, to the bishops and people of France, to the Bavarians and the Bohemians, the Flemish and the Germans, reiterating his conviction that God had called them to raise a second army of the faithful to protect the Holy Land.

The crowd of pilgrims was too great to be accommodated in the church of Saint-Mary-Magdalen; a platform was hastily erected in the fields just outside the town. From this platform Bernard could see, with satisfaction, a veritable army streaming into Vézelay, filling the roads that led to the village and spilling over the tilled fields and the gentle rolling hills that held the village as in a cup. Behind him was the huddle of houses and the narrow streets leading up to the church: a typical construction produced by ill-advised souls, decorated on every surface with the monstrous forms and deformed shapes that Bernard abominated, carvings whose only purpose was to give amusement and pleasure to those who should be contemplating the state of their souls. He was much happier here, in the open air, where nothing would distract his listeners.

Benoît de Périgné, hovering on the fringes of the crowd with Eleanor's Gascon musician to keep him company, was also happy that the preaching was to be outside, mainly because he stood a better chance of slipping away unnoticed from this position halfway up the hill opposite Bernard's platform.

The valley was all but filled with people now, common and noble alike jostling for the front rows where they would be most likely to hear the saintly monk's words of inspiration. Well, in practice the nobles filled the area closest to the platform with no argument from the burghers and peasants who'd put down their tools to make this pilgrimage. That, too, suited Benoît. He would be able to hear as much as he wanted from this hillside, and he didn't want to have to push his way through a tight-packed crowd of touchy nobles when he was ready to leave.

"I don't know why you had to be here at all," grumbled Cercle-le-Monde. "You could have been halfway to Sicily by this time."

"Why Sicily?"

Cercle-le-Monde regarded his unworldly, clerkly companion with some surprise. "It's the best place to go when you can't be with the court. To begin with, anyway. Roger is generous to the arts, and there are more beautiful women at his court than anywhere else in Christendom. He likes men of learning, too," he added. "You should be able to find a good place with him. Learn some Arabic, you could be a translator, maybe even rise to kadi—judge—in his courts."

"I'd rather go to Outremer," Benoît said. "Somebody has to look after her." He wondered why Cercle-le-Monde kept saying "you" rather than "we" when he spoke of Sicily. But more than that, he wondered where Eleanor was right now. He knew Louis had insisted on her accompanying him to Vézelay. Surely she should have been beside him on the platform. Was she ill? Nobody told him anything anymore, not since she'd dismissed him in Paris with the cryptic comment that there would be enough deaths in Outremer without his adding to the number. He'd dug into his own purse to make his way here, just to see her one last time, and now it seemed he was to be cheated of that sight.

"There'll be enough people to watch out for a queen, wherever she goes," Cercle-le-Monde pointed out. "And you'd not be one of them, not now that the king's jealousy has lighted on you."

"I've done nothing!" If he loved her, that was his secret. She had always been too high for him; he knew that, if the king didn't.

"Neither did William of Lezay. But he spoke a few careless words at Talmont, and you know what came of that."

"I've heard stories," Benoît admitted. He was about to ask Cercle-le-Monde about the truth of those stories, for the Gascon troubadour seemed to have an uncanny ability to know all that went on around Eleanor, even when he'd been some other place at the time. But a hush fell over the crowd, and Benoît fell silent automatically. The abbot of Clairvaux was ready to speak.

He seemed emaciated to the point of death, with a coarse robe falling loose about his bony frame, eyes glittering like candles in a corpse's eye sockets: a man whose austerities were notorious and unrelenting. But his voice was strong and firm, carrying over the crowd so that even Benoît could hear him clearly.

"O time of chastisement and ruin!" Bernard lamented. "The Lord of Heaven is dispossessed of His land, and the men of this time do nothing to save their Savior. The land made holy by His blood will be defiled by dogs; pagan filth will defile the shrines of our fathers! And you mighty men of valor can think of nothing but your own lands. Worms before Christ, you think yourselves noble knights, but you who defend your own treasures and think nothing of the treasure that He has laid up for us in heaven, you shall inherit only the dung heap that belongs to worms. How our Lord must grieve! He who suffered on the cross for us looks down now and finds not one soul who sorrows for him, who will rescue His holy sepulcher from the defilement of the pagans! God is merciful; He has taken care for our salvation, He desires that we should enter with him into paradise, and we are throwing away His sacrifice and spitting on His memory. You selfish souls who hear my words and will not hear, who will speak for you when God's holy shrines are defiled with pagan filth? Where will you make pilgrimage to get forgiveness of your sins? Where will your descendants set up shrines in your memory? Our Lord and all the saints are weeping to know that you despise them and betray their sacrifice, as no doubt you would betray your own mothers. You shed Christian blood, you attack each other and crave savagery and bloodshed above all things, but you will not take up a cause in which you can fight to the glory of God."

Benoît's head swam. He could scarcely breathe. The words of the saint were like a burning wind about him. He *was* selfish. He had loved learning too much; he had forgotten his family and his boyhood vows; he had brought trouble on his lady whom he adored by letting that adoration be seen. He was damned, and God wept for him, and there was only one way of salvation open. He moved forward, two steps, three. Something hung on his arm, impeding him. He shook it off, and music strummed in his ear: a dance tune of the south, low and inviting. He stopped where he stood and shook his head fiercely to clear it of these buzzing sounds. What had he been thinking just now?

"The man of Clairvaux has his magic," said Cercle-le-Monde in a cautious half whisper, "and I have mine." His fingers danced across air, and the student songs of the tavern made a subtle mockery of Bernard's passionate preaching.

"This Crusade is not for you," Cercle-le-Monde said. "Go to Sicily."

"*She* is going."

"She has no choice. You do."

"Will you come to Sicily?"

The troubadour's eyes shifted. "I must find service somewhere, must I not?"

While they spoke, the roar of the crowd had drowned out Bernard's words. The people before them pressed on the platform, crushing themselves against the wood, begging for crosses. Bernard handed out the white crosses that had been prepared until his supply was exhausted, and still they begged for more. The king's libertine brother Robert was clasping Bernard's feet, begging for a cross to take up. Benoît saw men he knew from court, sensible hard-bitten soldiers and subtle politicians, weeping and clasping crosses. Ivo of Soissons had one; Eleanor's vassal Geoffrey de Rancon had plastered a white cross upon the greasy front of his tunic. The whole world was transfigured with love of God and desire to save His Holy Land. Benoît felt cold and removed, set apart from the happy throng and their salvation. One part of him longed to join the mob at Bernard's feet, but Cercle-le-Monde was still calling that low music from the air, and he was able to stay where he was despite the urge to join them.

A woman screeched and fastened her hands in Bernard's coarse white tunic. A shred of wool came away in her fingers and she waved it above her head, proudly displaying her trophy until someone else snatched it away from her.

Bernard stepped back, away from the pressing crowd, holding out his hands and promising something; Benoît could see his lips move but could no longer hear the words above the crowd's ecstatic chant of *"Deus vult! Deus vult!"* God wills it! He understood the meaning, though, when Bernard pulled off his robe and stood before the crowd in a thin tunic that showed his emaciated joints. Someone handed up a short eating knife and Bernard methodically hacked his white robe into strips that he handed out, two short strips to each reaching hand. Those who got the fragments twisted them into a crosslike shape and joyfully carried them away.

A new shout, clear as a trumpet call through the chill air, rang above and through the roaring of the mob. Benoît twisted his head and looked behind them, up the gentle slope of the green hill to the west. Over the brow of that hill, as he watched, came a troop of fantastically dressed riders on horses white as snow. Ribbons and slashed sleeves and silken banners and long unbound hair like black and golden and auburn silk streamed behind them as the little group of women thundered down the hill and through a crowd that parted to let them by, silent for the moment with shock at their audacity. And at the head of the group rode Eleanor, queen of France, duchess of Aquitaine, countess of Poitou. Gilt half-armor curved over her lovely breasts; a network of chains light as silk girdled her slender waist and dangled over her thighs. Riding astride like any knight, bearing a pennon of silken ribbons, she galloped to the very foot of the platform where Bernard stood and bowed her head without dismounting. The white horse stamped and snorted, and counts and barons who'd been mobbing the saint for shreds of his holy tunic edged out of the way of the palfrey's stamping hooves and wildly rolling eyes.

"Your words have touched my heart and my sinful soul, Abbot," Eleanor announced in a light clear voice that somehow carried to the farthest reaches of the crowd. "My ladies and I will ride to Jerusalem with this army."

Bernard could do nothing but hand her, wordlessly, the last shred of white woolen cloth from his tunic. Louis looked on with a pinched face as his glittering, golden wife pinned the improvised cross over her breast. She looked up at him then, chin high, and her smile was brighter than her polished armor and sharper than any blade. She would go on this Crusade, as her lord had ordered. But she would go on her own terms.

Chapter Twelve

In the week before the festival of Saint Denis, the Crusaders reached Constantinople. The day before the army arrived, the emperor sent ambassadors with unwelcome news: the German army and their leader Conrad of Hohenstaufen had already crossed the Bosporus and marched into Asia to fight the Turks. Louis, still waiting for the contingent of his own army that had taken ship at Brindisi, was unwilling to follow the Germans. His knights were angry, thinking that their chance for glory was being taken away, that the Germans would kill all the Turks and leave nothing for them to do. And the emperor of Constantinople entreated Louis with fair promises to meet with him inside the city and to make the same agreements that Conrad had made—whatever those might be.

Louis responded to all these pressures in his usual manner. He ordered the army to halt before Constantinople and wait while he decided what to do.

Eleanor had not been included in the meetings with the ambassadors, though she had seen them from a distance as she and her ladies rode out for exercise and to escape the achingly slow pace of the march. Nor had Louis asked her advice as to how best to deal with the political pressures on him from all sides. She believed that they would have to enter the city, if only for a day; they were dependent on the emperor for boats to ferry the army across the Bosporus. So she waited in her own tent, with her ladies around her, and collected what crumbs of information she could. Cercle-le-Monde was her best source of gossip; denied permission to travel with the French king, he had managed to get himself officially attached to the Lusignan household. But as the weeks of march stretched on, the attachment seemed more and more tenuous. He somehow managed to drift unobtrusively around the camp, avoiding Louis's notice and spending far more time with Eleanor than with Black Hugh of Lusignan, until it seemed that Louis had forgotten all about the decision to leave him in Paris. Louis even called on him for a song from time to time—some metrical saint's life, of course, not one of the troubadour's own lighthearted compositions.

"These Greeks of Constantinople call themselves Romans, pretending to be the unworthy descendants of a noble race," the royal chaplain announced. Eleanor bowed her head and tried to listen attentively. Odo of Deuil had been privileged to attend the king during his audience with the Greek ambassadors; surely he had learned something then. She knew already that these Greeks styled themselves the heirs to Rome, and their city the Empire of New Rome. She had her own letters from the empress—sad letters from a sad and lonely woman in a foreign land, who hoped that Eleanor would be her friend. But she would learn as much as she could of this strange place before she ventured into it. It was said that they laughed at Westerners, called them barbarians who did not know polite manners.

"Their city, which we term Constantinople in memory of the great Christian emperor who founded it, they call Byzantium. Hence the common name of the coinage—"

"I know, I know," Eleanor snapped. "We have paid enough good *livres d'or* for enough black and stinking bread by this time. I have heard the Greeks calling the coins bezants, and so has everybody else in this army. By my faith and Saint Radegonde, priest, have you learned nothing from these ambassadors but what any pilgrim with the army could have told you these three weeks since?"

It appeared that he had not. Eleanor dismissed him impatiently and sat very still on the folding stool in her tent, half listening to the whispers of her ladies, half listening only to the soft wind that came off the shores of the Bosporus.

"In Constantinople the very air is silk, soft as a lover's caress," Faenze said with a sigh.

"I had not thought—" began Bertille, and broke off as Faenze stamped on her foot. The comment about Robert of Dreux's rough caresses went unspoken. For a time at least. The king's young brother was married now, to the widow of the count of Perche, but she had not come on the Crusade with him.

"In Constantinople," sighed Ada, the most pious of Eleanor's ladies and the only one of whom the king's chaplain approved, "they say there are so many churches that the bells are ringing all day long, and every minute there is, somewhere in the city, a procession of priests in jewels and silk vestments richer than a king's robes, chanting prayers inside churches so large that they can swallow up the light of a hundred wax tapers."

"In Constantinople," said another, "the emperor sleeps in a room hung all with purple silk, and his wife bears his sons in that room, and so the heirs to the empire are known as porphyrogenitus—born in the purple."

"But he sleeps lightly, with candles burning, and in fear of his life, for all the emperors of Constantinople die by violence."

"Or poison," corrected another. "Or if one should be allowed to live, the next emperor blinds and castrates him and imprisons him in a monastery."

"In Constantinople there is a church called Holy Wisdom, so large that it could contain all of Paris, and during the singing of the liturgy the very angels from heaven fly down to hover about the head of the emperor and join in, so sweet is that music."

"In Constantinople the emperor sits on a golden throne that can fly through the air, and his throne room is full of birds, each one carved from a single emerald, and singing as if they were alive."

"In Constantinople, Turks and Saracens ride freely about the streets, as if they were honest Christians."

"In Constantinople the emperor has a pleasure palace in the center of a lake, and its walls and ceiling all of colored glass, and it can be entered only by an underground passage, and when the emperor goes therein to take his pleasure, by a signal fountains spring forth and play over the glass, and all within is jeweled light running like a river."

"In Constantinople there are two monks and three eunuchs to every whole man, and the eunuchs have the running of the empire."

"Thierry Galeran will *like* Constantinople," commented one lady, and Eleanor smiled. Then the fantastical tales wreathed round her ears again, like the scented smoke of incense during a foreign Mass.

"In Constantinople the houses rise like towers into the sky. The streets are dark ravines between the towers, and the poor smother in the darkness."

"In Constantinople there is a market every day and all day, as great as our fair of Saint Denis, and the whole market is covered by a roof of silk held up by jeweled columns."

"In Constantinople there is a pillar of prophecy setting forth the day and the hour wherein the city shall perish, but no man yet living can read the language of the prophecy."

"In Constantinople the hunting park of the emperor contains every kind of wild beast and bird and fish that lives, two by two as Noah had them in the ark, and the unicorn rules over them all."

Eleanor impatiently shook her head and rose to her feet. Their tents had been pitched before the city walls for half a day now, and Louis awaited the emperor's summons like a child waiting for permission to leave the room, and she felt like a child herself, doing nothing but reading over the empress's lonely letters and listening to tales out of old romances. "Which of these things may be true, we shall learn in good time," she said. "Who will ride out with me?"

From the high tower of the city wall, just outside his palace of Blachernae, the emperor of Byzantium could see the Frankish encampment in his own hunting park, the occasional glitter of lances and bright armor showing through the dust that encrusted all the barbarians, the disorderly jumble of horse lines and latrines and tents pitched in casual, random groups like a child's blocks strewn upon the floor. Behind that muddle rose the three stories of the simple lodge Manuel kept in the middle of the Philopation. It would have provided room enough to lodge the king, this mild Louis whose letters said so much about God's will and so little about his army's plans, but not for the horde who followed him. At least they would not ruin the park; that had already been accomplished by the German barbarians who preceded them, cutting down the trees for firewood, fouling the land, and killing his preserved hunting game to roast upon their barbarous fires.

The gate below this watchtower was open, and a long procession of his own people wound through it, the priests chanting and swinging their censers to perfume the air and discourage demons, the nobles riding on gently pacing palfreys with reins and saddles of braided silk. Whatever the intentions of this Louis, he and his people should be welcomed as if they were the friends they claimed to be.

And with any luck, they could be sped across the Bosporus to fight the Turks, like the Holy Roman Emperor Conrad and his German army last week, before the pretense of innocuous friendship wore thin on either side.

"Disorganized," sniffed the strategus of the Eastern Theme, who had chosen the honor of watching by his emperor's side above the delights of gathering firsthand information about the Frankish army. "They'll foul their own camp within a week, and in a fortnight there'll be plague among them. I could take them now with a few troops of Turcopole archers."

"They are said to acquit themselves well in fighting," Manuel responded absently to his war leader's boast. "You might lose a few men—and make more enemies. Who knows how many more of these Franks come after them? We will let them go in peace." God knew he had done all that he might to ensure that peace, straining his treasury to see that food and markets were sent out through Greece to meet the advancing barbarian army, ordering repairs to the city walls, and issuing new armor to his own troops. The rumors that came before the army said that this was an even larger host than had threatened Byzantium in his father's time: mailed knights enough to cover the entire triangle of land on which the holy city stood, an army of infantry so great they would drink the Golden Horn dry.

Rumor had, of course, exaggerated. But not by as much as Manuel had hoped. "There is no reason to look for trouble," he said now, firmly. "We will receive this Frankish king as we did our brother-in-law of Germany, and like Conrad, he will give us his homage and his promise that he will do no harm to us Romans on his way to battle. Then they will pass on their way."

"They may be many, but they know nothing of the Turkish ways of war. They will die in the sands of Syria," predicted the strategus.

"Even the sands of the desert are not sufficient to swallow up this horde," a lesser official said gloomily. "How many of them are there? We thought the Germans an innumerable host, yet here are as many Franks again as we counted Germans, and who knows how many come after?"

His comment unleashed a spate of pessimistic rumors.

"It was said in Thessaly that their cavalry forces alone covered the whole surface of the land."

"The largest rivers hardly sufficed to supply them drink."

"Nor could all the stores of Thessaly's fertile fields feed them."

"The province of Thessaly," said Manuel Comnenus, the Most Serene Basileus of New Rome, "was not required to bear the burden alone. We have placed provisions in their path and shall continue to sell to them from our markets while they remain within the boundaries of the empire."

"How will they supply themselves after they go beyond the range of our ships?"

"Since they say God has called them to this war, perhaps He will feed them. In any event, what they do beyond our borders is their concern . . . and perhaps God's. Ours is only to see that they go from here in peace, and that they take oath before they go to respect our territories and not to plunder Christian lands."

"How can you trust the oaths of barbarians?" spoke up the patriarch of New Rome from Manuel's other side. "They know neither sense nor decency. The ambassadors you sent yesterday report that there are *women* riding with the army."

Manuel shrugged. Women followed an army as seagulls followed garbage; it was a fact of nature, regrettable but unchangeable, and he was not in a mood to argue with the patriarch about it.

"Not just the usual prostitutes and camp followers," the patriarch said sharply, as though reading Manuel's thoughts, "but women of noble families, riding shamelessly astride like men. Have ever you heard the like?"

Manuel shrugged again and tried to suppress the thought that his own wife might have fit naturally into such an entourage. The Empress Irene, born Bertha of Sulzbach, had never acquired the grace and style and sense of ritualized beauty that ruled his court. She was firmly, almost aggressively, as barbarian as the day she arrived to claim the marriage his father had promised: treading flat-footed over the intricacies of court etiquette, disdaining cosmetics and adornments in favor of a natural face which, truth to tell, would have benefited from some artificial aids. Also, she was somewhat thick in the waist. Yes, he could imagine Bertha-Irene on horseback, brandishing her battle-ax and bearing down on the enemy with a face of grim determination.

"It will not be necessary for you to meet these shameless women, Patriarch," Manuel said gravely. "As for the state of their souls, that—like their chances against the Turks—is for the Franks, not us, to concern themselves with. Why, they are barely Christians as it is; remember the heresies the Emperor Conrad espoused?"

His brother-in-law. It would not have been polite for Manuel himself to take issue with Conrad's heretical views concerning the nature of the Godhead, but he would have no objection if the patriarch were distracted now into a harmless theological argument. Manuel had long ago developed the ability to listen and respond to theological discussions while letting his eye rove over the room, picking out the prettiest and most willing girls in his wife's retinue.

Of course, here there were no pretty girls to watch, only the undisciplined rabble of pilgrims, goats, cavalrymen, and barbarian nobles, and his own welcoming committee approaching in a formal cloud of incense-scented silk robes. And, probably, some barbarian women with shoulders like wrestlers and faces like stone walls, howling and waving their lances in the air. Perhaps, Manuel thought, he should be glad that the dignity of an emperor precluded his visiting the Frankish camp in person. Mud, rags, and ugly women.

And the patriarch was not ready to be distracted. "One among them they called Goldenfoot, because her gown is bordered with gold. She rides before the other noble ladies, inciting them to disrespect and unseemly actions. You can see them from here." He spat over the battlements; the wind from the north blew his spittle back into his long beard, while the emperor tried to keep his mouth from twitching. Rather than meet the patriarch's angry eyes, he pretended to squint at the Frankish camp, where these immodest noblewomen were said to be parading themselves. How could anyone make out details in that disorderly, stinking tumult? He saw dogs and beggars and pilgrims and pikemen and knights, all equally muddy and tired from the long march across the barbarous western lands. And approaching the filthy camp, now, his ambassadors were a double line of bright silks, scarlet and emerald and jacinth blazing against the dun-colored dirt of the barbarians: every color but the purple reserved for emperors.

A flash of light, as from a burnished lance point, caught Manuel's eye. A moment later, the space between his ambassadors and the Frankish camp was filled with horses, white and dapple and bay, mares running free with only the lightest of bridles to guide them. The long cloaks of the riders streamed out behind them, mingling with long windblown tresses of gold and black and brown. And in the forefront of the troop of women was one so slender his two hands could have gone about her waist, with honey-brown hair falling about her shoulders, its natural light echoed and enhanced by the dazzle of gold at waist and neck and hem.

Not like Bertha-Irene. No. He'd been wrong; this Amazon was nothing like his serious German wife.

The patriarch hawked and made as if to spit again, but swallowed instead as a fresh breeze filled their faces with the stench of the barbarian camp. "How can you treat with a man who lets his wife display herself so shamelessly?"

"What?" Manuel demanded.

The patriarch raised his staff and pointed with a shaking arm. "That one there, spattering mud in the faces of your envoys with her horse's hooves. Goldenfoot. That immodest one," he said, "is what the king of the Franks has taken to wife. Why bother to treat with such a rabble? What use will his promises be? No matter what oaths you demand of him, do you think a man who cannot keep his own wife at home with her spindle can control this army?"

Manuel smiled into the wind. The smell of the camp was not so foul as all that: strange and barbarian and sharp with wood smoke. The smell of life. "Perhaps not," he said slowly, "but the negotiations should be . . . interesting, don't you think?"

The patriarch looked sharply at Manuel, but the emperor's face was shuttered, stiff and remote as that of the icon he resembled when the imperial crown framed his face in hanging pearls and haloed his head with gold and precious stones.

In that first dazzling ride through the city, Eleanor could almost believe that all the whispered tales and rumors of Constantinople were true. They entered the city through an arch so high that three men standing on one another's shoulders could not have reached the keystone; above the arch, the walls of the city towered, ancient, impregnable, heavy with the weight of history and prophecy. Banners of silk fluttered from the windows of the tall palaces on the other side of the gate, and the narrow street through which they rode was sprinkled with flowers. The air was heavy with the scent of strange perfumes, poured out like water in the fountains that dazzled under the October sun, and girls in thin silk robes sang songs of welcome as they passed, their high foreign voices sweet and incomprehensible as the speech of birds.

"Truly this city is the wonder of the world," she sighed to Louis.

His chaplain Odo rode on the king's other side and answered for him. "They are not Christians, or not truly so. And while their rich dwell in marble palaces, the hovels of the poor crowd around and poison the air with their stench. A great king would have cleared all this away." A contemptuous sweep of his arm indicated a cluster of poor wooden dwellings, huddled in the shadow of one of the silk-decorated mansions and sinking into the noisome mud that filled the low side of the street.

Eleanor leaned forward to look across her husband at Odo; she divided her smile equally between the two men who seemed so often to think and speak as one. "Very true. In a well-regulated city, no rider would be in danger from pigs running loose in the street and foraging for scraps. How could one call such a place civilized?"

Louis chewed on his lower lip. His pale face was blotched from the heat of the sun; now a red flush rose up his neck. "I never asked for this burden," he said in a low voice.

Eleanor sat back, feeling obscurely ashamed of herself. She had meant only to remind that self-righteous monk that Paris itself was nothing to be so proud of, with its streets filled with mud and beggars and half-wild pigs scavenging the midden heaps. Now she had also reminded Louis of his brother's untimely death and how he had been taken from the monastery to be trained for the throne after Philippe's horse shied at a pig in the street and threw him to his death. *Not* the best subject for Louis to be thinking of, not as they were on their way to claim the dubious friendship and halfhearted support of this Greek emperor. And she had not meant to make him unhappy.

Not this time, anyway. Eleanor thought of their daughter Marie, growing up in Paris while they made this mad pilgrimage-war to the farthest ends of the earth, and told herself that Louis deserved to be unhappy.

All the same, she could have wished for a little more confidence in him—and in herself—when, after a very short ride, they dismounted before the emperor's palace of Blachernae. Three stories of pillars and arches covered in gold and silver mosaic rose before them; a host of twittering, bird-voiced, soft-faced beings in jeweled robes awaited them in the porch. Accustomed to the dour visage of Thierry Galeran, Eleanor hardly knew what to make of these men-women at first; then she understood that they must be the famous eunuchs of Constantinople, and her lips twitched with suppressed amusement. Perhaps the Templar might not love Constantinople so well as predicted, when he saw what soft useless things were the eunuchs who were said to be the true rulers of the empire.

They passed through hall after hall, through a long gallery whose columns glittered with pictures all in gold and the brilliant colors of spring flowers. Even the floor upon which Eleanor walked was a mosaic. She stepped across seas full of sirens and storms, came safely to land on an island of flowers, moved at a eunuch's direction across a dazzling labyrinth of silver lines, and saw before her a throne and an idol of gold and pearls.

No, not an idol—a black-browed man of middle height, whose thin clever face and amber-colored eyes should have been eclipsed by the glory that surrounded him. He sat upon gold worked like feathers and flowers, curling delicacies of metal that blazed with jewels in the uncertain light. His brow was encircled with pearls and diamonds, ropes of pearls hung down like a lady's braids to frame his face, and a cap of gold, supporting these jewels, was itself suspended from the ceiling by golden chains. But the man within this splendor dominated it and all the room by the intensity of his face, the eyes that burned and saw everything and nothing.

Incense perfumed the room; a low, sacred chanting hummed through Eleanor's ears. They worshipped this emperor as the likeness of Christ on earth, it was said. She bent her knee in a courteous gesture of respect; behind her, she could hear the rustling of stiff linen robes as the lesser members of their party, the bishops of Langres and Lisieux, her woman Faenze and the king's young brother Robert, sank to their knees at the sight of this blazing glory.

Beside her, Louis made as if to kneel, awkwardly, and the chaplain Odo stood stiff as any stick, his rigid back and clenched hands eloquently expressing his distaste for the corruption of religion and decency he saw in Constantinople.

Before Louis could complete his gesture, the man with the thin, dark face had moved from his golden setting, leaving the crown of pearls and diamonds hanging incongruously above an empty throne. He offered one hand to Louis and the other to Eleanor, saying something in his strange tongue; the gesture bid them rise, not to bow their heads to him. The eunuchs who had shown them in and the chanting priests stiffened in outrage to match Odo's.

His hand clasped her fingers for a moment. It was warm and dry; she thought she could feel the pulse of his blood, like a bird's heart beating against the thin cage of its chest.

The emperor led them to two low chairs placed one on either side of the throne. Seated, they were like children at his feet. The bishops Godfrey and Arnulf, the king's brother Robert, and Eleanor's woman Faenze stood uneasily in a small group, looking dingy against the silken tapestries and dwarfed by the high arched ceiling that lifted its columns of gold mosaic into the shadows of a dome. Count

Thierry of Flanders stood with arms akimbo, surveying the glittering room with small clever eyes that seemed to reckon up the worth of every object in livres and deniers. His wife Sybille stared about her with frank enjoyment.

He is clever, Eleanor thought. *He shows us great courtesy and at the same time makes us small beside him.* Unwilling admiration warred with concern for her husband, who might be maneuvered into giving up all his advantages by this clever man. And there was a third feeling, all but eclipsing the other two.

Nobody told me he was so young. Why that should have been important, she could not say, but she looked up into the dark, confident face of a man not yet thirty, and she felt a quiver of fear that had nothing to do with the emperor's diplomatic skills.

One of the soft-faced eunuchs who had let them to this room stepped forward in a rustle of silk. "I am the interpreter from the Bureau of the Barbarians, the voice of the basileus," he announced in a singsong Latin that hissed and whispered over the sibilants.

Manuel spoke, looking at Eleanor. She blushed and dropped her eyes. *He is only a man. A man dressed up like a saint's image . . . that's silly, even blasphemous. I will not be impressed. I will not!* But she knew it was not the emperor's stiff silken robes, his gold throne, and his jeweled crown that made her unwilling to meet his gaze.

The interpreter looked at Louis, not at Eleanor, as he translated the emperor's words. "The basileus asks of your present state and your wishes for the future."

Louis shifted uncomfortably on his low stool and gnawed at his lower lip before replying. "We have no wish save to cross peacefully through the lands of the Greeks and to rescue our fellow Christians from the infidel."

The interpreter bowed three times before repeating Louis's words in Greek. Eleanor looked behind the emperor's throne, at the cluster of priests and eunuchs gathered there. One man, at least, was no eunuch; younger than Manuel and almost as richly dressed as the emperor, he was looking at the Franks with open curiosity. His glance wandered over the entire group, but it seemed to Eleanor that it always returned to Faenze.

Manuel spoke to the interpreter again and received a quick, low-voiced reply. The young noble who had been watching Faenze said something; Manuel smiled and nodded.

Behind Eleanor, the Frankish party shifted and shuffled their feet. She heard the distinct *chink* of mail and wondered who had been fool enough to come with a mail shirt under his robe. If the Greeks noticed, the action could be taken as an insult.

"What are they gabbling on about now?" muttered Bishop Godfrey of Langres in his low, gravelly voice. "Some treachery, I make no doubt."

His fellow legate, Arnulf of Lisieux, glanced at the group near the throne. "You are too quick to suspicion. We have been offered only fair words as yet. And this emperor is not, I think, as thick-headed as a French knight. He's not fool enough to betray us with our army camped outside his walls."

"No. He'll wait until we have crossed the Bosporus and cannot besiege his city. *Most* reassuring."

Manuel leaned forward a fraction of an inch, only enough to set the ropes of pearls swaying against his high cheekbones, and the quarreling bishops fell silent. They listened as attentively to his speech as if they could understand each word, then listened again while the self-important interpreter translated.

"My lord joins his prayers to yours for the victory that only God can give and promises to supply you with all that lies within his own power. Are you in need of boats to ferry your army across the Bosporus?"

"We are," Louis answered quickly, "but not until the rest of our forces arrive."

Manuel's face stiffened. "The rest of your forces?"

"The marquis of Montferrat and the lords of Savoy and Auvergne took their armies by ship from Brindisi. We promised to await them here."

The emperor Manuel's face was a dark mask, stiff as a painted saint on a board. He spoke quickly, looking at Louis, one hand moving in an encircling gesture that seemed to include the Frankish retinue.

"Until that time, then," the interpreter said, "the basileus hopes that you will enjoy the pleasures of our city, as we in turn hope to benefit from your company among us. You need not do homage to us until your companions have arrived."

Robert of Dreux stiffened. *"Homage!"* His voice rang out briefly, sudden and loud for a moment, then lost among the wisps of incense and the encircling golden gleams of the high vaulted ceiling. "Tell this painted king we have marched here to save Christians, not to be insulted by Greeks. Tell him our army—"

He broke off with a quick indrawn breath. Beside him, Bishop Arnulf of Lisieux shifted his weight, feet hidden under his long formal robe.

"In our country," Louis replied tranquilly, "it is not the custom for sovereigns to do homage to other sovereigns."

The interpreter began translating Manuel's words almost before the emperor had finished speaking. Eleanor had the sense that this argument had been debated before—with Conrad of Hohenstaufen, perhaps? It was a little thing, the interpreter insisted. Perhaps his words had been misunderstood. Certainly there was no question of asking the king of the Franks to do homage for his own lands! But as the army of the Franks marched on toward Jerusalem, was it not their intent to liberate those lands formerly held by Christians and now conquered by the Saracens? And since the Crusaders expected the basileus to feed their army and furnish guides, should not this be looked upon as a joint effort? In which case, surely it was only reasonable that those cities formerly held by the empire should be returned to Manuel, just as those cities formerly held by the Franks should be returned to them. The emperor asked only that Louis swear homage in advance for any cities of the empire that he might subsequently liberate, agreeing now that he would hold those cities only through and by permission of the emperor.

The interpreter finished by pointing out that Conrad of Hohenstaufen had already sworn such an oath before his armies passed on into Asia.

Eleanor wondered if they would be allowed to go on without swearing to Manuel. Could they even cross the Bosporus without his help? And once on the other side, how would they fare without guides or markets?

"I cannot answer these things now," Louis said peevishly. "My head hurts. These are complex questions. I must take council with my barons before I can give you my decision."

"Of course, of course," said the interpreter, mimicking Manuel's soothing tones. "You shall be escorted to your lodgings now."

Robert of Dreux moved suddenly, and the clanking sound of mail under his tunic was clear as the ringing of a bell. Eleanor fell into a fit of coughing while Robert demanded to know if the emperor meant to separate them from the rest of the Christian army.

"We are all Christians here," said the interpreter. "We hope that the most noble king of the Franks and his retinue are pleased with their lodging in the Philopation. The rest of the army will, I regret, have to camp in the surrounding park, which was a more pleasant place some months ago, with caves and ponds for shelter, with trees for shade, and stocked with wild game for the emperor's hunting amusement . . . Well, at least the caves and ponds remain. There was some small difficulty with the German army."

All through the interpreter's smooth speech, Eleanor could feel Manuel's eyes on her, amused and knowing. She stared at the tiny squares of gilt and azure tiles that made up the mosaic walls, looking neither at the basileus nor at her husband while the interpreter went on to express Manuel's hope that Louis and Eleanor would accept his escort to visit the holy places within the city after they had rested.

The lisping eunuch did not join their party on the tour of the holy sites of Constantinople; his place as interpreter was supplied by the young man Eleanor had noticed in Manuel's entourage, the one who seemed so taken with Faenze. He introduced himself as Alexios, the emperor's nephew, and apologized in advance for any difficulty that might be caused by his imperfect French; the emperor wished only to do his distinguished guests the utmost honor by having them escorted by a member of his own family. "My uncle regrets that he cannot join you himself," Alexios said, looking straight through the dark, thin-faced man who stood not two paces from him, "but imperial protocol forbids his meeting you again until the banquet of welcome."

Louis said, "But——" and Eleanor trod on his foot, at the same time giving his little brother Robert a forbidding stare. Before either of them could say anything else, she thanked Alexios for his services, said truthfully that his mastery of the French language was most impressive, and added that she *quite understood that the most serene basileus was not present,* giving Louis another meaningful look as she said the last words.

The Greek party gave a collective sigh of relief as it became clear that the Franks had understood and accepted the polite fiction that allowed Manuel Comnenus to walk among them, free of his hampering ceremonial robe and crown and also free, perhaps, of some of the formalities that kept the emperor of Constantinople fenced in between protocol and tradition.

In the church of the Holy Apostles they saw the iconostasis of beaten silver with images of the twelve apostles, and the column to which Our Lord was bound before He was put on the cross. In the church of Christos Pantokrator they admired the golden mosaics set between the arches, and the marble slab on which Our Lord was laid when He was taken down from the cross. In the church of the Blessed Virgin of the Pharos they saw two vessels of gold hanging from heavy silver chains, one of which, Alexios told them, contained the image of Edessa—the cloth with the divine features of Our Lord imprinted on it—and the other, the tile under which the cloth had been hidden, which also showed the face of Christ.

"They venerate the holy relics of Edessa, but they could not lift a hand to save that city from the heathen," muttered Godfrey of Langres.

"We have also in this chapel," Alexios said over the bishop's resentful murmuring, "two pieces of the True Cross, the iron of the lance with which Our Lord had His side pierced, the crown of thorns, two of the nails that were driven through His hands and feet, and the girdle of the Blessed Virgin."

Louis glanced at Eleanor. "We should remain and pray to Our Lady," he said to her, "that she may grant us a child."

"She has already done so," Eleanor said through her teeth. That bright-eyed boy, the emperor's nephew, most assuredly understood every word they said. She did not care to have her marital difficulties discussed before these Greeks, nor to hear Louis dismiss the daughter who had been born out of her body in twelve stifling hours of torment on a summer day as if she did not exist at all.

"An heir," Louis amended.

"I believe," Eleanor said sweetly, "we are to be conducted next to the church of the Holy Wisdom. Is that not true, Alexios?"

The ennui she had begun to feel at this endless parade of gold and silver and sacred things vanished when they entered under the high dome of the church of Sancta Sophia, the Holy Wisdom. The vast dimness surrounded them like an ancient forest in which the trunks of the trees were columns of porphyry and marble, glimmering in the light of a hundred silver chandeliers that descended on silver chains from a heaven of blue and silver tiles that framed holy faces in gold mosaic. Forgetting her companions, Eleanor moved slowly forward over a pavement of mosaic and marble that seemed to be strewn with purple flowers. The distant chanting of some Greek rite might have been birdsong, or the rippling of water from a secret spring; the incense that scented the air might have been the rich smell of crushed pine needles in the highland forests of the Auvergne. She felt herself at once to be very far away from anything she knew and to be coming home again, walking the labyrinthine path to the heart of the forest that Cercle-le-Monde had once shown her.

That dark anonymous man, the basileus, paced beside her, keeping step with her on soft, silent slippers of gilded leather. Somewhere in the distance she could hear Alexios explaining something to the rest of their party.

"Truly this is a wonder of the world," she said, forgetting that the emperor required an interpreter to understand her. "I see why you Greeks call us barbarians!" If only Abbot Suger could see this place . . . no, perhaps better not; he might lose all heart for his building and rebuilding of Saint-Denis if he saw how the Greeks had outstripped him in splendor, centuries before his abbey church was even thought of.

The emperor beckoned for Alexios and said something to him in the soft liquid accents of the Greek tongue.

"My . . . relative . . . wishes the queen to understand that France has brought here a greater wonder than any he has had the honor of showing her," Alexios said. His eyes followed Faenze, where Robert of Dreux gripped her arm to keep her by his side, but Manuel watched Eleanor and saw the blush with which she received the compliment.

What is the matter with me? He will think Frankish women are too barbaric even to flirt competently! But it wasn't the extravagant words that put her out of countenance. It was the man watching her. Not the basileus, that icon in gold and pearls and stiff embroidered brocades; it was the young man, the man in a loose silken tunic under which his body moved with the ease of the athlete, the man who had chosen to walk beside her while Louis lost himself in a dream of holy relics, and Thierry of Flanders no doubt mentally priced and sold each item in the church.

The basileus—the emperor, Eleanor reminded herself. The emperor upon whose ships they depended to cross the Bosporus, upon whose markets they depended to feed the army. The emperor who was married to one of her own countrywomen— at least, the German Bertha seemed like a countrywoman of hers beside all these elegant, scornful, foreign Greeks.

"I look forward to meeting the basilissa," Eleanor said firmly.

"It is not customary . . ." Alexios began, then was interrupted by a sharp command from Manuel. After a brief exchange, he turned back to Eleanor. "Although it is not our custom for the basilissa to attend the state banquets of the basileus, she will naturally be eager to meet visitors from her own land. Therefore tonight's will *not* be a state banquet, and the basilissa Irene will join us then."

Far away in the darkness that sparkled intermittently as the flames of the candles fell on bejeweled icons and elaborate works in gold and silver, a procession of Byzantine priests moved slowly through the great space of the church of the Holy Wisdom. Their chant seemed strange and foreign to Eleanor, with those high sweet voices rising above the deep regular pulse of the men's chanting. Women? No, of course—eunuchs.

The music was lovely, the walls and pillars of white and green and red stone were beautiful, the incense that wafted from the censers before the profession was sweet . . . and she needed to see the sky over her head, instead of this artificial sky of blue and silver and gold mosaic with the solemn faces of saints and apostles looking down at her. "You mentioned a pillar of prophecy," Eleanor said, "I would see it now." She turned away from the chanting priests and moved toward the great double doors of the church, toward the blue and golden light of day that she could see only as if through a distant window, so far away were those open doors.

Louis followed her; so, after a moment's hesitation, did the rest of the party. At the church entrance they paused while Alexios offered to have their horses brought around to spare them the long, tiring walk down the Mese.

"The Mese—that is this grand street before us?" asked Sybille of Flanders, pointing to the long open-air bazaar that stretched away from the steps of the church. Her eyes sparkled with anticipation. "Perfumers," she whispered to Eleanor, "and I see jewelers farther down, and workers in ivory. . . ."

Eleanor grinned in response. There could be such a thing as too many holy relics. "We will walk," she said firmly to Alexios. "Pray arrange to have our horses brought around to the square where stands this wondrous column; we will return to the Philopation from there. If it pleases you, my lord?" she said belatedly with a bow toward Louis.

"What? Oh—I—yes, certainly, whatever you like," Louis said. He looked bemused, as if he had left some vital part of himself back in the churches with all their holy relics in their richly worked cases. "This is indeed a most wonderful city," he said to Alexios. "Please convey to the emperor—"

"*When you happen to see him,*" Eleanor interjected firmly.

"—that we are most grateful to him for allowing us to visit these holy places."

Manuel smiled and said something to Alexios. The boy shook his head firmly. Eleanor arched one brow. "Do you not interpret for us, Prince Alexios?"

"N—Nothing to signify," Alexios stammered.

"Please tell us about this column before the church," Faenze begged. "Is this not the wondrous column of prophecy of which you spoke, Prince Alexios?"

Alexios gave her a grateful smile and moved slightly, putting Faenze between himself and Eleanor. "No, this is the Column of the Emperor's Protection. Do you not see the great man of copper on the copper horse? That is Heraclius the emperor."

All the Franks craned their necks upwards looking along the length of the great marble and copper pillar with its bands of iron. High above them a flat slab of stone, as long and as wide as the floor of Eleanor's private chapel in Paris, supported the copper horse and rider. One of the rider's hands reached out to the east, as if to push back the Turks who pressed ever closer to Constantinople; the other verdigris-green hand held a globe of gold surmounted with a cross.

"What does the writing on the base of the pillar say?" Faenze asked.

"That the Saracens shall never have truce from him."

Bishop Godfrey gave a most unbecoming snort. "Well, it is clearly not a statue of your present emperor, then. For have we not heard that he has just signed a treaty with the Seljuk sultan of Konya?"

Manuel's sharp cheekbones flushed dark with anger before Alexios had finished translating the comment, and he spoke sharply in Greek.

"If the most serene basileus were present," Alexios said, "he would remind his distinguished guests that the political situation here in the East is somewhat more complex than that in their lands, where they have the happiness to be very far removed from the infidels."

"All heretics and traitors speak such," muttered Odo, "excusing their lies and betrayal with explanations too complicated for an honest man to untangle."

Faenze squeezed Alexios's hand. "There is no need for you to weary yourself in translating every foolish word we say to . . . your friend," she murmured, and Alexios gave her a grateful smile.

"Indeed, this is no day to waste in arguing politics," Eleanor said sweetly. "I wish to walk down this street called Mese, and so does Sybille. You will give me the support of your arm, my lord bishop?" At least she could separate Godfrey of Langres from the Greeks. Controlling Odo was beyond her; he was liable to declare himself defiled by the touch of a woman. "Prince Alexios, I know my lord has no interest in the worldly things shown in this bazaar. Perhaps you could beguile the walk for him by telling him more of the miracles worked by the holy relics we have just seen." That should keep their young interpreter too busy to relay any more tactless comments to Manuel.

After the first few steps into the bazaar, Eleanor was too dazzled and delighted to worry about keeping her discourteous companions under control. Anyway, Louis should have been doing that; let him keep a rein on their tongues, for once! She needed to *look*.

The stalls of the perfumers scented the air with the essence of flowers and fruits; rose predominated, but geranium and violet competed, as well as something that reminded Eleanor of her sendal rosary of scented wood, and other deep, musky fragrances that made her feel dizzy and transported. She was almost relieved to pass on to the booths where rolls of cloth spilled over the sides of the stalls, lining the street with splashes of brilliant, jewellike color.

"How do they get such deep tones?" Sybille marveled, fingering a length of silk with gold figures worked against a deep rose-pink background. "And such intricate figures upon the ground? Thierry, we should send some of our Flemish weavers to apprentice here."

"The weaving and the dyeing of these particular cloths is done in the imperial workshops," Alexios said apologetically, "and bar . . . foreigners are not permitted to join the guild."

Sybille's eyes sparkled and Eleanor could guess that she was revolving ways around this prohibition. "That is a pretty color," she said, "but it would hardly suit you, Sybille."

Sybille held the silk for a moment against her cheek, where it warred violently with the reddish gold of her hair, and sighed. "Be you my mirror, Faenze," she commanded. "Is it so *very* bad?"

"It . . . does not set off your coloring, my lady," Faenze said tactfully.

Behind them, Alexios discoursed in a low murmur on the lives of saints revered in Byzantium, while Louis occasionally said "Amen" or "Great is the glory of God."

Sybille dropped the silk with a sigh. "Devil fly away with the Angevin blood," she said. "My father Fulk left me the red in his hair and the green in his eyes, and my pretty brother Geoffrey got the pure gold and the blue of the sky." She gave Eleanor a conspiratorial smile. "If only you had seen Geoffrey, you'd never have taken the French prince," she whispered. "Geoffrey outshines him as one of these Greek golden bezants outshines a French silver penny. You know they call him Geoffrey the Beautiful?"

"You've mentioned it," Eleanor said. In the long journey out from France she had learned more than enough about Sybille's admiration for her younger brother. "They also call him Geoffrey the husband of the Empress Matilda, remember?"

Sybille sighed. "She's not good enough for him . . . all she does is waste his time making him fight her hopeless battle for England. *You* already had your lands."

Had, Eleanor thought. *Had.* But since her marriage to Louis, the rule of Aquitaine and Poitou was his. She had had to beg his adviser Suger to get mercy for her people. . . . Unprofitable thoughts. She picked up a sea-green silk and showed it to Sybille. "This is more becoming to you."

"I am sick of wearing green and blue," Sybille said. "But I'll take a length of it anyway, if only as an example to our Flemings. And you should have this purple." She smiled at the merchant, held up a bezant and waggled her red-gold brows inquiringly. When he shook his head, she held up two more bezants and stretched out the length of silk, indicating how much she wanted. Eleanor lifted up the end of the length of purple silk and opened her palm.

More head shaking, and a spate of incomprehensible Greek, were her only response.

The others in the party had paced on ahead of the three women, all but Godfrey of Langres, who stayed glowering by Eleanor's side. Now Alexios broke off his tale of Saint Simeon and his vision of the nameless glory of God to return and interpret for the women.

With many expressions of deep regret he explained that the silk from the imperial workshops was not to be sold to foreigners, and that the purple and red silks especially were reserved for the imperial family and could not under any circumstances be worn by commoners.

"But my sister has a dress with two panels of purple silk from Constantinople," Eleanor protested, "and in any case, the dukes of Aquitaine are hardly 'commoners.'"

Alexios shook his head. "The stuff in your sister's dress is probably an imitation of our purple, from Sicily. Is it truly as deep and rich as this?"

"No," Eleanor said, "at least, not since we had to wash it . . ."

"No one has mastered the secrets of the imperial silk guild," Alexios said proudly, "and no one ever will. Would it please the ladies to accompany us on to the Forum of Theodosius, where the horses await us?"

There was more than enough to look at on the Mese to console Eleanor for the loss of the purple silk, although she had a feeling that Sybille was still cogitating plans to get some samples for her Flemish weavers to imitate in wool. After the booths of the textile sellers came those of the jewelers and goldsmiths, with their great cabochons of ruby or emerald set in delicate filigree or repoussé, their damascened bowls, their crosses and reliquaries bright with patterns of blue enamels so deep and brilliant that they gave the illusion of looking into a piece of the sky. Then came the carvings in ivory, caskets and book covers adorned with classical and religious motifs, and, after that, less precious goods, from gilt leather and embroideries in gold thread to the stalls of ordinary pottery and metalwork and finally the humble provision merchants offering salt fish, honey, and mare's milk. And filling the space between the booths was a throng of people who must have come from the four quarters of the earth. A troop of green-eyed barbarians dressed all in furs made way for a Byzantine lady carried in a gold-curtained litter, with only the tips of her perfumed fingers showing through an opening in the curtains; men as black as if they had been painted, tall fair-skinned Russian soldiers with heavy silver bracelets on their bare arms, turbaned infidels whose skin was even darker than that of the sunburnt men of Sicily; a Greek nobleman riding a white horse whose prancings and curvettings threatened the benches on which the potters' wares were set out. And all these people made way without being asked for the little group of Franks with their two Greek companions; not even their shadows fell upon the thin dark man who walked in the center of the group.

"I have heard," Eleanor said to Alexios, "that it is your emperor's pleasure to walk the streets of the city incognito, that he may see for himself the condition of the people."

Alexios nodded agreement.

"How does he do it? Does he paint his face, or wear a mask?"

"My lady?"

"I have the strangest feeling," Eleanor said, "that everybody in this great city of Constantinople is able to recognize him on sight."

"Ah—the pillar you desired to see is just ahead, my lady," Alexios said. "Allow me to clear away the merchants who are blocking your view."

A few quiet words from Alexios, a nod toward their party, and the sellers of koumiss and salted greens whose portable stalls were set up around the column hastily removed themselves.

"You should not tease Alexios," Faenze whispered to Eleanor. "He has a hard task—and a difficult position, for although he is not the emperor's heir, he might be set up as one by one of the many rival factions in the city, and so he is always most careful to demonstrate his complete loyalty to Manuel. Heirs . . . and emperors . . . have a way of dying unpleasantly here. But all Alexios really wants is to set up his own household and live quietly, outside the capital. His family has a villa on the other side of the Golden Horn, and there are vineyards attached to it that will be his portion."

It occurred to Eleanor, not for the first time, that Alexios seemed to have managed to say a great deal to Faenze in between his double duties of guiding the Franks and interpreting for Manuel. And that young Robert of Dreux was looking even sulkier than usual.

Once the area around the pillar was clear, the Franks approached and ran their hands lightly over the intricate bas-reliefs that decorated every inch.

"It must be fifty ells in height!" muttered Thierry of Flanders, craning his neck to see to the top.

"Sometimes we have had a hermit to make his life upon the top of the pillar," said Alexios, "relying for his subsistence on a basket that he let down to be filled by the charitable."

"Is it . . . ah . . . inhabited at present?" Thierry asked, backing away slightly.

"Regrettably, no."

"Just as well," Thierry said with his great booming laugh. "I shouldn't like to worry about being hit on the head with a basket . . . or with the other things the hermit probably dropped down!"

There were no grotesqueries of demons and half-human figures such as Eleanor was used to seeing in Western churches, no amusingly deformed beasts. Everything was worked so realistically that she half expected to see one of the galloping horses on the lower part of the column break free and clatter onto the pavement, to hear the hiss of the arrow as the archer on the horse loosed the string of his taut bow.

The stag they hunted raised a proud head crowned by a delicate tracery of antlers; a little above the hunt, a robed man raised a torch whose flame seemed alive, only caught for the moment in the stillness of stone, before a carved bust sitting atop a carved pillar; farther still, a crowned figure tumbled from the walls of a round tower.

"On this column," Alexios said proudly, "is pictured and written all the events and all the conquests that have happened in Byzantium and those that are yet to happen. This scene prophesied the death of the basileus's father in hunting," he explained, indicating the hunting scene at the base of the column. "And this prophesied the iconoclasts of three hundred years ago, who destroyed all the holy icons they could find."

"Then there is no order to the scenes?" Louis asked.

"None that we have been able to understand."

Eleanor pointed to the image of the falling king. "And this? What tale does it tell?"

"One that has not yet been told, my lady," Alexios said. "Perhaps it foreshadows the end of Byzantium; perhaps the last emperor will be thrown from the city walls. There are many images whose meaning is not yet clear. We cannot read those that tell of time to come. But after the event has happened, our wise men can ponder the images here and interpret those which foretold it." He paused. "Perhaps there will be no one left to tell the meaning of that scene."

On their return to the Philopation, the Franks who had been lucky enough to be included in the tour of the city told the others all that they could remember about it.

"I swear to you," said Robert of Dreux to the courtiers who hadn't gone, "in this church that they call the Holy Wisdom there cannot be fewer than a hundred chandeliers of silver, and every one hanging by a silver chain as thick as a man's arm."

Thierry of Flanders moved his fingers for a moment, and his thick lips moved silently. "I would calculate that not one of those chandeliers could be worth less than two hundred marks of silver. And that's not counting the chains . . . let me see—"

"But the silver is the least of the wealth," Robert interrupted him. "There was this altar . . . its top was made of gold and precious stones broken up and crushed all together, and it must have been six ells long—"

"Four and two-thirds," Thierry corrected. "I measured by the length from my fingertips to my nose."

Robert colored and started to say something disparaging about so-called nobles who measured everything as if it were a bolt of cloth, but his discontented mutter was drowned out by the deep, calm voice of the bishop of Langres.

"The walls of the city are none so strong," Godfrey said. "I noted several places where the stonework is crumbling."

"The masters of Greek fire probably need not concern themselves with the strength of walls," Arnulf of Lisieux pointed out. "You *have* heard of Greek fire? It spreads like oil over all that it touches, and it burns with a magical flame that cannot be put out by water or earth—"

"A child's story," Godfrey of Langres interrupted. "If it were so potent a weapon, be sure the emperor would have shown it to us! They take us to see their holy relics because all they have to defend the city is their faith that the saints will work them another miracle at need," he said scornfully.

"There is also the great chain across the Golden Horn to prevent ships from approaching that side of the city," Arnulf mentioned.

"But as we have no ships, that need not concern us!"

The wonders of Constantinople were forgotten in favor of a long wrangle about whether the Crusaders *could* take the city if they weren't good Christians and vowed to go on to Jerusalem at all costs.

From the windows of the royal suite in the Philopation, Eleanor could look over the hunting park and up to the city walls, with the emperor's white palace of Blachernae towering above them. To her left were the dark waters of the Golden Horn; before her, the evening sun stretched out long golden fingers and gilded the walls of Constantinople. Smoke rising from the campfires of the Crusading army teased her nostrils with the acrid scents of burning wood and dung and sizzling fat, rose like a veil between her and the golden city so that the walls seemed to dance in the smoky air.

"A messenger left these things for you," Faenze told her.

She looked at a bundle of blue silk and at a letter secured by a golden seal. "A letter from the emperor? This will be for my husband. The messenger made a mistake."

"He said to tell you that Louis has had gifts appropriate to his tastes and station," Faenze recited gravely, "a small icon of our Saint Spiridon and a finger bone of Saint Basil the Younger enclosed in a reliquary of gold."

Eleanor's fingers brushed the blue silk. It felt soft and cool as the evening sky above them.

"That's only the wrapping," Faenze said. "Shall I—?"

Under her small, deft hands the outer covering of silk fell away, revealing an ivory casket. Carved into the ivory were the figures of a man and a woman under an overarching tree. They were dressed in diaphanous tunics whose folds were so delicately carved, they seemed to float on the cool breeze from the Golden Horn.

"It *might* be an image from the story of Saint Anne," Faenze said dubiously. "Praying beneath the laurel bush?"

The minute, incised leaves could have been laurel leaves. Eleanor touched the carved ivory face of the girl. She was turning away from the young man who reached out to her. The girl's breast was round and firm, even the nipple delineated under the thinnest carving of an ivory tunic; her raised arms turned into branches that entwined with the tree that shaded the two figures, and her feet were sprouting roots that seemed to move and sink into the earth, as though the carving were alive.

"I think it is no saints' tale," Eleanor said.

"What could be valuable enough to enclose in such a chest?"

"The casket itself is the gift." Eleanor stooped and gathered up the blue silk that had enclosed it. "*And* the wrapping. It was meant for show, obviously; even the emperors of Constantinople cannot be foolish enough to throw away good lengths of silk like this."

But Faenze had opened the ivory box while Eleanor was gathering and folding the blue stuff. "I think," she said slowly, "they have riches beyond anything we have imagined."

Nestled within the white sides of the casket, folds of silk glowed like jewels: the true Byzantine purple, the imperial purple, woven with shimmering figures of gold and emerald thread that seemed to dance as Faenze gently lifted the fabric and laid it across Eleanor's outstretched hands. The silk slid across her fingers, light and delicate as a lover's caress, and as the fabric moved it released a subtle, lingering fragrance that made Eleanor think of flowers under a summer sun: not roses or lilies, but some exotic Eastern flower she had never seen. When Faenze let the folds of silk fall, the weight of the accumulated lengths was heavy on her hands, and the scent rose in dizzying clouds. Eleanor felt as if she were holding all Constantinople in her hands, the prophecies and the mysteries and the glittering wealth; the perfumed air around the silk carried with it the clouds of incense and the strange chanting music and the columned forest of the Holy Wisdom, and Manuel's dark eyes always upon her.

"A very suitable gift," Louis's cool, measured voice commented. He had entered silently, as usual; she had learned long ago not to act startled when he appeared without warning. When she complained of being surprised, he was hurt and said that a wife ought never to be doing anything that she objected to her husband's seeing.

Now she stood quite still as he crossed the room and took up one of the folds of silk, pinching the fabric between finger and thumb that reminded her of Thierry's merchantlike evaluation of all the wealth he saw in Constantinople. "The royal purple. Most appropriate. It is the gift of one king to another; he wishes to show that he honors me as his equal."

Eleanor let the silk slide from her arms. It slithered to the floor around the casket. Faenze gasped and knelt to gather it up again.

"Is something troubling you?" Louis asked. "You look . . ." He frowned. "The day has tired you. I shall send to Manuel and make your excuses. You need not attend this banquet if you are feeling ill."

Eleanor forced a smile. "Pray do not, husband. I am not ill or tired in the least, and it would be most impolite of me to absent myself from the banquet when the Empress Irene means to attend specifically for my sake."

Louis looked pensive. "I do not wish you to trouble yourself with affairs of state. You should allow me to take care of these things for you; they are not for a weak woman. Perhaps I should not have brought you with me."

Eleanor bit back the tart rejoinder that it was somewhat late to have thought of that. "But it is my duty to support you, husband, and if my presence can in any way ease the strain of negotiating with this emperor, then of course I must wish to accompany you."

"You have never shirked your duty," Louis said, somewhat reluctantly, as though he found this a questionable virtue in a woman. "But what brought the frown to your face, then?"

Eleanor briefly contemplated throwing her head back and howling like a wolf at the rising moon. Must she forever account not only for her movements but also for her expressions, her thoughts, her prayers, and her dreams? "It was nothing," she assured Louis. He only meant to be considerate. It was not his fault that the way he watched and questioned her was so *irritating.* But she had to come up with an explanation; she knew from long experience that he would not stop until he had one. "It was the gold thread in that figured silk," she lied. "It is full of little sharp ends and edges; it hurt my hands."

Louis gave her a relieved smile, and she let out the tiny breath she had been holding. "It did not trouble me," he said, "but your skin is so delicate. Ah, well, these Byzantines are great ones for the show of gold, even if it costs them discomfort, but give me a good honest woolen robe."

"A monk's robe, belike," Faenze murmured under her breath, so low that Louis did not catch the words.

When Louis finally left them alone to prepare for the banquet, the fragile scent that had perfumed the silk had dissipated. The room smelled only of the smoke from the army's campfires.

Chapter Thirteen

They entered the Sacred Palace by the hall known as *Chalce*, the Bronze Hall, a great domed room filled with bronze and marble statues so finely wrought that the folds of bronze draperies seemed to flutter in the breeze, the marble flesh seemed merely pale and not stone-white.

"It is against nature for anything made by men to appear so natural," Louis said uneasily.

"Your friend Bernard of Clairvaux would approve," Eleanor teased him. "Has he not often preached against the unnatural monstrosities our Western masons carve? Here there is nothing that could not have come from life."

But she, too, felt some unease at being surrounded by these still forms whose carved eyes seemed to look through her, at some distant past or future that had no connection with the living moment.

"Are these images of saints?" Louis asked Alexios, who had come to escort them and interpret for them.

The young man smiled. "No, of gods and goddesses of pagan times. This is Apollo, god of song—you see his lyre? And here," he said, turning to a statue of a woman, bare to the waist and proudly displaying her full, white breasts, "here is Aphrodite, goddess of love, with her mischievous son Eros who shoots the arrows of love into men and women."

Louis's lips compressed into a firm, disapproving line.

"It is a pretty fancy," Eleanor said quickly, before Louis could express his opinion of a supposedly Christian emperor who filled his halls with statues of pagan gods, "even if we know better than to believe in such things now."

Alexios smiled. "Ah, my lady, some of us have been humbled before the power of Eros. Who knows—he may even aim some of his arrows at our Western visitors." He looked at Faenze as he spoke, and she blushed and lowered her eyes.

There were more halls to traverse before them, separate marble buildings joined by twining pathways of gold mosaic tile.

"This place is like a labyrinth," Sybille of Flanders whispered to Eleanor. "Shall we be trapped forever, do you think, if our guide disappears suddenly?"

Eleanor smiled and shook her head. As they came farther into the precincts of the Sacred Palace, she too felt as though they were moving into a place where all the laws of the natural world were suspended, like the magical kingdoms under the earth where people sometimes disappeared for seven years that seemed like a single night.

"Do you suppose it is safe to eat the food here?" she whispered back. "Or will a single bite doom us to remain forever?"

Sybille sighed deeply. "I could imagine worse fates. It will be hard to go back to marching with the army after a taste of this luxury."

Eleanor glanced at Faenze. "I suspect we may be required to leave a hostage before we depart."

The dining hall was lit by heavy silver candelabra that set all the upper air of the domed room ablaze, while leaving the tables beneath in a net of flickering lights and shadows. The eunuch who had acted as their first translator was waiting here to interpret the order of seating as decreed by the parakoimomenos, the chamberlain of the imperial household. Louis and his brother, and the count and countess of Flanders, were seated at tables to the right of the Imperial table, with the eunuch as their interpreter. Alexios led Eleanor and Faenze to a place on the emperor's left and remained with them there.

"It is our custom to have certain entertainments while we dine," he told them. "That man"—he indicated a white-haired priest sitting with Louis—"is to recite the lives of Saint Spiridon and of Saint Basil the Younger, in metrical verse, that the king may know the holy stories of those whose icon and relic he is to take with him."

"How . . . interesting," Faenze said flatly.

Alexios gave her a conspiratorial grin. "The emperor desires to arrange entertainment to everyone's taste. Translating the saints' lives is a very difficult task, so he
has assigned his best interpreter to that table. We, over here, shall be hearing a new
sort of tale called a *romance*."

"I know," Eleanor said quickly. "Cercle-le-Monde here has told me one such
tale, all of lovers lost in a wood and such foolishness." She nodded at the troubadour, who had been given a cushion near their table—with, but not of, the noble
party. He sat cross-legged, dark head bent over his vielle as if the proper tuning of
the strings were his only interest in life.

"Trifles," Alexios agreed, "but delicious ones, do you not agree?"

Eleanor was saved from answering by the arrival of the emperor and his retinue.
Manuel was robed like a statue, in stiff purple so heavily sewn with gold thread
that the fabric could scarcely be seen. To his right, a tall woman with fair hair and a
discontented frown took her place. Eleanor hardly needed Alexios's whispers to tell
her that this was the Empress Irene, once Bertha of Sulzbach. Her Teutonic fairness
and unbending posture made her stand out among the supple, dark Greeks.

On the emperor's left, closer to Eleanor's table, were seated a young man and
woman who seemed to her to resemble Alexios—or was it only that all Greeks
looked alike to her? No, Alexios told them that these were his cousins John and
Theodora.

The first course consisted of a collection of little dishes filled with spicy and
salty foods. While the wagons bearing the dishes were rolled around the tables for
the diners to make their selection, a monk read homilies from Saint John
Chrysostom—or so Alexios told them—a team of acrobats balanced three men
high under the central chandelier, and a brown-skinned man with a length of cloth
wrapped around his head balanced a dish of olives on a long pole set on his head.
Faenze gasped and clapped her hands together when he began to juggle a set of
sharp tined utensils that sparkled in the candlelight, while the dish of olives swayed
perilously but never quite fell off the pole. The entertainment concluded with his
making the sharp golden utensils fly out of their circle to land neatly, one before
each guest at the table. Eleanor picked hers up and looked at it curiously. It had two
tines, like a broken pitchfork; the ends were sharp, but the edges were so dull that
she did not see how she was to cut her meat with it.

When the hot dishes were handed around, she understood. Everything had already been cut up into bite-size pieces, mixed with strange piquant sauces. All she had to do was spear a bite on the end of this thing and convey the meat to her mouth. She watched Alexios surreptitiously to make sure she understood the procedure, then she was able to help Faenze, who was struggling to use her utensil as a dining knife.

While they ate, the promised entertainment began with a melancholy-sounding flourish on a strange kind of lute. The Greek jongleur's voice was rich and resonant; even without understanding the words, Eleanor was swayed by the sensual impact of the sounds.

"He invites all those who have been subjected to love's torments to come and hear a tale of passion and suffering, of lovers lost and happily united again," Alexios translated in an undertone.

It seemed to Eleanor that the emperor was watching her. She half turned away from him and listened attentively to Alexios's translation. The hero of the story began by declaring his immunity to Eros, who resolved to be revenged on him by bringing him to a woman whom he could not help but love. Yet he did not allow the hero to see the woman at first, but tantalized him by showing only the garden where they were to meet. A wall of colored marble enclosed this garden, which in turn enclosed an inner courtyard, "a fragment of paradise, the dwelling place of pleasure and spring of sweetness." Within this courtyard was a pool that was magically kept warm and perfumed, with a mosaic of flowers and fruits upon its walls that made it seem like a place where summer ruled even in the bleakness of winter, and it was here, the poet told them, that the hero was destined to find and love the lady of his heart. But sweet fulfillment could not yet be his, for he had not yet made his submission to Eros, and so first he was shown the lady from afar.

"She rode a horse as white as milk," the poet sang, "and the hem of her garment was worked in gold, so that she was known as Goldenfoot. Slender she was a young tree, and her hair was the color of new bark, soft and light, and twined in two plaits that knotted up his heart and held it prisoner."

Eleanor felt that the room was growing hot and close. She pushed back the light brown plait that had fallen forward over her breast and looked up to find Manuel smiling. Beside him, the young Greek girl Theodora pouted and touched his hand. Bertha-Irene pointedly looked away, leaning toward Louis's table to listen to the holy tales of the saints.

On Eleanor's side of the room, the Greek singer's resonant voice carried the story forward on a wave of sensual melody. "The apples of her breasts shone through her scarlet garment, and a look from her eyes ravished the soul of the onlooker."

When the singer paused at the end of this description, Eleanor nodded to Cercle-le-Monde.

"It is the custom among our people that guests shall offer entertainment to match that of the hosts," she said, ignoring Faenze's startled look. "Let us have a song of your own, Cercle-le-Monde. I have a fancy to hear that one that begins '*Ben sai qe lor es mal estan.*' I will translate for you," she told Alexios sweetly, "and you shall do the same for the emperor."

Cercle-le-Monde glanced up for a moment, flashing a questioning look at Eleanor. She nodded firmly. After a preliminary sweep across the strings of the vielle, he began to sing:

> *"Ben sai qe lor es mal estan*
> *als molleiratz car se fan gai*
> *domnejador ni drudejan."*

"In the northern Frankish tongue," Eleanor told Alexios, "one would render his song thus: 'It's disgusting to see husbands acting like libertines, and those who do will receive their just reward; false lovers are cheated in their turn.'" She smiled again at Manuel, whose face had darkened as though he understood before Alexios could translate. "Pray convey to the emperor my apologies that I have not the skill in languages to render the sweet rhymes and pretty turns of phrase with which Cercle-le-Monde ornaments the verse."

After a brief exchange, Alexios told her, "The emperor says that your command of the Frankish language is doubtless excellent, but you have yet to listen to the language of the heart." He looked at Faenze as he spoke, and her face seemed to light up from within. Eleanor felt sad and old beside these two young people. What would it be like to love where you liked, to think first of whether you wanted to lie in bed with a man and not of how his lands and armies joined with yours? A brief memory of a tall golden man laughing in the sunlight pierced her heart. . . . But she had not loved William of Lezay. And she was married to Louis.

The Greek singer took over the entertainment again, narrating the reproof of

Eros to the hero. "None can escape my archery; why do you wander away? Though you flee to the ends of the earth, there I will be waiting for you. Become the servant of Eros, and enter into the garden of all delight. There may you know your lady, and she you, and all the sweetness of desire fulfilled will be my gift to you."

Eleanor nodded to Cercle-le-Monde when the Greek paused, and he launched into a song that might have been made for the occasion, of the difference between the false love of Lust and the true love of Amor, and how those who settled for Lust only cheated themselves.

The dishes of meats in rich sauces were removed, and golden bowls full of ripe fruit and sweet pastries were lowered from the ceiling by some silent mechanism invisible to the diners. Eleanor took a flaky pastry from the dish before her. It was filled with fine-ground nut meats and honey, spiced with nutmeg and cinnamon like the posset her grandmother used to mix for every bride bed, every wedding in Poitou. The honey dripped onto her fingers and she licked them shamelessly, tasting golden sunshine and sweetness in every drop.

In the Greek romance, the lovers were at last united, in that walled garden where flowers and fruits overhung a magical pool. The Greek sang meltingly of the sweetness of their embraces, the rare and wondrous pleasure so great that their hearts beat faster and their souls were well-nigh driven from their bodies. As Alexios translated, his hand touched Faenze's; Eleanor could see a pulse beating in her throat, as though that one touch had given her all the pleasure the poet sang of. Was it like that for some lovers, then? In the years since she married Louis she had come to believe that this intoxication of desire was an invention of the poets to give them something to sing about, a pretense that nobody challenged because it was so much prettier than the reality.

The Greek was finished, but the diners were not. Eleanor looked meaningfully at Cercle-le-Monde. He gave her a long grave look back and said, "Gentles, for this entertainment my poor words are only base metal next to the gold of the Greeks. I pray you accept therefore a song made by a nobleman, the lord of Blaye, as the best that our nation can offer in recompense." And before Eleanor could stop him he began that song which Jaufré Rudel had made for her when she left the Languedoc for Paris:

"Amors de terra loindana,
per vos totz lo cors mi dol;

Love from a distant land,
for you I suffer
and can find no remedy
unless I may follow
the call of Love into
some garden . . .

"A poor effort," said Eleanor to Alexios, "hardly worth the trouble of translating."
Manuel said something in Greek.

"My lord says that the sweet music alone conveys the meaning," Alexios told her.

As the Frankish party was leaving the Sacred Palace, a eunuch hurried up with a
purse of gold bezants for Cercle-le-Monde, the emperor's thanks for his singing.

"It is as well the emperor paid you," Eleanor said. "I myself do not feel inclined
to do so."

"Dear wife," Louis said with his sweet smile, "we must take care of our depen-
dents. These light songs are not to my taste, I confess, but we owe the man thanks
for having pleased the emperor. It was a most edifying evening, do you not think?"

Eleanor knelt before the heavy wooden crucifix that had been brought, so
Bertha-Irene proudly informed her, all the way from Germany as part of
her bridal furnishings. From this angle she looked up at Christ's realistically
pierced feet, with the painted drops of blood oozing out around the real iron
nail. Faced with this reminder of the sufferings of Our Lord, it was wrong to
think about the fact that her knees were beginning to ache and that the cold of
the marble floor was striking inward to chill her bones. Besides, she was three
years younger than Bertha of Sulzbach. She could certainly kneel here as long as
the empress did.

Bertha's head was bowed; she did not fidget or look up at the crucifix. Her lips moved in quiet prayer, beseeching the lord to whom they prayed to send her and Eleanor the sons and heirs their husbands needed.

"Amen," she said at last, and Eleanor echoed fervently.

"And as the Blessed Virgin did rejoice in thy birth, O Jesu, so should we thy servants rejoice..." Bertha began again, and Eleanor's heart sank. By Saint Radegonde, she would be a cripple incapable of either riding or childbearing if she did not get to stand up soon!

By the time Bertha ran out of prayers, the uncushioned ivory stool that she offered Eleanor seemed like the height of luxurious comfort.

"I pray daily to Our Lord for at least two hours," Bertha told Eleanor brightly. "Surely He will soon send me a child! And every Friday I go to the church of the Pharos to pray before the girdle of the Blessed Virgin."

"You have been married only a year," Eleanor said. "Surely soon your union will be blessed."

Bertha sighed. "We have wasted so much time already! We should have been married four years ago, when I first came here... but then the old emperor died, and Manuel was so busy with his new duties.... It was a very hard time for me."

"It must have been," Eleanor said with sympathy. "It's hard to grow used to living in a strange place. Paris is a fine city, but it is cold and gray beside my homeland. And you had so much farther to go ... But it must be easier now? You've had time to learn their language, and your husband is such a fine-looking man...."

"Oh, do you think so?" Bertha shrugged. "My people do not much admire these little dark men. But marriage is not for our pleasure, after all, but for the begetting of heirs. I do not mind it so much now. One can get used to anything. But if I were with child, we would not have to do any of ..." A hint of red tinged her clear, fair skin. "*You* know."

Eleanor thought of Louis's furtive visits to her bed, the hasty and clumsy couplings that sometimes left her aching for something, she knew not what ... thinking there must be *something* more to the love the poets sang of than *this*. But if Bertha felt no more joy in Manuel's embraces than she had of Louis, perhaps it was all a silly game men had, to pretend it was so important.

"My grandmother," she said, "told me once that if a man and a woman share a drink made with the ... parts ... of a male hare, then she will bear a male child. But if only one drinks, then it will be a girl."

"That's pagan superstition," Bertha said. "We ought only to pray to Our Lord and the Blessed Virgin. My old nurse," she added thoughtfully, "swore that eating pine nuts would do it."

"Or a bath in crushed pine needles, but while you're in it, you have to say the right prayer. It's perfectly all right," Eleanor said. "Even a priest couldn't object. You just say seven times, '*Maria virgo peperit Christum, Elisabet sterelis peperit Iohannem baptistam.*'"

"Some people say it helps to draw a pattern like this." Bertha traced a quick double spiral in the air.

"On what?"

"Anything. A bit of parchment, I guess. Then you wear it around your neck and it helps to quicken the womb. The only thing is . . . you can't use ink, that doesn't work. You have to draw it in your woman's blood. So you have to wait for the right time. . . ."

"At least you don't have to *eat* it," Eleanor said. "Dangereuse told me about one where you take walnuts and crush them up small and bake them into a cake with a bit of that blood, and then . . ."

"Ugh! With my people," Bertha said, "it was hazelnuts, not walnuts. Did you ever try it, though?"

"No," Eleanor lied. "Did *you?*"

Bertha's fair skin turned pink. It was not a becoming color for her. "I think I would try anything," she murmured, "not to have to . . . *you* know. He has no shame; he does not observe the days of abstinence, says those are rules of our church and they don't apply to him; and he wants to do all sorts of things that have *nothing* to do with making a child. You know the sort of disgusting ideas men get. . . . Of course I've made it perfectly clear to him I will have none of that, and I won't do anything with him on Thursdays, or during Lent, or on a saint's day." She sighed again. "But there are a lot of other days. If only my womb would quicken!"

When Eleanor returned from her visit to the empress, the Philopation was oddly quiet. Louis and most of his advisers were gathered in one room, arguing over some communication from Manuel. The Templar Thierry Galeran intercepted her on her way to her own rooms and told her that she was wanted in the council.

"Louis wants *my* opinion?" she said in surprise. The man who had not troubled to tell her how he meant to punish her own people of Poitiers would hardly ask her advice on how to deal with the Greeks . . . would he?

"Some women's matters," Galeran said. "Don't keep him waiting."

Eleanor sighed inwardly, remembering the day when, as a young girl, she had told Dangereuse that she could not understand why her father allowed men to stay in his service who were rude to her. "They are humble enough to your father," Dangereuse said dryly, "and it does not hurt me if they sneer that I was a paramour to his father. I had my William's love. Very little matters beside that."

Now Eleanor understood what Dangereuse had left unsaid: that her father was not likely to dismiss men who were useful to him just because they sometimes failed in courtesy to a woman of his household. She was queen of France now . . . but Louis liked and trusted this dour Templar who had made himself a eunuch to preserve his vow of chastity. *Revered* the man. Eleanor could not dismiss him from the king's household. She could complain about him, like any common wife whining to her husband, or she could rise above it as Dangereuse had done, and at least keep her dignity.

The men were arguing when she entered the room they had turned into a council chamber, with red faces and fists banging on the table and voices too loud for them to have heard her if she spoke. She caught fragments of sentences, disjointed phrases knocking against one another like swords clashing against armor as half the great lords on the Crusade shouted at once.

"Ridiculous vanity—" someone began.

"No homage!" The king's young brother pounded his fist to underline the words. "Absolutely not!"

"He gave ships to Conrad without this requirement, why not to us?"

"We should hire our own ships!"

"They're not even proper Christians!"

"It is only a matter of form." The quiet voice of Arnulf of Lisieux cut through the shouting like a small, slender knife that could slide through the chinks in a suit of mail. "The Emperor Conrad is already bound to Manuel by the ties of kinship; his wife Gertrude was sister to the empress. Between our lord Louis and Constantinople there are no such ties. Before assisting us to cross the Bosporus, the emperor wishes some assurance that we will respect his lands."

"Why don't we hire our own ships, then?" Robert of Dreux demanded.

Louis sighed. "We cannot. Manuel has commanded too many of the private merchant ships for his war with Sicily."

"So he *says*," the bishop of Langres grumbled. "More damned heathen trickery."

Thierry of Flanders shook his head glumly. "If it's trickery, they're all in it together. I could find but one for hire. Most of the damned heathens won't even talk to us."

Geoffrey de Rancon looked up, eyes bright with an idea. "We could start carrying men over the Bosporus in that one ship while you distract the Greeks by pretending to argue over fine points of the agreement," he suggested to Louis.

"And what," Godfrey of Langres snapped before Louis could speak, "do you propose to do when our army is hopelessly split, one half on this side of the Bosporus and one half on the other? I thought even in the Languedoc they raised men with more military sense than that!"

Geoffrey de Rancon's face darkened ominously. "Priest, what do you know of war?"

"More than you, it would seem!"

"Gentlemen, peace, peace!" Louis entreated, white hands upraised. Of them all, he was the only one who seemed tranquil and unruffled by the debate; he, Eleanor corrected her thought, and Arnulf of Lisieux, who sat beside him, his long, supple body coiled like a racing hound at rest. "It ill beseems a Christian monarch to deal in deceit. We will indeed discuss the emperor's demand in more detail, but without pretense, only with a true and honest desire to find terms that shall satisfy him without compromising our own sovereignty. Meanwhile, let the emperor's messenger return to us, to discuss the matter for which we have summoned the queen." He nodded to Eleanor and she came forward.

Muttering darkly that they had greater need of action than of more Greek talk, Geoffrey de Rancon left the council table and so cleared a space for her. As she took her seat on the carved ivory stool he had vacated, most of the other lords stood and took their leave of Louis. "Women's business," Thierry of Flanders said. "You won't be needing us."

Eleanor suppressed a flicker of irritation as the council chamber emptied. Louis ought to have dismissed them, and they should have waited for his word. He was not careful enough of his dignity. But that was an old annoyance, quickly forgotten as she saw Alexios enter, smiling at her under his black mop of wildly curling hair.

"Robert," Louis said to his brother, "you have our permission to depart. As Thierry said, this is women's business, not worth wasting your time on."

Robert shoved his stool back with such violence that it overturned as he stood. A chip of carved and gilded wood broke off one corner and bounced across the marble floor. He strode out of the room without the courtesy of a greeting to Alexios or a farewell to Louis.

Now, of all the Franks, only Louis and Arnulf of Lisieux remained, and Louis was standing. "This second matter with which this man has been charged is more in your realm than mine, my dear," he told Eleanor, "and I have other, more pressing matters to see to. I feel confident that you will see the wisdom of acceding to his request." He glanced at the bishop of Lisieux. "I fear you must remain; it would hardly be proper to leave the ladies alone."

Eleanor let out a very small sigh as Louis, too, left. Whatever it was Alexios wanted, how was she supposed to negotiate with him when Louis had all but commanded her to agree—and in his hearing, too? And what did he mean, *ladies?* She had not suddenly grown a second head, had she?

Alexios bowed to her and smiled warmly. "My lady, the Emperor Manuel, desiring that his people and yours should be united by bonds as warm as those of brotherly amity which join him with the Holy Roman Emperor—"

"I don't quite see how that can be worked out," Eleanor interrupted. "Your emperor is already married to Bertha . . . Irene, I mean; he can't very well marry Constance as well." Besides, Louis's sister was betrothed to Eustace, the son of the English king. Betrothals could be broken . . . but surely Manuel didn't mean to put aside the Holy Roman Emperor's sister-in-law for Constance? Eleanor half closed her eyes, imagining the scandal that would create and the schism between the two Crusading armies.

Alexios's brilliant smile dimmed. "Well . . . perhaps not *quite* so close," he said. "But surely my lady would agree that some alliance between our nations would benefit us all? Purely as a matter of diplomacy?"

"Oh, sit down," Eleanor said, suddenly catching on, "and say what you mean. You want to marry Faenze, don't you?"

Alexios lowered his body to the nearest stool, slowly and carefully as though he though it would bite him. "You . . . noticed?"

"I'm not blind," Eleanor said. "Anybody would have seen the way you two look at one another." And anybody who jumped to conclusions might have drawn the wrong ones from the way Manuel watched her at times. Her face felt warm, and she remembered that she was supposed to be negotiating, not just talking. "The girl is in my care," she told Alexios, "and it is my responsibility to see that she is properly provided for."

"The emperor has charged me to say," Alexios said slowly, "that he fully understands your concerns. Any lady of the Franks who chooses to remain in Byzantium will possess as a gift from the emperor a country palace overlooking the Golden Horn, together with vineyards and other lands sufficient to maintain her in the style of the emperor's own family."

"This is indeed a generous offer," Eleanor said. Faenze would be doing well for herself . . . if she were minded to give up her home and everything that was familiar for Alexios. And Eleanor rather thought she would be willing to do that in any case . . . but there was no need to say as much! "I assume these properties would be made over at the time the marriage is celebrated?"

To her surprise, Alexios looked down and blushed. "Where marriage is possible, that would be the arrangement," he said. "Where it is not, the matter might be settled . . . more informally."

Eleanor clenched her teeth against a sudden wave of anger. Had Faenze told Alexios the truth about her troubled past, and had he decided that a girl who was no longer virgin was not worth the honor of marriage? "Faenze has lived virtuously in my household," she snapped. "I will not consent to leaving her here as your light-of-love, Alexios!"

Alexios's eyes widened. "Oh, no. I love Faenze and my dearest wish is to marry her," he assured Eleanor, so earnestly that she could not but believe him—especially when he went on to quibble about the need to have the ceremony performed according to the Greek rite. Eleanor cut him off in the middle of a long and hopelessly confused sentence about the possibility that Faenze might prefer to be married first according to the Latin rite, but that she would have to be baptized into the Greek church afterward, and the patriarch might object . . .

"If you mean to marry the girl," she said, "and if there is time to see that she is dowered as the emperor suggests, then I have no objection. It will be up to you to persuade Faenze that she should abandon her church and home to live in a strange country. The change has been difficult for some," she said, thinking of tense, unhappy Bertha-Irene. "It is a matter you should both think on. I shall send for her now."

"No—that is—wait a moment!" Alexios blurted out. "I have not finished."

Eleanor raised her brows and waited.

"The emperor particularly wishes me to point out to you the many advantages of living in a great city like Byzantium, the center of civilized life," Alexios said hurriedly, stumbling over the syllables of the French tongue. "Here is all that any lady may desire—music and art and fine silks, the riches of the world passing through our markets, and most of all, the sweetness of Eros who rules all of us, even emperors and queens. In a case where marriage was not possible," he said, lowering his voice, "the lady would not even be required to adopt our faith. There is no objection to foreigners practicing their own rites in privacy."

Eleanor could feel Arnulf of Lisieux watching her; she would not turn her head to meet his dark, sardonic gaze. "In my country," she said at last, "we have the strange barbarian habit of preferring to make love directly, not through messengers. There is no reason for you to tell me these things. Faenze is the one you should be speaking to."

Alexios dropped his voice still further, so that Eleanor could scarcely hear him. She doubted that the bishop of Lisieux would be able to make out his words at all. "The emperor anticipated this and bade me ask whether you were well acquainted with Louis before your marriage. Or was that arranged before you and he had ever exchanged a single glance as man and woman?"

"You may tell the emperor from me that he asks questions that are none of his business," Eleanor snapped. She rose. "I shall send Faenze to you now. You may wait here."

Arnulf rose from his seat and followed her from the council room. "It is none of my affair," he said quietly as they walked toward the royal suite, "but—"

"You are right," Eleanor said. "It is none of your affair."

"They are fools," Arnulf remarked in a detached tone, "who would set two great Christian monarchs by the ears only to satisfy a passing desire. If the emperor is foolish, I am glad to see that the queen of France is wise . . . too wise to trade the duchy of Aquitaine for a house on the shores of the Golden Horn."

Faenze was waiting in Eleanor's rooms, sitting quietly with her hands folded in her lap. The tension that whitened her slim fingers belied her calm pose. Of course, the Philopation must be buzzing with the news of Manuel's dual request. While the lords who commanded the army fumed over the demand that they do homage to this foreign ruler, Faenze at least would be waiting to hear about the other half of the demand—in Eleanor's opinion, the more important half. Homage to a ruler who lived halfway across the world from France was only a form. Faenze's marriage to Alexios would be a new life for her.

"He is waiting," Eleanor said with a half smile. "The decision is yours, Faenze . . . but . . . are you *sure*? They are so different from us, these Greeks. I think Bertha of Sulzbach has not been happy as Irene of Constantinople."

Faenze started eagerly from her seat. "I would not have to change my name," she said, "and Alexios loves me. It would not be one of these marriages made between estates and titles. . . ." She blushed and looked away.

"Like Bertha's with Manuel," Eleanor said quickly, before either of them was tempted to mention her own marriage to Louis.

"Exactly," Faenze said with relief.

"Go to him and talk it over," Eleanor said. "And Faenze? Be sure—be very sure that this is what you want." The girl would be alone here, with only that stiff German empress and a handful of Latin merchants to remind her of her home. Should she warn her again? No. Faenze was very sure that the love she shared with Alexios would be enough to sustain her all the rest of her life. And yet they had only glanced at one another a few times, had only enjoyed a few minutes' surreptitious conversation. How could she be so sure?

She has surrendered to that laughing pagan god, Eros, Eleanor thought. Commoners may do so, I suppose. Perhaps for them, those foolish songs of gardens enclosed and lovers' meetings may mean something.

Faenze lingered to tell Eleanor that another invitation had been sent for her to pray with Bertha-Irene that evening. "Alexios brought it . . . my lord Louis was here; he approves," she said.

"He would," said Eleanor dryly. She had no desire to wear out her knee bones in another lengthy session before the gilded images of saints she had never heard of. But, after Faenze had gone to her love, she took up the scroll left by Alexios and examined it curiously. The previous message had been verbal; this was more formal, written in letters of scarlet upon a parchment with gilt edges, an Imperial invitation.

The words also were as stiff and formal as one would expect of Bertha-Irene, requesting Eleanor's company in an evening prayer at a shrine in the Sacred Palace. The easiest access to this shrine was by the sea stairs; a boat would be waiting at sunset to convey the queen, if she deigned to accept the invitation.

All very proper. But at the bottom of the scroll was a gloss in the sweet words of home, the langue d'oc, which hardly anybody in Louis's entourage would be able to read.

> *e non puosc trobar meizina*
> *si non vau al sieu reclam*
> *ab atraic d'amor doussana . . .*

> And can find no remedy
> unless I may follow
> the call of love . . .

Eleanor rolled the parchment into a tight wand no thicker than her finger and tied the purple ribbon of silk around it, jerking it into taut knots that creased the ribbon beyond repair. An unfamiliar, aching emptiness filled her breast. "In a garden or behind a curtain," she said under her breath, finishing the verse that Cercle-le-Monde had sung against her wishes at that banquet. It was not the empress who had sent this "invitation to prayer"—and the god Manuel wished her to pray to was no Christian god but laughing Eros. Assuredly she would not go.

The imagined laughter of the pagan god filled her ears, a gay descant that danced above the hum of the Mass and the monks' chants of prayer.

Along the shore where the army was encamped, the emperor's ships brought food and other necessities so that the Frankish Crusaders could buy what they needed without entering the city of Constantinople. More than necessities, Faenze thought, trying to look through her lashes at the dark-haired women in all but transparent garments who leaned from the deck of the nearest ship and waved invitations to the soldiers. Sweaty, red-faced men, their clothes stained and dusty from the long march across Europe, jostled for their turns on board the floating brothel. One of them, shoved by a comrade's elbow, took two staggering steps backward and all but overturned the long table where the money changers sat before stacks of gold bezants and silver marks. There were silver vessels there, too: patens and chalices that the priests with the army had brought to serve Mass before the great lords, silver washing basins and other things that had seemed very fine at home but here were accounted crude work, valued only for the weight of their metal. The trader at the end of the table yelled at the Fleming and rearranged his stack of silver vessels with neat, precise movements.

"Don't stare at those women!" the young count of Dreux growled. His hand closed painfully tight about her arm. Only two years younger than her, Faenze thought, but this brother of the king's was no more than an overgrown sulky boy who pouted when he couldn't get what he wanted.

"Why not?" she demanded. "You were the one who wanted to walk through the market. You were the one who wanted to talk. And you are the one who treats me as if I were no more than one of *them*." She jerked her chin toward the brothel ship. Soon she would be away from all this mud and stink and brawling, the treasured wife of a gentle man who read poetry to her and wanted to keep her in luxury, who was giving her her own house and lands so that she need not feel dependent on him after her people left. As if she'd miss this! It had seemed the least she could do, in charity, to walk with Robert of Dreux this one last time. Besides, she dreaded the scene he would doubtless have made if she refused him.

"You are not a common whore, to stare at such bawdy sights," Robert said.

Faenze laughed bitterly. "Common? No, I am the whore of the king's brother!"

"You think this perfumed Greek boy would have you if he knew?" Robert's free hand fell hard on her shoulder, forcing her to turn and face him.

"He knows!" Faenze flung in his face. "Would I cheat him so? He knows—everything—and so he, at least, knows exactly why I do not regret for one minute leaving my native land! What have I ever had in France but hard words and being used by men? What have I ever had of our church but being blamed for what I was powerless to prevent? I shall be a Greek now, Robert. A Greek wife attending a Greek church, and married to a Greek, and proud of it!" She had not meant their last conversation to go like this. She had imagined a sad, sweet scene in which she told Robert some pretty lies to soften her departure, something about memories she would always cherish. But when he held her so tightly, all she could remember was how much she hated his hands on her body, the nights when she had told herself it did not matter, the times when she had taken unwilling pleasure in his use of her and hated herself afterward. It would not be like that with Alexios; when the Greek priest baptized her, she told herself, she would be reborn, and all the unhappy past no more than a dream.

"You don't mean it," Robert said. "You know you are *mine*. If you were in your senses, you would never leave me for some mincing Greek with curled hair. These people are not even real Christians. I can't let you do this, Faenze."

"You do not own me. Go home, Robert, and exercise your marital rights on the countess of Perche. *She* has been given you by the king. *I*," Faenze pointed out, "have not. You never thought me worth marrying."

"You're not," Robert said between his teeth, "but you're worth rescuing. I am going to save you from yourself."

"Robert, I do not *want* to be rescued. I want to stay here and marry Alexios. Truly, that is what I have chosen!"

In their walking they had come to the end of the long line of the money changers' tables. Beyond them, another ship bobbed at anchor: the single ship the count of Flanders had been able to hire for their whole army.

"You are out of your senses," Robert said, "and anyway, it is not for women to choose in these matters. You should be guided by your male relatives."

"My *brothers?*" Faenze laughed in his face.

"In their absence, by me," Robert said, and something in his face made her suddenly afraid. "Faenze, I will not permit this. Come aboard the ship now, with me. I will take you out of reach of this Greek and all the emperor's men. My own men are already there, waiting the signal to sail."

Faenze looked wildly about her. Suddenly Robert's desire to talk with her on this crowded, muddy shore made perfect sense. She could see no one she knew. The nobles of Louis's entourage did not have to come to the market, the emperor himself saw to the supplying of the Philopation. Here were only the knights and the foot soldiers and the camp followers who trailed after the army, the ragged pilgrims she had laughed at when she rode at ease with Eleanor's women and saw them tramping through the mud and asking if every stinking village they passed might not be Jerusalem. She'd thought them stupid, but they were cleverer than she: they would see Jerusalem.

"I will not go with you," she said, trying to pull away. But his hands were hard and strong with years of swordplay and tilting, of carrying sword and lance since he was barely tall enough to lift a wooden practice blade. A stupid, sulky, overgrown boy, with the strength of a man to carry out his will.

"Help me!" she cried out, looking from side to side for some friendly face. "Franks, to me! This man—" She thought the Fleming who had been quarreling with the money changer looked up at them.

Robert swept her against his body, crushing her there with one arm while his other hand went over her mouth. "Hola, friend," he called out. "Why are you letting these Greeks keep all the wealth? I am the king's brother, and he has said that we should spoil the heathens and take their gold for our own!"

The soldier's eyes widened. "In truth?"

The money changers were frantically grabbing up their wealth. The man nearest them slid a pile of gold bezants into the skirt of his gown, stuffed silver coins into his sleeves.

"See how they are trying to sneak away like thieves?" Robert shouted back. "Stop them! It is the king's will!"

Faenze wriggled desperately in Robert's grasp, tried to bite his hand, but the sweating fingers on her mouth slid down to her throat and a hard pressure blackened her vision. The last thing she heard was a shout of, "Haro! Haroooo!" from the Flemings. The last thing she saw, before the world went dark, was a shower of golden coins falling into the mud before her and a man's grasping hand being trampled by another's boot.

The woman's hair was like straw, stiff and coarse with whatever preparations she used to bleach it to that unnatural yellow color, probably trying to match those strange light brown eyes with the golden flecks, the eyes that had given her the name she used as a camp follower. And none of that, of course, mattered in the least, nor did the rents in her gown or the splatter of mud that dotted its draggling hem. All that mattered was the tale she was gasping out in her hoarse voice. Eleanor stared into the woman's eyes as though she could read there the meaning of her words, without waiting for Sybille to interpret. The woman was a Fleming, one of those who'd come in the trail of Thierry's army, and so was her man, who had started the shameful riot in the market that afternoon. She didn't want him hanged; Eleanor had understood that much, but what she did not yet know was why Sybille had brought the woman to her.

"Sybille, *I* can say nothing to Thierry of how he does justice among his own men," she interrupted the outpouring of guttural Flemish words mixed with sobs. "If you wish to intercede for him—"

"Too late," Sybille said dryly. She spoke in French, and very quickly, as if in the hope that the camp follower would not understand her. "He has already been hanged—on the word of *your* husband—though I do not believe mine objected. But this woman says he did not start the looting."

A wail of raw pain came from the woman's throat, a sound more animal than human. Eleanor could not bear to look into the golden eyes that had been fixed on her face with such entreaty.

"It is too late now," she said unhappily. Of course one could not expect perfect justice and fairness. A man who would control this turbulent army of knights and pilgrims from all over the Christian world must be seen to act quickly and with a firm hand. And if someone was hanged unjustly, and if women cried, what was new in all that?

"She says," Sybille said, more slowly, "that the king's brother began it, that he told her man and the other soldiers the king had said they might do as they would with the Greeks, that they were not Christians and that it was good to take their gold."

Surely even Robert was not such a fool as that? But . . . Louis would never hang his brother. He might well have ordered a dozen soldiers killed as an example, to show firmness while he vacillated about what to do with Robert. And when he did act, sometimes he was guilty of . . . excess.

She stared at the wall and saw not the patterned marble of Constantinople but the gray stones of an old keep on the Breton coast. A sunny, blood-dappled court-yard, the sound of chopping wood, only it was bone and flesh that was being chopped off, the hands of men whose only fault was to serve William of Lezay . . .

"Then let the council question Robert," she said. "What does she think I can do?"

A burst of Flemish from the weeping woman; Sybille nodded impatiently and said, "*Ja, ja,*" several times, as one listening to a tale she had already heard. "Gerda Goldeneyes says that Robert cannot be brought before the council, because when the riot began he hastened aboard the ship my husband had hired for the Crusaders and it took him and all his men across the Bosporus. And with him he took one of your women."

Eleanor felt cold. "Faenze . . ." She had missed the girl, assumed she was in some corner of the Philopation whispering with Alexios. "Did she go with him willingly?" She bent over Gerda as though she could shake truth out of the coarse lion's mane that fell over the golden eyes. "Tell me! She did not!"

Gerda shook her head and wept into her hands while Sybille questioned her in their harsh tongue. Broken words and sobs alternated with sharp questions while Eleanor felt the chill of loss and danger sinking deeper, into her bones. "It's a pity she understood about her man," Sybille said dryly at last. "It is hard to get much sense out of her now. She claims she could not see, she was knocked down in the riot and took shelter under a table. She saw the girl with Robert and knew her, she thinks she heard her cry out, but there were other women screaming, you understand? She doesn't know exactly what happened. But . . . the ship is gone." She laughed shakily. "Dear Christ, help us, the ship has crossed, Thierry is raging to heaven, a man's been hanged for looting, and God knows how many others died in the riot . . . and I'm going to give my blue gown to a blowzy camp follower." She laughed again. "It's all I can think of to do."

"Oh, I do believe we can do more than that," Eleanor said, turning so quickly that the trailing skirts of her gown rustled across the floor and brushed the knees of the sobbing woman.

She did not wait for summons or permission to enter; no one would have heard her, anyway. Through the hanging curtain that gave a semblance of privacy, she could hear the council room echoing with the same pointless arguments she'd heard before. Except that now there was a new edge of—what? Desperation? Or plain viciousness? Something that set her teeth on edge even as she lifted the curtain and fell to her knees before Louis.

"My lord, I beg your help!"

"Not *now*, my love." Louis rested one hand on her hair.

"Faenze—"

"Who?"

"My waiting woman. Your brother Robert has taken her and the ship and crossed the Bosporus."

"So we have already heard," said Thierry of Flanders in dry tones that reminded her of Sybille.

"And a damned good idea, too!" Geoffrey de Rancon shouted. "He at least won't do homage to the emperor! So should we all cross before complying with these insulting demands!"

"My lord, he has taken my waiting woman against her will," Eleanor said. "Will you do nothing?"

Someone snickered and made a coarse joke. Eleanor tried to close her ears to the arguments and the laughter while she waited, eyes fixed on Louis. His pale, narrow face betrayed nothing. He glanced at Arnulf, then at Geoffrey. "What can I do?" he said at last. "Those who have already crossed the Bosporus are beyond my reach. Can I make ships for the rest of the army appear out of thin air?"

"Robert has insulted your majesty and that of the emperor." Eleanor tried to find arguments that would touch Louis's pride. "I am sure Manuel would give you a ship to pursue him if you requested—"

"*I* say," Geoffrey de Rancon interrupted, "we make no more *humble requests* of these heathen Greeks! Let us take the city instead!"

"An action that will surely inspire the emperor to trust us and give us the ships we require for the crossing," Arnulf of Lisieux said with a sharp edge of sarcasm in his voice.

"Once we hold the city, we can dictate our own terms!"

"And we shall be rich—"

"I could rebuild Taillebourg with the contents of just one of those churches the king's brother told us of!"

"And I could buy back the half of my fief from the damned Jew moneylenders—"

Louis's eyes widened. He was no longer looking at Eleanor; no one was. "My vow was to save the Holy Land," he said quietly. "If no one else remembers that promise, I shall go on alone, but I shall not stop until I see the place where Our Lord died for our sins."

His calm statement was lost in the tempest of debate and greed that had swept over the council. One man shouted the virtues of attacking the city walls where they had been seen to crumble, while another argued for a stealthy entrance into the city and taking the emperor hostage. The bishop of Langres pointed out that the city's water supply came by great conduits leading from the mountains; by cutting those conduits they would be able to force the Greeks into submission. "And if this city alone is taken, it will not be necessary to conquer the other Greeks in their cities, for they will yield obedience voluntarily to him who possesses their capital."

"What if they have reservoirs within the city? I have heard they build great tanks under the ground—"

"However big," Godfrey of Langres snapped, "they are surely not of infinite capacity!"

Arnulf of Lisieux raised his eyes and his hands to heaven. "By all means," he said, "if slaughtering Christians wipes out sins, let us take the city. If it is as important to die for the sake of gaining wealth as it is to maintain our vows, then let us throw away our souls for a handful of silver! There is, after all, precedent."

Odo of Deuil, the king's chaplain, stared down his nose at Arnulf and asserted that it must be clear to the meanest intelligence that the Greeks were not true Christians. "If our priests consecrate Mass on Greek altars, the Greeks afterward purify them with propitiatory offerings and ablutions, as if they had been defiled. If one of our men wishes to marry a Greek, they rebaptize him in their rite before they make the pact. Instead of partaking only of the sacred host during the Eucharist, their people partake also of the wine, as though the Mass were an occasion for drunken rejoicing. And worst of all, they assert that the Holy Spirit proceeds from the Father alone, and not equally from the Father and the Son. Furthermore—"

"There you are," said the bishop of Langres with satisfaction. "What more do we need? When they removed the *filioque* from the Creed, they denied Christ. They are more like Jews than Christians!" He turned to Louis. "It is time to show your strength, my lord, to revenge their insults. Constantinople is a barrier between us and our Christian brothers in the Holy Land. Without the emperor's meddling, Edessa might not have fallen. Let us take this city and open up a free road to the East!"

The late afternoon sun slanted in at the windows and gilded the bishop's graying head; the light poured across the marble floor like the shower of gold so many Crusaders envisioned when they thought of the city whose golden walls overlooked their camp. Louis, at the head of the table and farthest from the windows, was not touched by the light, nor was Arnulf of Lisieux, who greeted the shouts of approval from the great lords with his sardonic smile.

At the setting of the sun, a boat will be waiting to convey you to the place of meeting. . . .

No one noticed when Eleanor left the room.

She had assumed that Alexios would accompany the boatman—the one Greek she could talk to and the one who would surely help her to bring back Faenze. But instead of Alexios, the men waiting at the small pier below the Philopation were two smooth-faced eunuchs in court dress who shook their heads when she addressed them. They responded neither to French nor to Latin nor even to her few words of Italian. Perhaps Alexios was waiting for her at the Sacred Palace . . . or perhaps, after all, this invitation really did come from Bertha-Irene.

The waters parted by the boat's silent passage seemed dark and menacing, untouched by the last light that played about the walls and towers and gilded cupolas of Constantinople. A cool breeze ruffled the water. Eleanor shivered and looked up at the great city that seemed to float above her, suspended in the golden light, with no real connection to this lower world of darkness and damp and wavelets slapping against stone walls. What did she know of these people? She must have been mad to leave the camp so, without telling her other women where she was going. She saw herself sinking through the dark waters, mouth full of the salty taste of death, and the rippled surface closing above her with a satisfied whisper.

Mad imaginings! Bertha-Irene had no reason to hate her.

Not yet.

Not now, and not ever, Eleanor told herself. If she was going to Manuel now, it was only to warn him of the Crusaders' treacherous plans and to beg his help in rescuing Faenze. And if she was going to Bertha-Irene, then the empress could help her reach Manuel for the same reason. Whoever had sent this message, there was no treason in her answering it.

The boat came to a halt at a crumbling pier where the sea had eaten away at the carved faces of marble lions. It bumped gently against the marble again and again while the boatman, who had not spoken, scrambled out to hold the mooring rope, and one of the eunuchs offered his hand to assist Eleanor onto the pier.

Before her, the remains of a once-grand marble stairway rose from shadow into an oblique sunset light that cruelly revealed cracks and crumbling steps and the shallow ovals worn by many feet. The other eunuch said something in melodious Greek and gestured upward, then both men returned to the boat.

"Wait," Eleanor said, "how shall I—"

The boat drew away as silently as it had brought her there, leaving her alone on a battered and neglected marble landing where stone lions and gryphons gazed through her with their eyeless, sea-worn heads. Eleanor took a deep breath of the cool, damp, slightly salty air, looked up at the sunlight that gilded the upper steps, lifted her scarlet skirts, and began to climb.

She had no intention of reaching the top breathless and sweaty and discomposed; she stepped slowly, at a queen's deliberate pace. It seemed to her that the setting sun kept pace with her, so that the golden light above and beyond receded as she climbed, and she was always in the shadow.

At the very top of the stairs, the light shone level across gilt mosaic pavements and marble columns. Here, at least, there was no neglect—or, no, Eleanor noted the signs of hasty repair and renovation. Until very recently, the gardens around this palace had been let grow wild; whoever had clipped them back could impose a semblance of order but could not disguise the undisciplined tangle of thorny vines underneath the surface. And the gilding of the tiles before her shone unevenly where, here and there, the golden glow of fired glass was replaced by gold paint upon new stones.

It had been said that the Sacred Palace was so large and comprised so many separate buildings that the emperor himself could not use more than a fraction of the rooms. Eleanor had laughed at that as one of the exaggerations of the Byzantine legend, but the evidence was before her now.

What had not been said was that the emperor whose wealth aroused the Crusaders to such a frenzy of lust was unable to keep the unused portions of his own palaces in order. Was he so poorly served? Eleanor wondered. Or had he spent more than he could afford on fitting up his fleet for this war with Sicily, and was the grandeur of their reception no more than gilding over a secret poverty?

But the small building before her spoke not of sudden poverty but of long neglect hastily remedied. Entering, Eleanor found silken cushions and tapestries hung in mad profusion to cover the marble walls. An inner archway beckoned her into a small courtyard with a fountain in the center bubbling scented water that brought the memory of summer roses into the sharp autumnal air. Torches were fixed into sconces on each of the four inner walls of the courtyard, showing in their trembling light a mosaic of flowers and fruits that carried on the illusion of summer. Braziers burning sweet incense were placed in each corner to take the chill from the evening air.

Eleanor touched the water that bubbled from the fountain; it was warm and left the scent of roses on her fingers.

The words of the Greek romance came back to her: *A fragment of paradise, the dwelling place of pleasure and spring of sweetness.*

It was the pagan God she was meant to pray to here; this whole building was an altar to Eros.

"By my faith and Saint Radegonde," Eleanor said between her teeth, "I am not a sheep to be brought to the sacrifice!"

She spied a further arch beyond the fountain. A few swift steps brought her from torchlight and perfumed smoke to the pale light of the evening sky and the cool, almost biting air of the October night. The mosaic path that led away from this temple of Eros was overgrown and cracked where wild grasses had forced themselves through the grout. On either side, the grass grew waist-high, dry pale stalks heavy with seed heads that whispered against her skirts as she moved slowly from Manuel's garden to the untended wilderness beyond. The light from the torches inside the courtyard shone through the arch and threw her shadow before her, a long, wild, wavering shape of darkness against the sighing sea of grass. Dark square shadows at the end of the path must be unused buildings, long-abandoned parts of the Sacred Palace. Far beyond them, a twinkle of lights along the brow of the hill showed the limits of the living palace. And beyond that, there was only darkness sprinkled with points of light: the sleeping city of Constantinople and the stars above it.

Eleanor shivered in the night wind. It seemed to whisper in her ears of cold and darkness, to carry tales of ancient suffering and loss. This cold night wind was the sort that could carry the army of the dead into the heavens, skeletal warriors on ghostly horses. Such a wind could blow stronger and colder still, could blow all the golden city of Constantinople into an illusion of smoke and mirrors that would vanish with the coming of the morning.

The torchlight that lit the path and picked out sparkles of gold among the broken tiles dimmed, and Eleanor caught her breath, but it was only a man coming through the arch as she had come a few moments earlier.

Only a young, thin-faced, dark man in a silken tunic, not the gilded idol, the emperor who sat upon a jeweled throne in a crown that framed his face with jewels. Only a man.

His arms were strong and warm and alive about her. Eleanor felt an aching emptiness, infinitely painful and infinitely sweet, like nothing she had felt with Louis. Stepping back away from him felt like stepping away from a part of her own living flesh, like giving herself to that night wind and the army of the dead.

Surrounded by that chill wind, she faced the man who was also the emperor, whose face was a dark unreadable shape against the golden light of the torches. "We must have an interpreter," she said slowly and as clearly as she could, praying that he would understand. "I must talk to you."

He answered in heavy, accented, but understandable French. "We have no need of more words, you and I."

"You speak our language?" Surprise made her almost forget the ache of desire. "But then—" Her mind raced. What had been said before this man? What of their secrets did he know?

"Not well. Not enough for . . . diplomacy. Enough for us." And he made to take her in his arms again.

"I did not come for that!" Eleanor pushed him away with both hands. Her palms tingled where she touched him. His chest was well muscled under the silk, she could feel the contours of his body, hard and well formed . . . *she would not think about that*. "There is trouble in the camp. . . . Do you wish to save your city?"

That, at least, caught his attention. He offered her his arm, with no attempt at lovemaking, and she retraced her steps into the torchlit courtyard where she could watch his face as they talked. He knew already about the riot, of course, and said that he had taken appropriate steps. The Crusaders' discussion of sacking the city did not surprise him. "This was always my grandfather's fear, when your people came first from the West," he said slowly. "Conrad would not attack the city of his . . ." He shrugged and waved his hands, giving up on the Western kinship terms. "Like-brother," he said at last. "But your Louis . . ."

"He does not wish it," said Eleanor, "but he is young." *Older than this Manuel.* The excuse rang hollow to her. "He may be . . . he may give in to his advisers. And there is more. You must help me."

Manuel smiled slightly. "To Goldenfoot," he said, "all honor, a home in Byzantium, whatever she desires . . ."

Eleanor stamped her foot with frustration. "You are mad! This is not about me, it is my woman who needs your help. The girl Alexios loves." She told him what she had learned of the riot and how Robert had used it as cover for carrying off

Faenze, taking her and his men across the Bosporus in the single ship the Franks had been able to hire.

"And what should I do?" Manuel asked, as calm as though he had not understood the situation.

Eleanor stared at his handsome, unreadable, foreign face. "You are the emperor. You have ships and men. You can go after her. . . ."

"A Greek army fights a Frankish lord and his soldiers to take away a Frankish girl," Manuel said without expression. "Do you wish war? This is no way to avert it."

Eleanor bit her lip, considering. He was right; he could not openly pursue the king's brother and instigate a battle for Faenze, not without precipitating the war between Greek and Frank that they both wished to avoid.

"I have taken steps," Manuel said again. "I have recalled some part of the fleet that I had hoped to send against Sicily." He shrugged. "Roger of Sicily has offended us gravely by his attacks on Greek cities, but we can spare a few ships in the service of Christ. By tomorrow night three of my ships will be at your lords' disposal. So may all you Franks cross the Bosporus, putting them beyond reach of our walls . . . and then perhaps you will be able to find Alexios's Faenze as well. Does this please you, queen of my heart?"

"There is no need for honeyed words," Eleanor said. *Faenze.* Would tomorrow be too late for her? She could only pray not.

"Forgive me. My poor command of your language," Manuel apologized with a half smile. "I have learned my phrases from Frankish songs of love."

"We also," Eleanor warned him, "have songs of war. What if my people will not cross now? Too many of them are hungry for war." And for the riches that had so carelessly been displayed to them; but she was ashamed to say that.

"They will get war enough from the Turks," Manuel said, "and as for hunger . . . The market is closed now; no one can expect me to provide food and goods for men who loot. But with the fleet, I have also recalled the merchant ships that were to provide for the fighting ones. There will be new ships and a new market . . . on the far side of the Bosporus. If your army would eat, they will cross."

Eleanor nodded slowly. It seemed likely that the provision of ships and food would outweigh the chance of loot offered by Constantinople. With this information, Arnulf and the other sensible men in the Crusading army should be able to dampen the hot tempers of the lords who were already drooling over the wealth of the city.

There had really been no need for her to come. The emperor of Constantinople needed no warning, no guidance from her, and he offered her no help for Faenze, save a chance to cross after Robert and Faenze and to do what she might on the far side of the Bosporus. But when she said as much, Manuel shook his head and placed one hand lightly on her arm. His touch was warm through the silken sleeve and the linen undertunic. "You will go with your army," he said in tones of deep regret.

Eleanor gave him a sharp smile. "You would not have it otherwise," she told him. "Constantinople is too precious for you to risk a war with our Crusaders. And you *know* that Louis would surely join those who were urging the sack of Constantinople if I stayed here . . . if I were mad enough to stay . . . if I were fool enough to trade all Aquitaine and Poitou for a house on the Golden Horn!"

"If you were on this side the Bosporus, and Louis and all his army on the other . . ."

"Your French is poorer than I thought," Eleanor said slowly and clearly. "The duchess of Aquitaine is no man's concubine . . . not even an emperor's." But she did not withdraw the arm he touched, and when his other hand came up to cup her chin, she did not move away.

"But even kings and emperors . . . and duchesses . . . must make their sacrifice to Eros," Manuel murmured. His dark, clever face was very close to hers now. She could smell the perfume that scented his tunic, and beneath that, the musky male scent of his body so close to hers, so different from Louis's.

"I am no sheep to be led to sacrifice," Eleanor said, but still she did not move away.

"No. But the pagan Greeks of old wrote that sometimes, in time of great need, a king would go consenting, to save his people. So might a queen go."

"As the price of the ships?" Eleanor's brows arched, and she took a half step backward. "I think you mistake your company. If it is a whore you want, there are women enough in Constantinople to satisfy your need." She remembered the dark girl who had clung to Manuel's sleeve on the night of the banquet. His own niece!

"It is a queen I desire tonight," Manuel said, "and there is no price and no payment save what is freely offered and freely given."

Amors de terra loindana . . .

Chapter Fourteen

ercle-le-Monde shifted his pack and gazed morosely across the choppy black waters of the Bosporus. The short crossing had thoroughly unsettled his stomach, an unfortunate weakness for one with his name. *"Dex,* but I never planned to circle this much of the world, or knew it extended so far!" he muttered under his breath. At least the worst was behind them now—no more water. They were to march overland the rest of the way.

Waiting for the ship had been worse, anticipation churning his stomach, than this second long wait while the army assembled itself and prepared for the march. The king and his personal retinue had been the last to cross, and as the queen's man, Cercle-le-Monde had waited to take ship with her. Waited while the king and the nobles debated up to the last minute as to the exact terms of homage the emperor would require, waited while the army went half mad over rumors that the German army ahead of them had already defeated the Turks at Konya and would reach Jerusalem first, waited while Louis finally promised Manuel homage in advance over any lands and cities belonging to Constantinople that he might reconquer from the Turks on his way to Jerusalem.

The days they spent in Constantinople had been gilded by the October sun, but on this morning of departure the sun was weak and pale in the sky and the winds that flicked Cercle-le-Monde's cloak whispered that winter was coming, winter in a place of unfamiliar mountains and enemies who knew this land far better than they could ever hope to learn it . . .

He shook his head impatiently, as if to shake the buzzing dreams out of it, and looked at his lady. *She* at least was not apprehensive of what might lie ahead. Since the day when Manuel agreed to bring back his fleet to ferry the Crusaders across the Bosporus, she had been vibrant and confident as he had not seen her in many years—not since the day of that wedding in Poitiers, when showers of jewel-studded comfits distracted the southern nobles from the quiet departure of their young duchess.

He had made a song about that day, when the lady of Aquitaine deserted them from the north and took the sun with her, leaving her Poitevins to a winter of mourning. What they needed now, he thought, looking at the damp foot soldiers and pilgrims thronging the shore, was another song, one to remind them of the reason for this march, one to put into the army some of that spirit of life he saw blazing in his golden lady on her white horse.

exilla regis prodeunt," Cercle-le-Monde sang in his high, carrying tenor, the voice trained to fill a castle hall—or a battlefield. "The standard of the king comes forth."

The banners of each contingent fluttered free under the pale autumn sun: the blue and gold of France, the white cross of Savoy, the golden lion of Aquitaine, the stark sable and silver of the Knights Templar. The foot soldiers nearest Cercle-le-Monde took up the song.

> "Vexilla regis prodeunt,
> Fulget crucis mysterium,
> Qua vita mortem portulit,
> Et morte vitam protulit."

Some fifty leagues to the southeast, on the road to the Turkish stronghold of Konya, arrows whistled through the encampment of the German army. The lightly armed horsemen with their strange pointed helms and their agile little ponies had first descended in the half-light of dawn, buzzing around the camp like wasps who could send out their deadly stings in all directions. They had struck and disappeared into the forested hills before the German knights could arm and ride out against them. Twice parties of mailed knights tried to ride out from the camp and follow the Turkish attackers; archers hidden in the trees shot their horses out from under them, then practiced finding gaps in the armor of the lumbering, overburdened knights. Very few made it back to the dubious safety of the camp. One of those who did reach the German lines gasped out his story in ever-weakening sighs, until the squire who was trying to remove his armor found that a deep arrow wound in his side had caused internal bleeding. He died before the greaves were unlaced from his feet.

> *"Quai vulnerata lanceae*
> *Mucrone diro, criminum,*
> *Ut nos lavaret sordibus,*
> *Manavit unda et sanguine."*

The French army sang lustily of the wound in their Savior's side and the blood that had washed them all clean of sin. The bishops of Langres and Lisieux joined in the chant, lifting strong voices to encourage the wavering. The banners of Savoy and Montferrat followed those of France, and among them the lusty Crusading hymn lost some of its strength; the king's uncle, Amadeus of Savoy, was old enough to prefer a quiet discussion of Turcopole tactics to the rousing cadences of the song.

Unable to pursue the Turcopole attackers, dying one by one from arrow shots loosed by solitary men who appeared and disappeared like evil spirits of the forest that surrounded them, the Germans decided during a brief lull in the attack to break camp and march for Konya. If they were quick enough, they might be able to form a defensive line of march before the Turks returned. Baggage and tents would have to be abandoned, the wounded were lucky if any man took the time to slit their throats and save them from death at heathen hands. The army had become a mass of sodden, muddy, demoralized men stumbling into something that might charitably have been described as a marching formation. The Emperor Conrad's nephew, Frederick of Swabia, rode up and down the lines and exhorted his men with pungent Swabian oaths to keep their fornicating shields *up* and their dung-eating heads *down* and their worthless, maggot-food bodies in *line*.

243

As the straggling column moved out of camp, the light dimmed suddenly, as though night had fallen in the middle of the day. Fearful soldiers looked up, distracted and then terrified by the sight of a black hole eating the pallid sun—and through the sky they stared at came the whir of arrows, a spiked rain that fell with deadly effect and destroyed all Frederick's efforts to achieve some semblance of order in the army.

In the rear guard, and grumbling mightily that the southerners always got the short end of the stick, marched the men of the Languedoc: Black Hugh of Lusignan, Geoffrey de Rancon, and others who had cut their teeth on songs like sword blades and swords like songs, in the ceaseless strife that occupied the barons of Aquitaine whenever their lord looked away. When his knights cried out in alarm at the partial eclipse of the sun, Geoffrey de Rancon bellowed at them that they were no better than gossipy old women.

"It's a good sign," he declared. "It's a sign of that Turkish defeat we were hearing about. Now shut up and sing, and look lively about it!"

> *"Impleta sunt, quae concinit*
> *David fideli carmine . . ."*

Singing of the sacred wood and the sacred tree on which Our Lord made His sacrifice, the men of France and Savoy, Auvergne and Montferrat, Flanders and Burgundy, Aquitaine and Poitou marched forth to their own certain victory and salvation.

In the forests before Konya, the blood of German soldiers watered the trees, and their bodies were left to enrich the soil of the woods. The foot soldiers were the first to die; after them, the Turks pursued the knights who tried desperately to outride them on winding, unfamiliar trails. The branches of the trees choked them and the hidden gullies of ancient streambeds broke their horses' legs, and heathen shouts filled their ears as they died, two or three together fighting back to back at the last, or one man hurled from his horse and mercifully stunned by the fall. A handful escaped, chancing by luck on paths that did not end in a tangle of underbrush and that were not already haunted by enemy soldiers. With Germans darting in all directions like rats before the harvesters' sickles, the Turkish harvesters could hardly spare time and energy to chase them all and mow them down.

Of seventy thousand mailed knights and twice that many foot soldiers, fewer than ten thousand escaped the slaughter after the army was broken in that dark wood; ten thousand of two hundred thousand, spared to face hunger, cold, and the rest of the Turkish nation.

Among them were the emperor and his nephew.

In the first days of the march south along the coast, Eleanor loved it all: the morning and evening smoke of the campfires, the cold clean winds off the mountains, the icy streams they washed in, the slow unfolding of new hills and forests. They saw no Turks; the only Greeks were those on the market ships that followed the army and supplied them with provisions. She felt as if she were reborn and riding into a world made new with promise. The leaves on the trees were filled with green light, the droplets of water that clung to their edges and that sprinkled the riders were like a continual light baptism in water more holy than any stale basinful in a church font. Belle-Belle, the pretty white palfrey that Amicie de Périgné had bought for her in Hungary, tossed her head and almost danced along the narrow path. A lucky chance, that, having her master of horse join the Crusade; she had not been so well mounted since she went to Paris. The earth beneath her palfrey's feet and the trees rising above their heads were her cathedral, the graceful arch of the branches more lovely than anything little Abbot Suger could cause to be made in stone, the mosaic of green leaves and pale blue sky finer than any window of stained- and leaded-glass pieces.

"You," Sybille of Flanders said once when they were riding together, "are *enjoying* this."

Eleanor laughed. "Mea culpa! Would you rather I sighed and moaned and took to a litter like Mathilde?" She glanced behind them, where the covered litters favored by the count of Savoy's wife—and, to be honest, by most of the ladies who had come this far—slowed the army's progress even worse than the ragtag of impoverished pilgrims marching behind the foot soldiers.

"No," Sybille said dryly. "I would rather my bones were as young as yours. *I* enjoyed our month in Constantinople." She sighed with pleasurable memories.

Pleasure and memory of a different sort ran through Eleanor's body, a liquidity of desire that sang through her own bones and trembled in the soft responsive flesh. That night—her skin had been on fire; she had discovered what Cercle-le-Monde and the others sang about.

But it had been one night, not even that, really, two stolen hours of joy, to set against a life and a duchy and the land of Aquitaine. Not enough to weigh in the balance.

"Constantinople," she said firmly, "was a dream." *Or an awakening.* "This is real, and we are alive and in it, and I will not willingly miss one breath I take in this world while I live in it. I want to see everything and know everything and do everything and . . ." She had to pause for breath, and Sybille laughed softly.

"You sound like my brother Geoffrey. You two are very like."

"Are we?" Eleanor asked idly. She remembered when Geoffrey had been discussed as a possible match for her, when she was fifteen and the unprotected heiress of Aquitaine. But he'd never been a real possibility; he was already married to Matilda, the widow of the old German emperor and possibly the heir to England, and divorces took time.

"Tall and fair—yes, these days of riding in the sun have gilded your hair, you know, though it's not the true gold of Geoffrey's—and so sure of yourselves, so hungry for life." Sybille sighed. "The two of you together would have been something to see. . . . Do you sometimes wish you had been born a common peasant, free to marry the handsomest boy at the village dance? Women of our station—and men, too—are never free to marry to please themselves."

"Sometimes," Eleanor said, "pleasure and policy go hand in hand."

Sybille glanced toward the van, where Louis's gold and blue banner waved above the heads of his mounted knights, with beside it the white and red cross of the Knights Templar.

And sometimes they can be made to do so. A resolve as yet unexpressed was quickening in Eleanor, something slow and hidden, like a flicker of life within her belly. Divorces took time . . . but they were possible. Nearly everybody in Europe was related within one of the church's forbidden degrees, if one looked back far enough. She and Louis had a relationship too distant for scandal but not too distant for the church to ignore, if anyone chose to point it out. Bernard of Clairvaux had already pointed it out, in fact, though his protests had gone unnoticed in the general scandal of Raoul's putting aside his wife Leonora to marry little Petronilla. The excuse for *that* divorce had been a bar of consanguinity between Raoul and Leonora, and Bernard had written to his friends that Louis had no right to concern himself with other people's relationships when he himself was openly living with a woman who was his cousin in the third degree. Eleanor could go over the genealogies in her head; Robert the Pious, king of France, was Louis's direct ancestor, and his granddaughter Audiard of Burgundy had married into the Poitevin line and was Eleanor's great-grandmother. She was not precisely sure that she could call herself Louis's cousin, but some relationship within the forbidden degrees surely existed. And there had been no papal dispensation for that hasty wedding.

She spurred her horse to ride well ahead of Sybille, who could not stand the bone-jarring canter of her own mount. Better the mud splashed up by the mounted knights ahead of them than this continuous trickle of irritating conversation. She wanted to be alone with her own thoughts and memories. She could never have remained in Constantinople; she would never forget two hours stolen from politics and ceremony for the worship of an older god than any the church knew.

Louis had not visited her bed while they were in Constantinople, nor since then. She had never looked forward to his visits. Now, knowing what sweetness could be between a man and a woman, she dreaded them. And he would almost certainly leave her alone on the march; he was not a man to make love in a tent in the middle of an army camp, knowing the soldiers outside would be envying and speculating.

The road they followed left the coast at a rocky promontory that gave no place for the horses' hooves and turned slightly inland to go up through pine forests, up and up toward the clear, clean air of the mountains. Eleanor took deep breaths of the resinous air and thought, carefully, of nothing at all. Not of the past, for she had left Constantinople and would never return; not of the future, for there was something there she was not quite ready to look at yet. It was enough to be alive, in this moment, breathing in leaf mold and the scent of resin and the cold November air . . . almost perfect, save for an underlying sweetish taint that crept in and spoiled it for her.

At the next bend in the road, they came upon the first corpses, and the sweet smell of decay filled everybody's nostrils and Eleanor bent retching over her saddle until someone shoved a pomander into her hand.

"They're Germans," reported a squire who dismounted to examine the bodies. "All Germans . . . No Turks, not one."

"I wonder," said somebody in the hush that followed this discovery, "why the Turks didn't take their armor?"

The answer to that question became clear as they rode on along the winding coastal road. There were so many dead, tens upon tens upon hundreds, beyond any man's counting, so many that the Turks had not even bothered to strip any but the richest of the fallen.

They had to ride farther than they had meant that day, to find a place to camp where the stench of death did not hang closer than the smoke over their campfires. A rocky promontory off the road seemed good to the army's leaders, a clean place and one that could be guarded during the night by a single line of men placed across the narrow neck of the little peninsula.

After that day, the order of march was changed. The king's royal person was too valuable to be placed in the van, where they might expect first to encounter the Turks. Louis and the knights and barons of France took up the rear guard, with other groups arranged before them in order of importance . . . with one exception. Eleanor refused to ride in the mud stirred up by thousands of marching knights and befouled by their horses. The ladies who traveled in litters might stay safe in the rear if they liked; she would ride at the head of the army. To Louis's vague protestations of fear for her safety, she answered that she had no fear where her men of the south were with her, and *they* had no fear of meeting the Turks they had come to fight. A lift of her chin and a challenging glance brought Black Hugh of Lusignan to her side, and a moment later the younger sons who represented Angoulême and La Marche joined him, with Hautefort and Turenne and the viscount of Limoges not far behind. Louis sighed and named Geoffrey de Rancon and his uncle of Savoy as leaders of the vanguard—one southerner, one Frenchman.

As the march south along the coast progressed, it became easier in one respect: time and climate and marauding animals stripped the dead, leaving nothing behind but bones and armor. Much of the discarded armor was picked up by pilgrims or poorly equipped foot soldiers; by the time the army reached Nicaea, it looked as much German as French.

At Nicaea, Robert of Dreux found them. He and his men had turned back to escort the demoralized remnants of the German army to meet the French. Horses were scarce; no one under the rank of baron rode, not even the women. At the rear of the tatterdemalion column Eleanor saw a familiar green dress, now faded and stained with splotches of rusty brown. The woman in the dress had flung a thread-bare shawl half over her head and face, holding it with one tanned arm in a way that gave her almost the look of the few Turkish women they'd seen from a distance, but where the dress fell away from shoulders too thin to support it, the skin was white as any Frankish maid's.

"Faenze!" Eleanor plunged through the crowd of curious Frenchmen and caught the tanned arm. The woman twisted violently to free herself, and Eleanor glimpsed the gleam of steel flashing in her free hand; then one of Black Hugh's men had her by the wrists. "Hellcat! You want to kill our duchess?"

"It was a mistake," Eleanor said. "I surprised her." She studied Faenze's eyes. They looked half wild, peeping through the tangle of hair that must not have been properly combed since Constantinople, and there was an ugly swollen line running down the side of her cheek, from eye socket to jaw. "Faenze? You know me?"

Faenze gave a creaking laugh. "My . . . my lady. I did not know who touched me. I have taught these animals to be careful how they grab at a French lady!"

"By Saint Sebastian, she has and all!" said one of the German soldiers nearest her, in a thick accent that Eleanor could hardly understand, but his voice seemed almost admiring.

"Come with me," Eleanor said.

"Wait a minute!" The exhausted, filthy foot soldiers moved forward. "You doesn't taking her anyplace she doesn't wanting to be going," said the man who'd spoken first. "You getting that, fine lady?"

"My good man," Black Hugh drawled, "you happen to be speaking to the duchess of Aquitaine."

"Doesn't caring if I be speaking to queen of France—"

"Well," Hugh said reluctantly, "that, too, as it happens."

"This little lady been our luck, see? Anybody hurts her, he going having me to talk to—me, Dieter Wall-eyes!" The German thumped his chest.

After Dieter Wall-eyes and his friends had been assured of Faenze's safety with the fine lady who'd grabbed her arm, Eleanor was finally able to take the girl to her tent. She sent her other ladies away and bathed Faenze with her own hands, put a poultice of pounded yarrow and oil of Saint-John's-wort on the ragged scar that marred her cheek, and dressed her in the first gown she pulled out of the baggage.

"Now," she said, after getting most of a bowl of warm broth down Faenze, "tell me . . . whatever you want to," she hastily substituted for her first impulse to ask for everything that had happened, "and then we shall see about getting you back to Alexios."

Faenze touched the poultice with which Eleanor had covered her cheek. "He will not want me . . . now." She laughed again, that rusty, creaking laugh that reminded Eleanor of the ravens feasting on dead German bodies. "But neither will Robert."

"Did he do this to you?" Eleanor touched the poultice over the terrible, jagged scar.

Faenze's lips twitched. "Yes, but I did worse to him—and in a place nobody sees!"

"Faenze!" In the midst of grief and shock, Eleanor felt a cracked, lunatic laughter bubbling within her to match Faenze's. "You didn't . . . impair his ability to give the countess of Perche a son?"

"Only half of it," Faenze said, "but it seems to have given him a distaste for me. He threw me out to march with the soldiers' women. . . . He had the knife by then . . . he didn't feel like using me as a woman, but he held me down and used the . . . *I don't want to talk about it.*"

"I'll have him hanged," Eleanor said. Unable to sit, she paced the tent, four paces, turn and back, turn and back. "No, first I'll have someone finish the job you started. With a dull knife. *Then* I'll have him hanged."

"The king's brother? I don't think so," Faenze said dryly. Her voice sounded calmer, as though she were gradually coming back to herself. She fondled the blade she had kept by her through all the bathing and dressing, not a lady's knife, but a hefty dagger with a leather-wrapped hilt and a blade worn thin by many sharpenings. "The first soldier who tried to make free with me, I kicked him where it hurts and . . . I thought he would kill me, but he started laughing and said it was a rare thing to meet an honest woman in a baggage train and I should have his second-best knife if I thought I'd have the guts to use it. I only had to use it once or twice . . . then the men started calling me Lady Luck, and no one tried anymore. No one who knew me, anyway."

Louis refused flatly even to consider sending Faenze back north to Constantinople with an escort from the French army, and Eleanor's own vassals agreed for once with his reasoning. The Turks were hovering just out of sight, pouncing to pick off any who lagged behind the army or who became separated from it. Look what happened to Gerhard of Meilhac and his squire when they went hawking, they said. No, let the lady wait for a Greek provision ship, she could get back easily enough that way . . . if she really wanted to go.

But the ships the emperor had sent to provision the army had been growing fewer, and the coastal road turned inward after that rocky promontory, winding up into the mountains, where the concealing trees grew close on either side and they never knew when a flight of arrows would come hissing at them. Between the mountains were streams swollen with winter rains, where the marching army was forced to bunch up while lines of pack animals helped the men across one by one. The Turks liked those spots; arrows loosed from the mountaintops were sure of finding some target in the crowd of men and animals. Food was whatever they could terrorize the Greek villagers into giving up—never enough; fodder for the animals was whatever leafy bits remained on winter-lashed trees and bushes. The knights saw to it that their horses got the best of what there was, so the packmules one by one foundered and died, and the villagers were repaid for loss of their winter stores by carrying off the richest parts of the abandoned baggage.

"We are marching with Death," the knights grumbled. Faenze, riding pillion behind Eleanor, thought that she rode with Life. Eleanor glowed with a seductive, luxuriant vitality that drew longing looks from all the men who rode with her. Her cheeks were bright from the stinging cold of the mountain winds, her breasts were high and full against the fine fabric of her gown, and a feverish vitality infused her words and gestures. She kept the men of Provence and Aquitaine, the Poitevins and the Limousins, cheerful and defiant with the marching songs that Cercle-le-Monde invented and that she sang in her high, clear voice.

"Where death is closest, life is sweetest," she told Faenze once. "Do you not feel it? How shall we go back to being immured in stone walls after the freedom of the road?"

"With deep gratitude to God, if He allows us to live so long," Sybille of Flanders suggested. She cast a measuring glance at Eleanor's waistline and later spoke quietly to Faenze, saying it was strange that her lady should bloom so in hardship. Had she noticed anything odd since she returned to wait on Eleanor? Sickness in the morning, tenderness about the breasts?

"My lady prayed for a child," Faenze said. "In Constantinople she prayed with the empress. If God chose to grant her prayer—"

"Then He chose a damnably uncomfortable time to do so," said Sybille. "Do *you* pray that it is not so, child, for how we shall take a pregnant woman over these mountains all the way to Jerusalem I do not even wish to imagine."

The road turned back to the coast at Ephesus, and there was a ship from Manuel and messengers who warned the king that the Turks had a large force waiting ahead. "Those who harried you up to now were nothing, stragglers, freebooters, brigands," the messengers said earnestly. "Ahead of you is an army twice the size of that which defeated the Germans. Take refuge here where we have walls to protect you."

When Louis refused to consider retreat, the messengers warned him that the emperor was seriously displeased to hear how his men had been threatening and pillaging the Greek villages along their way.

"We must eat! If the emperor would protect his people, let him provide provisions as he agreed," Godfrey of Langres said angrily before Louis could speak.

"The emperor cannot provide for you when you take these mountain roads," the principal messenger said. "If you will remain at Ephesus, we will see what can be done. If not . . ." He shrugged. "Our people are angry; they say you Franks are worse than the Turks. The emperor may not be able to restrain his people from vengeance in the future."

"The restraining hand of the emperor," Arnulf of Lisieux said, "has not been notably evident up to now."

"Then," Cercle-le-Monde reported to the ladies, "Conrad of Hohenstaufen claimed he had been feeling ill and would return to Constantinople by this ship . . . for his health."

"When half the survivors of his army have marched on ahead of us?" exclaimed Eleanor. "How can he abandon them?"

"His nephew Frederick remains with us as his deputy." Cercle-le-Monde regarded Faenze thoughtfully. She was thinner and browner, as were they all. The scar along her cheek was somewhat healed now, but all Eleanor's applications of ointments and charms had not prevented the infected wound from leaving a rough, raised line that would mar her beauty forever. "The Greek ship will be leaving soon."

Faenze touched her cheek and shook her head slightly.

"Faenze, you should go," Eleanor said. "Alexios will not care about. . . . Oh, talk some sense into her, Cercle-le-Monde! You are always so eager to sing about the delights of love, perhaps you can bring these two lovers together again!"

"I cannot go now," Faenze said flatly when Cercle-le-Monde got her alone. "Maybe later."

"There may be no *later* for any of us."

"Then *you* take ship with the Greeks, if you are so eager to run away and leave her! I cannot. She must have some woman she can trust with her, now of all times."

Cercle-le-Monde's fingers drummed a rough tarantella on the canvas of the tent. "Even Louis would not be such a fool as to get a woman with child in the midst of this death march," he said, but without conviction.

"Louis," Faenze said in a very low voice, "has not been to her bed since before we reached Constantinople . . . and she *is* with child, perhaps six weeks gone."

Cercle-le-Monde whistled, long and low. "What does she say?"

"She says nothing, and she will suffer me to say nothing. But I know the signs," Faenze said. "She is certainly with child. We are all so thin now that perhaps it can be concealed a month or two longer, but the time must come when it is known. *Now* do you see why I cannot leave her?"

"Perhaps," Cercle-le-Monde said, "I had better begin to tell Louis tales of miracles, when I am sent to amuse him. It may serve to prepare his mind."

A fter Ephesus, the winter rains began in earnest, swelling already flooded streams. At Decervium, the army was half on one side and half on the other of a knee-deep, foamy brown stream when a wall of water roared out of the mountains and swept away tents, baggage, all who had the misfortune to be in the river. They spent the rest of the brief winter day marching upstream to find a place where it was possible to cross the water, and most of the night shivering beside sullen fires of rain-drenched, green sticks.

"We should give thanks to God's mercy that the Turks did not fall upon us while the army was divided," Louis said.

"And maybe we should ask God exactly where the Turks are, since they were not waiting here," Thierry of Flanders said in an undertone.

Two days later they found out.

The Greek peasants they had captured as guides had promised them that the great river ahead, the Maeander, flowed out into a wide valley where it was all little streams and shifting rocks, unpleasant but not difficult to cross. Ordinarily this might have been true. When they reached the valley, though, the "little streams" were joined together into one racing, roaring mass of turbulent, muddy water. The scouting party Thierry sent upstream to seek out a ford came back in disarray, with arrows sticking out of two horses, panting a story of Turkish forces on the mountaintop.

"Can't be," Ivo of Soissons said, "they're on the far side of the river. Look!"

"They're everywhere," said Guillaume de Macon, "and we're trapped."

After a hasty conference, it was decided that the army would have to fight its way upstream again, to the one place the scouts had found that might be possible to ford.

"It's full of Turks!" one of the surviving scouts protested.

"Turks," Thierry of Flanders said, "can be shifted. Water is more difficult. Let us reach the ford, we shall see what can be done about the heathen."

In close order, with the women, the wounded, and the remaining baggage protected as best they could be in the center of the army, the French advanced slowly up the rocky slopes of the valley, constantly harassed by Turkish archers who appeared from the concealment of the trees, fired off a few arrows, and disappeared again.

"You five," Geoffrey de Rancon told his men, "you with the best horses, group behind me. Next time those cowardly heathen appear, we'll chase them down."

"You'll do no such thing," said Everard de Barres, grand master of the Templars. "Didn't you learn anything from the Germans' experience?"

"Germans!" Geoffrey de Rancon spat on the ground. "Easy to kill, and all dead. What should I learn from them but the road to heaven—or hell?"

"Not all dead," Everard said, "and young Frederick told us something of Turkish tactics. The main body of their men is out of sight; if you follow the Turkish archers, they'll lead you into a trap and you'll be cut down. So if you want to follow the Germans to hell"—he shrugged elaborately—"I *would* have no particular objection, save that we may need even thick-headed southern knights to defend the ford when we get to it."

Geoffrey gave in when Louis supported the Templar, but not without muttering and grumbling.

After two days of their miserable, slow progress back into the hills, the army reached the ford the scouts had reported: thirty feet of foaming water and treacherous currents, with a Turkish force on the far bank jeering at them.

"Let me go first," Henry, the young son of the count of Champagne, begged. "My men can scatter them and make it safe to cross. They can't take a charge of our men in full armor."

"Good lad." Geoffrey de Rancon thoughtfully examined his sword. "I'll go with you. My gentlemen are getting bored."

"Wait—we need to make a plan!" Everard de Barres shouted, but too late. The men of Champagne and Languedoc were already urging their horses into the muddy water after Henry and Geoffrey, shouting defiance at the Turks, who loosed a shower of arrows upon them.

"There's more of the pagan bastards coming on this side! Let's get to work, Flemings!" Thierry of Flanders barked, wheeling his horse. Shoulder to shoulder with the master of the Temple, he rode to meet the Turkish force advancing from the shelter of the trees. The weight of horses and armed men shook the unstable, waterlogged earth. The Turks, unprepared for a cavalry charge and unable to form their own lines after being dispersed among the trees, turned and fled. Those few who remained the Franks cut down with great sweeping blows of their heavy swords. Turkish silks and leather, so light and handy for maneuvering, were no protection in the melee against the weight of Frankish iron.

"We could get more," Thierry protested when Everard de Barres swung his arm up and shouted an order to retreat. "Did you see the *jewels* on some of these corpses?"

"Better than that," Everard said, "we can get across the river now. Look!"

The men of Champagne and Languedoc had had a similar success with their charge against the Turks on the far side of the Maeander. The ford was clear now, and the army was already making its snaillike way across.

At least I got these gold chains," Thierry said when they were comparing notes that evening, "and an emerald the size of a pigeon's egg from this one heathen's turban. I wish we'd had time to search the bodies."

"There'll be more," Geoffrey de Rancon said with a wolfish grin.

"Quite likely there will," said Everard de Barres, "since most of them escaped into the mountains. Don't think it will be so easy next time."

But there was no "next time," no more satisfying melees and charges. The Turks had learned their lesson. Massed in an open place, they could not stand up to a charge from the Frankish heavy cavalry. But they could retreat into their mountain fastnesses to regroup, could attack the marching column with darting advances of archers who appeared and disappeared like swarms of wasps, could use their better knowledge of the terrain to select places where the French could not form up for a charge. From the Maeander to Laodicea, the Crusaders were never left in peace, never had the chance for a good fight on what they considered fair terms, never dry and never fed.

At Laodicea, where there should have been food and shelter, there was a deserted town that had already been sacked by the Turks; the Greeks had fled into their own mountain hiding places. It was impossible to get enough food to provision the army for the march to the next safe place, the fortified Byzantine city of Adalia; it was hopeless to wait for the Turkish attack at Laodicea. Men made short-tempered by hunger and cold and the continual buzzing danger of Turkish attacks that picked off one or two at a time tightened their belts and grumbled at one another. When three separate quarrels between northern Frenchmen and those of the Languedoc turned into three separate and bloody fights, Everard de Barres overrode the king's hesitation and decreed that the order of march from Laodicea should separate the two groups. Geoffrey de Rancon demanded the honor of the vanguard for Languedoc, and Everard cheerfully agreed.

Louis was petulant that Eleanor chose to ride with her men of the south instead of remaining in the rear with him and the French lords. "Cercle-le-Monde, fall back to the rear and amuse the king," Eleanor said desperately. "I *cannot . . .*" She bit her lip. It would be improper in a queen to complain to her servant that she could not bear the king's eyes always on her, his continual soft suggestions that she must be tired and should ride in a litter like the other ladies, the vague undercurrent of mistrust on his part and distaste on hers that had drifted like a miasma between them since Constantinople. Since the hours with Manuel, Eleanor knew she could not willingly lie with Louis again. What she would do about that, when the time came that he had privacy enough and desired her, she did not know. Nor did she know what she would do about the child growing within her, the child of whom she had not spoken with anyone—not even Faenze, who watched her with a cool, gray, measuring look, made no irritating suggestions about rest and hot possets, but somehow made sure that Eleanor ate her share of their coarse meals and did not tire herself wandering about the evening camps.

But, of course, there was no need to explain anything to Cercle-le-Monde. He was her man, and if she desired him to spend this day of march entertaining the king, he would go with no questions asked.

She thought that perhaps he did not need to ask anybody. It was seven weeks now since they had left Constantinople. How soon would her condition be obvious . . . and what would she do then? Perhaps more to the point, what would Louis do?

The winter rains had mercifully stopped for a few days, and as the vanguard marched out of Laodicea, the gray clouds that had hung overhead began to part, showing tattered ribbons of pale blue sky. A lusty, swinging song in the sweet language of the south began somewhere behind them, among the men of Lusignan, and spread up and down the ranks. Eleanor recognized with a grin one of the more improper verses of that exceedingly improper troubadour poet, her grandfather, Duke William of Aquitaine.

> "As the wood is cut, the thicker it grows,
> And what is taken, nobody knows.
> He who's lost nothing had nothing to lose,
> And ladies should love wherever they choose."

"And why not?" she said aloud, spurring her horse forward so that only Faenze and Sybille kept up with her.

The last wisps of cloud blew away in the crisp mountain winds; the sky was blue above her, the dry grass golden beneath her horse's feet. Her hair, burnt as much gold as brown by the days of march when she most improperly left off her veil, curled and crackled around her ears like a wild thing set free by sun and dry air after all these mournful days of rain.

"I shall have a son this time," she said without preamble, "a son to hold

Aquitaine for me." Suddenly all was clear as the rain-washed air of these hills. Louis would put her aside, of course. It would be a great scandal...but she would go home, to Aquitaine, and she would have a son to hold the lands after her.

"Are you mad?" whispered Faenze.

Eleanor laughed aloud. "Why, yes, perhaps I am a little mad...and wholly happy. Rejoice with me. You will like Poitou, Faenze. We will go home to Poitou, and I will have my son there, and we will marry you to some handsome young vassal of mine—oh, we have courtly men in the south, men who know how to dance and how to sing and how to love a lady. We will all be happy again." It was so simple, when you thought about it clearly. The marriage to Louis was a dreadful mistake, but mistakes could be undone. She would tell Louis all the truth that night, when they camped in the valley before Mount Cadmos...or perhaps not just yet; better to tell him when they reached Antioch. "I have a kinsman in Antioch, did you know that?" she said happily to Sybille. "My uncle Raymond—I can just remember him, he left for Outremer when I was a little girl." A big, blond, laughing man who had picked her up by the knees and slung her upside down over his shoulder, again and again, while she shrieked with delight and old Radegonde squawked that he was a scandalous rascal and he must not frighten her little lady. "He married Constance of Antioch, and now he holds the town in her right. They say," she said a little sadly, "that it was a love match, not just a marriage for his own advantage." The path narrowed, and she drew ahead of Faenze and Sybille, content to ride with her face in the wind and her mind drifting back to Aquitaine. Someday she too would know sweet love, not for a night but for a lifetime. And not as the concubine of some Eastern emperor, but as duchess of Aquitaine and countess of Poitou. She would take the right man next time; she knew what she was about now.

The hooves of war horses shook the path, and Black Hugh of Lusignan came up beside her, shouldering her horse to the inner edge against the cliff. Clods of dirt crumbled away from the edge under his destrier's hooves; this mountain track was not wide enough for two to ride abreast.

"You must not ride so far ahead of the army," he chid her. "Not that *I* care about your safety, of course, but I don't want the king to hang me for letting his precious lady be attacked by the Turks."

Eleanor glanced up through her lashes and laughed at him. Oh, the joy of talking in her own tongue to someone who didn't need every word spelled out and then had to run to the chaplain to make sure there was no sin in their talk! "Oh, well, Black Hugh, save your worries. My lord of Rancon has charge of the van; he's the one who would suffer, not you."

"Ah, but we should all have to face Saint Peter someday and explain how we let the loveliest lady in Aquitaine be taken by the heathen," Black Hugh said, "and I was never much hand at excusing myself."

"You should be by now," Eleanor said demurely. "I understand your family have had some need to practice.... How is the bishop of Niort these days?" The Lusignans were a byword in Aquitaine for turbulent quarrels, scandalous marriages and divorces, constant disagreements with the church and with their neighbors. Her own father had cursed them roundly for the most troublesome of all his stiff-necked vassals, and old Radegonde had said darkly that one could expect no more of a family descended from that Melusine, the one who changed to a serpent every Saturday night in her bath until her husband peeped through the door and discovered her secret. The latest scandal was that the bishop had excommunicated Hugh for living openly with a concubine while still married to Geoffrey de Rancon's daughter Bergone. Hugh had kept the bishop as a "guest" on short rations in an unheated tower until the excommunication was lifted ... then paid him a silver mark for each day of his enforced stay, "to make sure there were no hard feelings."

Black Hugh laughed and threw up his hand to acknowledge a hit. "The bishop has probably forgiven me. I'm not so sure about Bergone ... but she likes praying better than screwing, anyway. You'll notice her father is still speaking to me. But it did seem like a good time to make pilgrimage to Jerusalem. Besides, it's worth more to me than to most."

"It is? How?"

"I have so many more sins to be forgiven!"

Eleanor laughed with him.

"And by God, I'd commit another one this night, if I thought I'd get the chance," he said with a frankly lustful glance at the gown that strained over Eleanor's full breasts. She was thin everywhere else, but her bosom seemed to be preparing in advance for the child that would not be born for seven months yet.

"Sir," Eleanor said in mock anger, "this is improper talk for a man on his way to the Holy Land. You should do penance.... Let me see." She smiled to herself, considering what to demand. "My troubadour remains with the rear of the army, to entertain the king. You shall take his place tonight. My ladies and I will hear a *sir-vente* on the valiant exploits of our army on its march to the Holy Land."

Black Hugh pretended to wince. "I would prefer a *tenson* on married and un-married love." A *tenson* was a poem written in alternating verses spoken by a man and a woman.

"Why, sir," Eleanor said with a grin, "I do believe we have just had that! The sentence stands; see that you obey it tonight." She kicked her horse into a trot, to pull ahead of Hugh and put an end to the conversation. She wanted to be alone, with the cold winter wind in her face and the blue sky ahead of her and the limit-less space stretching down from the narrow mountain path, to feel herself flying with no rules of priests and kings to weight her down, into a golden future where Aquitaine was hers and she was Aquitaine.

The palfrey checked and stepped clumsily to one side, jolting her out of the dream. At the same moment a piercing cry shrilled through the air: the call of the Turkish archers. Eleanor pulled on the reins to hold the frightened horse back, tried to back it against the cliffside to make room for the men of Lusignan who were gallop-ing forward to attack the Turks, but some fool was behind her and nudging his horse between her and the cliff. Outward on the path the palfrey danced, two steps, three, and clods of earth broke off and fell outward from its hooves. She felt herself slip-ping sideways, trying to manage the horse and urge it back into the safe center of the path, but there was no safe place: only rocks and slippery mud and other, heavier horses, and a rain of arrows whistling about them all. The palfrey screamed and arched its neck and curvetted to the right, into emptiness. There was a shout behind her, and a swarthy hand trying to grab at her reins, but no hand could stop the horse's fall. Branches whipped across her face and tore her hands. She grabbed the thorny branches in a death grip and they checked her fall, but not soon enough to save her slamming belly-first into an outcropping of rock that knocked the breath from her. Something white thundered down the muddy slope, screaming as it went. A branch pulled free of the mud with a sucking sound, and she felt the weight of her body set-tling heavily upon the rocks that had caught her. So sharp they seemed, piercing right through to her back, where the pain gathered and clenched just above her hips . . . How strange; the branch she clung to was wrapping itself about her wrists now, pulling her up and away from the rocks. But its thorns still pierced her hands. She held to them, held to that small pain as though it were the only real thing in the world.

"Let *go*, damn it," growled a voice she had known in life. "I've got you now." Black Hugh hauled her unceremoniously over the edge of the path, stood her up, and dusted her off with brisk slaps. "Determined to get me in trouble, aren't you? I *told* you I didn't want to be hanged for losing the queen."

"Then you'd best let somebody with more sense take her in charge." Where had Geoffrey de Rancon come from? Eleanor looked about her, half dazed. The Turks were routed. Her horse was somewhere far below, screaming in pain until Hugh told one of his own archers to put an arrow through the poor beast's brain.

He took her up behind him for the descent down the mountain; on that narrow path, there was no other choice. Eleanor could feel her muscles stiffening all the jolting way down. The Turks did not reappear, but on the naked downslope with its treacherous screes of loose stones, bones gleamed white among the stones in mute witness that some survivors of the German army, those who had not retreated with Conrad to Nicaea, had made it this far.

In the valley, waiting for the baggage and the rear guard to complete the crossing of the mountain, Eleanor slipped off Hugh's saddle with relief. The mass of aches and scrapes that had pained her at first had settled down now into just one steady, throbbing pain that came and went at irregular intervals, like a fist clenching in the small of her back.

Geoffrey de Rancon spoke with the Lusignan and then came stumping over, weighted by his clanking mail coat, to where Eleanor sat against a tree. "I suppose you'll be wanting a litter now," he said. "Just as well. Women shouldn't try to control their own horses on a march like this."

"I rode down the mountain," Eleanor said, "and I shall be quite able to ride when we resume the march tomorrow."

"Tomorrow!" Geoffrey de Rancon looked up at the sun. "We've half a day's light left. We can be at the top of Cadmos by sunset."

"I thought the king's orders were that we should camp here and cross Cadmos tomorrow, when the army is all together." Eleanor looked up at the treacherous paths they had just traversed, slipping and sliding until each man or animal picked its own way across the scree by little, narrow paths no more than a footstep wide. The baggage animals and their guards were not yet visible at the crest of the mountain. Even supposing those Turks who attacked them had been routed, would it not take the rest of the short winter day for the rear of the army to get to this valley?

Geoffrey snorted. "The *king*, saving your presence, has no military sense. We'd be damned fools to camp in a valley where the Turks can ring us around and shoot down at their pleasure."

"I suppose you may be right. Our marching plans were made without good knowledge of the terrain. Nor did we expect the Turks to attack so soon." Amadeus of Savoy had joined them quietly. As the king's uncle, Eleanor supposed he had authority to override the king's commands.

"We know more now. My men caught a couple of Greeks hiding in the caves. They told us the top of Cadmos is as flat and fine a pasture as we could hope for, and overlooks the surrounding land in all direction, so that nobody can sneak up on us. We'll water the horses here, then push on."

"If the queen is well enough to continue..." Amadeus's voice trailed off. He looked gray and tired himself. His own wife Mathilde was riding in a litter, with the baggage; no doubt he would have been happier to wait until she caught up with them. But Eleanor realized with a sinking feeling that he would not countermand Geoffrey de Rancon's commands... or the king's. He was true kin to Louis; he would worry and fret and never make a decision at all.

He had given her an excuse. She could plead illness, the shock of her fall, and refuse to move, and it was just possible Geoffrey de Rancon would remain in the valley with her. It was certain, she thought, that Black Hugh of Lusignan would do so... even if it meant disobeying Geoffrey's direct orders. She remembered his mocking voice. "I would really prefer not to be hanged for losing the queen." No doubt he would also object to being hanged for disobeying the leader of the vanguard... and Amadeus of Savoy would be no help.

Besides, she was not ill. Not really. A little stiff from her fall, that was all. The nagging pain in her back that came and went would ease with movement, Eleanor told herself. It was nothing serious. It couldn't be. Hadn't she fallen from a horse more times than she could count, emulating her uncle Raymond's tricks and those of the squires who practiced with him? Raymond always said she bounced like a child's tossy ball.

You were nine then. You're twenty-five now, a warning voice in the back of her head told her.

Twenty-five was not old, not old enough to give up the freedom of riding to be bounced in a covered box, not old enough to give up on life. "I can ride on as long

262

as you can," Eleanor told Geoffrey de Rancon. "Shall we make a race of it, or will we stop at the top of Cadmos?"

The pack animal he commandeered for her was a sad change from Belle-Belle, her white palfrey; it had a spine-crunching trot and a shambling walk that made her sway from side to side to keep her balance. Eleanor set her teeth and promised herself that she would not complain. "But there are better horses left in this army," she told Faenze, "and by my faith and Saint Radegonde, tomorrow I'll be mounted as befits a queen! Amicie will see to that." What was the use in having a master of horse with the army, if he could not keep her mounted better than this?

Faenze offered to change horses with her, but Eleanor laughed away the offer. Faenze's mare Gringolet was a perfect mount for her, so calm and lazy she could scarcely be troubled to step over a rock in her path, so greedy she was still almost barrel-shaped after the privations of the long march. Attacked by Turkish archers, Gringolet would simply have backed up and gone hindfirst over the cliff, instead of fighting for the precious seconds that had given Eleanor a chance to grab at safety.

A sharp twinge of pain cut her laugh short, and for a moment she felt her lips pulling tight in the kind of grimace she'd seen on Dangereuse, those days when her grandmother complained of aching bones.

"What is it?"

"Nothing," Eleanor said. "Nothing." It must be this sorry, spavined beast's awkward gait that made her feel as if spears of fire were shooting up her spine with each step; that, and the bruises from the fall. At least it could not be long, now, until they stopped and made camp. She glanced uneasily upward at the pale winter sky, now deepening and streaked with tones of rose and gilt. How long, now, until darkness overtook them? With all the twists and turns of the mountain trails, it was impossible to judge how far ahead of her was Geoffrey de Rancon with the standard of the van, or how far behind the rear guard of the army lagged. Geoffrey might already be making camp at the summit of the mountain. Louis and the French knights might be close behind the cluster of men-at-arms who rode close around her in case of another Turkish attack.

In that case, why could she not hear them singing? The marching songs of France and Burgundy, Flanders and Poitiers had carried them across Europe and

263

into Asia. Now, though the men of Lusignan were chanting the hymn that had seen them out of Constantinople, no answering echo came from the rear guard.

"Vexilla regis prodeunt,
Fulget crucis mysterium,
Qua vita mortem portulit,
Et morte vitam protulit."

The words proclaiming the banner of the king hung thin in the frosty air, bounced back mockingly from the sheer sides of the mountains into which they traveled. And no reassuring echo came from the French who should have been close behind them.

The pain was growing worse. It shot through her hips and robbed her thighs of the strength to hold on to this miserable, bony excuse for a horse. It began to rise and fall in waves. At the trough of the wave, she could see the darkening mountain-side, hear the lonely sound of the song ahead; at its crest, a whirling blackness shot through with crimson sparks of pain engulfed her. She came out of one such wave to find Faenze riding close beside her, Gringolet keeping step with Eleanor's mount while Faenze put an arm about her waist.

"Not much farther now," Faenze kept saying . . . or had she said it only once? The waves were coming harder and faster now; Eleanor was aware of little but the spinning funnel of pain and the damp stickiness between her thighs. It seemed as though she did not come out of the waves at all, now. No. There were two kinds of darkness. There was the darkness within her, with its bloodred sparks of pain, and there was the darkness that surrounded them all, with its sparks of torch-light.

"So we did not have time to reach the top after all," she said conversationally to Faenze, who seemed to have grown a broad placid face topped with braids of flaxen hair.

"She's wandering," said Faenze's voice from somewhere behind her. Eleanor squinted at the torchlit face before her and eventually placed it.

"You," she said, "are Geoffrey's sister. Not that I've ever met Geoffrey, you un-derstand, but I have heard many good things said of him."

"Most of them from me," said Sybille of Flanders. "Isn't that tent up yet? We need to get her inside, and quickly."

Tent. Ah, yes. This was solid ground she was lying on, not that devil-curst mare's spiny back. How nice. But then why did she still hurt in waves, as if the horse's gait were still jolting her?

Another wave, deeper and stronger, came roaring through her body, and she groaned.

"*Not now,*" said Sybille urgently, but under her breath. "Here is my lord of Rancon, come to inquire after your health. . . . The queen is somewhat fatigued, and sore shaken from her earlier fall, but she will be doing well enough by morning," she said over her shoulder, too brightly. "Ah . . . is there any news of the rear guard?"

"Damned French must have camped in the valley," Geoffrey de Rancon said. "They'll have to catch up with us tomorrow."

Tomorrow . . . wasn't there something she had meant to do tomorrow? She couldn't *think.* Faenze wanted her to stand up now, to walk into the tent, and for some reason the girl was practically clinging to her back, so they must make a fine sight shuffling forward together.

"There." Faenze sounded breathless. "No one saw the blood?"

"Too dark, anyway," said Sybille. "But tomorrow . . ."

"We'll think of something."

Tomorrow. Oh, yes. "My horse," Eleanor whispered.

"Belle-Belle?"

"Dead. I *know.*" She had to husband her words now, let each phrase out between the crests of the waves that were now breaking continuously over her head. "Other one . . . I rode tonight . . ."

"I cleaned the saddle off myself," Faenze told her. No one will notice the blood, and if they do, what's a few bloodstains in an army?"

"Devil take the saddle!" She had to stop a moment and attend to the pain; it was trying to tear her apart at the hips now. "The *horse.* Cook it for soup. Make sure . . . nobody ever rides . . . damned bone-cruncher again."

"Doesn't she realize what's happening?" Sybille's voice, farther away now.

"Perhaps it's better so. She *wanted* this child."

"Son," Eleanor corrected from the cloud of pain. "Heir to Aquitaine. *My* heir."

The leader of the Turkish archers and light cavalry ordered them to keep their distance after that first impulsive attack, watching from crevices and forested slopes for some opportunity to do real damage to the invaders. No such opportunity offered while the vanguard of the French army made its organized, tightly compacted march to the top of Mount Cadmos.

The rear of the army was less compact. The French nobility might be no more quarrelsome than those of Languedoc, but there was no one man at the rear with the authority and commanding presence of a Geoffrey de Rancon or a Black Hugh of Lusignan. Louis abhorred strife. When the Burgundians insisted on preceding the French, or the count of Soissons fell into a quarrel with the heir to Champagne, he thought it as well that they should straggle along in widely separated marching groups. This slowed the progress of the rear even more, so that they were only descending the narrow, rocky path where Eleanor had fallen when the short winter day faded into dusk.

Tughril of Konya, commander of the Sultan's armies, watched the rear guard's halting progress with equal degrees of disbelief and satisfaction. "Truly is it written," he said under his breath, "that the unbelievers, being blind to Allah, shall stray from the way, and that we have prepared a painful chastisement for them. Allah has struck them with madness and blindness, to split their army so, and to leave their men struggling on strange pathways in the darkness." His teeth gleamed white in the gathering dusk. "*Now*, my children! God is great!"

"Allahu akbar!"

The screaming voices seemed to the French to plunge on them out of the darkening sky like monstrous birds of prey, slashing with steel claws that raked to the bone wherever they struck. From the heights came flights of arrows that panicked the horses; closer were the little dark men with steel that could cut through mail armor like magic. Some rallied and struck back; more went over the cliff in the confusion of the attack, until the gorge below was filled with the screams of wounded men and horses. Ivo of Soissons and Henry of Champagne nodded at one another, dropping their aimless quarrel about somebody's mistress back home, and formed their two groups of knights into a tight knot that guarded the rear of the army. Against the arrows and the darting Turks coming out of unknown side paths there was no guard. Men slipped in the blood of their predecessors, dismounted to lead terrified horses over dead bodies and oozing piles of intestines, only to feel the sudden bite of a Turkish sword from nowhere. In the shouting and the confusion, more than one knight, laying blindly about him with a two-handed grip on his heavy Frankish sword, cut down more Frankish foot soldiers than Turkish attackers. As the horses went down one by one, the knights, weighed down by their armor, were lumbering targets for the Turks with their wickedly curved, sharp swords.

The king's confessor, unarmed and not weighed down by baggage, judged that his best hope lay in reaching the valley where the vanguard should have camped. He shouted as much to the king's other attendants over his shoulder before taking off. Kicking and lashing his mule unmercifully, he forced the beast blind down a dark gorge of sliding rocks and grasping branches, slithering and stumbling, until the ground leveled beneath them and they were alone in darkness.

"Where *are* the damned southerners?" cried a squire who'd followed him. "Are they all dead too?"

There was no smell of blood and death in this valley. Odo looked up at the black bulk of Mount Cadmos, at the stars hovering over it . . . and the dots of torchlight that seemed to be so near the stars.

"They've gone ahead."

"And left us to be slaughtered? God curse them."

Out of the hell of blood and screams and flying arrows, Odo found himself able to think more clearly. "As a monk of the abbey of Deuil, I can only call upon the Lord and summon others to battle. I shall make my own way up the mountain, at whatever risk to myself, and send the army of the south to do battle with the infidels. You can go back and defend our king."

"I think," said the squire, "it is really my duty to protect you. What if, alone and unaided, you should fail to reach the southerners' camp? We must make sure that someone hears our cry for aid."

In the confusion of the night battle, some of Louis's guard had taken Odo's and the squire's departure as meaning that they were needed farther forward. Others found themselves fully occupied in fending off the Turks who had circled uphill around the rear guard and now plunged down the mountainside at them. Louis's horse threw up its nose and screamed when a pile of steaming guts landed at its feet; there was a desperate scramble and he found himself unmounted, unarmed, undefended. Hugging the cliff, he found a foothold in an outcropping of rock and a handhold in a scrubby bush that grew from some pocket of soil. He pulled himself up off the path and was able to stand firmly enough, with his face to the cliff and his feet planted on the ledge of rock that had given support to the bush. At the level of his ankles, there were the sparks of swords striking mail, swords striking rocks, shouts and curses, and the gurgling last cries of dying men. Louis felt upward with his fingertips, praying for a crevice or another bush within reach.

The baggage train, between the rear and the van, struggled slowly through the valley where they were supposed to have camped. An onslaught of Turks galloping through the valley disposed of the wounded who were drawn on litters among the baggage. That done, they enjoyed themselves for a few minutes by slashing open packs with their sabers and cutting the throats of the pack animals. While they were laughing at the sight of meal spilled to the ground and rising in white clouds, Mathilde of Savoy hustled the younger women behind the curtains of her litter and stood outside it.

"Crazy infidels! Get out of here before my husband comes back to cut you to pieces!" she screeched.

The dark men laughed and spoke among themselves in nonsense syllables like the twittering of birds, but one young rider reined in his horse and someone else brought a torch so that he could examine her face.

"Mother of warriors," he said in halting but understandable French, "if you were young to bear more sons with your spirit, I would take you as my share of the spoil."

Mathilde stood her ground, knees trembling. "For once, I thank God that I am very old and very evil-tempered," she told him, praying that the girls crowded into her litter would have the sense to keep silent. "Else I might be tempted to improve the breeding stock of your race. None of *my* sons would be in this valley, killing wounded men and helpless women, when the real fighting was elsewhere!"

The young Turk laughed and saluted her with his lance. The head was dark with blood. "Your Franks are not much sport. I have worked harder hunting rabbits." But he wheeled his horse and motioned his men away from the baggage train.

There was no hope of rescuing more baggage than the surviving women could carry on their backs. They fumbled in the dark for whatever they imagined might be most useful, gathering up what they could find in their skirts, and froze like the frightened rabbits the Turk had compared Franks to when a crashing noise sounded from the thick bushes clustering about the rocky side of the valley.

"Not a Turk," Mathilde said with relief at the sound of an unmistakable French curse.

"Your king." Louis pushed aside the last of the bushes and strode to meet her.

"What happened? Where—"

"Every one of our knights left a pile of dead infidels around him before he fell," Louis said. "I barely escaped with my life. The army is destroyed!"

After that, the belated arrival of the Savoyards was something of an anticlimax for everyone except Mathilde, who greeted her husband with an uplifted chin and a demand to know why he hadn't been there sooner, when he might have been of some use.

"We came back to the rescue as soon as your chaplain brought us the news," Amadeus of Savoy told the king. "If we can bring the rest of our men down into the valley to form a defensive line—"

"Too late to do anything but succor our survivors," Louis said.

A joyous whoop from the top of Mount Cadmos announced that the Turks had discovered the other half of the French army. Amadeus wheeled and led his weary men back up the mountain path, shouting the war cries of Savoy and trying to sound like a whole army coming to the aid of Black Hugh of Lusignan and the other men of the south.

The southerners in their camp had the advantage of space to fight in and some little advance warning, time to form a circle of mailed knights around the camp who repulsed most of the Turks until their attackers tired of the game and fell back into their mountain hiding places. One suicidal young Turk broke through the line of knights and charged across the camp, trampling foot soldiers and slashing wildly with his saber, leaving a trail of dead and bleeding men and collapsed tents behind him. One was the queen's. Amicie de Périgné, from his vantage point in the horse lines, brought the crazy Turk down with an arrow through the throat as he reached the far side of the camp.

Sybille of Flanders pushed the heavy folds of canvas off her head and looked at the pale oval of Faenze's face in the darkness. "That Turk stabbed one of our men in the gut," she said. "I know what that kind of scream means. Bring him over here."

"Why? We can't save—"

"No one," Sybille said impatiently, "will wonder why the queen's bed is bloody if they see a wounded man collapsed over it. Oh, if you see any we *can* help, try and bring them over, too. Unless, of course, a few more Turks decide to pay us a visit."

But the Turks harassing the Mount Cadmos camp withdrew before Amadeus of Savoy's charge; those who had decimated the rear half of the army were already gone. There was nothing for the survivors to do but pick up the pieces and go forward. Sybille found her hands full with tending the wounded who were found and brought for the women to nurse. Mathilde of Savoy, gray-faced with exhaustion, worked beside her. They were joined, one by one, by waiting women, whores, any who could hold a torch or wash a wound.

"Women's work," Sybille said through her teeth once, "washing and sewing. They make the mess, we clean up after them." At least there was no more need to explain the blood on Eleanor's skirts. The girl had courage, Sybille had to give her that; the short agony of the miscarriage over, she had insisted on rising to work with the others.

"Faith and Saint Radegonde," she said when Faenze tried to get her to lie down, "I had rather die on my feet than smothered under a tent, wondering what is happening now!" She looked pale in the torchlight, but no worse than the wounded men who would have to march in the morning. Sybille smothered her misgivings. They were all in the same danger here. By what Faenze had whispered, the pregnancy could not have been far advanced, only two months or so. Some women miscarried at this stage without even realizing what was happening to them. Eleanor had not been so fortunate. That fall from her horse might have done some other damage.

Sybille pushed sweaty hair from her forehead with the back of one wrist and called to a blowzy, yellow-haired woman who looked vaguely familiar. . . . Ah, yes, the Flemish whore who'd brought Eleanor the news when the king's brother kidnapped Faenze from Constantinople. It was the blue gown she wore that looked familiar; Sybille had given it her as a reward for coming to them. "Gerda," she said, "hold that torch lower." She needed to decide if there was any hope of patching up this man with the slashed thigh and the boots full of blood. He had been carried in by a comrade, but perhaps with a good bandage he'd be able to walk on the morrow. . . . If he couldn't, she had best spend her effort on somebody who might be saved. She dismissed her worries about the French queen. If Eleanor was able to stand, she might as well do so. She would have to do so in the morning anyway; those who could not march with the army could die here or be left for the Turks to kill. There were no good choices left for any of them.

The stragglers who came in with wounded companions brought bits and pieces of news with them. Thierry of Flanders and most of his men were safe enough, having pursued one party of Turks down a side path until their assailants disappeared into the forest, but their horses were near foundered and they would not be rejoining the camp until morning. Gautier de Montjay was dead, someone had seen the arrow through his throat. Most of the king's escort were dead.

"My brother?" a young man with a thick Norman accent demanded. "Itiers de Meingnac? Has anybody seen him?"

One of the wounded men lying on the ground lifted his head painfully. "You won't be seeing him again, lad."

The names of the dead mounted up, a clamor in Sybille's ears: the count of Warenne, his brother, Manasses de Bulles, Renald de Tours, Everard de . . ."

"Not the grand master of the Templars!" Sybille could not believe that the most disciplined body of men in the army had gone down to the Turkish assault.

"No, no," her informant assured her, "not Everard de *Barres,* Everard de *Breteuil,* you know, the cross-eyed one."

She noticed that Eleanor looked up whenever a new group of men arrived. Who was she waiting for? Her Louis was safe enough, he'd escaped while his men died in the dark. Thierry was safe too. Sybille supposed she ought to thank God for that, but she felt superstitiously that she would save the prayers until she actually saw her barrel-shaped man swaggering forward and insulting his comrades.

Dawn came so cold and slow they hardly knew it; only the torches were less and less help, and the sky looked less like a deep black well and more like burnished steel. As the sun rose higher, some of the winter clouds burned off, and they could see sparks of light and color across the valley where the Turks had regrouped. The

Templars were busy about the army, organizing small groups and planning some kind of marching order. Louis sat by the royal tent, hands limp between his knees, watching without interest.

One last group came straggling up the mountain path. A thin thread of song came with them, an untranslatably filthy Flemish tavern song carried by a strong bass voice. Sybille rocked back on her heels and sighed with deep relief as her Thierry came into sight, as filthy as the song he was belting out but alive, upright, even able to lead his horse.

"That's your man?" the whore called Gerda Goldeneyes said. "Lucky. Mine, he won't be coming back. Somebody saw . . ." Her face twisted for a moment. "I find another," she said after catching her breath. "We all lucky, us, here this morning."

Those still looking for surviving friends or relatives all but mobbed Thierry's band of Flemings with their questions. "If they're not here now, they're not coming," Thierry shouted over the cries and queries. "We passed nothing but corpses."

Eleanor was wasting her efforts, trying to ease a gut-wounded soldier who would never be able to march with the army. Sybille was about to tell her to work on somebody with a better chance when the man groaned and his head fell back against the girl's arm, eyes open and staring.

"Lucky?" she said wryly to Gerda.

The whore shrugged. "How long you want to live with your guts spilling out?"

Eleanor rose from her knees, settling the man as gently on the ground as though he were still able to feel her movements. Blood had clotted in the folds of her skirts, so that they clung together and kept her from taking a full step. She moved very slowly and carefully toward Thierry, and the other questioners looked at her face and made way for the queen.

The question she asked Thierry was blown away on the mountain winds, but Sybille heard the answer. "The jongleur, old Round-the-World? Nay, lass, I saw his body. Died with Warenne and the rest of the king's guard."

Eleanor walked back to her half-collapsed tent with the same slow, careful steps, and sat so abruptly that Sybille thought she had better go to her, and then thought she had better not. The French queen took something from the rubbish in the tent—an ivory box, its top smashed by the hooves of a Turkish horseman. Folds of rich purple silk fell from the box, blown out behind her like the banners of a lost army.

Chapter Fifteen

They had been fortunate, Faenze supposed, that this one of the three ships from Adalia boasted two private cabins, one of which had been reserved for the use of the noble ladies and their waiting women. If she were really a good person, she would be grateful for the privacy and comfort of a walled room where she could change from one salt-encrusted gown to another, sponge herself off with salt water, and sleep safely packed in a tight row of mattresses filled with other women.

But after so many storm-tossed days and nights of a voyage that should have taken only three days, with drinking water rationed until every throat was parched, women forbidden to come out on deck during the stormy weather, and the cabin smelling like a place in which fourteen women had eaten and slept and been seasick for weeks and weeks—and *her* lady looking more like a ghost with every day that passed, without even the strength to complain about the miserable conditions—Faenze was finding it hard to be properly grateful to God for anything.

Until this morning, when the port of San Simeon was sighted at last. As they entered the calm of the harbor, Faenze had dared to slip out on deck and had practically forced Eleanor to come with her.

"Does it matter?" Eleanor had said in that quiet, resigned voice that gave Faenze the creeping shivers. Her lady Eleanor had never been *resigned* to anything before. When there was music she danced, when there was no music she made or commanded some, when there was sunshine she stripped off her veils and rode bare-headed with her face turned up to the sun, and when it rained she cursed God and winter cheerfully and without shame. She could feast in the hall of the emperor at Constantinople, and she could make a meal of half-roasted horse meat eaten around a sputtering campfire seem like a feast when she complimented the squire who'd burned the meat on his cooking and thanked Lord Hunger and Lady Appetite for the fine sauce they gave the meal. Every day, good or bad, was a glorious adventure with Eleanor.... Until Mount Cadmos.

What had it been that finally quenched the spirit in her? Losing the child who had barely existed, who never should have been begotten and who could never be spoken of? The other hurts she had taken in that fall onto the rocks, that turned what should have been an easy, early miscarriage into a long night of blood and agony, and left her in pain from her back and hip for weeks afterward? The death of that sardonic troubadour of hers? Or the sight of Louis, alive and whole among men wounded in his service, relating a tale that improved daily of how he had found a high rock to set his back against and had hewed down attacking Turks until the way was clear for his escape?

Or was it the whispers that went around the army after that disaster? Eleanor had been heard to say under her breath, more than once, that she had been punished for her sins. Faenze thought she meant the child she'd gotten with Manuel and lost on Cadmos. That sour chaplain of the king's, Odo of Deuil, who dutifully wrote down every word Louis said of his own heroism in the night battle, thought—and said to others—that the queen repented of her self-will in insisting that the vanguard of the army march on beyond the agreed stopping place, just because she wished to camp in a pleasant spot with a fine view.

"It wasn't *like* that," Faenze protested. "It was my lord Geoffrey de Rancon wanted to march on—"

"A vassal of Aquitaine, if I am not mistaken. Do you pretend the queen could not order one of her own vassals to stop where she chose?"

There were men in plenty who could have backed up Faenze's story, and everybody knew that Eleanor, lacking the support of her husband, had no true power over the men who were nominally her vassals—whatever she ordered, Louis could countermand. But the lords who had accompanied the vanguard were too busy shifting blame from themselves to care where else it landed.

"Why not say it was the queen's choice?" Black Hugh of Lusignan demanded when Faenze cornered him. "She was there too—and she has nothing to lose."

"I thought you . . . cared for her."

"She's a fine spirited lass," Hugh said, "and if she were free, damned if I wouldn't find some way to dispose of Bergone and marry her myself. Aquitaine would be happy to have a fine figure of a man like me for duke. But Louis has Eleanor, and he's got his French castellans and seneschals watching every part of her lands, so what's the good of spinning dreams? I like the queen, girl, but I like my own neck and my own lands of Lusignan a sight better. If somebody hangs for this, it won't be me . . . nor yet my father-in-law."

Geoffrey de Rancon might have been hanged, if he had not shared command with the king's own uncle of Savoy. But Louis was not about to hang Amadeus of Savoy. It was convenient for everybody to blame the disaster of Cadmos on a woman's self-will—much more convenient than admitting that somebody in power had made fatal mistakes.

All the same, after Cadmos there was no more chance for the great lords who had been directing the army to make any more stupid mistakes. After consultation with Everard de Barres, Louis had turned over military command to the Knights Templar. Founded to protect pilgrims in the Holy Land, their order knew more than any of the home-grown French about fighting in this country, and the discipline that kept them shaggy and dirty, because cleanliness was considered self-indulgence, also trained them to instant obedience to their commander.

They were a dour group of men who disapproved of almost anything that made life worthwhile. Their Order forbade them to take wives and children, to tell jokes or stories, to enjoy the songs of troubadours or the performances of jugglers, to eat more than necessary to sustain life and strength, to dress fashionably or to tend their hair beyond hacking it off when it got long enough to need combing. And, individually and collectively, they could be recognized in the dark because their religious avoidance of bathing made them smell even worse than the rest of the army.

But they were good soldiers, superbly organized, and adept at fighting the natives of this land. Once the knights of the army were divided into small groups, each under the command of a Templar, they learned to stand under the darting Turkish attacks without breaking away in pursuit when it was hopeless, to attack only on signal, and to return on the same signal. The archers, also under Templar command, now marched not according to precedence but wherever they could best hold off the Turks from day to day, depending on the terrain.

Much of the terrain had been burned and despoiled by Turkish war lords who were quite happy to let the Greek villagers under their rule starve, if it meant the invaders would also starve. Horses and men alike dropped on the road, dying from starvation or wounds or the fever that came after the wounds or the chest cough that came with the renewal of the winter rains. The dying men were killed to save them falling into the hands of the Turks; the baggage the army could no longer carry was burned to prevent the Turks benefiting from it. The horses were more use; those they could eat.

Eleanor did not collapse physically on the nightmare march from Cadmos to Adalia. She even grew stronger, walking a good portion of each day to spare the horses. It was just, Faenze thought uneasily, that she seemed no longer quite there. She said little, and that little made no sense or less than none.

The coastal town of Adalia should have been a refuge. Instead it was almost their death trap. Intermittently besieged by the Turks, with plague rife in the city, the governor sent a messenger who advised that the Franks should consider themselves lucky to be outside, with a chance to get away. *No*, Adalia had no food for them. *No*, they could not enter the city; Governor Landulph had too many mouths to feed already while he waited for the emperor to send relief. "My best advice to you is to march on," he said, "and quickly, before the Turks return and trap you between our walls and their lines."

The leaders of the army withdrew and debated.

"Seize the messenger," Geoffrey de Rancon suggested, "as a hostage."

"It is against God's law to take hostage an envoy," Louis said. "Besides, the Greeks are our allies; how then shall we make war with them?"

"Easily enough," the bishop of Langres said. "Their walls are rotten and half their fighting men are sick, according to this messenger."

Arnulf of Lisieux arched one black eyebrow. "Well, Godfrey, if it seems good to you to fight and die for the privilege of entering a starving city where you will very likely catch the plague, you may attempt it with my blessing."

Godfrey of Langres's full face turned dark red. "I need no blessing from another bishop. We are of equal rank before God."

"The city's not worth taking," Thierry of Flanders said, "and I doubt the governor will open the gates to us even if we threaten to hang the messenger. He's too scared of the Turks. He's right, too. We don't want to hang about here and get trapped between the lines."

"It's another forty days' march to Antioch."

"Three days," said Thierry, "by sea."

"Where are we going to get ships, you idiot?"

Thierry grinned. "From the emperor of Constantinople, who is sending men to relieve the siege of Adalia. How did you *think* the Byzantine army was going to get here—by winged chariot?"

There was plague within the camp and a plague of Turks outside it before the Byzantine ships arrived, and then there were only three of them, not even enough to carry all the nobles of the army. Louis vacillated. Was it a sin to leave the others here at Adalia to fight their way south? Who should go on the ships? Those of the highest rank? The knights whose horses had already died? The pilgrims who had no arms and no knowledge of the art of war to defend themselves?

"*Not* the pilgrims," said Thierry brusquely. "They're a damned bloody nuisance and I for one don't care if they never reach the Holy Land. What use are they going to be there or anywhere else?" And he began setting out the order of passengers without waiting for Louis to concur, simultaneously beginning a series of quarrels, scuffles, and desperate dice games for passage space.

One of the loudest and most public of the quarrels was with his own wife.

"You're staying here and sending the French king off safely? You're crazy!" Sybille announced.

"Look here, woman!" Thierry dropped his voice to a low rumble. "Louis is about as damn useless as the damn pilgrims. The man can't make a decision to save his life ... or anybody else's. Once we get rid of him and his household, the Templars and I will organize this crew. We might be able to fight our way south. Louis for damn sure can't."

"I don't think even you can do it," Sybille said, "but I must admit, it should be interesting to watch."

"You won't be watching. You're sailing with the queen's household."

"I—am—not!"

"Look, you idiot, if I don't get back, somebody's going to have to be regent for our kid until he's old enough to defend his rights. Once the word of my death gets out, he won't be Philip of Flanders, he'll be Philip of Nowhere in Particular, or locked up to keep him out of the way, if he's lucky. *You* should know there's no shortage of claimants," Thierry said. Sybille had been, briefly, married to William Clito before his claim on Flanders had been overridden by Thierry's. About that time, the relationship between Sybille and William was found to fall within the forbidden degrees of consanguinity, forcing a divorce. "Only," Thierry said, remembering his main argument, "there won't be any news of my death, because I am not going to waste time debating and praying and waiting for God's will to be known. I'm going to get this army to Antioch. Where I will meet you. IS THAT CLEAR?"

When Sybille joined Eleanor and Mathilde of Savoy on the *Eleutheria*, Faenze thought that Thierry of Flanders might just possibly have the gift of command that would be needed to get the rest of the army from Adalia to Antioch. It couldn't be significantly harder than persuading Sybille on board without him had been.

She'd felt almost safe then, ready to relax and stop worrying about Eleanor. By sea they were supposed to be just three days from Antioch, where there would be rest and food and a city the Turks could not take and a kinsman for her lady to stay with. . . . Three days! More like three weeks, it had been; she'd lost count of the days sometime in that second week of gray choppy seas and ladies heaving their guts into the nearest basin, or onto the deck if no basin were presented them. They said the knights hadn't done much better, but at least they were allowed out on deck where the salty wind whipped across the ship and cleared away the stink. Faenze wondered how Louis of France had borne the journey and whether he minded very much being where he couldn't see Eleanor for all this time.

But now, at last, here was San Simeon, and beyond the flat marshy lands of the port, the mountains rose, girdled about by the city walls of Antioch, with the citadel crowning the highest hill and outlined in black against the rising sun. Faenze looked at all those nice solid walls, with their guard towers spaced so close together that the guards must be able to lean out and gossip with each other during the night watches, and thought she had never seen anything so beautiful and safe looking. Two sets of walls at least, and the citadel above all; no one who slept in the city of Antioch need fear being awakened by a charge of mounted Turks riding across her bedding.

The bells in all the churches were ringing for some festival or other, and there was a gay procession of mounted knights and ladies coming down to the mouth of the harbor. Dressed all in bright silks, they were, and their heads bare and their hair blowing in the brisk spring breeze; no mail helms, no armor, no boiled leather, and Blessed Virgin, how fine and fat and healthy they all were—even the horses!

"Look," she said to Eleanor, "it must be some saint's day they are celebrating. Oh, isn't it all beautiful? I can't wait to go ashore! Where does your uncle live? Does he know we are coming?"

"Raymond?" Eleanor said vaguely. "I don't know. How would he know . . . oh, well, it doesn't matter."

Beside her, Sybille of Flanders caught her breath in something between a sob and a gasp. "Look—Thierry! How did he come here before us?"

Faenze squinted across the sun-splashed water. "It is too far away to make out faces."

"It was the set of his shoulders I recognized," Sybille said, "or thought I did . . ." There was a brittle, hysterical edge to her laugh. "We've all been too long at sea, I think. Of course the army could not have marched this far in three weeks. I do know that."

At one time Eleanor would have started an argument about just how fast an army could move through hostile terrain when inspired by necessity. Now she only stared blankly over the rail as if she did not care whether the army had caught up with them or not.

What she needed was good fresh food, Faenze thought. Broth with wine and an egg beaten into it, and a clean room to sleep in with fresh breezes blowing through it, because she knew how her lady hated the stale smell of the cabin. She would pick up in no time now that they were finally safe. She *had* to.

Disembarking was a tedious affair of sidling along the planks that sailors pushed out from the ship to a stone jetty. The knights mostly disdained the plank bridge and jumped for land, laughing at each other and making bets on who would miss his step and fall in. Mathilde de Savoy looked unhappily at the narrow planks.

"It's better than some of those mountain paths we've ridden up," Sybille said. "Come on!"

The improvised bridge was wide enough for only one at a time. Faenze gently pushed Eleanor in front of her—she had grown rather used to pushing the queen around, since without some impetus her lady could not be bothered to eat or walk or do anything else. She supposed someday she would get in trouble for it, when

Eleanor noticed how impertinent she was being. That would be a good day for them all.

Now she clenched her fists and watched Eleanor walk like a sleepwalker down the slanting bridge, seemingly unaware of how the planks quivered and gapped to reveal the dark harbor waters. And now the procession she'd seen coming down from Antioch had reached the jetty, and a big golden-haired man at the head of the procession swung down from his horse and took Eleanor by the shoulders and lifted her bodily the last two steps onto solid land. Beyond her, Sybille was laughing and crying and hugging a short, broad-shouldered man whose face was buried in her shoulder.

"Get on with it, then," hissed one of Mathilde's waiting women, poking Faenze. "The rest of us would like to set foot on land too, someday!"

Raymond looked surprised when asked how he had been warned of their arrival. "Why, I've had men watching for your ships ever since the first ones arrived. We were sorely concerned that you were so long delayed. Were the storms so bad?"

"The first ones?"

"Thierry of Flanders," Raymond said, "and Archimbaud de Bourbon, and their households. And a bunch of Knights Templar." He grinned and pinched his nose. "So holy the good knights are, they smelled worse than the horses!"

"I don't understand," Eleanor said. "They were to organize the army to march south. Surely they didn't find enough ships for the whole army?" She looked at Sybille and Thierry. The count of Flanders looked away from her. "The land route was impossible," he mumbled. "We tried . . . I swear by Saint Bartholomew, we *tried*. The Turks were too many. Only logical thing was to save those we could, when we got two more ships."

Two more ships. Seven thousand soldiers. Eleanor felt sick and dizzy. "How many did you leave to the mercy of the Turks?"

"We brought away as many as we could," Thierry said and escaped her questioning to make a fuss about finding Sybille the gentlest mount among those Raymond had brought down to welcome his noble guests.

There were not nearly enough horses for everybody to ride up to the citadel. The noblest rode, the others walked or begged a pillion seat. Eleanor took Faenze up behind her and was grateful for the company. There was too much assaulting her senses as the horses picked their way up to the walled city. From Constantinople to Adalia they had marched through steel-gray winter. Antioch was spring in a forcing house being urged on to early summer: flowering trees and flowers hanging in baskets outside square white houses, a blaze of sun on colored silks that could hurt the eyes of someone accustomed to a winter landscape and an army of skeletons . . . an army of the dead, left trapped between plague and the Turks . . . She closed down her mind, locked that away with all the other unbearable memories, fastened on the details of the scene around her. There were people, too many people, all jostling and calling out in the streets in a babble of tongues that was worse than the student nations at Paris: Spaniards and Italians and Germans and Hungarians—she recognized that harsh language, every sentence exploding in a shower of consonants and falling downward like a shower of pebbles hitting the ground, from the days of the army's march through Hungary.

"They are all dressed like princes," she said wonderingly.

The big blond man who said he was her uncle Raymond broke off whatever he had been saying, and she guessed that she had interrupted him when he was talking about something else entirely. That seemed to happen a lot, lately. It was hard to listen, hard to keep her thoughts on what was going on about her; safer to keep silent.

When one did not listen, one could not hear the crying of a child who had never been born. Who should never have been conceived. Who was not—absolutely not—to be spoken of before Louis or anyone else who did not already know what had happened on the night of the Mount Cadmos disaster.

Safer, all around, to be silent.

But Raymond did not appear to have taken offense. After a brief check, he agreed that he had thought the same thing when he first came to the East. "Taffetas, brocades, silks, and even cotton are so cheap here that the commonest man can dress—and live—like a prince at home. And as for princes—well, you shall see for yourself how we live!" He gave a deep, rolling, satisfied chuckle and went on telling Eleanor what a fine land this was, how rich and fertile and beloved of the sun like their own home country—all in all, to hear him tell it, the Latin kingdoms of the East were the flower of civilization, and his own principality of Antioch the finest of them all.

Between the inner and outer wall there was a market, with open stalls and sheep bawling and vendors shouting over the noise of the animals. Here bearded and tur-baned Turks outnumbered all the Latins, ten to one. Faenze, riding behind Eleanor, clasped her tightly. "There are so many Turks!" she said. "Is it safe?"

Raymond chuckled again and told them that they were back in civilization; if men of different faiths could not keep peace in the city, how would they trade? "Most of the peasants are fellahin—Moslems," he said. "One cannot get a Frank to dirty his hands with working the land here. But not all Turks. Those are Druzes," he said, waving a hand to his left, "and this is a Bedawi family: you can tell them by the weight of silver and turquoise on the women. You will learn these little details soon enough," he assured them.

"And what is that man over there?" Faenze asked, looking at a hawk-faced, brown-skinned man who stood a head taller than most of those around him, sur-veying the crowd with dark, scornful eyes. "Is he a Turkish emir, or what?"

Raymond burst into laughter so good-humored that although Faenze blushed when he explained her mistake, she could not take offense. "Nay, lass, that's my good friend Jacob, as good a Christian as any of us, but born here in Syria. There are lots of native Christians, you know," he said, "funny little sects, probably hereti-cal, but we're a long way from Rome. Monophysites, Copts, Maronites . . . If you're interested in theology, you can get as good an argument going as you'd have in Paris . . . or Constantinople. And if you're not interested in theology, well, the Syr-ian Christians are a useful buffer between us and the Moslems—not first-class men, you know, not as good fighters as real Frankish knights, but still, they're *Chris-tians*, and that's worth something. There aren't enough of us true Franks out here to do everything. You should stay, you know," he said, looking hard at Eleanor. "You should all stay. You're needed here."

Faenze thought privately that he did not need to take Eleanor's hand and press it between both of his while making this statement. She wriggled on her pillion un-til their horse was uncomfortable enough to take two quick steps sideways, and then Eleanor needed both her hands on the reins.

Eleanor and her household stayed with the prince of Antioch; Louis and his with the patriarch. The division was agreeable to both of them. At least, Louis did not complain, and Eleanor did not greatly care one way or another. Raymond's palace was as good a place as any in which to rest. Lacking the oppressive opulence of Byzantine palaces, it was more like the small castles that dotted the southern shores of her father's lands: a large, comfortable square stone building three stories high, all arranged about a central courtyard where a fountain cooled the air and fell back into a mosaic-covered pool. Latticework and green-tinted glass screened the outer windows from the street.

Raymond's young wife, Constance, through whom he held the title of prince of Antioch, welcomed them warmly and seemed graciously unaware of the ironic contrasts that rose up like walls of iron spikes wherever Eleanor looked. Constance also was an heiress, but she had not had to leave her home to secure her inheritance; her husband had traveled to Outremer to marry her, he owed his position in life to her. Constance was four years younger than Eleanor but already had two babies playing at her feet, golden little girls who looked like miniatures of Raymond. And Eleanor came like a starving beggar in rags to this gracious house of falling water and mosaic pictures, of music and laughter and the gaiety that reminded her of her father's court in Aquitaine. . . .

One must not, of course, be sullen or envious—or worse, discourteous. Eleanor summoned up the image of her grandmother Dangereuse, straightbacked, cool, and courteous even to the clerics who taxed her with being the duke's concubine. She managed the appropriate exclamations of delight over Constance's lovely little girls, over the meal that had been prepared for her, over anything and everything that was brought out for her appreciation and comfort. Thank you. The rooms look very comfortable, I am sure we will be happy here. So good of you to lend me a gown for the evening. Yes, we will certainly have to visit the silk drapers tomorrow, you are right, I am sorely in need of almost everything. Thank you. Thank you. Thank you. Oh, yes, your girls are delightful, and they have such a look of Raymond when he was young.

"I'm only thirty-four now," Raymond said, soft and pretend-dangerous. "There just might be a few more good years in the old man yet. Time for this child to give me a son, anyway!" and he laughed and tousled Constance's head with one hand, and brushed Eleanor's with the other one, and made a joke of being a poor old man who was driven to distraction by these naughty girls. Eleanor tried to smile at his antics, wondered if she had gotten it right, wondered if she remembered how to laugh. She felt as though an immeasurable distance separated her from Raymond and his family, as though she were looking up at human life from the bottom of the ocean and trying to understand how it felt, what these people were laughing about. Perhaps she had really died on Mount Cadmos, perhaps she was a ghost sitting at the feast. Tomorrow she would vanish and they would tell stories for a hundred years of how the dead queen of the Franks had appeared at her kinsman's house in Antioch for one night. . . .

> *"Quant la douch'aura a'amarcis,*
> *el fuoilla chai de sul verzan"*

There had been no preliminary tuning of strings to warn her. For one breathless moment the tenor voice might have been Cercle-le-Monde's; then it grated slightly on a high note and the illusion was broken. Raymond smiled and began a laughing apology for his squire Gautier, who had wanted to honor Eleanor with a song of her own land but whose young voice had not, perhaps, quite the range required. Later she would remember the words; at the time she was unaware of anything except the grief and pain that filled her to overflowing.

"No!" She stood too quickly, felt dizzy. "No music—I want no music! I will have no singing, do you hear?"

It was not she, after all, who was the ghost at this feast.

Eleanor slept for the better part of two days, waking to find that she had been provided with new gowns by Constance's sewing women and that everyone was being excessively polite about the unfortunate incident with the singer. The gowns were not such as would have once been to her taste—the stuff, though fine, had obviously been chosen to flatter Constance's flaxen beauty, soft shades of pink and blue with discreetly subtle patterns woven into the heavier silks. "It doesn't matter," she said when Faenze complained that the pink was disastrous against Eleanor's sunburnt face, and "It's not worth the trouble, just cut it," when Faenze wanted to spend a morning teasing out the last tangles that had matted in the fine hair at the nape of her neck.

The polished metal of her mirror—another gift from her kinsfolk, she supposed—showed a face grown disconcertingly brown and thin, surrounded by a wild tangle of light brown hair that sun and wind had bleached into a fantastic medley of colors, some pale as straw, some reddish-gold, and a vagrant few glinting with pure silver. All Faenze's careful work with the ivory lion comb could not persuade the fine, dry, crisp strands around her face to lie decently flat in the long plaits that hung down over her shoulders.

"My lady Constance invites you to join her and her ladies in the bower," Faenze told her, "if you are feeling rested enough."

Three weeks cooped up in a tiny ship's cabin with seasick women . . . "Maybe," Eleanor said. The bower and the talk of women held no appeal for her right now, but neither did anything else. What did it matter? Perhaps fresh air would help. She had grown so accustomed to living and sleeping outside that the cool dark rooms of the palace with their latticed windows felt like a cage. "I shall go for a walk," she said. "Alone."

A page, seeing her in the hall, took to his heels, and a moment later a brightly dressed young man with curled hair saluted her politely, offering the count's compliments and suggesting that she might like to look over the interior of the palace, since it would be unwise for her to go out into the city at this time; the noonday sun was dangerous for visitors from the north.

"It can scarcely be worse than the sun of Provence!" Eleanor protested, remembering the warm, sun-drenched limestone hills of her childhood travels in Duke William's wake.

"The prince your uncle would never forgive me if I allowed you to come to harm in his city," the squire said firmly.

"We'll just discuss that with the prince my uncle," Eleanor said.

"As you wish." The young man looked quite satisfied to take her to Raymond, whom they found in a long room overlooking the courtyard fountain. Raymond and two others were bent over a map of the Christian holdings in Outremer.

"May I look?" She had not seen a map of this part of the world since they left Paris, and what the scribes showed in Paris was so manifestly incorrect that it had been less than no help in understanding the turns of their journey.

"It's badly out of date," said a broad-shouldered young man whom Eleanor recognized as the squire whom she had insulted. Gautier, that was his name. Their eyes met and he blushed and started stammering apologies for having disturbed her with his clumsy attempt at making music.

"*You*, Gautier," Eleanor said, "have nothing to apologize for. I pray you will forgive me my discourtesy. . . ." Impossible to explain. "Someone I cared for," she said over the squire's attempts to stop her apologizing, "used to sing that song. . . . He . . ." *He died at Cadmos. So many deaths at Cadmos . . . If I had not sinned, would God have spared us Cadmos?* No good thinking of that now. The map . . . the map was neutral, safe, an intellectual problem. "What is wrong with this map?"

Raymond's finger pointed at a tiny castle drawn in the upper right-hand corner of the map. "See there? Edessa. Fell to Zengi four years ago. Since then his son, Nureddin, has been picking off our castles east of the Orontes one by one. The Turks hold all *this* now." His hand came down over the eastern line of castles from Edessa to Hama. "Joscelin of Edessa is holding out at Turbessel, here. He's going to want Louis to help him get back Edessa."

"Move your hand," Eleanor said. "I can't see what's between here and Edessa."

"Turks," the third man said. He had been looking out the window at the fountain when Eleanor entered. Now, as he turned back toward the map table, she recognized the sleek dark head and sardonic smile of Arnulf, bishop of Lisieux. "Lots and lots of nasty Turks. I wish Count Joscelin joy of this army; they have much more enthusiasm for sacking Christian cities than for fighting Turks."

"Well, now that they're here," Raymond said, "they will presumably do *something*. The question is, what is in the best interests of the Latin states here in the long term? Not establishing an isolated Christian state at Edessa, where it'll be totally surrounded by the Turks. If that's all we do, they'll have it back within the year. Not taking the army south to Jerusalem; from Krak des Chevaliers to Krak de Montréal we've still got a good defensive line of fortresses. Besides, Damascus isn't going to attack us."

"Why not?" Eleanor asked idly.

"Muinaddin got Damascus when Zengi died. He's Nureddin's younger brother. . . ."

"And he's afraid Nureddin will keep moving south until he takes Damascus too?" Eleanor said. The names were strange and hard on the tongue, but the patterns of inheritance and war and families divided against one another must be the same as at home.

"Exactly." Raymond beamed. "Right now, between Nureddin to the north and Saifaddin at Mosul, we Franks are Muinaddin's best friends. Last thing we need is an army of ignorant newcomers, no offense, stirring up trouble down south with the one Moslem ruler who's willing to make deals with us."

"No." The shape of the kingdoms, and the dangers they faced, were becoming clear to Eleanor. She moved closer to the table. "Obviously the threat's in the north and east. But we can't hold Edessa unless we can supply it, so first we need to . . . can we get a corridor from the coast at Alexandrezea?" She pointed at the dot signifying a tiny port north of Antioch. "Across here . . ."

"Mountains," Raymond said, "and a fortress at Tell Bashir that could swoop down on our transport any time. Now, *here* it's flat and open, and we know the defenses of the castles Nureddin's taken, we ought to, we built most of them." He indicated the broad sweep of land east of Antioch, still shown on the map as belonging to the Latin kingdoms. "Artah, for instance . . ."

Artah was very close to Antioch. Eleanor frowned. "When did Nureddin take that?"

"Last spring," Raymond said. He looked up from the map. An insistent quality in his silence forced Eleanor to look up and meet his gaze: direct, strong, unapologetic. And eyes as blue as the summer sky, with laugh lines at the corners . . . "I know what you're thinking," he said, "and you have it. After Edessa, Nureddin started picking off our northeastern defenses one by one. Antioch is his logical next target . . . and I wasn't sure I could hold it until your people arrived. You are a gift from God," he said.

"Aleppo first," Eleanor said, looking back at the map, "or Caesarea? They're the only logical targets."

"And logic has, of course, been *such* a determining factor with this army," Arnulf of Lisieux murmured.

"Aleppo," Raymond said.

"Why?"

"One of Nureddin's main bases, now. Take that, you cripple his armies in this area. Caesarea—Shaizar, the Moslems call it—isn't as important."

"And therefore probably not as well defended."

"Probably not," Raymond allowed with a grin, "but with your cavalry, we *can* take Aleppo. Who'd have a pawn when he could capture a knight . . . or settle for a knight," he added with a caress in his voice, "when he might have a queen?"

His deep voice made Eleanor shiver. Oh, how she had *missed* all this—the heady mixture of power and politics, flirtation and innuendo, that was the gay life of the south! The French knights and clerics would have thought it unmanly to debate military strategy with a woman, and since they lacked practice at saying anything but what little was in their heads, would either not flirt with her or would go at it all too seriously.

The falling waters of the courtyard fountain laughed and chimed softly against the mosaic pool, and the noonday sun turned the droplets into jewels that rose up into the air and fell back again, absorbed and thrown up again and again. Eleanor felt the pattern of water and light and air catching her as in a net, drawing her mind into soothing patterns she had so long forgotten. *So . . . we dance, we rise, we fall and become one with the water . . . we dance again . . .* As long as she concentrated on these problems of politics and strategy, she did not have to think about Cadmos . . . no, don't name it . . . the black hole she had fallen into. . . . Her fingers pressed against her chest, finding something hard and round under her gown. The stone bead Cercle-le-Monde had given her, unimaginably old, out of the earth and the centuries past to her. The stone endured, the earth renewed, the water fell. Could she put the black hole of the past, the army of skeletons and the bloody graves on Cadmos, behind her and dance again? A selfish energy throbbed within her. *They are dead, but I am still alive. It is not time to stop dancing yet . . . and this, this management of men and affairs, is something I can* do. *They* need *me.*

"I beg your pardon?" Arnulf of Lisieux had said something, and she had not been attending. Oh . . . he wanted to discuss how they should present Raymond's plan to the leaders of the army.

"Somehow," he pointed out, "we will have to get it into the thick heads of men like Godfrey of Langres and . . . well, others of that sort . . . that not all Moslems are equal, not all are enemies, and that it makes a *difference* when and where we attack first in winning back these lands."

"Men like Geoffrey de Rancon, you mean," Eleanor said dryly. "You need not be so overcourteous that you do not speak his name in my presence! We have our boneheaded knights in the south also." She appropriated Raymond's cushioned chair with the lacelike carvings that decorated the back and legs, sat down before the map, and frowned in concentration as she studied the various directions the army might take from Antioch: north and east to Edessa, south to Jerusalem, or out into the desert toward Damascus. "What do you do when faced with an enemy who has drawn up forces that greatly outweigh yours, *Uncle* Raymond?" No harm in reminding him that their relationship made his style of flirtation more than slightly improper. She knew better than to take it seriously, of course, but Louis and that dour chaplain of his did not understand the Provençal manner. And this was no time to risk offending her husband.

"Are you suggesting that we *pray?*"

"I did not ask the bishop of Lisieux," Eleanor rebuked Arnulf coolly, without turning her head to look at his sardonic face, "but as I recall, he had more skill at the chessboard than to be reduced to prayer in the face of adversity. We outflank the enemy, of course. I can present your plan to Louis directly. He is intelligent enough to see the advantages, and once he has made his decision, he will be able to overrule any who oppose it."

Raymond's blue eyes crinkled at the corners. "I *told* them you would think of it for yourself," he said with a laugh and a triumphant glance at Arnulf and his squire.

So the whole discussion had been staged to maneuver her into presenting Raymond's case to the king! Eleanor arched her brows and decided that she did not necessarily object to being manipulated . . . in a good cause . . . and she was quite old and clever enough to make sure that her kinsman did not manipulate her into anything she really did not want to do.

"We had best discuss exactly how to present the plan," she said. "I need to know more . . . much, much more . . . about the lines of power and inheritance in these kingdoms, so that I do not make any mistakes with Louis. *Our* people I know, but if we want to make sure that this plan succeeds, I need also to know who will support it and who will lose from it here in Outremer." She glanced at the men gathered around the table, all three waiting on *her* word, *her* decision. "I want to know who holds each fief in Outremer, whom he holds it from, where his loyalties lie and where his debts are, whether he gained his lands by conquest or inheritance or . . . a fortunate marriage!" She deliberately slowed and accented the last words and laughed up at her kinsman—she could not think of him as "uncle," he was only eight years older than she—and was pleased to see a look of surprise in his eyes. "And then I need to know the same of the Moslems. Have Zengi's three sons divided all the Moslem lands among them, or are there other powers we should take into account? Do their men hold land of their lords as ours do? How is the fertile land divided now, and how might that change—would we take all, or should we share some with the emir of Damascus?"

"It will take all day to gather that information!" Raymond protested.

Eleanor met his eyes levelly this time, all joking aside. "Several days, quite likely. If you do not know all the relevant details, then pray send for those who do. And," she added, conscious for the first time how little she had eaten in the past weeks, "send for cooked foods, too, and some refreshing drink."

Raymond gave her a mocking bow. "Stuffed and gilded peacock and marzipan subtleties, I presume?"

"I would not so strain your hospitality, dear uncle. Whatever local fare your cooks can supply will be more than adequate." Eleanor glanced at the squire Gautier, who seemed to have little to contribute to this discussion. "And music," she said with a smile especially for him, "music would be most welcome to ease the long hours of learning that my poor head must undergo. Perhaps you know some songs of this land that would be new to me, Gautier?" It was the most tactful way she could think of to say, *Don't sing Cercle-le-Monde's songs.* She was much recovered . . . she had fallen into the water and risen to dance again . . . but that dance, perhaps, she was not quite ready to undertake.

For five days Eleanor and an assortment of clerks, scribes, well-traveled merchants, and anybody else with information about the internal structure of the Latin kingdoms and the Moslem states surrounding them pored over maps and documents of seisin and the laws of the Crusader states. After half a day of animated discussion about the exact proportion of money to armed men that *fiefs de besant,* or fiefs whose value was in tolls or rents rather than land, owed to their lords, and the status of such fief-holders as members of the king's High Court in Jerusalem, Raymond announced that pressing business required his presence elsewhere.

"Good," Eleanor said. "I mean, good fortune. Oh, and could you ask the patriarch of Antioch for the loan of some of his clerks? I am still not quite clear on the division of property between Christian and Moslem smallholders along the Orontes."

When food appeared, Eleanor nibbled absentmindedly on whatever was brought and sometimes remembered to compliment Constance's cooks—although there was a near explosion in the kitchen on the day that she finished off a dish of quail in clove and malmsey sauce and sent thanks for the delicious sugared violets.

The head cook himself accompanied the tray of sweetmeats that was sent to the courtyard at dusk that day. When the sun fell low enough to leave the courtyard in partial shade, Eleanor had fallen into the habit of dismissing the clerks with whom she spent the day and relaxing on a cushioned bench in the courtyard where Constance and her ladies and any visitors they had joined her. Gautier was with Raymond and no longer available to make music for them, but there were always new singers and entertainers desirous of showing their skills to the visiting queen of France. Visitors flocked to the prince's house, too, curious about this glamorous young queen who had survived such a perilous journey, and many of the nobles who had come with Louis found their way to the courtyard as well. Franks and Levantines gossiped and argued, music and the tinkle of falling water and the scent of flowering trees softened the air, and Eleanor listened and learned the details and feelings that made a living reality of the parchment documents she had been studying during the day.

She was slightly annoyed when the ceremonial entrance of a servant carrying an enormous brass tray of sweetmeats interrupted the revealing argument between a Syrian-born Frankish knight and Black Hugh of Lusignan.

The head cook, an imposing figure in a high Moslem-style turban and a brocaded purple tunic only slightly marked with grease spots, preceded the servant and stood slightly to one side while the boy knelt before Eleanor to display the selection on the tray.

"*These,*" the cook said, "gracious majesty, are sugared violets."

"And very beautifully done," Eleanor said.

"These are pastries filled with a preserve of apricots and nuts. And these are grapes in wine."

"Yes?"

"There is no flesh of bird or animal here. I would not commit the solecism of serving *quail in malmsey sauce* as an evening sweetmeat, any more than I would send *sugared violets* to the noontime dinner table."

"Of course not," Eleanor agreed so warmly that the cook wondered, for a minute, if some malicious servant had scrambled her message. "Now tell me, sir—"

"Malouf," the cook said, "just Malouf."

"Tell me, Sir Malouf, where do you get all these delicious fruits? Are they all grown locally? And how can you have fresh fruit so early in the year?"

"Sir" Malouf relaxed and told Eleanor rather more than most people would have wanted to know about the orchards of Syria and Transjordan and Damascus, the trade routes and the markets where farmers from enemy states quietly slipped over the border to sell produce from warmer southern climates at inflated prices.

Sounds of jingling mail, tired horses, laughing men came dimly through the thick walls of the palace surrounding the courtyard. Malouf spoke more loudly. Constance, who had been twiddling with a bit of embroidery while Eleanor indulged her strange taste for talking with all sorts of common people and even servants, brightened and sat up like a fading rose that had just been revived with cool water. "Raymond is back—and safely, or they would not all sound so cheerful!"

"More than cheerful," Eleanor concurred, once her attention was drawn to the noises coming from the stables. Raymond's great, full laugh rang out over the voices of the other men. The sound reminded her of her grandfather recounting tales of his old conquests . . . except that the old troubadour had been frail and ancient in her childhood. Raymond had the laugh of a man in the fullness of his strength; he sounded as his father, her grandfather, must have done when he was actually enjoying the life of nonstop battles and seductions and feuds he recounted in old age with such gusto. A young, strong man, golden as the sun . . . no wonder Constance wilted when he was away and revived when he returned. "Where has he been?"

Constance gave her a strange look. "He didn't tell you?"

"Maybe," Eleanor conceded. "I've been busy."

At that moment Raymond strode in through the double doors that led to the outer buildings, still in half-armor, clasping his helm under one arm and barely slowing as young Gautier chased after him and tried to do a proper squire's service by unfastening the rest of his lord's mail. Both men were coated with the fine white dust of the country; their faces were masks of dust streaked with lines of sweat, and a smell of unwashed horses and men surrounded them like an invisible cloud.

Constance gave a small shriek as Raymond approached her. "You are as filthy as a Bedawi camel driver! Let Gautier tend you, my lord, and let you *both* go and wash; then you shall have as many kisses of greeting as you desire."

Raymond laughed, clasped Constance about the waist, and swung her into the air. She squeaked with excitement and pretended dismay, returned his kiss, then mimed coughing and choking and held her nose as soon as he set her back down.

"Ha, Eleanor!" Raymond turned to her. "Not still buried in musty parchments?"

"I am ready to approach Louis," she told him. "I know now exactly what arguments—"

"No need," Raymond said cheerfully. "I've his promise of support before the council."

"You have?"

Raymond's blue eyes shifted slightly, fixing on the arched windows behind her. "Well—as good as his word on it. While you were educating yourself about Outremer, I just borrowed a few of his knights and rode out to take a look at the defenses of Aleppo. Nureddin did some damage to the walls when he took the city, and he's been too busy trying to conquer the rest of the world to have the fortifications properly repaired. Everard de Barres agrees with me that we should be able to take it easily, and he says Louis always takes his advice on military matters."

Since Cadmos, Louis had done more than take the Templar's advice, he had turned the army over to him entirely. But . . . Eleanor frowned. Antioch was not Cadmos; there were more problems here than the simple one of staying alive until they could reach the safety of the Frankish states in Outremer.

"If the grand master of the Templars is with us, that is good," she said, "but it may not be enough. This is not just a military question, Raymond—it is also political. You should know that better than I." Her days of study, gossip, and questioning had shown her the complex web of alliances, feuds, loyalties, and rivalries that barely held the Latin kingdoms of Outremer together. Only the constant threat of the Turks and the shortage of knights kept the separate states from breaking into constant internecine warfare. And the Crusaders had remedied that second problem. . . . "Raymond." She said what should not need to be pointed out. "There will be at least a dozen different interests represented at the council meeting, a score of voices arguing that the military force of the Crusade should be put to this or that objective. Your desire to attack Aleppo might be seen as just another self-serving demand. We must make sure that Louis understands the overall strategy that would be served by making Aleppo and Caesarea—Shaizar—our first targets."

And overall strategy had never been Louis's strength.

"Oh, stop worrying, puss," Raymond told her. "You want to be sure that I appreciate all your plotting and planning. Well, I do. It kept the ones who stayed here out of mischief while I was leading the expedition to Aleppo, and I'm duly grateful.

Now doesn't a poor old kinsman get a kiss for wearing himself out in the Syrian sun?"

Eleanor dodged behind the bench she had been sitting on. "*Not* before he washes off the Syrian dust," she told him. "And the Frankish sweat as well! I've no mind to take this fine sendal gown back to France marked with such souvenirs of our voyage."

"Fine," Raymond said, "don't take it back to France. Now——"

He spread out his arms. Eleanor assessed the slight bend in his knees, the shifting of weight, and fled into the safety afforded by Constance's giggling ladies just as her uncle leapt over the bench with a great clanking of mail.

"You're getting old and slow, Raymond!" Constance teased.

Raymond looked wounded. "Hey. It's not every man my age who can still mount a horse——"

"——or a bench," interpolated Gautier with a snicker.

"——*or a bench*," Raymond went on without pausing, "in full armor."

"Half-armor," Gautier said pertly. "At least I got *some* of it off him before he started playing around."

"Anyway," Raymond demanded, "I captured *you*, didn't I?"

Constance looked up at him through her lashes. "Maybe I wanted to be caught . . . and maybe your niece doesn't!" She gave him a little push and pretended to scold. "Now get on to the baths, you and all your great big sweaty friends. I don't know what our guests will be thinking—such horseplay with the queen of France, of all things!"

Raymond grinned. "When I come back, she'll think how much cleaner and pleasanter we Franks of Outremer are. Everard de Barres didn't go straight to the baths, you know. *He* doesn't use them at all. Against his Templar vows. And L—one of the other Franks says they are dangerously sensual pleasures and not appropriate for Christian men."

On the next day it was the ladies' turn to use the private bathhouse that was an integral part of the place. Eleanor and Faenze joined Constance and her ladies in the pool of deliciously warm, silken, flower-scented water. Through the water, a mosaic pattern of flowers and leaves seemed to waver like a greenish illusion, the forest of a dream. Eleanor sat back on one of the steps and let her eyes wander over the graceful patterns of the mosaic while Faenze rubbed suds into her hair, piled the water-weighted mass up on top of her head, and massaged the back of her neck with skillful fingers. The design of intertwining green leaves and vines was so subtle that she could never quite trace it long enough to be sure just how it repeated. Someone would splash and disturb the water, or a cluster of soap bubbles would drift across and obscure the view. It was curiously soothing to look at, though; she felt as though she herself were following the sinuous curves of the vine, like the curves and turns of her own life. Darkness and light, danger and safety, death and life, all alternated and all were renewed. If she could just look at the pattern long enough, find her way into the heart of this forest, would she know the shape ordained for her own life? Would she be able to find her way again?

Nonsense. I know where I am going and what I am doing. What was the point of losing herself in a maze of speculation when there were practical, immediate tasks to deal with? She must get out of the lazy comfort of the bath, dry her hair, and have Faenze dress her in something appropriate for making an impression on Louis. No matter how confident Raymond might be of Louis's support, Eleanor wanted a chance to impress him with the political and strategic superiority of attacking Aleppo before the council meeting.

"Rinse my hair, Faenze," she said, interrupting the light gossip of the ladies. "We cannot spend all day lounging in the baths."

"Why not?" Constance asked lazily. "Or do you wish to visit the bazaars yourself today, instead of having the merchants bring their goods here for you to select from? I *told* you that gilt samite was not the best—"

"It will serve," Eleanor said. "I have not time to worry about my dresses today." During the preceding days of study and argument, she had scandalized Constance by seeing to the repair of her own wardrobe in the quickest manner possible, sending for a few merchants of fine fabrics and trimmings to bring a selection of their wares for her to look over. No trader in Antioch refused a summons to the household of the prince. On one day she bought silks and whisper-light fine cottons, on the next day braids and trims, and by the end of the week Constance's sewing women had put together what Eleanor considered a fitting selection of gowns for a great queen traveling through the East and her waiting women. Constance clearly felt that Eleanor had cheated herself of all the pleasures to be had in trailing through the bazaars, fingering furs and silks and having merchants open bales of new-brought wares. Creating a queen's wardrobe could have taken an enjoyable six months of debate over colors and costs, sleeves and bodices. It was almost indecent to make vital decisions so quickly, not to mention the cost of buying everything without preliminary haggling!

"Next week," she promised Constance, "you shall show me the bazaars. I will be depending on your knowledge of the city to help me replace all the small things we lost on our way here." She did, actually, regret having to replace her wardrobe by proxy. She imagined the bazaars of Antioch as a fairyland of brilliant colors and gossamer-fine silks and gold-threaded brocades, and there was really no substitute for taking a fold of fabric between your own finger and thumb to gauge its drape and weave. But there would be time enough to enjoy herself later, while the army they had brought to the Holy Land marched out to take Aleppo. And tomorrow, Joscelin of Edessa was expected to reach Antioch. His supporters had already persuaded Louis that it would not be fair to decide the next move of the Crusade without giving Count Joscelin a hearing. Eleanor felt it would be only wise to make sure Louis had all the information she had so painstakingly gathered, proving beyond a doubt that it would be suicidal to attempt retaking Edessa before they had reconquered Aleppo and Caesarea, before any formal meeting.

Covered in a loose-fitting gown of whisper-light woven cotton, as airy as a spring breeze against her damp skin, Eleanor sat by a window and let Faenze comb out her wet hair. Once it dried, she could dress more formally—the gold samite Constance had scorned as imperfect work might be a good choice—and make her visit to the patriarch's household where her husband resided.

The young men of Raymond's household were laughing and playing around in the courtyard this morning, vying to see who could make the most extravagant boast of his plans for taking Aleppo. Eleanor listened with half an ear to their horseplay and their shouted wagers. Who would be first over the walls, would take the most ransoms, would kill the most Turks?

"They never think," she said to Faenze, "that perhaps the Turks will kill some of *them*."

Faenze divided her mistress's hair into two sections, plaited one half loosely to keep it out of the way and dropped it forward over Eleanor's bosom while she concentrated on combing out the other section. "If young men thought about being killed, how could we have wars? Cowards should go into the church."

A man's steps sounded on the stairs as she was speaking. "We would all be a sight better off," said Raymond of Antioch, "if *one* man at least had gone into the church as he was supposed to do." He glared at Eleanor. "Do you *know* what the stinking, two-tongued, treacherous sod has done?"

"The council meeting is tomorrow."

"Today," Raymond corrected her with bitter satisfaction. "Count Joscelin arrived in midmorning and demanded that Louis immediately pledge his support to attack Edessa. Naturally your husband called all his great lords and bishops to advise him. God forbid he should make an intelligent decision on his own!"

"And they *advised* him to attack Edessa first? I don't believe it! Thierry at least is not so stupid. And you had his promise..."

Raymond leaned against the door frame. "Oh, no," he said. "Nothing so sensible and reasonable as taking Edessa will do for the holy Louis. Oh, he listened to me. He listened to Raymond of Tripoli. He listened to Joscelin. *And* he listened to the patriarch of Jerusalem, who wanted him to know that Conrad of Hohenstaufen was already in the Holy Land, having taken ship from Constantinople to Acre. And then he folded his holy hands and announced that his vow of Crusade obliged him to complete his pilgrimage by visiting the sacred shrines of Jerusalem before he could consider any acts of war."

"Jerusalem." Eleanor closed her eyes briefly and called to mind the maps she had studied with Raymond and his advisers. Of course Jerusalem was the center of the world, the most holy place known, and of course they would make their pilgrimage there. Eventually. But Jerusalem was also in the center of the Frankish domains, well protected on all sides. Whereas here in Antioch—"

"There must be some mistake," she said. "I will speak with him myself."

"My lady! Your hair—"

"I can plait the other half myself," Eleanor said. "Raymond, you will escort me?"

"It might work out better if Louis didn't see me right now," Raymond said frankly.

"Why? Did you call him a two-tongued, treacherous sod to his face?"

"Umm... harsh words were exchanged," Raymond admitted. "Mind you, I've a perfect right to be angry. He as good as promised me his support, then turns around like this . . . but just at the moment, I do not think I am the king's favorite person."

"It's not about whether he likes you," Eleanor said, "it's about how to use the army most effectively. Can't he see that?"

"God send you may cause him to see it," said Raymond, "but I think you'll do better without me."

In the end it was Gautier who, for propriety, escorted Eleanor through the streets of Antioch to the patriarch's house. Here she came face to face with Louis at the shaded porch that protected the front of the building from the Syrian sun.

"My lord! You are not going out? I came to see you."

"How kind of you," Louis said. "What made your need of me so urgent? I understand you have been quite happy in the prince's household."

"My uncle and his wife have been very kind. And I have been busy." Eleanor took a breath. "Busy learning about these lands. The political situation is complicated—"

"I do not require instruction from my wife in these matters," Louis interrupted.

"You need instruction from *somebody!*"

"Come inside." Louis took her arm in an ungentle grasp. "If you are determined to quarrel with me, you shall not do so in the street like a peasant woman. There has been more than enough gossip about you already!"

The rooms inside the patriarch's house were cool and bare, pooled with blue shadows from the whitewashed walls and furnished as sparsely as any monk's cell. Eleanor strode back and forth in the room Louis led her to, while he sat on a hard wooden stool and watched her coldly.

"You must see that the danger is in the north," she said, "where Nureddin's troops are concentrated. Why should we bring our army south to Jerusalem? We will only have to march back this way to fight the Turks."

"There is no shortage of infidels to do battle with," Louis said, "and I will lead *my* army where I will. These decisions are not yours to make. I have vowed to go to Jerusalem." She felt pinned against the white wall by his icy stare. "I have made a private vow that I will not eat meat or wear silk or enjoy the embraces of my wife until we have made our pilgrimage to Jerusalem, and then God will grant us a son."

"You have His word on it, I suppose? Be careful of the promises of the great."
Eleanor flashed. "Raymond thought he had your word that you would support him
against Aleppo."

"God has not sent me to this land to support the pretensions of a Provençal
fortune hunter," Louis said. "If your uncle is so lost in dalliance and soft Eastern
ways that he cannot keep the princedom he gained through marriage with the lady
Constance, that is not my problem to solve."

Eleanor's brows arched. "Oh? You have some objection to men who profit by
their marriage? And I suppose you do not enjoy the revenues of Aquitaine and the
feudal service of my vassals?"

"That is beside the point," Louis said. "We march for Jerusalem in the morning.
Prepare your household."

"Take *your* army, then," Eleanor said. "I will stay here with my vassals."

"As my wife, you go where I go!"

"Perhaps I am not your wife," Eleanor cried. "We are related within the forbidden degrees—we had no dispensation for the marriage—perhaps *that* is why God has
not given us the son you desire so ardently. It is time for us to separate." It seemed
wonderfully, beautifully clear now. "You go on to Jerusalem. I shall stay here with my
kinsman. My men of the south are more than enough to defend Antioch."

Louis drew in a long, hissing breath. "So," he said, quietly, "it is as I thought—or
worse. Eleanor, I will not allow you to shame yourself and me in this way. You cannot
remain here as Raymond's leman."

"As Raymond's— You're mad."

"No. I *was* mad, mad with love for you, mad enough to deny all the filthy gossip
that your behavior here has caused. Now I am sane enough for both of us. You will
come to Jerusalem with me, you will forget this unclean love, you will be a dutiful
wife again. Christ will enter your heart and all will be well." Louis's eyes shone as
though he could see a vision of unearthly beauty.

Eleanor shook her head in disbelief. "Don't you hear *anything* I say? This is not
about Raymond," she said, as she had done to her uncle. "It is about how best to use
the army. It would be foolish to march south now, when—"

"Peace! It is not your place to instruct me," Louis informed her, "but mine to
instruct you. I have failed of my duty to you by leaving you too long in Raymond's
household. Do you think it pleases me to hear about your shameless behavior with

him? Fondling and kissing in public—they say he behaves not like uncle and niece, but like some infidel potentate who keeps a dozen wives at once. I am surprised the lady Constance countenances such behavior, but then, she was born out here; perhaps she knows no better."

"You're mad," Eleanor said again. "I—you do not understand our southern manners."

"Indeed I do not," Louis snapped. "My mother would die before she would parade herself through the streets dressed like that. I thought you had learned some decency in Paris, but it seems I was mistaken. You come before me like *that* and expect me to believe that you are pleading Raymond's cause only for political reasons?"

Eleanor glanced down at the fine white robe that she had not troubled to change before leaving. It was not as impressive as the samite gown she had planned to wear, but it was perfectly decent—except, perhaps, where the heavy plaits of her hair, still damp from the bath, had dampened the fabric so that it clung to her bosom. She crossed her arms and glared at Louis.

"If you would *listen* to my reasons, perhaps you might be able to understand them. Raymond—"

"I thank you," Louis interrupted. "I need hear no more of your dearly beloved *uncle*. Until I saw you I had not believed the rumors. But if you will fling yourself out of the house dressed like a whore from the stews, only to quarrel with me on Raymond's behalf, why should I not believe you whore with him in private too?"

"Because I tell you it's nonsense!"

"Is it? *Is* it? Half Antioch thinks he has made you his newest mistress and laughs at me for letting you stay there!"

"Then half Antioch is wrong," Eleanor said.

"Prove it to me." Louis stood up and grasped her shoulders, drawing her close to him. "Prove to me that you are faithful."

"In God's name, how? If you have not the sense to discard foolish gossip for yourself, how shall I prove it to you? Will you humiliate me by asking my ladies whether I have not slept among them, in the same chamber, every night since we have come to Antioch?"

"Lust keeps no timetable. Who knows where you have been in the afternoons?

What trysts you may have kept in the mornings? You are in his house, it would be easy—"

"When exactly do you think he lay with me? Before or after his journey to scout out the Turkish defenses of Aleppo? The man has not even *been* in Antioch most of this time, Louis!"

"Prove your honesty." Louis released his grip on her shoulders and fumbled at the breast of his own gown, bringing out a tiny box of gold filigree on the end of a fine chain. "Swear by this piece of the True Cross, which the patriarch of Jerusalem brought me only this morning, that you have never lain with any man but me."

Eleanor put out a hand to take the reliquary. The heat of it surprised her; she jerked her fingers away. Of course, it had been lying next to Louis's skin, but should it be quite so hot? Now that she paused for a moment, she could feel the waves of heat emanating from Louis. His hands were shaking, too; he had been leaning on her as much to steady himself as to hold her.

"Go on," Louis urged. "It will not burn you . . . not if you are honest."

"My lord, you are ill," Eleanor said, trying to keep her voice calm and soothing. "I believe you have taken a fever from this Eastern sun. Will you not lie down and allow me to make up a soothing drink?"

"I'll have none of your witch brews. Only your oath. Swear to me. Swear on the Cross that you have never played me false."

Eleanor raised her hand to the reliquary again, then drew back. The thin, dark face of the Byzantine emperor seemed to rise between her and the splinter of wood in its golden case.

"Swear!"

The wind swooped outside the shuttered windows of the patriarch's house. It wailed through latticework and stone like a thin, distant crying . . . the crying of a child who had never drawn breath in this world. . . .

If Louis was hot, she felt cold, cold as stone, cold as an unmarked grave in a foreign land. She stared at the dull shine of the golden case and could not speak for the grief that choked her.

Louis stepped back. "You will come with me to Jerusalem," he said. "You will do penance for your sin, and we will be joined together again, and there will be no more talk of consanguinity and divorce."

Eleanor shook her head.

"Oh, yes," Louis said softly. "You *will* obey. Galeran!"

The Templar eunuch stepped into the doorway, so swiftly that he must have been listening all along.

"The queen is overtired," Louis told him. "She will rest here until we are ready to march. You will watch to see that no one disturbs her. Send servants to the prince's house to pack her belongings."

Chapter Sixteen

The young duke of Normandy was in a mood to be irritated by everything—the August heat, the flies that swarmed maddeningly about the riders, the slow pace of the cavalcade, and, above all, the fact that he and his father were actually on their way to Paris to submit their quarrel with Louis to arbitration rather than fighting it out properly on the Norman-French border at Mantes where both armies were drawn up.

Geoffrey's lazy, patronizing explanations of the political situation were only an added irritation, like the horseflies and the sweat trickling down inside his armor.

"Look, Henry," Geoffrey said, "we can't fight it out if the other chap refuses to stand up and fight, see?"

"Louis is lying about being too sick to leave Paris," Henry grumbled. "I know he's lying. He always has an attack of fever when it's convenient."

"Probably," Geoffrey conceded. "He doesn't like to fight. Look at that disaster he called a Crusade!"

"Disaster?"

"Oh, that's right," Geoffrey said silkily, "you were off not conquering England while Louis was off not saving Outremer."

Henry was so red-faced from the heat that any blushes were concealed among the beads of sweat that decorated his freckles. "I may not have beaten Stephen this time, but I did better."

"Yes?"

"I found out that all I have to do is leave him alone and he'll defeat himself. He's so afraid of everybody that he's alienating all his possible allies. He tried to throw Vacarius out of England for lecturing on law; that's got the clerks against him. That idiot Eustace got the archdeacon of York killed, and at the same time Stephen refused the pope's legate safe-conduct through England to Ireland; that's got the pope and the rest of the church against him. He's playing fast and loose with his grants to the barons; half of them are totally out of control and the other half are ready to shift their loyalties to any man who'll confirm them in their charters and keep his word. England wants law. I can give it to them. Let Stephen keep vacillating, and—if my mother will just stay out of it—the English will be *begging* me to take the crown in a few years."

Geoffrey concealed a smile and decided not even to mention that people desirous of stability just might not see it in the person of an eighteen-year-old gamecock who kept raiding their shores. Henry's analysis of the political situation was remarkably good for a boy of his age. Stephen would probably be able to muddle on in England for five or six more years, and by then Henry would have the maturity to present himself as a credible candidate for the throne—especially with the experience he was gaining since Geoffrey had formally handed over his mother's inheritance and named the boy duke of Normandy.

"Good. Then you *do* see that there are times when *not* fighting can be the surest way to winning."

"But I don't see that this is one of them," Henry declared. "We could have attacked Louis's army whether or not he was there, couldn't we?"

"Yes," Geoffrey said patiently, "but we couldn't have destroyed it. These silly border wars—you take my castle, I take one of yours, and let's burn the town just for fun—will go on indefinitely unless we make some kind of deal with Louis. He's not strong enough to destroy Normandy and Anjou, and we're not strong enough to take on France and Aquitaine. Wars are expensive. I want to stop putting out fires and start building up our territories. Do you have any idea what it cost us when Robert of Dreux burnt Séez? A whole productive town that won't be worth anything in taxes for a solid ten years now!"

"Well, we got his castle at La Nue," Henry said.

"Yes, if this were a chess game that would be even, but in chess the pieces stand up again for the next game. It's just wasteful when you burn and break your pieces and have to keep playing anyway. We have to look at what all this border fighting is doing to the economy, don't you see?"

Henry did not particularly want to hear Geoffrey's lecture on Building up the Economy and Peaceful Is Rich once again. It wasn't that he disagreed, really, it was just that he'd heard it too often already. Time for a tactful change of subject. "You never did tell me how Louis fucked up the Crusade," he said hopefully. "I heard some gossip, of course. . . ."

Geoffrey grinned. "In a nutshell, the silly bugger lost half of his men on the march because he didn't know how to defend against Turkish attacks, left Antioch to the mercies of Nureddin instead of shoving him back when he had a chance, attacked the only Arab city that was friendly to us and failed miserably, wasted a year moping around in Jerusalem while his little brother tried to take over the French throne, then sailed back and struck commemorative medals and had Te Deums sung in all the churches. If Abbot Suger hadn't been minding the store, Robert would have France and Aquitaine would have split off into a bunch of independent baronies before Louis got back."

"And Suger's not looking out for Louis anymore." The little abbot had died in January, worn out before his time from managing the kingdom of the Franks for Louis the Fat and his ineffectual son Louis the Pious.

"Which," said Geoffrey cheerfully, "is what makes it a good time to make deals with Louis. I don't mind giving him back that bastard Gerald Berlai if I can get him to stop helping Eustace go after Normandy for a while. Fair trade." He thought that over for a while. "Better than fair; Gerald is such an idiot, he'll alienate the Poitevins if he's put in charge again. Between Gerald Berlai in charge of Poitou and Geoffrey de Rancon as seneschal for Aquitaine, the whole of the south should be ripe for revolt pretty soon. That'll keep Louis too busy to trouble us in Normandy and Anjou."

"But you told the messenger you meant to keep Gerald in chains for the rest of his life in revenge for what he did to our monks of Saint-Aubin!"

Geoffrey chuckled. "Of course I did. Why should I tell Louis that I'm sick and tired of listening to Gerald's yapping and would pay to have him taken off my hands? That's no way to bargain. I want reparations for all the money I spent besieging Montreuil, and I want Louis to repudiate Eustace's claims against Normandy."

Henry was unwillingly impressed. "And you think you can get all that for one prisoner?"

"No harm in trying!"

"And anyway," Henry said, cheering up, "I'll get to see the French queen. I hear she's worth a visit to Paris!"

"You've seen her," Geoffrey said. "When you were a little boy. Remember when we went to Paris to see Abbot Suger consecrate his new-built church? I took you to Bernard of Clairvaux to get his blessing?"

"He didn't like me," Henry said cheerfully. "I remember *that*. 'From the devil he comes, and to the devil he'll go,' he said."

"Remember the woman who was with him just before we went in? She went past us in the hall. . . ."

Rustle of silk skirts, a cloud of sharp sweet perfume, a woman with tears in her eyes and a body straight as a fine sword.

"*Definitely* worth a trip to Paris," Henry said. "Too bad I was too young to appreciate her when she was in her prime."

"By the gossip from Outremer," Geoffrey said, "she's still prime, though I never did hear the right of it. Some said the king wanted to divorce her for adultery with her uncle, and some said she wanted to divorce him for being an incompetent fool. Arnulf!" he called to one of the men riding just behind them. "Come up here. My son wants to hear about the scandal."

The bishop of Lisieux spurred his dun palfrey to draw level with Henry. The white dust kicked up by the leading riders had given both the palfrey and the bishop a look of prematurely white hair. "Which scandal?" Arnulf inquired pleasantly. "Petronilla running away with Raoul de Vermandois?"

"That's history, not scandal. After they've got three children and the pope unexcommunicated them and Louis and Thibaut quit fighting over it, it doesn't count as gossip anymore," Geoffrey said repressively. "About Louis and Eleanor on the Crusade. You were there. What actually happened? Did she want to divorce him, or was he trying to dump her? And what did the pope have to say about it?"

"I saw that girl the day she decided to marry Louis," Arnulf said. "Did I ever tell you about that? Looked like a queen even then—she couldn't have been more than, oh, fifteen or sixteen. Her father had just died and she knew as soon as the news got out she'd be prey to every fortune-hunting baron in Poitou and Aquitaine. The archbishop and his advisers were making lists of possible husbands.... You were spoken of," he said to Geoffrey, "but I pointed out that you were married already."

"Thank you," Geoffrey said. "I think." He shook his head. "No, it's for the best. I couldn't have held Anjou and Aquitaine both, not at that time."

"Also," said Henry, "my mother might have killed you if you tried to divorce her for a fifteen-year-old duchess."

"There is that," Geoffrey agreed.

"Anyway, young Louis was her idea. That will of Duke William's, leaving her in the French king's wardship?"

"Yes?"

"Forged. I was there when they decided—when she *told* the archbishop to do it. Then she had the man who'd brought the news of her father's death *and* everyone he'd spoken to kept prisoner in Bordeaux until her messenger could get to the old king with the news of Duke William's death. Including me," he said ruefully. "I played a *lot* of chess with young Eleanor while we waited. She was mightily pleased with herself for having thought of a young husband who would be powerful enough to keep Aquitaine and her safe. Of course, she'd never met Louis.... I thought at the time she might rue the bargain someday. But you don't tell the duchess of Aquitaine she's making a mistake."

"And was it a mistake?" Henry asked. "I heard they haven't any sons because they married within the forbidden degrees without getting the pope's dispensation."

Arnulf dismissively waved one slender hand. "I doubt that Our Lord is such a niggler over details. If marrying your relatives within the seventh degree of consanguinity were a sin, the noble families of Christendom would die out in a generation; you trace things back far enough, everybody's related to everybody else. Anyway, I did hear that Pope Eugenius formally absolved them of any sin when that question was raised, on their way back from Sicily. More than that, he told them to stop quarreling like foolish children and saw them bedded together in his own house, like a second bride night. And what came of that? Another daughter!"

"What about Antioch?"

Arnulf raised his black, slanting brows. "What *about* Antioch?"

"You were there," Geoffrey said impatiently. "Is it true she played the wanton with her own uncle and Louis wanted to put her aside for it, but that Abbot Suger wouldn't hear of his giving up her lands?"

"Does it matter?"

"Well," Geoffrey said, more slowly this time, "it might. . . . After all, Suger's not advising the king now. Bernard of Clairvaux is the strongest voice in young Louis's court, and he cares nothing for worldly considerations and has often criticized the queen for being too light-minded. And everybody knows that Pope Eugenius asks Bernard's advice before he takes a crap, let alone any bigger decision. If the case for divorce were brought again, the results might be different, don't you think?"

Arnulf gave Geoffrey a long, considering look. They were both tall men; they could exchange glances over Henry's tousled red head. "So that's why you agreed to come to Paris for this arbitration?"

"It is a factor," Geoffrey said. "One of many."

"Well, then." Arnulf considered his next words carefully. "I myself never believed she had sinned with her uncle. In fact," he said, remembering those crowded days in Antioch, the hasty assembling of facts and figures by day and the "social" evenings of ascertaining where the loyalties of the most powerful men lay, "I don't think she would have had *time;* they were both too busy planning how to bring the Crusaders and the Latins of Outremer together in an assault on Aleppo. But if you ask me to swear it—well, the only ones who could know the truth of it for sure are Raymond and Eleanor themselves. And Raymond's dead. So if you want to ask Eleanor," he said with a smile, "have the goodness to warn me first, so that I can watch from a safe distance!"

"Hot-tempered, is she?"

"Any woman would be, asked a question like that. And with Eleanor . . . personally, I'd rather walk through Greek fire stark naked and carrying a lighted torch."

"There's a Knight Templar among Louis's counselors," Geoffrey said. "Thierry Galeran. You know him?"

Arnulf's lips tightened. "The eunuch. Yes. He was among Louis's retinue on the Crusade. A very . . . pious man, I suppose, according to his lights. He kept the Templar rule so strictly that you could smell him coming from two leagues away, especially in the summer."

"I met a Templar who told me that Thierry told him that Louis asked Eleanor that very question, asked her to swear her innocence on a holy relic, and she could not do it."

Arnulf threw up his hands. "And I know a man who knows a man who knows a monk whose sow littered six greyhounds, only somehow nobody can tell you the name of the monastery where it happened but only that it was someplace very far away. No, I cannot *swear* that nothing untoward happened in Antioch. But I know Eleanor, and I know Louis, and I can tell you one thing that I *will* swear to: if she were married to a man who knew what to do with a woman, instead of that half monk, she would never betray him. She wouldn't bother," he said, half to himself, "the sins of the flesh simply aren't that important to her. A man who captured her mind would have her, body and soul. The important question, I think," he said, "is, do you think you can hold Anjou and Normandy and Aquitaine *now?*"

"I don't have to hold Normandy," Geoffrey said, clapping his son on the shoulder. "Normandy does very well with its new young duke."

"Normandy and Anjou together are too strong for Louis's peace of mind," Arnulf pointed out. "That's why you keep having these border squabbles. If Aquitaine were joined to those two, Louis might never sleep sound in his bed again."

"In that case," Geoffrey said with a grin, "let's be considerate and not even mention the possibility to him. After all, it's not imminent. Eleanor is still married."

Henry turned his shoulder on Arnulf and stared at his father. The fact that he had to look up slightly to do so in no way diminished the quality of menace in his eyes. "So," he said, "are you."

The long summer had left Paris stifling, hot, and stinking. In the Great Hall where Louis had assembled his nobles and advisers to witness the humbling of the Angevins, the smell of large unwashed men and dogs mingled with the pestilential airs that rose in the heat from the cesspools of the city. The armholes of Petronilla's long green bliaut cut into the flesh beneath her arms. The overdress had been cut out several years ago, before three pregnancies changed her from a slim girl to a generously built, deep-bosomed matron. But it was the finest garment she possessed, and nothing less would have done justice to the day—or so Eleanor insisted.

Petronilla surreptitiously wiped away the sweat that gathered around the tight band of her wimple and looked at her sister with envy. Eleanor was older than she was and had borne two children herself, even if they were both only girls; she had no right to look so straight and slender, so cool and untroubled by the heat and the pressing crowd. The white band around her face was crisp and smooth, and the bulky plaits of her light brown hair fell below her waist with no need for padding out such as Petronilla's tiring woman had to do with long strands of wool concealed inside the skimpy ends of the braids. "They're late," she said. "How long do you want to wait here?"

"As long as it takes," Eleanor said blithely. "By my faith and Saint Radegonde, I have been so *bored* lately. Don't you want to see the count of Anjou for yourself? When I was on Crusade, his sister Sybille never ceased to fill my ears with tales of his perfection—the very model of manly beauty, chivalry, and scholarship all in one, or so she claimed."

Petronilla sighed under her breath. It was a pity that Eleanor could not find enough to amuse her in a woman's proper realm of childbearing, sewing, and overseeing the comfort of her household, and so insisted on pushing her way into assemblies like this where men would debate on men's affairs at interminable length. It wasn't improper, exactly; Eleanor was not the only noble lady who had come in the expectation of seeing the upstart count of Anjou humbled before the righteous wrath of Bernard of Clairvaux. It was just . . . well . . . *boring.* Waiting was boring, and listening to Geoffrey of Anjou debate borders and feudal obligations with Louis was undoubtedly going to be even more boring, and most likely he'd just give in to anything Louis wanted. Agreeing to let Bernard of Clairvaux arbitrate between them was tantamount to giving in to Louis before he started, and this Geoffrey must know that. Petronilla sighed again and resisted the urge to tug her bliaut down where the tight armholes were cutting into her flesh, and suggested without much hope that she might at least go back to Eleanor's bower and take a little nap while they waited for the Angevins to show up.

"Not *now,*" Eleanor whispered. "Something's about to happen, don't you hear all those horses outside? I'd never forgive myself if I let you miss this, Petronilla."

Petronilla looked across the faces of the assembled nobility of France and saw nothing she hadn't seen a hundred times before. Louis had seated himself in his fine chair with its high carved back, raised a little from the floor by a dais draped in fine blue wool embroidered with golden flowers. The low stools that had been provided for Geoffrey Plantagenet and his son would make them feel like children awaiting their father's scolding . . . if Louis could only carry it off with appropriate dignity. His face was pale and sweating under the crown he had donned for the occasion, either from the fever he claimed had prevented his marching to take on the Angevin troops in battle or from the weight of his long, heavily embroidered gown and floor-sweeping cloak.

Beside his chair on the left stood her dear Raoul, holding the mace that symbolized his status as seneschal of all France. Although nearly sixty now, he was still a fine figure of a man, broad-shouldered and ruddy-faced—twice the man that Eleanor's Louis was, at twice his age! *And* he had given her a son . . . Petronilla hastily turned her thoughts away from young Raoul in his sheltered monastery. Folk said the boy's leprosy was a curse on her marriage to Raoul, but how could that be, when she had borne two healthy girls since? God willing, soon there would be another son to be a proper heir to Vermandois. . . . She would pray Bernard of Clairvaux to intercede for her in that matter; he would surely be in a good mood after putting the upstart Angevin in his place.

She glanced uneasily at the saintly monk of Clairvaux, seated on Louis's other side, and wondered if he was ever in a good mood. His coarse brown robe, stained and torn, was like a rebuke to the worldly glory around him. His nose was wrinkled in distaste as he looked over the finely dressed courtiers—not from his own smell, presumably, a man who was too holy ever to wash properly must get used to the smell, but in disapproval of all these silks and satins, these mincing pointed shoes and painted faces. Petronilla shifted her weight and thought that perhaps she would change into something plainer—and looser—before approaching Bernard. She might wash off the fine dusting of blanchet her woman had applied that morning to give her rosy face a fashionably pale look, too, although the sweat trickling down her cheeks had probably taken care of that.

The heavy double doors at the end of the great hall swung open, and a murmur of anticipation ran through the courtiers like a fresh wind through the heavy stands of wheat that surrounded the city at this time, awaiting the harvest.

"Here he comes," Eleanor murmured unnecessarily. Her hand gripped Petronilla's arm a little too tightly, leaving the imprint of each separate finger under the long green sleeve.

The man who walked—no, swaggered—into the hall was a head taller than Louis. Where the French king's heavy ceremonial robes overpowered him, this man's travel-stained leathers set off the golden crown of his own hair and emphasized the muscular contours of his body. Blue eyes blazed from a face set in lines of anger.

Petronilla drew in her breath and forgot about the boredom of politics. Here was no penitent come to beg forgiveness for his cruelty to a prisoner and ask for the lifting of his excommunication. This was a man as proud and defiant in the heart of the French king's lands as he would be at the head of his own army.

She scarcely had eyes for the lesser men who followed him, the stocky red-haired boy and the dark bishop whose white miter of authority sat oddly above his own travel-stained garments and the rest of Geoffrey's small guard. But a gasp of astonishment from the men around her drew her attention to the last man in the little procession.

Gerald Berlai, baron of Montreuil and seneschal of the king's borders with Anjou, had been brought to this meeting of "reconciliation" like a common criminal instead of a noble prisoner awaiting ransom. Chains ran from the iron bands about his wrists to a belt at his waist; another chain joined his feet, forcing him to take mincing steps like a lady. He clanked dolefully at each step.

Louis leaned forward, his face even paler than before, but Bernard spoke before he could open his mouth.

"Vile and rapacious sinner, how dare you approach us in this manner?"

"He's all of that," Geoffrey said cheerfully, jerking his thumb at Gerald Berlai as though he really thought the monk was addressing his prisoner, "but I think he's repenting now. And if he's not sorry yet, I'll be happy to load on some more chains."

Bernard's mouth worked convulsively and thin lines of spittle gleamed on his thin lips. "You—you—I have excommunicated you for this!"

"Then you can't do it again, can you?" Geoffrey nodded to the monk, propped one foot on the low stool that had been provided for him to sit on, and looked up at Louis with a grin. "I did not come here to debate religion," he said. "I came to treat with the most noble, brave, and puissant Louis, king of the French, over some little disputes at our borders that are growing costly for both our realms. Surely we can talk freely together, man to man, and settle these little problems today?"

Louis glanced at Bernard as though waiting for permission, but the monk's lips were clamped together now and he stood in a sulfurous silence that reminded Petronilla of the air before a summer storm.

"Why, yes—of course—as a good Christian, I have no desire for war between us," Louis stammered.

"Indeed you do not." Geoffrey inclined his head in a semblance of a polite bow. "That has been evident in all your actions."

The stocky redhead standing beside Geoffrey sputtered at this statement but was silenced by a glance from the count's blue eyes. The boy propped one foot on his own stool, and for a moment the similarity of poses brought forth the underlying family resemblance between them: this must be the son, Petronilla thought, the boy who'd been brought here to do homage for Normandy. Then the boy began fiddling with some complex knot of leather laces that he had been holding, and the resemblance faded: he looked more like an unruly apprentice to some craftsman than the son of a count and a duke in his own right.

Louis took Geoffrey's statement at face value, or pretended to, and proceeded to outline what he said would be a fair settlement between them. Geoffrey should formally cede the disputed lands of the Vexin, Henry should do homage for Normandy and acknowledge Louis as his overlord, and Gerald Berlai should be freed on his promise not to rebuild the razed citadel of Montreuil.

"And what do I get out of it?" Geoffrey asked.

Louis raised his brows. "Peace between our realms and ourselves. Is that not what we both desire?"

"Surely," said Geoffrey, "but that's not *all* I want. I want you publicly to repudiate Eustace's claims against Normandy and promise that you will no longer support his attempts to take my son's inheritance—"

"Once the boy has done homage to me as his liege lord," Louis said stiffly, "that goes without saying."

"Doubtless," Geoffrey agreed, "but I'd just as soon have it said and witnessed, if you don't mind."

"As you wish. Would there be anything else?" Louis asked with the faintest trace of sarcasm.

"There would indeed." Geoffrey straightened to his full height and stood facing Louis, no trace of laughter on his face now. "I want full reparations for the damages this brigand has wreaked on my lands and on the monks under my protection." He nodded at Gerald Berlai. "And there'll be no more talk of my taking his promise for anything. Why should I trust the word of a man who has no more honor than a weasel in a henhouse? For years he's been holed up in Montreuil with bastards almost as bad as him, like Rogon de Coue and Paien Bafer, ravaging the lands you set him to guard almost as badly as he used to attack Angers and Saumur."

"But he has mended his ways. You have not complained of his depredations in Angers for some years——"

"Right," Eleanor said, not quite beneath her breath, "now he specializes in extorting double taxes from *my* people on his own side of the border."

Fortunately, her voice was drowned out by Geoffrey's interruption. "He hasn't been *able* to raid into Angers since I built two castles between Loudun and Montreuil to bar the way," he snapped, "and now that I've blocked off Saumur the same way with Coudray and Saint-Martin, he can't get at my lands that way either. So now he's going after the monks of Mairon. Or didn't anybody mention that little matter to you, my gracious king of the French? This piece of vermin was regularly taking the monks captive and extorting ransoms for them, torturing them too, until Saint Aubin himself appeared to me in a dream and told me it was my duty to stop them. I put in three summers besieging Montreuil until Saint Aubin told me to burn the castle by hurling cauldrons of flaming oil from my trebuchets——"

"He did not either," young Henry interrupted indignantly. "That was *my* idea, and I got it from reading your copy of Vegetius."

"Well, then, it was the saint who inspired you to read a book instead of twitching around with your hounds and your hawks, and—put that damned tangle of jesses away, boy, we're dealing with serious matters here!" Geoffrey bellowed at his son. His cheeks were flushed with rage and his hands trembled; he seemed close to one of the legendary Angevin fits of demonic temper. The barely suppressed rage only made him more compelling. If Bernard of Clairvaux was the gloom before a summer storm, the count of Anjou was the lightning flashing around the edges of the cloud.

"At last," Geoffrey said, looking back at Louis, "the castle burning around them, this brigand and his cronies bolted like serpents from their lair. Paien was killed in the sortie, Rogon died of wounds, but this one lived to see me burn his false charters over Mairon in the presence of Bishop Norman and the abbot Robert de Latour-Landry. And your tame monk there had *me* excommunicated for my treatment of this ferret-faced scavenger! Why didn't he excommunicate Gerald Berlai instead, years ago?"

"Heresy, defiance, deadly sin!" Bernard burst forth before Louis could answer. "The world, set in wickedness, deludes with vain pride this degenerate soul forgetful of his own condition. O vain labor indeed, to search after vanity! Hear the word of the Lord, Geoffrey called the Plantagenet, and repent before the devil takes you in your black Angevin bile! Release this innocent man whom you have misused so cruelly, give him into the keeping of my mild and merciful lord Louis, and I shall even now lift the ban of excommunication over you. This is your last warning and your last chance to redeem yourself!"

"Release him? By the head of Saint Denis, man, I'd have hanged him when I took him if the Truce of God had not been in effect while your mild and merciful lord was off doing nothing in Outremer!" Geoffrey thrust his head forward toward Bernard, and his powerful shoulders worked under the leather harness as though he were barely able to restrain himself from physically attacking the man of God. "I count it an honor to be excommunicated for taking this worthless piece of shit prisoner, and if it is indeed a sin . . ." He paused, straightened, and raised both arms toward the ceiling. "If protecting my lands and people from a brigand is a sin, then I pray God not to forgive my fault but rather to strike me dead on the instant!"

In the alarmed hush that followed Geoffrey's prayer, Bernard spoke again. His voice was low and gravelly now, and his eyes had rolled back into his head until only the whites showed. "Not in this instant, sinner, but within the month shall you answer to One greater than I. Repent now for your soul's sake, or you shall rejoin the devil who sent you forth before the new moon rises over the river Loire."

"Is this how you make treaties?" Geoffrey shouted at Louis. "By having your pet monk foam at the mouth and prophesy disasters for anybody who won't lie down and let your robber barons trample on him? This is a travesty! Let me know when you're ready to speak for yourself instead of leaning on this crazy soi-disant saint, and *then* we can negotiate—if I'm still in the mood!"

Turning his back on the king, he stamped out of the hall, followed by his son Henry and the rest of his entourage. Gerald Berlai made a show of stumbling pitifully in his chains, but the effort was wasted; all eyes were on the Plantagenet's back. Petronilla held her breath until the man was out of the hall, half expecting to see the finger of God strike him down before her very eyes.

Beside her, Eleanor drew a long breath of satisfaction. "Now *there*," she said in a low voice, "there goes a *man*—and such a man! Everything Sybille said of him was true. Come to my bower, Petronilla. We cannot talk among all these yapping lordlings."

Petronilla mentally thanked Saint Radegonde that the babble around them covered her sister's comments. Eleanor's recovery from the hard pregnancy and harder birth of Alix, the child conceived during the return from Outremer, had been slow and difficult, but in these last months, as she regained her strength, Eleanor seemed also to have gained a new and shining surface, glittering with a cold defiance like crystals of ice—and with it, a new carelessness. She took no care what she said, or before whom. She had complained before three of Louis's favorites that she was married not to a man, but a monk. She had told poor Abbot Suger that he should have let Robert of Dreux alone when he returned from Outremer with the idea of seizing the crown while Louis dallied in Jerusalem, because a king who *did* something was better than one who only prayed. She had told Louis himself that she wished the count of Anjou *would* hang Gerald Berlai and, while he was at it, all the other Frenchmen whom Louis had set in charge of her lands in the south.

All she needed now, Petronilla thought, was to be caught praising the man who had just defied not only Louis but also Bernard of Clairvaux. Didn't she know that queens had been put aside for less? Especially queens who had given their lord only two daughters in fourteen years of marriage?

As soon as they reached the relative privacy of the bower, where Eleanor dismissed all her women except Faenze, Petronilla hinted delicately at these concerns. She was shocked when Eleanor laughed in her face.

"Put me aside? Ah, sweet Jesu, would that Louis could make such a decision! What do you *think* I've been praying for since dear old Suger died? Louis is dancing to Bernard's tune now, and so is the pope. Bernard has already said that Louis and I are related within the forbidden degrees—"

"Pope Eugenius gave you his dispensation for that," Petronilla reminded her, "when you came back from Outremer."

"Faenze! Let loose my hair; these plaits are giving me the headache. I do not speak of Outremer," Eleanor said to Petronilla, tearing off the linen band around her face while Faenze worked at the heavy plaits of fair brown hair, "or of what came after. That is all *over*. Over and done with," she went on in a dreamy tone as the ends of her unbound hair began to crackle around her waist and hips, "over and dead . . ." She stroked an ivory comb in the shape of a lion; half the lion's claws were gone now, and a crack in the lion's mane was stained rusty brown, but she still treasured the thing. "Dead, like my uncle Raymond. He died defending Antioch, you know, died because my holy lord Louis wanted to be a pilgrim and not a soldier. He refused Raymond the use of our armies out of spite—and the next year Nureddin sent Raymond's head and right arm to Baghdad. . . . All that is over now." She stopped sharply. "I do not think of it anymore. And soon I need not think of my monk of a husband, either. All I have been waiting for is to pick on a man who can hold Aquitaine for me against Louis—and this time," she said, deliberately running her fingers through the loosened plaits until her hair crackled all around her like a cloak of summer lightning, "*this* time I am too wise to choose a husband sight unseen."

"You haven't seen one now," Petronilla said. She felt like someone shouting warnings at the rising sea, telling it of the rocks it must shortly break against. "Geoffrey's married too. Even if you manage to end your own marriage, what of his?"

Eleanor stretched and arched her back like a cat, ran her hands down a waist still reed-slim after two pregnancies and rested them on the gentle swell of her hips. "Oh, I've heard about *that* marriage. Matilda is twelve years older than he and notoriously hard to get along with."

Sometimes a storm tide could drive the sea over the rocks as if they did not even exist.

"And heiress to England."

Eleanor dismissed that too. "She may think so, but in all these years of fighting she's hardly persuaded the English to see it her way. And when did Geoffrey ever help her in that battle? That fire-haired son of his already has Normandy, and every few years he goes over and makes a gesture at claiming England—he and Matilda can continue that game whether or not Geoffrey stays in it. The Plantagenet cares nothing for a misty island at the western edge of the world," she said blithely, "nor do I. That is a game for pawns at the far reaches of the board. But joining Anjou to Aquitaine—*that*," she said with satisfaction, "is a move worthy of a queen and a knight."

"I don't play chess," Petronilla said hopelessly, "but Eleanor, this is not a game. Even if Geoffrey agreed with you, would Louis let you join Anjou and Aquitaine?" Men could build breakwaters to contain the worst storm tide.

"I do not propose to ask him," Eleanor said. She pushed the freed masses of light brown hair away from her face. Even in this hot, damp air, the individual strands curled and snapped with energy and clung to her forehead like waves curling into a tempestuous froth. "I propose only to be troubled in my conscience again over the matter of our consanguinity and to wonder whether it is for this sin that God has denied us a son." She smiled brilliantly at Petronilla. "The holy Bernard will be quite willing to agree that I am a sinner and a liability to the throne, don't you think?"

"Think of the scandal! And—he is under ban of excommunication . . ."

Eleanor's smile took on an icy sparkle. "Why, Petronilla, you yourself showed me how foolish it is to allow scandals and excommunications to stand in the way of true love!"

Benoît de Périgné had drifted as far south as Sicily by the time Eleanor and Louis were shipwrecked there on their way home from the Crusade. He had rejoined her service there and thought, by now, that nothing she could command of him would surprise him. But he was surprised by the message Faenze brought.

"Are you sure?" he asked. "I had wagered myself she would be wanting speech with Geoffrey Plantagenet by now." A wager he was happy enough to lose, to be sure. Foolish to suffer heartburning and jealousy over a woman so far above him, but Benoît had long since concluded with resignation that he was an incurable fool.

"My lady would hardly wish to meet with a man who has just so rudely defied her lord," Faenze said with a demure dropping of her lashes that told Benoît he would have cause enough for his jealousy before the Angevins left Paris. "The bishop of Lisieux is an old friend whom she has known since childhood, a companion of the Crusade. What could be more natural than that she should invite him to visit her while he is in Paris?"

"I don't know," Benoît said sourly, "but I suspect I'll be finding out." Natural—ha! He might not have had the privilege of listening in the bower while Eleanor had that animated discussion with her sister, but he had served his lady long enough to know when she was up to something.

He carried the message, though, with all the respect appropriate from a clerk of the queen's household to a bishop, and guided the bishop of Lisieux back to Eleanor's rooms, and watched, gnawing the inside of his cheek, while Eleanor rose to greet the man with both hands outstretched in warm welcome.

"Arnulf, old friend!" she exclaimed. "It has been too long since you have visited Paris. Come, sit and take a cup of wine with me and tell me how you fare out in the barbarous lands of the Normans."

"Not so barbarous as all that," Arnulf said with a smile. "The Empress Matilda keeps a goodly court in Rouen. Perhaps there are not so many musicians and poets as you attract, my lady, but there are men of learning and wit who might amuse you. Perhaps you will visit her someday."

"I doubt it," said Eleanor. "What a pity that she did not come with her husband! She might have moderated his wrath. Or perhaps not. I hear that they live very much apart, and that her influence over him is slight."

Arnulf looked into his wine cup. "One hears many rumors. Not all of them are to be believed—as you and I should know, being in a position to contrast our personal knowledge of the journey to Outremer with the wild and outlandish stories going around Europe about that same journey."

"Indeed," Eleanor agreed with a taut smile, "there is an art in knowing what to believe and what to disregard, what to broadcast to the world and what to keep secret. I believe you were once much annoyed with me for insisting that you follow my guidance in such matters."

Arnulf grinned. "Was I? If so, I have now much more cause to be grateful to you, my lady. Yes, I was eager enough to get to England with the news of your father's death, to win preferment from Stephen, and not over-happy to be kept instead at Bordeaux. . . ."

"So bored that you had nothing better to do than to play chess with a fifteen-year-old-heiress . . ."

"Who usually won," Arnulf finished, and they enjoyed the comfortable laughter of very old friends. "No, my lady, you did me a good turn there. Stephen's star is sinking, and I am happy to serve the Angevins. They, at least, take my advice."

"As Louis never did," Eleanor said ruefully. "I cannot blame you for leaving his service for Geoffrey's when he sent you to negotiate." She looked him full in the face, holding his gaze with wide-open eyes whose color shifted bewilderingly from the faint green of spring to the blue of a summer sky. "I do not know," she said, slowly enough to impart great weight to her words, "that I should blame anyone for wishing to make such a change."

"In some ways," Arnulf replied, "we servants of God are more free than great nobles, who are bound by oaths of liegeance . . . and marriage."

"And yet," Eleanor said, tapping the side of her own cup with one finger, "one who has watched the game of politics long enough, as you and I have, sees that allegiances change over time. You, Arnulf, always serve God, but within your duty to Him you have found your personal allegiance at one time with Stephen, at another with Louis, and now with the count of Anjou, who is friend to neither of your previous masters. Is it not so?"

"At least," Arnulf said, "I have the benefit of knowing always who is my ultimate liege lord."

"I too," Eleanor said. "As you exist for and within God's grace, Arnulf, so do I exist for and within Aquitaine. And what is best for Aquitaine may change over time."

She rose and handed her untouched cup to Faenze, signaling that the interview was over. "This dispute between Louis and the count of Anjou is most unfortunate," she said. "If any weak words of mine should help to placate the count and set him in a better frame of mind toward my lord husband, I should consider it my duty to speak those words."

Arnulf nodded slowly. "I am sure that Geoffrey will be most gratified to hear of your desire for peace. But I am only a humble cleric, my lady; I cannot speak for my master."

"Perhaps," Eleanor said, "his fiery temper would be cooled if he were to walk in the royal gardens behind the Great Hall. There is a pleasant orchard at the tip of the Île de la Cité, with a fountain continually supplied by the waters of the Seine; it can be a refreshing place to take the air on these hot summer evenings. But then, I am only a woman—what do I know of affairs of state? How would you advise your lord to deal with this regrettable quarrel, Arnulf?"

Arnulf bowed as he rose and prepared to take his departure. "I think, my lady," he said, "I should advise him to cool his temper by a walk in the gardens."

The Île de la Cité, the heart of Paris and of the French realm, was shaped like a boat that parted the waters of the Seine. From the center of the isle, the Grand Pont to the north and the Petit Pont to the south connected the isle with the growing commercial district on the Right Bank and the crowded, disputatious university district on the Left. The bridges and the connecting street were noisy with daylong traffic, with the grinding of the water mills that floated under the arches of the bridges, and with the cries of tradesmen and the debates of students, but the walls of the palace and the rooms within absorbed those sounds, and the narrow triangular gardens sheltered by the palace were a place of relative peace and quiet—except on those days when the royal authorities opened them to the students. The students, of course, were not allowed to enter through the palace; a wooden gate at the very tip of the island interrupted the crumbling wall that surrounded the garden and allowed entry, when it was unlocked, to any who were bold enough to navigate the tricky shoals and currents created by the two tiny strips of half-submerged island that rose within sight of the isle itself.

Naturally no "student days" were allowed when the king was entertaining an important delegation from Anjou. As the hour of Vespers approached, a few servants were at work in the kitchen garden that abutted the Great Hall, with its beds of pot vegetables, dittany, leeks, and sorrel, but beyond the trellis of pliable wood that separated this practical area from the pleasaunce no one save the royal family walked in the evenings.

Sweet and healing herbs grew as low hedges and ground cover in the second garden, surrounding hopeful beds of roses and the lilies whose flower Louis had adopted as his symbol. The lilies were gone now, and the few roses whose petals remained drooped sadly in the August heat, but the creeping mint sprawled luxuriously over the garden paths, releasing a sweet and pungent scent wherever Eleanor stepped. Someone had taken care to water the useful herbs, the pennyroyal and thyme and spikenard, the feverfew and angelica. At the borders of this garden, the wild ragwort sent up tall golden spikes—no need to care for that one, it grew like a weed, uninvited and untended, like the love that its flowers were said to excite. Petronilla complained that the blooms of ragwort made her sneeze, but Eleanor would not have it cleared away; it was something wild and free in this carefully clipped and controlled place. "And have we not all need of love?" she had demanded of her sister. Well, perhaps not. She had done well enough without. But a tremor of excitement made her hands shake as she entered the third and final garden, the pleasaunce where the fruit trees clustered against the sunny southwestern wall—medlars and quinces, pears and pomegranates, all crowded together to produce more show than fruit. And she broke off a spear of golden ragwort as she passed through the low stone arch.

Benches of stone, made of the carved blocks left by the ancients, were ranged between groups of trees along the dilapidated wall. Eleanor took a seat on a block of stone whose one carved face showed half an arm reaching for a bunch of grapes just out of its reach, and idly studied the fragments of inscriptions that showed here and there on the lower stones of the wall, bits of Latin words all but indecipherable with time and lichen: DEDIT . . . HIC . . . XLV . . . There was no sense to be had in them; better to think of the present and immediate future. Geoffrey would come along the same path she had taken, she would hear his steps in the herb garden. What would she say when he came to here?

Would words even be necessary?

She fell into a pleasant dream of the future as it could be, herself married not to a failed monk but to a man with the strength to hold Aquitaine against all enemies, even the power of France itself, a tall, golden man laughing in the sunset . . . A faint memory of strong hands swinging her up in the air, of her own delighted shrieks, terror and excitement combined . . . A man as golden as the flowers she still held in one hand, and as wild, too, a veritable weed growing up in the French king's garden, to confound and frustrate him!

The lapping of the Seine against the outer wall turned to splashes and the unmistakable sound of a boat banging against the small quay outside the gate. Eleanor sighed in frustration. Whoever it was would be thwarted by the locked gate and would go away in a minute—she hoped the visitor gave up before Geoffrey arrived. Around this pleasaunce, the old stone wall had been built up with modern courses of brickwork until it was too high for her to look over and simply send this would-be intruder about his business. And the dignified image she meant to present to Geoffrey would be completely spoiled if his first sight of her were of her standing on the bench, leaning over the wall to shout at some encroaching student. Forcing her limbs to relax, she rested her back against a tree whose roots had cracked the ancient wall and whose thick trunk bore testimony to the centuries that had passed since those stones were first laid. She looked away from the distracting sounds of the boat and the Seine, toward the stone archway framed with a shower of golden ragwort where Geoffrey Plantagenet would appear. The setting sun would blind her at first, he would be no more than a shadow framed in golden light. She shivered with anticipation, then started at the unmistakable creak of hinges behind her.

"Who do you think you are?" she snapped at the shabby young man whose hand pushed open the wooden gate from the little quay. "Get out of here at once, this garden is reserved for the royal family."

"I rather thought," said Henry, duke of Normandy, in dulcet tones, "that we Plantagenets might soon be counted as part of the family. Or did I misunderstand the message sent by my lord of Lisieux?"

Eleanor glared at the boy. Short, snub-nosed, dressed in an old stained tunic so short that it showed all the patches on his hose, he looked more like some worthless apprentice boy than the new duke of Normandy. The setting sun lit up his face unmercifully, showing every freckle and turning his red hair into a crown of flame that reminded her of Bernard's prediction: "From the devil he comes, and to the devil he'll go!"

"I sent *you* no message," she said. "Now go away and play somewhere else, will you? I have affairs of state to discuss with your father."

Instead of accepting her dismissal, Henry took three steps forward and sat cross-legged at her feet. "Geoffrey won't be coming," he said. "He didn't get your message, you see. I did."

"How did you suborn Arnulf?"

Henry grinned. "I am not," he said, in the same oversweet tones he had used at first, "*entirely* unfitted to rule my heritage." His eyes sparkled with mischievous delight, and Eleanor could tell he expected her to try and tease the secret out of him. In that, at least, she could disappoint the boy. Instead of questioning him, she pretended to yawn behind one white hand.

"What games you play with your father's messengers do not concern me," she said, "though I should think *you* might be concerned if he finds out about them."

Henry shrugged. "I am better qualified than he to discuss these affairs . . . of state."

Eleanor laughed. "*You?* You don't even know what I wanted to see him about!"

"Oh, yes, I do," Henry said, "and I can assure you that he would not suit your purposes at all. You dare not divorce Louis until you've made sure of a new husband who will be strong enough to hold you and your lands; otherwise you'll be captured and married to the first brigand who is fast enough and clever enough to catch you—someone like Gerald Berlai."

"Him, at least, I need not fear," Eleanor pointed out, "since your father apparently means to keep him in chains for the rest of his natural life."

"There are dozens more like him, and worse. Do I have to name them? Lady, half the vassals of Louis, and all of your own, will be waiting for you the minute the church declares you free. Geoffrey de Rancon," he said softly, "has grown well accustomed to holding power in your dower lands. And his wife Audrée died three years past. Don't you think he will be interested in this opportunity to own direct the lands he now oversees?"

Eleanor shivered in spite of herself. She would never forgive Louis for making Geoffrey seneschal of Poitou on his return from the Crusade, a mark of favor designed to show that he did not blame Geoffrey for the disaster of Mount Cadmos.

"Once divorced from Louis," Henry said, "you are any man's prey. I don't say it is right, but it is the way of the world. You must plan another marriage before you can even think of leaving him."

Eleanor examined her fingernails, pretending indifference. "What makes you think I would even wish a divorce?"

"I've seen you," Henry said, "and I've seen him. You're wasted on Louis; you want a real man, and it's time you had one." His knowing smile made her feel warm all over.

"My, what a precocious child it is," she said mockingly. "Since you understand my situation so well, had you not best go and bring me your father, so that we can discuss it face to face rather than through the intermediary of a boy who thinks his dukedom makes him a man?"

"My father," Henry said, "cannot provide you with the husband you need. He's married already."

Eleanor shrugged. "If he looks hard enough, he can find some common ancestor who will give him and Matilda the excuse of consanguinity for a divorce. I don't say it is right," she quoted Henry's words back at him, "but it is the way of the world!"

"I, on the other hand," Henry went on as if she had not spoken, "am free to marry where I will."

Eleanor suppressed her first instinct to burst into laughter. Men got nasty if you mocked them, especially young gamecocks like this. "How nice for you," she said. "If you are so eager to wed, I am sure Geoffrey will be able to arrange a suitable match. As duke of Normandy you will be a most eligible young man."

"As heir to England," Henry said, "I am even more eligible. And I have already seen the woman I want to wed. It is only a matter of waiting until she too is free." He shifted position slightly, resting one arm on the bench beside Eleanor. She could feel the heat of his body. "Actually," he said conversationally, "I first saw her some years ago, leaving an interview with Bernard of Clairvaux. A woman like a sword blade, I thought, straight and sharp."

"You couldn't have been more than seven years old at the time! Don't try to tell me you were *that* precocious, devil's spawn or no!"

"At the time," Henry said, "all I thought was that if I had a lady like that, I would not be such a fool as to make her weep."

Eleanor doubted that. There would be storms and quarrels and tears in plenty for any woman foolish enough to marry one of the Plantagenet devil's brood. *But at least*, a traitor thought suggested, *it would not be boring. Too bad he's not old enough for you.* "Perhaps you had better first ascertain whether your ladylove reciprocates your interest," she suggested, moving slightly away from the boy as she spoke.

"She will," Henry said, "as soon as she understands the situation." He stood in one smooth movement and leaned over the bench, resting his hands on the wall behind Eleanor and trapping her between them. "My father," he said in a soft voice that carried an aura of menace, "is *not available*. Believe me, you'd be wise to accept that and make other arrangements."

"My arrangements," Eleanor said, "are no concern of yours!" She should dismiss him, *now*, before his young male arrogance led him into some insult to her. No, she realized with a deep internal shiver, before *she* was led into treating him like a man, into taking his pretensions seriously. It was hard to reject his talk as a boy's grandiose fantasies, now with his strength and energy surrounding her. A woman could rest on that strength, recharge her own. Someday, with the right partner, he could move mountains and make empires. *As could I . . . with the right partner.* But Geoffrey, not this boy, was the right partner. She had determined that as soon as she saw him defy Louis and Bernard. She should not be swayed now by the pleasures of being courted by this young bundle of energy and desire. "You may go now; I have nothing to discuss with you."

"I have Normandy," Henry said reasonably, but without moving, "and I'm going to inherit Anjou. I have a legitimate concern with the matter of who holds the lands along my southern marches." He grinned, and Eleanor felt an unwilling kinship with this audacious boy. "I think it should be me."

"It's going to be me," Eleanor said, "no matter whom I marry."

"If you marry me, then it'll be the same thing. *Think*," Henry said, "Aquitaine,

Anjou, and Normandy joined together, and England joined to that again. We would be unstoppable. France, Burgundy, Champagne together would be nothing against us, and besides, they can never stay on good terms long enough to make a lasting union. You and I would have the beginnings of an empire."

Eleanor drew in her breath, shaken despite herself by the vision Henry presented to her. She had not thought seriously about his claim to England, nor about his expectation of inheriting Anjou. But then—how seriously were such things to be taken?

"If you are so eager for empire," she pointed out, "then the same lands would be yours after your father's death. Instead of inheriting Anjou alone, you would inherit Anjou and Aquitaine together."

"There are certain disadvantages to that arrangement," Henry said.

"Perhaps from your point of view." Eleanor shrugged. "Not from mine."

"Oh, no? And how strong would Anjou and Aquitaine be, if Normandy made war on you? Probably," Henry pointed out, "aided by the king of France, who would not be pleased to find you had divorced him only to give Aquitaine to the count of Anjou."

"I give Aquitaine to *no one*," Eleanor said sharply. She was beginning to enjoy this argument for its own sake, even if the premises were ridiculous. "Besides, if you rose in rebellion against your own father, he would be quite justified in taking back the dukedom of Normandy that he has given you."

"Ah," Henry said, "but I hold Normandy by right of my mother Matilda, who would not be your friend in these circumstances."

"Geoffrey's sister is married to Thierry of Flanders," Eleanor mentioned casually. "Could Normandy sustain attacks from north and south at once?"

"Don't be too sure of Thierry's family loyalty," Henry said. "He might not wish to alienate the future king of England."

"And you, my young duke, should not be so sure of that inheritance!" Eleanor said sharply. "Your mother has fought long enough for England without results."

"Ah," Henry said, "but I am not my mother. When I fight, I get results . . . and I get what I want." His freckled face came closer to hers; she could see the dancing lights of gold and green in his eyes, could feel the intensity with which he was willing her to agree.

"Not always!" But she almost took him seriously in spite of herself. Impossible to dismiss this young gamecock as a boy; he was a man, and one who knew what he wanted.

"Invariably." His mouth came down over hers, hard and hot and demanding, and she responded despite herself for one intoxicating moment. When she broke away, her breath came short and quick. So, she noted with satisfaction, did his.

"Sit down," she said. "Over there." She pointed to the next bench.

"Why?"

Eleanor laughed up at him. She could feel all his heat and his desire for her now, and it warmed her and at the same time gave her confidence that she could master this brilliant young spark of Angevin fire. "Because if I am to divorce Louis," she said, "there had best be no slightest hint of impropriety between me and the man I mean to marry."

Henry stepped back a pace, his face blazing with excitement. "You see the mutual advantages of our arrangement, then?"

Eleanor lowered her eyes. That tunic of his really was indecently short; did the boy realize how revealing it was? "I certainly do," she said over a bubble of laughter, and then, before he could be quite sure of her meaning, "I have never met a man who could maintain such a stimulating political discussion!" And she meant that too, she realized with some surprise. Arguing with Henry was more fun than being courted by any of the nobles or troubadours who made a show of sighing at her feet. The woman who married Henry Plantagenet might be angry, jealous, furious at times. But she wouldn't be bored, and their marriage bed would be . . . Another shiver, this time one of delicious anticipation, passed through Eleanor.

Chapter Seventeen

Louis was not surprised when, on the day after his defiant departure from the Great Hall, Geoffrey Plantagenet returned to humbly beg forgiveness and sue for peace. Nor was Bernard of Clairvaux, Louis's chief adviser since the death in January of little Abbot Suger.

"Your curse has brought him to a consciousness of sin and a desire to make his peace with us," Louis told Bernard.

"He would do better to make his peace with Our Lord," Bernard said. "It was not a curse but a prophecy. The Angevin is a dead man." He advised Louis to seize this opportunity of making favorable terms while Geoffrey was in this humbled mood. He believed implicitly in the vision that had shown him the count of Anjou's approaching death and warned Louis that young Henry might be even brasher and more difficult to deal with than Geoffrey had been.

The wrongs of Geoffrey's prisoner, so important the day before, were all but forgotten as clerks and nobles hastily cobbled together an agreement wherein Geoffrey renounced all claims to the disputed land of the Vexin and Louis graciously permitted young Henry to do homage to him for his dukedom of Normandy.

"I don't like it," Raoul de Vermandois fretted.

"Why not?"

"What does Geoffrey gain from this?"

"The assurance that we will support his son's claim to Normandy and will no longer recognize Eustace's attempts to take that land?"

"That young cub is more than capable of holding Normandy without help," Raoul growled, "certainly without giving you such a bribe as undisputed possession of the Vexin. There's something behind this."

"A man close to death may wish to see his affairs settled in peace and his soul clean of unlawful gains," Bernard asserted.

"Hah! *You* may think the castles Geoffrey took in the Vexin were unlawful gains, but what gives you the illusion he agrees with you?" Raoul demanded rudely.

But he could hardly argue with the completed agreement and the new-made peace between Anjou and France, both of such advantage to the young king he served. Raoul de Vermandois's bluff, soldierly style was out of fashion at court; Bernard of Clairvaux, riding high with his triumph over Geoffrey Plantagenet, encouraged young Louis to a style of spiritual high thinking that gave Raoul the hives. Immediately after the departure of the Angevins, Raoul requested leave to retire from court to look after his estates on the Flemish border, long neglected while he remained in Paris on the king's service.

If he had asked Petronilla's opinion before his departure, he might have gained some inkling of what was behind Geoffrey's uncharacteristic capitulation and might have remained in Paris to advise Louis most strenuously against his next decision. But Raoul had never been in the habit of thinking of women as more than pretty playthings. Eleanor's little sister had once appealed to him as a sweet child whose dependence on him made him feel young and strong again, but the intoxication of those first days was long gone. In the course of giving him three children, Petronilla had changed from a pliant young girl to a somewhat dumpy matron who no longer imagined the sun rose and set in the aging man she'd married amid such scandal. It was impossible for Raoul now to remember the brief madness of middle-aged passion that had swept him into excommunication and war for Petronilla's sake, equally impossible for him not to reflect that the young wife who had cost him so much turmoil had after all given him only two daughters and a leprous son hidden away in a monastery. If not exactly estranged, they were certainly not on such terms that he would invite her opinion on matters of court—indeed, it had never occurred to him that Petronilla had an opinion on anything weightier than the cut of a bliaut or the length of the new sleeves.

With Suger dead and Vermandois away from court, there was no one among the king's advisers who dared disagree with Bernard of Clairvaux. Bad things happened to those who clashed with that saintly man; those who might have doubted his influence with pope and king were shortly given clear proof of how much higher his influence went. On a hot September afternoon beside the Loire, Geoffrey Plantagenet called a halt to the ride home from Paris so that he could strip and cool himself in the river. The next day he died.

"Everyone knows that excessive bathing is dangerous to the health," grumbled an unbeliever.

"Henry and half the men with them swam too," countered the one who brought the tale, "and *they* didn't die the next day of a fever."

Bernard might claim his words were a prophecy, but Paris understood that he had cursed Geoffrey Plantagenet and the count had died. Some gentlemen with long memories whispered about the time back in '35 when Bernard had clashed with the Queen's father, William of Aquitaine. Odo of Deuil had heard the story many times and claimed the privilege of telling it. Excommunicated for his support of the false pope Anacletus, William had made the mistake of trying to attend mass at his church near Parthenay on a day when Bernard was preaching there. Confronted by Bernard and the sacred Host, rebuked in public for his sins, William had been touched by the finger of God on his heart, falling down in the dust and foaming at the mouth.

"And *he* died, too."

"Not for two years."

"Still. He was young and strong, like Geoffrey Plantagenet. And a sudden fever took him. And when he was on pilgrimage, too!"

"There is no escape from the wrath of God," Odo intoned piously, but his eyes were not upraised to heaven. Rather, he watched the lean form of Bernard, pacing step for step beside the young king whom he counseled.

With the recent example of Geoffrey's death, and the memory of Bernard's clashes with the queen's father, there was no one who really cared to argue against Bernard when he told Louis that his childless state was the result of marrying a proud woman of a sinful family and one, furthermore, with whom he was related within the forbidden decrees of consanguinity.

"Childless? I have given him two daughters," Eleanor said with some acerbity when this statement was related to her, "but, of course, in Bernard's eyes women are scarcely people. Never mind! I have no intention of arguing; quite the reverse." She smoothed her light honey-colored braids over her breasts and smiled into the mirror of polished bronze that reflected her image in a golden glow, then frowned in slight discontent. Was there the slightest blurring along the fine line of her jaw? And was it a fault in the mirror, or a true reflection of the years that had passed since she married Louis? Years during which she had hardly lived, save for the brief burning triumphs and tragedies of the Crusade; it was not fair that they should leave their marks on her skin just as if she had been truly alive all this time. Ridiculous! Her *real* life was just about to begin, and she felt no older than the girl who had married Louis in a shower of golden trinkets under the Bordeaux sun; younger, if anything.

Cautious discussions, hints, and messages gradually brought forth the opinion that if both parties to the marriage were troubled by their consanguinity and the consequent curse of childlessness, Pope Eugenius would not object to the convening of a council of bishops to discuss the divorce. But which bishops should be appointed, and where should they meet, and when?

September, October passed in a flutter of golden leaves and tentative agreements and suggested names. November brought winter, bare branches, the first suggestion of ice in the air. Eleanor felt the dying of the year like the sinking of her own hopes. How many more councils and discussions and agreements must pass before she would be free? Henry was about his own business in Normandy, and she was condemned to another icy winter looking at the Seine.

"I *must* get out of here," she complained to Petronilla, who sat comfortably beside a brazier stitching on her Garden of Paradise. Eleanor's fashionably long sleeves swished in the air as she stalked back and forth, frequently imperiling the shaky brazier.

"Yes," Petronilla agreed, "that would be more comfortable for everybody, I am sure." She bit off an end of thread, and old Radegonde scolded her in a creaky voice for not using the little shears that hung from her chatelaine. "I have been wondering why you don't."

Eleanor threw up her hands, and Petronilla prudently moved the brazier a few inches back toward the corner. "I? What have *I* to say in the matter? It is all the pope, and the bishops, and the saintly abbot of Clairvaux, sending back and forth and deciding how to accomplish this thing. When I try to hurry them up, they tell me that they move in God's time. Well, God may not be getting any older, but I certainly am!"

"Then you might as well be about the other business you must accomplish before you are free," Petronilla said. She set two stitches, carefully, into Eve's eye, then frowned and pulled one of them free again. "I think we want the gold there, don't you, Radegonde, to bring out the light of the eye?"

"God pluck the eye out!" Eleanor swore. "What other business?"

Petronilla looked up at her, smiling. "You used to be more clever, before . . ." She glanced at Radegonde and decided not to finish the sentence she had begun. If gossip about Eleanor's arrangement with Henry Plantagenet got out and spoiled the divorce, her sister would kill her. Slowly. "Before the plans for this divorce were agreed," she said instead. "Don't you and Louis need to agree on how to replace his men in Aquitaine with yours?"

Eleanor drew a long, shaky breath. "You are not so stupid after all, Petronilla. Of course! It might be more conventional to wait until after the divorce is pronounced, but princes need not wait upon convention. We should ride through Aquitaine together, seeing to the changes at each city and castle, so that no one will be in any doubt after the divorce that I have retained charge of my own dominions." She smiled, seeing in her mind's eye the sunny slopes of the south. "We could begin in Bordeaux. . . ."

Louis might not have been quite so ready as Eleanor to dispense with convention, but both Bernard of Clairvaux and Odo of Deuil encouraged the plan to begin the separation *chevauchée* at once.

"It won't offend the pope that we seem to anticipate his decision?" Louis asked.

Bernard assured him that he would personally write to Eugenius and explain that this was the best possible arrangement. After all, they all desired a peaceful transition. The pope loved each of his children in France and Aquitaine, noble and common alike, and as a good shepherd cares for his sheep, so the pope would be in favor of anything that preserved peace in the land during this difficult time.

"Besides," Odo of Deuil said when Louis had left, his religious doubts satisfied, "it leaves us more freedom to plan what happens after the divorce."

"That is in God's hands," Bernard said. He knew that Odo and the king's other advisers wished to make sure that Eleanor's next husband would be the right sort of man—someone deeply beholden to the king of France and too weak to oppose him—but he did not believe the matter required all the secretive whispering and plotting Odo brought to it. Women were weak and easily led; at the appropriate time—that is to say, as soon as the divorce had been pronounced—they would see to it that suitable candidates were brought before her, and she would be only too happy to choose one of them to keep her and her lands safe.

Neither of them thought that it might make any difference who replaced Louis's men in charge of the strongholds of Aquitaine. Whoever they were, they would owe homage to Eleanor, and through her to her new husband. The queen might as well be allowed to play in the south for the next few months, while men who understood the higher issues made the plans that counted, here in Paris.

The pale November sun of Bordeaux was only a weak reflection of the summer's fire, but the roads of her own country warmed Eleanor, as did the red wine of Bordeaux. Geoffrey du Lauroux, who had married her to Louis fifteen years ago, was now to be one of the church lords who would pronounce her divorce on grounds of consanguinity. He welcomed Eleanor and Louis urbanely, and all three tactfully avoided discussing the irony of the situation.

From Bordeaux they went inland to skirt the marshy edges of the Gulf of Poitou, then out again to the chilly coast at Talmont.

"A poor country, this." Louis was muffled in furs like an old man, and his lips and fingers were blue in the chill wind from the sea. Eleanor suppressed a smile. From Paris to Poitiers they had been escorted by Louis's men, but there in her own capital, Black Hugh of Lusignan had greeted them and demanded the honor of escorting his duchess through her own lands. The French, apart from Louis's own household, were more than happy to return across the Loire to lands where people spoke a comprehensible language and had a decent respect for the proprieties. Thenceforth the separation *chevauchée* was led and guarded by men of Poitou, while Eleanor and Hugh planned the route. It was, of course, necessary to visit each of the cities and major castles where the French were garrisoned, for Louis to promise the French new positions and their back pay while Eleanor named a man of her own country to take charge and raise men for the defense of the region. Hugh, who had been free to keep track of the lords of Poitou and Aquitaine while Eleanor was trapped in Paris, advised her on the choice of replacements, and Eleanor took his advice as often as it suited her. But the route from one city to the next was chosen by her, and it was on her planning that they rode through the marshy gulf territory rather than through the richer country inland. The divorce was not yet pronounced; there was no harm in leaving Louis with the impression that the lands he was losing with Eleanor were, on the whole, poor and unremarkable.

They might have spent Christmas in the comfort of Talmont, but that castle held too many bloody memories for Eleanor to feel comfortable there. She confirmed d'Aulnay in his charge of Talmont and pressed on northward. Christmas found the *chevauchée* at Saint-Jean-d'Angély, a small fishing port in the shelter of the island of Oléron, where the royal household turned fishers out of their huts and the soldiers were grateful for upturned boats as shelters. The cold wind brought chilblains to Louis's fingers and turned Eleanor's cheeks red.

"A short ride would bring us to your château at Saintes," Black Hugh murmured to Eleanor.

"It is not advisable," Eleanor murmured discreetly back, "for us to make this journey *too* comfortable."

They shared a conspiratorial smile. The lord of Lusignan went off to send some of his men inland to collect firewood for the royal party. On his return he was not overjoyed to find a newcomer by the queen's side, a lean, green-eyed man who was trying to teach her the proper way to eat Marennes oysters while she protested that she remembered those cold, salty lumps from childhood and doubted they had improved at all.

"I remember," the man teased her. "You were eight years old and I was fifteen, and I thought it funny to see the face you made when I gave you one and told you it was a sweetmeat."

Eleanor's face lit up. "Raoul! I almost knew you. I hope," she said with mock severity, "your manners have improved since then. Oh, Hugh," she greeted Lusignan, "this is my kinsman Raoul de la Faye, my . . ." She frowned and counted on her fingers. "Let's see, your father was a cadet of Châtellerault, so he would have been my mother's cousin, so that makes you . . ."

"Not cousin," Raoul corrected her. "The relationship was hardly that close."

"Close enough," Hugh remarked pleasantly, "to fall within the forbidden degrees."

Raoul's green eyes grew cold as the icy sea from which the oysters had been taken. "My lady knows that she can trust her kinsmen to care for her."

"It is the duty of all her liegemen," Hugh said.

"Excellent!" Eleanor cried. "You, Raoul, shall show your care for me by buying oysters from the peasants, and you, Hugh, can do your part by eating the nasty things!"

But in the end they all wound up feasting on oysters in the Charente style: cold salty oysters mixed with sizzling sausages that had been roasted on sticks over the fire, the whole washed down with a pale green wine that seemed to carry some of the salty tang of the ocean it resembled. The next day Raoul commandeered the greatest kettle and the services of an old wife, and produced a stew of fish and mussels so thick that the ladle stood up in it, and by the third day of their stay it had become an accepted thing that he would travel with them on the next stage of the journey.

Early in January they left the coast and turned inland along the course of the Charente river, leaving behind the peasants of Saint-Jean-d'Angély to their cold winter work of scraping oysters and mussels from the rocks at low tide. The winter light danced off the waters of the sea and the estuary and sparkled across the flat beds where the salt makers worked. Eleanor felt almost sad to be leaving this land of water and dancing light.

"Cheer up," said Raoul, riding beside her, "tonight we shall dine on mutton from the salt marshes. You have never tasted anything to rival this meat, which comes to the table already salted and savory from the salty grasses the sheep live on!"

Eleanor laughed up at him. "Do you never think of anything but your stomach?"

"Have a little respect for your poor old gouty uncle," Raoul teased her. "What pleasures are left to a man of my advanced age, save those of the table?"

"I have a feeling you do not restrict yourself entirely to those," Eleanor said, glancing up through her lashes.

The coastal soil of the Saintonge gave way after Saintes to a chalky upland where sheep and cattle grazed on either side of the slow, green Charente river. The cathedral of Angoulême rose above the valley on the plateau of the city. Louis wanted to linger there in the pleasing religious atmosphere created by the bishop and his attendant clergy. Not for the first time, Eleanor wondered why he had left his chaplain Odo behind in Paris.

It was at Angoulême that they heard the news: old Thibaut of Champagne had died at last, leaving Champagne to Henry and Blois to the younger son, also called Thibaut. Louis seemed surprisingly agitated by the information. Eleanor had no tears for the old man whose enmity had made her sister's marriage to Raoul de Vermandois the cause of war. "We . . . you should get on better with the sons," she said soothingly. "Henry at least is quite a reasonable person; he distinguished himself on the Crusade. Remember the skirmish at the Maeander?" Perhaps not the best subject to bring up with Louis, who had hardly distinguished himself for anything but dithering and weakness on the entire Crusade, but his eyes brightened and he began to talk of how many Turks he had personally killed on the night of the disaster at Mount Cadmos.

"Mount Cadmos. I remember, yes," Eleanor said neutrally and turned the conversation as soon as she decently could. Cadmos: a shred of purple silk blowing in the wind, an ivory casket shattered, a singing voice silenced forever. And for his part in that disaster, Louis had made Geoffrey de Rancon seneschal over Aquitaine—*her* Aquitaine!

When she instructed their escort to make ready for the ride to Poitiers, Louis complained that she ought to have planned the route so that they would go by Taillebourg. It would be only courteous for her to visit her seneschal in person on this journey.

"Your seneschal," Eleanor said as they were riding out of Angoulême, "not mine."

"But he is a Poitevin, and no Frenchman." Louis seemed honestly confused. "I had thought to please you by appointing him."

The man who had brought them to disaster at Cadmos, and then had blamed her frivolity, had claimed it was her choice to ride ahead and he had no option but to obey the queen . . . The jolting mountain ride, the fall that had lost her a son, for she felt sure Manuel's child would have been a son . . . Eleanor stared blankly at Louis and wondered if they did indeed come of the same race of beings.

"After all," Louis added peevishly, "he deserved some recompense for trying to save the army at Cadmos."

Having first made the decision that nearly destroyed it. But Louis's watery blue eyes gazed at her, limpid and clear and seeming to have no memory of the truth of that night. He had truly rewritten history; in his mind the disaster of Cadmos had been caused by a woman's foolishness and retrieved by the bravery of good knights, just as his ignominious scuttle to safety among the bushes had become a valiant singlehanded battle against dozens of Turks. In that moment he seemed more alien to her than any of the grotesques carved on the columns of ancient churches. How had she ever endured lying with him? It had been *wrong*, deeply wrong, like embracing a salamander or a spirit.

"In Poitiers," Eleanor said, spurring her horse, "we will discuss the matter of my future seneschal over Aquitaine and Poitou." She caught a gleam of hopeful excitement in Black Hugh's eyes. As Geoffrey's son-in-law, and one who had stood by her at Cadmos, he would be assuming he had the right to take over the guardianship of her lands. It would be almost a kind of inheritance. . . . How much else did he expect to take over?

She had scant time to think through the matter; a few pounding paces, and Hugh's horse drew level with hers on the road, just as Raoul de la Faye came up beside her on the other side.

"A queen should not ride ahead of her escort," Hugh said, a teasing twinkle in his dark eyes. "I believe I had occasion to warn you of that in Outremer."

"But the duchess of Aquitaine," Eleanor retorted, "can surely ride where she pleases in her own lands, particularly with the escort of such great chevaliers as you two!" And she set a pace that kept both Hugh and Raoul fully occupied with managing their own horses, and kept it up until her own palfrey was flagging with exhaustion. Not such a fine horse as her Belle-Belle, whom she had lost in that fall that also cost her Manuel's child. Well, she might yet bear the son of an emperor. Henry was not lacking in ambition, and who knew what they might build out of a realm that began with Normandy and Anjou and Aquitaine added together—not to mention the possibility of England, one day? And she would have a horse the equal of Belle-Belle, too, now that she was free to reside in Poitiers and give her own attention to the matter of the ducal stables.

As they neared Poitiers, the chalky meadows of the Charente gave way to dense woods of oak and chestnut, the southernmost fringes of the wooded bocage of northwestern Poitou. Here the road narrowed to a snaky trail winding through the forest. Unable to deflect unwanted attentions and assumptions by fast riding, Eleanor fell back and surrounded herself with her own ladies. The Poitevins were happy enough here in the bocage, but Faenze and the other Frenchwomen whispered nervously to themselves. They disliked this shady world in which the shadows of great twisted oaks suggested deformed robbers or hanged men swinging from the great branches, where the road opened out without warning into sun-dappled dells where pools and great stones encircled little fields glowing with light. Eleanor felt herself a girl again here; in such forests around Poitiers she had run free when her father the duke was away putting down the endless petty rebellions that plagued the land. Dangereuse would bring her and Petronilla out into the forest to gather mushrooms after a warm rain, or to knock down chestnuts out of the trees in autumn, just like any peasant family, or to learn her herbcraft at any season. Eleanor had been a poor pupil, ignoring the lectures in favor of spying on the animals that nested in the forest or, more dangerously, the landless peasants who hacked a poor living out of some of those infrequent water-girdled fields. But there were few enough of those! Only the bravest dared venture into these dark woods, haunted by legends of the loup-garou and the White Ladies.

In this winter season the trees were bare and one could glimpse the sky through a latticework of tangled branches, but the forest lost none of its fearful mystery for the outlanders thus. The dappled light of the pale sun created dancing shadows over ground and vines and trunks, so that the entire wood seemed to be moving like a sleeper made restless by strange dreams. Faenze's eyes grew wide as she stared about her, and twice her mount stumbled because she had failed to notice the ruts made by previous riders who had come through on a muddy day.

"Don't be so nervous, Faenze," Eleanor said. "There has not been a werewolf seen in these woods since my grandfather's time."

One of the other French girls crossed herself and murmured that it was unchancy to speak of such things.

"The woods are full of strange creatures," Eleanor said happily, "but they are no danger to those who belong to this soil." Black Hugh of Lusignan had fallen back to join their conversation, and she could not resist the urge to tease him. "Some families are even related to them by marriage."

Black Hugh laughed too loudly, breaking the icy winter stillness around them, and proceeded to regale the ladies with a slightly bawdy version of the legend about his ancestress Melusine, who turned into a serpent every Saturday night in her bath. When her husband's curiosity drove him to break his vow to leave her unobserved on Saturdays, and he saw the twining, glistening serpent tail spilling out of the water, she gave a great shriek and flew out of the window, never to be heard from again.

"Oh, don't be so nervous," he said, somewhat impatiently, when Faenze shrank from him. "It was all a very long time ago, you know."

"But did it truly happen?"

"I can show you," Hugh said solemnly, "the very window she flew out of. And it is true that from that time on the Lusignan men . . ."

The comparisons between snakes and portions of male anatomy that followed had the girls giggling and blushing. Once, Eleanor thought, she would have been worried lest Louis overhear the bawdy tone of their conversation; she would have dreaded a silent evening in the shadow of his thin-lipped disapproval. How good it would be to be done with all that!

She dampened the conversation only when Hugh began hinting that even now the Lusignans were particularly partial to royal beauties whom they found deep in the forest.

"How fortunate," she said dryly, "that you are already married, Hugh, or these foolish girls might think you were casting about for a wife!"

"A man may look to the future," said Hugh, softly enough that those riding around them could not hear, "and . . . a man may dream."

"Dreams have led many a man into a hopeless slough," Eleanor said, "and a man who is wedded to the daughter of the seneschal of Aquitaine would be foolish to look even higher!"

"But . . ."

Surely Hugh had meant to remind her of her hints that Geoffrey de Rancon would not long retain his position, but he fell silent, as did the others, on hearing the silvery tinkle of bells and the unearthly singing of high, sweet voices somewhere ahead of the cavalcade.

One of the forest clearings was ahead, a larger one than most, to judge by the pale gilt light that grew with every pace forward. "Sir Hugh, move your horse aside for a moment," Eleanor asked him. "I would prefer to ride at the front for a while."

Hugh did as she asked, but his arm shot out and caught her wrist as her palfrey sidled past him. "I will not have you riding ahead of me into any danger."

Eleanor twisted her arm against his thumb and broke free easily enough; he had not expected anything but grateful acquiescence. "If there is danger," she said, "it is not the sort that can be fended off by swords. And these are *my* lands."

Louis was crossing himself and saying the Pater Noster when Eleanor reached his side, at the cost of forcing half the fine gentlemen who escorted them into the briar-streaked verge of the narrow road. Here the fine, pale light was stronger, seeming to set the barren gray woods aglow, and she could glimpse moving figures in the clearing. They seemed to be circling or dancing around a high stone. . . . Her skin prickled despite herself, and she remembered old nursery tales of dancers who worshipped the ancient standing stones and made strange sacrifices there. And *those* were not safe stories lost in the mists of time, like Lusignan's serpent ancestress. She had heard the keepers of her father's forests report finding blood puddled in such great stones, or a ring of ashes about one, usually at the time of the new moon. And there were parts of the forest Dangereuse would not take the girls to . . . .

But surely not on the main road to Poitiers! The last screen of entangling bare branches scraped around the leading riders, and now Eleanor could see clearly. The great gray shape was no standing stone of ancient times but a simple country chapel, built by laying courses of the local stone atop one another with no mortar, nothing to hold it but the native wit of the builder. It was even topped with a small cross. And the white dancers were not the Ladies of the Forest but boys and girls in white robes, holding candles and crowned with wreaths of berries and evergreen leaves. They had been moving in a spiral procession around the chapel, chanting a hymn to Our Lady in high childish voices, but now they broke out of line and ran to admire the fine ladies and gentlemen who had interrupted the ceremony.

"We grow heathen ourselves from so much traveling," Eleanor teased Louis. "I'll wager even you did not recall it was the feast of Candlemas!" And before he could reprove her levity, she slipped from her palfrey and went forward, surrounded by the little Poitevins, to say a prayer at this shrine in the forest which, she could now see, marked a rudimentary crossroads; an even narrower track than the one they followed ran east and west from the clearing. One way would lead to the open land by the sea, the other, most likely, to Black Hugh's own castle of Lusignan.

The Virgin in her little chapel of rough stone walls was a stiff, primitive wooden carving, black no doubt with the smoke of all the candles that had been burned in her honor on uncounted Candlemasses past. She reminded Eleanor of the Dark Virgin in her crypt under the church at Poitiers. . . . That one, it was said, had been discovered in the forest and brought into Poitiers for her due honor. This one, it seemed, the peasants had kept for themselves. . . . She could not blame them;

she felt the same waves of immanent power coming from this stiff black figure that she had felt in the crypt at Poitiers. There was a strength in these dark, expressionless statues that surpassed anything she felt before the modern, beautiful carvings of the Virgin all gilded and wearing a blue cloak and a sweet smile.

She could not well pray for a son at this time. The Virgin would laugh at her and ask what she wanted, an heir to France for the man her flesh shrank from or an heir to Normandy by the young man she was not yet wedded to.

Lady, what shall I pray for, then?

The dark, inscrutable face looked down at her. No gentle loving smiles here but only stillness and dormant strength, the strength of great stones enduring years of wind and water, the strength of earth renewing itself with the dust of the stones, the strength of green things forcing their way up between the stones. Eleanor swayed between the conflicting forces and balances, sensing the world for a moment not as a single struggle between God and Satan but as a great net of individual impulses all pushing their way to the same end: *Grow. Live. Endure.* The wheel of the stars in the night sky, the wheel of the sun about the earth, the turning wheel of Fortune were all one. It was too much for her head to hold; she felt her body gasping for breath, as though she could take in wisdom with air. Understanding was almost within her grasp. . . . Her vision darkened and she felt herself falling, the great interconnected turning wheels fading, leaving her with only a handful of scattered dream-images familiar from long ago: the crown, the ship, the great wind unleashed.

"Is it all in the past, then?" she said aloud, feeling herself in a waking dream. "Or all to do over again?"

Hard hands supported her; the stones in the ground dug into her knees. She looked up and saw her master of horse, Amicie de Périgné, bending concerned above her.

"My lady. Are you unwell?"

Eleanor gave a shaky laugh. "Only dizzy with the grace of Our Lady, I think. I—am glad you came forward, Amicie."

"We are Poitevins," said Benoît from her other side. "The honor of guarding you belongs to *us*, not to Lusignan!"

How alike they were, with their long bony faces and their Poitevin pride, these bickering Périgné brothers! Yet both, in their different ways, had served her long and well. They had a family talent for loyalty . . . and stubbornness.

"Wait," she said as Amicie made to lift her up. "I have not . . ." She had not made any prayer yet; she had only been caught in the net of power that emanated from this Virgin of the earth. Only! Eleanor bent her head; the gesture could be taken for piety, only she and the Virgin knew that she was afraid to look up at the black carved face again for fear of seeing more than she was meant to know.

She settled for a brief prayer that she might be guided to do the right thing in the months ahead and warned of any dangers in her path.

At Poitiers they were met by Louis's chaplain Odo, who said he had ridden from Paris to bring the news of the count of Champagne's death. "We heard of that at Angoulême," Eleanor told him.

"I must confer with the king." Odo's pallid face shone with self-importance. "This bodes great changes."

"For France, perhaps," Eleanor said sweetly, "but not for *me*. The dukes of Aquitaine have little to do with the lords of Champagne."

She excused herself and left Louis and Odo to their political discussion, wondering a little, but not greatly perturbed, at the smirk that crossed the chaplain's face as she left. Well, he had never liked her; doubtless he was glad to see this unhappy marriage coming to an end. They were agreed on that one thing, at least. Meanwhile, she had more important matters to consider. The decision she had evaded at Taillebourg must be made here in Poitiers, and as publicly as possible.

In her father's day the Great Hall of the ducal residence would have been full of courtiers, troubadours, knights doing their yearly service, merchants with fine spices and other goods who had come up the long road from the Moorish lands far to the south. In the years of Eleanor's residence in Paris, no court had been kept up here, and the hall showed its neglect. She summoned Benoît to advise her. Should she order a great cleaning, see the tapestries brought out of their chests and hung upon the walls, the floors shoveled out and fresh rushes laid down?

"How long," Benoît asked, "do you expect to remain in Poitiers?"

Eleanor shrugged. "I may as well stay here until the divorce is pronounced, I suppose." The separation of her lands from Louis's would be completed when she appointed a seneschal over Aquitaine; there was nothing to return to Paris for. And she wanted to be safe in her own domains when she was free, not trapped in the north where she had no one of her own to protect her until Henry came. "Yes," she decided swiftly, "I shall take up residence in Poitiers now. The council of bishops can meet here as well as anywhere else." She would speak to Louis about it as soon as that sly, secretive chaplain of his left them in privacy.

"Benoît! You must write to each of my vassals, bidding them to attend my court at Poitiers. No, wait. I shall send only to those who hold directly from me, and order them to bring their liegemen; that will save the cost of so many messengers. Let Amicie prepare horses—no, first let me count how many we must absolutely have. Let me see, we must send for William of Angoulême, a pity I did not think of this when we were passing through that city; Thouars, of course; Châtellerault—my kinsman Raoul de Faye can carry the letter, since his lands are dependencies of Châtellerault, so that saves another messenger's fee; Ventadour, La Marche, Taillefer. . . Lusignan is here, so we needn't pay to summon him . . ." She went on enumerating her chief vassals from memory while Benoît scrambled to find inkhorn and parchment and make notes of the names. The Poitevin lords such as Thouars and Châtellerault were known to him, he was related to most of them, but he had never had dealings with such men as the vicomte de Turenne, on the Toulousan border, or the lords of Dordogne and Périgord.

Once he had the names straight, Benoît set up a writing station in a small room that had once been used as a storehouse, privately lamenting the lack of a proper chair with high arms and a footstool. He had to write like any common student, standing over the desk until his arms shook with fatigue, and he cursed the boy whose services he had commandeered to scrape the parchments. At least he always traveled with the his essential tools, the scraping blade and the knife for trimming his pens, a supply of quills, a blind point for ruling off the parchment, and an inkhorn with a tightly fitting cover. But where could he find red lead to make the capital letters stand out as they should, or ultramarine to line them?

"We don't have time for illuminations," Eleanor said. "Do the best you can. Soon enough we shall have everything you desire. You shall be my chancellor, Benoît, and direct scribes instead of writing yourself." Already, while he fussed about the writing materials, Faenze had seen to the cleaning of the Great Hall and the hanging of the tapestries. Brocaded silks and embroidered woolens packed away since the death of Dangereuse were draped over chairs and tables to conceal the neglected state of the furnishings; there was even a young lad with a vielle singing softly in the background. Musicians, Benoît thought, seemed to spring out of the ground wherever Eleanor stood. Cut one down, you found another half dozen sprouting in his place. He could almost sympathize with Louis's periodic attempts to clear the court of such frivolities.

The chapel and kitchen were still undergoing the assaults of Faenze's hastily assembled crew of servants, and Benoît was still bemoaning the lack of colors to make bright the ducal letters, when Louis came padding into the hall, Odo following him, to ask the meaning of all this uproar, the clamor and confusion that had disturbed his council with the chaplain.

"I cannot reside in a dirty and neglected hall," Eleanor said, "nor will I have my vassals come to such a place to do me homage." She explained her intention of staying in Poitiers until the divorce was final, and that she wished all the chief men of the realm to witness her appointment of a new seneschal.

"Geoffrey de Rancon has served us well," Louis said.

"I choose my own servants. Don't worry," Eleanor told him kindly, "you go on to Paris. You won't have to be here when I tell him his time is over."

"The lady means to remain in Poitiers?" Odo's voice was dry as the shed skin of a snake, rustling in the wind.

"I believe I just said so," Eleanor snapped, "and it would be no violation of your priestly vows to address me directly and with proper respect!"

Odo inclined his tonsured head. "I must have been mistaken," he said. "I thought you were as eager as my lord to correct this unhappy matter."

"I am," said Eleanor between her teeth, "and the pope can send his council of bishops here quite as well as to Paris."

A look she could not interpret passed between Odo and Louis. "That," said Odo courteously but firmly, "would be quite . . . inappropriate."

"Why so? Am I not countess of Poitou and duchess of Aquitaine?"

"And my lord," said Odo, "is king of France. It would be quite unsuitable for him to travel into your domains for the council regarding this divorce. The thing must be done properly, in Paris, with due respect for his rank and dignity."

"It was not beneath his dignity to make haste to Bordeaux to marry me!"

But Odo and, with his encouragement, Louis stood firm on the argument that it would be unacceptably undignified for the king's divorce to be pronounced anywhere save within his own domains. And Odo kept saying that if Eleanor refused to leave Poitiers, all sorts of arrangements would have to be made over again, and who knew how long it might take.

Eleanor bit her lip, considering, and turned to Benoît. "What do you think all this is about?" she asked in an undertone. "Are they trying to provoke me into staying, or into going?"

"Does it matter where the divorce is pronounced?"

"It might . . . if it takes longer this way . . ." Already it had been months since the divorce was agreed upon in principle. How long dared she wait? Suger's death had freed her of the one counselor who would never hear of Louis giving up Aquitaine, had left him dependent on the misogynistic Bernard who hated the free ways of southerners and urged him to rid himself of a wife who bore only girls. But Bernard was frail with the years of austerities he had practiced. "Bernard is for the divorce," she said, "but he might die. The *pope* might die. Anything could happen."

The boy with the vielle had been listening intelligently to the discussion. Now he modulated his soft song, from a *chanson d'amour* to one of the simple rhyming Latin songs spread by wandering students. The pure young voice sang:

> "*O fortuna*
> *Velut luna*
> *Statu variabilis . . .*"

> O Fortune
> like the moon
> always changing . . .

Eleanor gave him a sharp look. "Clever boy!" she said in a voice that could have cut diamonds.

He sang through her words and on to the next verse, comparing Fortune to a turning wheel.

> "*Sors imanis*
> *et inanis*
> *rota tu volubilis . . .*"

Within this single year the balance had shifted and given Eleanor a chance at freedom. Who knew when the wheel of fortune would turn again and close the doors that seemed to be opening?

"Very well," she said, turning back to Louis and Odo. "We shall compromise. Let the bishops meet in France, but close to the borders of Poitou, so that I may come home again as quickly as may be.

She suggested Tours; Odo mentioned Orléans; they agreed on Beaugency, halfway down the Loire between Orléans and Tours. Eleanor possessed a small manor outside Beaugency where she could reside while awaiting the council's decision, and from there she would have only a short ride down the Loire valley through Blois to Tours, then south across the river, to be once again in her own lands.

After the agreement was reached, Eleanor felt vaguely uneasy. She had expected Odo, in his vicarious pride for the king's position, to fight harder for Paris as the site of the divorce. Well, one of the bishops who was to decide the matter was Geoffrey du Lauroux, the archbishop of Bordeaux, who had married her and Louis fifteen years earlier. Perhaps Odo understood that it would be improper to ask the senior member of the conclave to travel farther than necessary.

Having almost won her battle to have the divorce pronounced on her own lands, Eleanor felt she could be gracious and accede to Louis's desire to leave Poitiers at once. She would be home soon enough, home to stay in the wooded, ferny, twisting ways of the bocage, with its ancient forests and green pools. She could ride on to France with Louis, as long as they went no farther than Beaugency.

So it was that the change in the seneschalship of Aquitaine was announced not to a grand convocation of the lords of the land who could be required to submit to the duchess's man as to herself, but to a hastily assembled group of men half in and half out of riding clothes, while Faenze and Eleanor's other waiting women scurried about packing up the tapestries that had so recently come out of storage. Eleanor stood on the slightly raised dais at the far end of the hall. It did not give her enough height to dominate the gathering of men preoccupied with their preparations for departure. She had to do that with her voice, first raising it high and sharp enough to capture their attention for a moment.

"Before leaving Poitiers, I must have a trustworthy man as seneschal over my lands."

That got their attention. Hugh of Lusignan, lounging on a bench to her right, looked brightly alert, expectant as a hound watching the table scraps. Raoul de la Faye stood to her left, at the head of the small group of men he had brought from Faye-la-Vineuse to add to her escort.

"Geoffrey de Rancon has served my lord of France well and faithfully," Eleanor said, now dropping her voice so that they had to watch her face and listen closely to be sure of catching every word, "but as we prepare for me to take over the governance of my own domains, I prefer to have a man of my choosing, a man of Poitou, a man bound to me by ties of kinship to govern in Poitiers during my absence."

Black Hugh nodded approvingly at the first two phrases, looked startled at the last, and then tried to suppress a grin. What did the man think, that she was going to announce their betrothal, and he still wedded to Geoffrey de Rancon's daughter?

"Therefore," she said after a pause filled with tension, "I name my kinsman Raoul de la Faye seneschal over Aquitaine and Poitou." She turned to Raoul. "Much as I regret parting from a kinsman so newly met, I fear you will have to remain in Poitiers for the time being, Raoul. I must have a man I can trust looking after my interests while we wait for the bishops in Beaugency to make their decision."

Black Hugh jumped to his feet. "You *promised*—"

"I made you no promises."

"But it was understood . . . You put Geoffrey de Rancon out of office, but the office passes to his son, or, since he has none, to his daughter's husband."

"The seneschal serves at the pleasure of the duke or duchess of Aquitaine," Eleanor said, more calmly than she felt. "The office is not hereditary. You have no grounds for complaint, Hugh."

Hugh's face grew even darker than the sun of the south had burnt it, and he swore a short and mercifully unintelligible oath between his teeth. "You wanted a man you could trust? That at least was wise, for God knows one can never trust a woman! If you leave Raoul de la Faye and his men here in Poitiers, my lady duchess, you may whistle for an escort into France. I shall take my men back to Lusignan!" He turned his back on her and stamped out of the hall.

"You've made an enemy there," Raoul de la Faye said in an undertone.

"How perceptive!" Eleanor raised her brows and saw Raoul's face redden. "Did you think he was a friend before? My father told me never to trust a Lusignan, and my grandmother taught me never to trust a man who courted for a new wife before he had cast off the old one. I'll have no hound who follows me only for the bones I throw him," she finished with a bravado she did not feel. It was a risky beginning to her rule as duchess, to alienate the Lusignans. But it would have been more risky still to accede to Hugh's assumptions that he had a natural right to be her chief counselor and seneschal.

"If you had not made me seneschal," Raoul said, "I would be free to ride on with you now, to protect you in France until the divorce. It is not too late to change your decision—you can call him back, or leave Geoffrey de Rancon in charge—"

Eleanor shook her head, smiling. "The best man to watch over my lands is the one who does not desire the position. You make me more sure of my choice with every word, Raoul. And I shall need no great escort in France; this is only a divorce, not a war. As soon as the bishops have come to Beaugency, they will confirm the separation, and two days later I can be home in Poitiers."

Chapter Eighteen

The bridge over the Loire at Beaugency must have been more than a hundred years old. Although it seemed to be in fine condition, most travelers went over it with caution, usually crossing themselves and saying a prayer.

"It *looks* sturdy enough," Benoît told Faenze, "but you never can tell about these fiend-built things."

Faenze glanced ahead, where Louis rode with Eleanor in a careful show of amity designed to let everyone understand that the divorce was something forced upon them by church law and had nothing to do with any difficulties in their personal relationship.

"Get on! *He* never called on the devil for aid, I'll say that much for him."

Benoît sighed. "Of course he didn't. Why would a king of France trouble about one little local bridge?"

"Comes in handy, doesn't it? We'd've had a long ride roundabout if it weren't here. I don't reckon kings like long detours better'n anybody else."

"Even if it were built by a king," Benoît said between his teeth, "it wouldn't have been this king, it would have been his grandfather. Maybe his *great*-grandfather. Maybe Charles le Magne, it looks old enough!"

"So is there a story about the bridge, or isn't there?"

"I was trying to tell you when you got me all distracted with nonsense about kings and grandfathers," Benoît said unfairly. "It was the mayor of Beaugency called up the devil, and he—the devil, not the mayor—said he would build the bridge in exchange for the first soul to cross it. Naturally the townsfolk were somewhat uneasy about the bargain, but the mayor swore on the relics of Saint Martin of Tours that he himself would be the first man to cross the bridge. So they figured that was all right. But when the bridge was done, the mayor let a cat out of a sack and threw a bucket of water on it, so the poor creature scurried across the bridge to get away from the water, and the devil got its soul and the mayor crossed safely enough. The devil saw he'd been tricked, but he didn't hold it against the mayor; he laughed so loud the top fell off of Caesar's Tower there." Benoît pointed to a square keep across the river. "And I guess he felt that was revenge enough, for he didn't keep laughing until the bridge itself fell down."

"Tower looks all right to me," Faenze said, squinting slightly. "Where's the missing bits, then."

"I suppose they rebuilt it," Benoît said.

Faenze thought a while longer while the slow cavalcade clip-clopped across the bridge and into the town of Beaugency. "I don't believe it," she said finally.

"Why not?"

"Silly. Cats don't *have* souls. I should think a great scholar who studied logic in Paris would've noticed that!"

Once their amity had been firmly and publicly established, Louis and Eleanor separated. He remained in Beaugency while she retired to her manor of Tavers, just outside the town.

"I don't like it," Benoît fretted on her behalf. "He'll have the bishops' ear. They'll take his side on everything."

Eleanor sighed. "Benoît, for once Louis and I are on the same side. I want my freedom from this marriage, and he wants a wife who'll give him an heir. I expect that as soon as the divorce is pronounced he'll have Odo scouring the records for some family with seven generations of seven sons and one marriageable daughter. No," she corrected herself with a slightly forced smile, "Odo is probably *already* searching for my replacement. Why would they wait?"

"But the charge of your daughters . . ."

Eleanor's face became quite expressionless. Benoît could not think why he suddenly remembered that her grandfather had once threatened to behead the bishop of Poitiers over some theological dispute. "Alix and Marie will remain in Louis's keeping, as is customary." She turned away, blinking rapidly. "There will be no discussion of that issue."

Later, when she sent him daily into Bordeaux to listen to the bishops' discussion of the case, Benoît learned that the disposition of Eleanor's daughters had been determined ahead of time. One of the conditions that Louis's advisers insisted upon was that Eleanor should make no claim on the girls.

"It is the custom," Faenze said when he told her this, "and what did you expect? Even Louis must sometimes worry that it's his seed, and not Eleanor's womb, that makes only girls and not so many of them. If he doesn't get lucky with the next wife, those two will be his only heirs."

"You are coarse."

"Realistic. What did you *think* would happen to the girls, Benoît? You can't expect him to leave the future princesses of France in the hands of a woman who does not love him and who might marry God knows who after she gets free of him. Besides," Faenze went on, "it is probably better for them not to have any change. Marie hardly knows Eleanor, she grew so accustomed to the care of her nurses and her own establishment during the years we spent in Outremer. And Alix . . . I believe Eleanor has been expecting this since Alix was born. Preparing for it. She took great care to find reliable nurses and ladies before the birth, and immediately afterward she handed Alix over to their care. She has hardly even seen the child."

"I suppose," Benoît said, "some women simply lack maternal feeling."

Faenze decided, upon consideration, not to box his ears, because he was only a man and couldn't help being an insensitive clod. But it was a near thing.

Geoffrey du Lauroux, who had solemnized Eleanor's marriage to Louis some fifteen years earlier, was one of the three bishops appointed by the pope to hear the arguments for her divorce. The others were the archbishops of Rheims and Rouen. With three such eminences and all their followers, not to mention the King and *his* household, the little town of Beaugency was strained to find decent lodgings for all the visitors. The king, the nobles, and the lords of the church were lodged in comfort, but mere knights and deacons were crammed six to a room, and as for the squires and clerks, they were lucky to get the shelter of a stable and some straw that wasn't too damp. As for the poor commoners who held the nobles' horses and dressed them and fed them and carried their chamber pots, one assumed that they found some corner to sleep in, but no one troubled overmuch about them.

"Trust me," Benoît reported to Faenze on the third day of the hearings, "you *don't* want to come into the town with me. If you take a step without looking down, you're likely to tread on some man-at-arms who's trying to catch a bit of sleep in his master's corner. As for the hearings—" He threw up his hands. "We're packed like pilchards in a barrel. The other day the king's chaplain sneezed and six people wiped their own noses, they were standing so close to him it felt like their own rheum. And you wouldn't *believe* the wild rumors that spread in that kind of crowd. There's talk about Outremer," he said darkly. "Not in the court, of course. But . . . Faenze, what exactly *did* happen there?"

"I can tell you what *didn't* happen," Faenze said quickly. "She never did, or said, or thought, anything the least bit improper with her uncle Raymond. That I can swear to. Anyway, it's none of their business."

"Maybe not," Benoît said, "but divorcing her for adultery makes a better story than that they've just discovered their consanguinity, which nobody believes for a minute. Of course nothing's being said in the court. Geoffrey du Lauroux sees to it that all's proper there. But outside, well, it's a French town and they were never too fond of us Poitevins. Some clerk from Rheims told me he knew for a fact that the queen wasn't present because she was all but mad with her shame and grief at being put aside by Louis."

"Better not let Eleanor hear that," Faenze said, "or we'll all be dragged into town to put on a dance in the town square."

"You wouldn't have *room* to dance," Benoît said. "It's too full of unnecessary followers milling about with nothing to do. I wish they'd get this over with. It's been arranged for months; you can't imagine the little details they find to argue about now. I suppose they want to make it all look good."

"I s'pose Geoffrey du Lauroux finds it a bit embarrassing to preside," Faenze hazarded, "seeing he was the one who married them in the first place. Won't he get in trouble for that?"

"Not likely! If there's one thing all parties are agreed upon, it's that this was all a terrible mistake and nobody suspected any relationship between Louis and Eleanor until they just happened to look at the genealogies in detail. Good thing Bernard of Clairvaux isn't here," Benoît said.

"Why? Isn't he for the divorce?"

"Yes, but he's not tactful. He's perfectly capable of pointing out that he has been complaining about the relationship since the day they married. Then Geoffrey du Lauroux *would* look bad—and so would Pope Eugenius, who told them three years ago not to worry about a thing."

After another week of interminable, nitpicking debates, the marriage between Louis of France and Eleanor of Aquitaine was declared invalid under the terms that had been agreed upon long before anybody met in Beaugency. Since they had married in good faith and in ignorance of their consanguinity, the children of the marriage were to be considered legitimate and would remain in the care of their father. The domains that Eleanor had possessed at the time of her marriage were to be restored to her. "Surprise, surprise," Benoît commented, "as if we hadn't spent the last few months changing over garrisons and castellans!" And both parties were free to marry again.

"What happens," Faenze asked slowly, "if she marries somebody *else* who is related to her as nearly as Louis?"

Benoît shrugged. "If she marries in her own rank, that'd be hard to avoid. You dig back four or five generations, all these noble families have intermarried so many times they're technically illegal. Just means it'll be easier to get it annulled if it doesn't work out." He reconsidered for a moment. "Or maybe not . . . The church likes to *look* as if these things are taken seriously. Someone who keeps coming back with the same story about marrying in good faith and then being shocked to discover a relationship within the forbidden decrees, well, the first time is one thing, but repeating it might annoy the pope. This time," he pronounced, "she'd better think hard before she takes a husband."

"Maybe," Faenze said, "she's already *thought*."

Benoît shook his head. "After Louis, she won't be so eager to tie herself to some man she's never met. Mark my words, she'll take on her own domains and keep all her suitors dangling while she thinks it over. She likes running things, you know; she might not be in such a hurry to hand over her lands to another husband." He didn't really believe that, but he liked the picture his words painted: his lady holding court in her own gracious southern lands, a court of music and poetry and dance, and some trusted friend who had known her nearly fifteen years to serve as her closest adviser.

The picture was rudely dispelled that very night.

"*Why* pack by torchlight and leave under the stars?" Benoît asked amid the flurry of servants running about the manor. "What's the matter with riding out in daylight like decent civilized people?"

Eleanor picked up her mirror of polished bronze and tilted it idly this way and that, sending reflected candle flames to dance up the walls while Faenze muttered rebelliously about the difficulty of finding anything in the clutter her lady strewed about her, let alone finding it by candlelight. "It's quite simple, Faenze," Eleanor told her. "Pick up something. If we want to take it with us, pack it. If we don't, then put it in the chests of things to be sent for later. When the room is empty, you're done." She looked back at Benoît. Her hair was loose about her shoulders, as if she were preparing for bed, and in the glow of the candlelight she looked absurdly young, as young as the madcap girl he'd found—and lost—during a student riot at the fair in Paris.

"I am not leaving," she explained seriously. "I am prostrate with grief and too ill to receive anyone. I shall have to rest here at my manor outside Beaugency *without seeing anyone* for several days, do you understand?"

"Who's going to believe that?" Benoît demanded.

Eleanor's smile was so sweet, he could not quite say why he felt a sense of danger in it. "Why, all those fools who've been spreading the rumors you told to Faenze. And, with luck, a few more nobly placed fools. I shall leave most of my household here to make it look good; I'll be taking only a small escort, and riding fast. *No*, Faenze, put all those gowns in store. I can't be hampered by a baggage train!"

"Not," Benoît said slowly, "an entirely stupid idea. You want to be well away from France before anyone knows it."

"With luck and God's grace," Eleanor corrected him, "well into Poitiers. We should be able to manage it, too; it is just to ride down the Loire to Blois, then Tours, then a little way south and I'll be safely home—while Louis and his advisers think I am still weeping here in Tavers."

"*Louis?*"

"He will wish to believe it," Eleanor said, "and that is three-quarters of the way to swallowing the story whole. Besides, I rely on Faenze to make it convincing. You had better rub a little ash into your eyes to redden them, Faenze. Oh, and perhaps you should make a little mess in the hall. Dishes overturned and that sort of thing. Louis is more likely," she said wryly, "to believe I've been throwing things than that I'm quietly weeping in my bower."

"I'm coming with you," Faenze declared.

"You don't need to," Benoît said. "*I'll* look after her."

"Neither of you is coming," Eleanor told them. "Faenze, no one will believe I'm here if my favorite lady in waiting is not to be seen. And Benoît, I have need of your services in another matter, something that calls for a man of superb discretion who can ride all night if need be."

"I thought that's just what you were planning to do!"

"I," Eleanor said patiently, "shall be riding south. You need to go north. Into Normandy. And you must give no one else the message I send with you, save only the man I shall charge you to find. Do you understand?"

Benoît blinked in confusion. There had been those scenes last August, when Eleanor was so taken by the way Geoffrey Plantagenet defied Louis to his face. But . . . "But Geoffrey's *dead*," he said slowly.

"His son," said Eleanor, "is not." A light danced in her eyes. "Indeed, I should say he is very much alive!"

"Which son—Henry or Geoffrey? Or do you mean to have both of them, and keep the Angevin domains intact?" Benoît was too angry to guard his tongue.

"There is a limit," Eleanor said icily, "to the presumption that I will forgive for the sake of old friendship." She spoiled the effect of this rebuke by sputtering with half-suppressed laughter. "Oh, Benoît, if you could see your face, it would curdle fresh milk! Henry, of course. Can you really see me marrying a younger son?"

"I can see—" Benoît clamped his teeth together so fast that he caught a fold of his cheek. The effort not to howl with pain helped him to suppress the words that wanted to come out. *I can see you marrying a younger man.* Twelve years younger, to be exact.

How can she think of such a thing?" he grumbled later, to Faenze, who had thought to bring him a packet of bread and broken meats from the kitchen to stow in his saddlebags. "He's an infant. Besides, last summer I thought it was the father she wanted. Is it just because Geoffrey's dead now?"

"You haven't met him, have you?"

"Not to talk to. I saw him, of course, back in August when Geoffrey dragged him along to court to do his homage to Louis." A sulky, square boy with unkempt red hair, who had no better manners than to play with a tangle of jesses while his betters were having diplomatic talks. Every feeling was outraged at the thought of his lady giving herself to that young oaf.

"Well, she's talked with him," Faenze said. "Maybe she sees something in him that we're missing."

Benoît tugged on the straps of his saddlebags and checked the girth around the horse. "Right. Normandy and Anjou and a claim on England, that's what she sees!"

"You'd rather have her wait meekly here for Louis to marry her off to some spineless vassal of his?"

"She doesn't *have* to marry. She's duchess of Aquitaine in her own right. She could keep her own court and . . ."

Faenze looked at him pityingly. "Even if she could. Even if her own vassals weren't likely to fall all over themselves fighting to see who gets the first chance to abduct her. Even if she *could* keep them all in check . . . Benoît, she's just thirty, and she has spent half her life married to that cold, stale milk pudding. Do you think she *wants* to sleep alone the rest of her life? Duchess she may be, but she's a healthy young woman and she wants what all the rest of us want: a man in her bed and children in her arms."

"You wouldn't understand. Some women are meant for a higher destiny."

"If you meet one outside a nunnery, let me know!" Faenze's lips and cheeks were red with cold or anger, and she looked more alive than Benoît had ever seen her.

"Faenze," he said, checking just before he mounted. "What about you? What do *you* want?"

Faenze looked back toward the hall doors. "I had my chance," she said. "In Constantinople . . . It wouldn't have worked, anyway, even if that bastard Robert hadn't forced me away. An emperor's nephew can't be marrying spoiled goods. Nobody would want to . . . It's different for *her*. She could have any man she wanted."

"A boy of eighteen!"

Faenze's lips twitched. "Look at it this way, Benoît. Who else would have the energy to keep up with her?"

enoît was well on his way to Bayeux before Eleanor and her chosen escort left Tavers, quietly, in the first glimmerings of light before dawn. The little village outside the manor slept; even the splashing of the horses as they forded the streams running into the Loire disturbed no one. Once out of the village, they could make better speed, but Eleanor was still cautious; she had outriders posted ahead and behind, and would move no faster than the man in front could spy out the land.

Less than half a league out of the village, her caution was rewarded. She pulled her horse up sharply and her knights crowded around her at the sound of hoofbeats coming toward them. It was Boson d'Aulbeterre, the man she'd sent ahead.

"Armed men, two score," he gasped as soon as he was near them, "under the banner of Thibaut of Blois."

Eleanor glanced to right and left. She had chosen, for speed, to ride with a minimal escort: only a dozen knights, and those the ones who had enough sense to do without the services of their squires for the journey.

Amicie de Périgné was calmly putting on his helm, as though nothing could be more natural than to fight against odds of more than three to one before breakfast. The other men looked equally ready to defend her. Nausea twisted her stomach. "There must be some other way," she said. "If we disguised me as a squire . . ."

Amicie shook his head. "Lady, you are betrayed. Easy enough to slip some man of his in among the servants at Tavers, with instructions to let him know as soon as you were divorced. And for a bonus," he said grimly, "the man will have told him you were coming this way, and there is but the one road along the river . . . and no bridge before Blois."

They could retreat to Tavers . . . but it was not built for defense . . . and what would she do there? Wait while Thibaut and half a dozen other claimants fought it out? Hope that Benoît would reach Henry in time for him to send rescue? But, dear Lord, she had been too confident; she had sent word for Henry to meet her at Poitiers.

Ahead was immediate disaster, behind a more delayed disaster, and to her left the glimmering waters of the Loire closed off the way to the south and safety. "Can we go that way?" She jerked her head to the right, to the north. "Does any man know this region?"

"Lady, I was fostered here," spoke up a young man, hardly more than a boy, whom she had chosen for her escort simply because his young freckled face reminded her of Henry. "There is a track through the forest toward Feularde."

"And what's Feularde? Three huts and some pigs? A lot of good that'll do us!" Boson snapped.

"Some people," the boy said, "do not like to go into the forest near Feularde. Especially in the dark. There've been lights seen there, dancing among the standing stones . . . And the peasants tell stories about the great stone atop the others."

"La Pierre Tournante." Eleanor remembered the tales now. "The Turning Stone, is that it, Hélie?"

"Yes, my lady. They say there is a great treasure lies beneath the stones, and at midnight on Candlemas, La Pierre Tournante turns to reveal the entrance to a secret chamber, but it turns so fast that whoever goes in will be trapped to starve there."

"What a pity," Eleanor said dryly, "that Candlemas is past. It might offer us a refuge from Thibaut."

"Peasant nonsense," Amicie muttered. "It won't scare off Thibaut's men."

But as nobody had any better suggestion, they dismounted and led their horses along the narrow track that Hélie pointed out. The March wind drove bare branches together and apart above their heads and set the leaves underfoot to scurrying in crackling whirls that danced and sank again.

"Demons dance tonight," muttered Boson.

"No," Eleanor said firmly, "the wind is the gift of my patron saint Radegonde, to cover the noise of our passage."

But when they reached the deep-shadowed clearing where five great stones rose up, roofed by a sixth stone too large by far for mortal men to lift, more than one of the men crossed himself surreptitiously. Eleanor's hand stole to the pierced stone that Cercle-le-Monde had given her so long ago. *This is the heart of the oldest forest, and it is to be found wherever you seek it . . . you may always find your way here again at need.* But that had been in the sweet south, in the spring, when all things grew fresh and new. Here she was still trapped in winter, in a forest of trees as bare and white as skeletons. And when her little group stopped, they could hear the sounds behind them: men on horseback, who had not troubled to dismount and creep quietly through the woods, cursing at the branches that slashed them across the face.

"They saw where we turned off. . . . It's no good, but at least we can have the stones at our back as we fight," muttered Amicie.

"No. Go under the stones," Hélie said. The freckles on his face stood out like spots of ink on a clean-scraped parchment, and he was shaking with the effort of contradicting the senior knight in the party.

"What good will that do? They'll see us, and I've no fancy to fight like a badger trapped in his sett."

"They won't. I'll turn them aside. Here, take my things!" Hélie had little enough to distinguish him as a knight, only a sword too long for him and a rusty helmet tied to the pack on his horse. He thrust the sword at Amicie and bent to the ground, came up with dirty hands and rubbed the grime on his face. "I was *fostered* here, I can talk like the locals. I'm a swineherd. You never came this way. I never saw you. Go on!"

Both men and horses were reluctant to thread their way between the two nearest standing stones, into the shadows beneath La Pierre Tournante. Eleanor drew a deep breath and smelled the mold under the leaves where Hélie had stirred it up, dirtying his face. There was life in that damp black mold, richness to feed the new growth of the spring. "Come, then," she said, very quietly, and lifted Cercle-le-Monde's blue-green stone bead on its chain so that they could see it, or at any rate see that she held something. "I had this talisman from just such a place of ancient stones. It will protect us all."

They followed where she led, and the darkness within the stones made the shadowy predawn light in the forest seem like the blaze of noonday by comparison. Amicie had some trouble with his horse. When he'd coaxed the beast through into the circle, he muttered rebelliously about preferring a good sword and a troop of well trained men-at-arms for protection over some rock with a hole in the middle.

"If you can raise men-at-arms from a circle of stone, pray do so," Eleanor snapped, but under her breath.

Boson paled and crossed himself as though he thought they would indeed find a circle of stone warriors surrounding them.

"Where's that boy gone? What if it was all a trick to get himself free of us?"

"*Hush*, Amicie."

While they were getting the horses into the stone circle, Hélie had ambled back down the track the way they had come. Now Thibaut's men were so close that they could hear the jingle of armor and the creak of harness. A thick, slurred voice accosted them, demanding to know why they had scared off his swine.

"Out of our way, peasant!"

Eleanor pulled off her veil and wrapped it around her palfrey's mouth, ran one soothing hand along the horse's neck. *Keep still, keep still, it's all right, nothing to worry about.*

"Ah, masters, but my swine, my little one with the black spots, she ran this way when she heard you coming, and the rest after her. They bean't used to fine lords riding through, that they bean't."

There was a sound of leather cracking on flesh, and Hélie blubbered for mercy.

"Wait, you idiot," said another voice, "don't beat the sense out of him. Do you mean to say we're the first riders who've come through here tonight, peasant?"

Hélie's voice raised in wails and lamentation for his swine and in vows to all the saints he could think of that never, no, never, did anyone ride along this poor little path. Why, couldn't the gracious lords see it was not clear enough for mounted men?

"The oaf has that part right," said someone in Thibaut's party, with feeling. "My face is so scoured by branches that I look like I'd been trying to rape a she-devil."

"You've tried everything else," someone sniggered.

The wind rose overhead; bare branches clattered against one another. Eleanor's hand closed tight over her stone bead, "Hold my mare," she whispered to Amicie, and with her free hand she began to unplait her long braids. The wind gained force as her hair floated free about her face. *Loose the knots in your hair and find a wind that will carry you where you will,* Dangereuse said in her mind. Twice now that wind had carried her to disaster, first to France and then in Sicily. Dared she try a third time?

She did not dare *not* try. She had been too long winning this freedom to give it up now to Thibaut of Blois.

She combed her fingers through the freed plaits and cold air whistled past her, whipping her unbound hair about her face and howling in the passages between the stones. Amicie was muttering prayers under his breath, but the wind drowned him out. The horses moved, unhappy, but the sound of their steps was lost in the snapping of twigs from winter-bare branches as a storm loosed by her great need spiraled about the stones and spread through the naked wood.

"This is an unlucky place," one of the men from Blois said. "Can you hear the demons laughing?"

"Idiot! It's only the wind in the——"

A branch cracked in the sudden gusts of wind and came plummeting down at their feet. Eleanor yanked viciously at the last tangle in her plaits and the sound of the wind rose to a demonic howl. Someone outside called on his saints for protection. So did Amicie, standing beside her; she could smell the fear on him.

"Enough!" It was their leader, but his voice sounded shaky. Eleanor trapped her flying hair, a handful in each fist, and the wind slowed until she could hear him better. "They never came this way, or they'd have run off the clod's precious swine before ever we bothered him. Give the lad a few sous and let's go back. They will have turned back to Tavers; we might be able to catch them up before they get there."

"If we're not trapped here forever," muttered an unhappy voice. "They say when the great stone turns . . ."

"Well, you don't see it turning, do you?" snapped the first man.

"*Something* moved."

"Shadows. The wind. Moonlight!"

Eleanor spared a hand to touch the stone bead at her neck. *If the stone turns, we are trapped forever. Have I escaped into prison?* The thought echoed like a struck gong in her head, like something that she had forgotten, something that was to come that she knew but had forgotten. . . . Perhaps she was only escaping into madness. With half her long hair freed, the wind gathered strength again, crying like an army of lost souls.

"I am *not* running from noises in the night," the leader said in answer to somebody's sotto voce comment. "It is simple reason. Thibaut won't be happy if we let them bolt into Tavers and he has to set siege. Neither will Odo."

Eleanor started at the familiar name.

"Who cares about the king's chaplain?"

"Thibaut does. He stands nearer the throne than anyone else. And after he went to the trouble of setting the divorce in Beaugency, for the lady to fall into Thibaut's hands like a ripe plum dropping from the tree, he'll not be well pleased if we let her get back to Tavers. I *told* you we should have stayed in Blois, she'd have ridden straight into captivity. But no, Thibaut had to send us out to 'make sure of her.' Hah! All we've done so far is alert her. Come on! I told you she would have scuttled back to her manor, and we've wasted too damn much time just because you thought you saw some trampled bushes at the turnoff of this path. Probably this idiot's swine that trampled them."

Gradually the voices moved off and Eleanor breathed again. Young Hélie came back, grinning under the dirt that besmeared his face. "Best wait," he cautioned them, "we want them well on the way to Tavers before we set out again."

"Not too far on the way," Eleanor said. "We've to get through Blois before they find out I'm not at Tavers. God send Faenze delays them long enough!" She felt shaky at the knees, but the ground was solid and firm enough beneath her feet, and her mare beside her was a warm and comforting bulk, and very real. She gave thanks to have come back again from the world of mystery into the world of plain facts and sharp wits, the world she could master.

"Blois! Are you mad? Knowing Thibaut plans to capture you?"

Eleanor stared through the shadows until Amicie dropped his eyes. "And exactly where would *you* propose to cross the Loire? At Beaugency? Do you think I should ride back to Louis, who plotted this treachery, and beg him for safe-conduct? We'll go through Blois."

"Thibaut will have everyone on the lookout for a noble lady."

"They won't see one," Eleanor told him, and after a moment's blank silence, "Well? Surely *one* of you has a change of clothing in his saddlebags?"

After another moment of silence, she said, "And the first one who tells me it's improper can strip and give me his tunic and braies, and ride back to Tavers naked."

After a moment there was a smothered laugh from Boson. "Lady, I've clothes to spare, but my garments would go around you twice. You'll have to rob young Hélie."

There was enough light by now to see Hélie's dirt-bedaubed face turning red—and to show the weal where one of Thibaut's men had struck him across his face. Eleanor touched the swelling line as lightly as she could. "Hélie, you have already saved me twice. Will you make it a third time? Lend me your garments and see what you can do with Boson's spares."

The changing was accomplished hurriedly, with some turning of backs and Eleanor's insistence that it was still dark enough to preserve everyone's modesty, and before it was fully light there left the hamlet of Feularde a somewhat less impressive group than had come in. With their armor and swords packed away, the knights might have been a group of merchants with two slovenly serving boys. One boy had a whiplash across his face and was wrapped in hand-me-down clothes somewhat too large for him; the other had his head wrapped up like a sufferer with toothache. Both were so dirty that it was hard to make out their features.

"This," Eleanor said after they had regained the main road without mishap, "is a *much* more comfortable costume for riding. Perhaps I shall set a new style. Amicie, try to slump in your saddle. You look too . . . knightly. Look at Boson, he's the very image of a fat, lazy merchant ambling home."

"That's what our old master-at-arms always said about him," Amicie retorted with a flash of malice.

They passed through Blois without attracting attention; it was market day and all sorts and conditions of people were crossing the bridge there. They rode on along the main road until Eleanor spied a path branching off southward into the forest. Eleanor turned to Hélie.

"Do you know this side of the river as well? Where does that path lead?"

"You don't want to take it," Hélie said. "They told me if you go too far south you'll be in Angevin territory."

Eleanor smiled. *"Excellent."*

"But my lady——" Amicie called as she turned off the main road.

"We're going to *Anjou?*"

"Where better?"

"You can't trust those Angevins."

"I shall have to," Eleanor said calmly. "I expect to marry one of them. If he gets my message in time, he may be in Poitiers before us. Come *on!*"

Young Curtmantle—I mean, the duke of Normandy? Naah, he's not here," the gatekeeper at Sées told Benoît.

"I was told he was revising the charter of the town's liberties."

"That was *last* week. Doesn't take young—our duke, I mean—long to cross out half the lines in the charter and tell a clerk to copy the new version. He's gone on up Falaise way."

Border guards rode out from Fulk's keep at Montrichard to block their way.

"Oh, well, that's all right," Amicie said as soon as he recognized their colors, "we can just tell them you're on your way to marry their master."

The stone bead lying on Eleanor's throat felt very cold, cold as the deep drifts of snow on the earth in shadowy places. "No. Wait. We're merchants, that's all. Keep to that story until you know who their master is."

"But if you're *marrying* him—"

"Geoffrey Plantagenet left more than one son."

Her instincts were proved right. It was young Geoffrey who held this keep, in defiance of the will that had left Anjou to Henry, and he would have liked nothing better than to keep his older brother's prize for himself. Fortunately greed, or the power in Cercle-le-Monde's stone, blinded him. He was too interested in the gold Amicie paid over as "passage toll" to wonder how such a shabby company came by such wealth, or to look closely at the fine-boned, beardless boy who rode with their serving men.

Young Henry? Oh, aye, he *was* here, but that was two nights since."

"Where'd he go?"

"How should I know?"

But the last of Benoît's gold revived the gate guard's memory, and he allowed that the duke *had* sent messengers summoning his chief men to a council at Lisieux.

Between Montrichard and Poitiers lay the forest, deep-shadowed, crisscrossed with winding trails left by poachers and deer, with here and there a clearing where a few peasants secretly tried to hack out a living under the shade of the oaks without paying either Angevin or Poitevin for the right to live.

"We've nothing to fear from the peasants," Eleanor said serenely when Amicie proposed bypassing the first such cluster of huts and muddy fields. "They'll not tell any lord of our passage for fear of attracting attention to their own existence."

"They're starving. They'd as soon cut our throats and make soup of our horses!"

Eleanor smiled serenely. "Why, Amicie, cannot I trust you and my other brave knights to defend me against a few ragged peasants? Put your armor back on, if it will make you feel better. We are nearly home." The stone bead was warm and vibrant against her skin; it seemed to thrum with excitement the nearer Poitou they came. Already she felt safe and at home; the great oaks that shaded them, the bent golden grass and the tracks of deer and rabbits were no different from the forests where Dangereuse tried to teach two willful girls her herb lore. While Petronilla sat at their grandmother's skirts, Eleanor had roamed where she would, gaining a sense of the forest that she used now to guide herself and her people home.

The danger, when it came, was so near Poitiers that they did not recognize it at first. The forest had thinned out around them until they came to a true road, one of those her grandfather had cleared and rebuilt from the traces of the straight old Roman track. Before coming out onto the road, Eleanor put back on her woman's clothes and washed at the icy trickle of a spring where there remained the molder-ing remains of a shrine to some forgotten saint. "Bring me safely to my capital," she prayed there, "and I will find out your name, lost saint, and rebuild this shrine and make it a place of pilgrimage."

Once on the straight road for Poitiers, she bade Amicie unfurl the banner that had been hidden in his saddlebags, and told Boson and Hélie to ride ahead, announcing her coming in every hamlet along the way. Here in her own lands, it was surely safer to be the countess of Poitou and duchess of Aquitaine than an anonymous servant boy riding with the grubbiest merchants who ever did business in Poitou. Peasants and children came out to gawk at her passage, and at the Monastery of Saint-Benoît the abbot himself came into the road to offer her rest and shelter for the night.

"Your grace will scarcely wish to enter Poitiers so travel-stained and with such a small entourage," he urged.

All Eleanor desired was to enter Poitiers at all, but she looked around at her dusty troop, reflected that she herself must look no better, and remembered that Saint-Benoît had been famed in her father's time for offering exceedingly comfort-able lodgings to wealthy ladies on pilgrimage.

"We shall pause here long enough to wash and rest," she decreed, "but I will be in Poitiers before nightfall."

"A few moments while we make our humble guest rooms fit for such noble company," the abbot suggested, "and I have here some new wine from Bordeaux; your grace would honor our abbey by giving her opinion of it."

Eleanor commanded her men to see to their horses and take a meal in the abbey hall, all but Hélie. "Someone must stay with the horses," she said apologetically to the abbot, "and I have very particular commands regarding my own palfrey, who is not accustomed to strangers."

Having, as quickly and quietly as possible, given those commands to Hélie, she accepted the abbot's arm as far as his private rooms. Perhaps she had been too many days in the forest; it should have been pure joy to sit in a cushioned chair, drinking wine from a goblet of chased silver and hearing the gossip of her own capital from the suave and worldly abbot of Saint-Benoît. But Eleanor felt restless and ill at ease in these surroundings, and the stone bead that had thrummed against her chest lay silent and cold. Well, it *was* a pagan relic; one could hardly expect it to feel very lively here. The guest rooms would have been better. The abbot's own rooms, where he received her while the other rooms were being cleaned, were too austere for her to feel truly welcome here. Bare white walls, a roughly carved crucifix, and a whip hanging on the wall, the tips of the lashes stained dark in mute witness to the abbot's holy self-flagellations. She was out of place here, she and the crimson cushions that had been hastily brought for her comfort and the silver goblet from which she drank her wine.

"Women need comfort," the abbot said. He made it sound like an eighth deadly sin. "Comfort and guidance, for their minds are not meant for ruling."

Eleanor smiled sweetly, sipped her wine, and resolved to investigate the charter of Saint-Benoît as soon as she took power. It was too much to hope that she could fill all the responsible posts in Poitiers with men who did not share the abbot's views; but by her faith and Saint Radegonde, she would at least find some who were bright enough not to say such things in her presence!

The clatter of horses and men in armor penetrated the thick whitewashed walls of the abbot's rooms, and Eleanor looked up in surprise and momentary alarm. But what was there to fear? She was so very close to home now. . . . Her father had always said that his worst enemies were those who dwelt the nearest to him; the closer they were, the more damage they could do.

"Black Hugh!" Eleanor set down the goblet and rose to welcome him with both hands outspread. "I might have known you would be first to greet me. Oh, it is good to see someone with whom I've shared so much, a man of my own land!" *How had he known she was here? Coincidence, or betrayal? Dared she ask?* "Will you ride with me to Poitiers, then, as we rode together so long ago in Outremer?" *Remind him of the fellowship of those days, pretend, it never crossed your mind he might be seeking revenge for her denial of the post he'd counted on. Even if he came in revenge, he might go along with the pretense of old friendship. Buy time; time, that had been her enemy for so many slow days and years, might now be her friend.*

"Aye," Hugh said with the ready smile that promised everything and meant nothing, "I mean to ride with you from here."

Eleanor had not spent so many years in the French court without perfecting her own version of that smile. It helped that she had to look up at him; tall men tended, she had noticed, to underrate those who were shorter and weaker than they. "How clever of you to find me here!"

Hugh nodded at the abbot, and Eleanor exhaled softly. If he was the source of Hugh's information, she was not lost—yet.

"Those grazing lands to the south of the abbey—" the abbot murmured.

"You'll have your reward," Hugh promised, offhand, "but not till the business is done. Come, lady, we've a long ride ahead!"

"Not so very far to Poitiers," Eleanor said. *Keep pretending you've no suspicion of him. He may yet decide not to betray you—and himself.*

"A little farther," Hugh said, "to Lusignan." His hand was hard on her arm. "Now don't embarrass yourself by making a scene. I'll be a good husband to you. Careful and forethoughty!" He laughed with triumph. "Haven't I paid men on all the roads to Poitiers to keep watch for your coming?"

"Bergone—"

"Alas," Hugh said, "we have found that we are related within the fifth degree, by her great-great-aunt's sister who married into the Lusignan family. We have separated by mutual agreement, and Bergone has retired into the convent of Fontevrault to pray forgiveness for our unwitting sin until the annulment of our marriage shall be completed." His smile was a white crescent flashing briefly in his dark-tanned face. "I may not be able to marry you officially for some months, but no one will hold it against us if we anticipate the decree. A young and hot-blooded countess, and one who has already known the embraces of a husband, can hardly be expected to deprive herself so."

"I will not go with you." Eleanor stood as stiff as she could, but the room seemed to be moving oddly about her.

"Sweetheart, you have no choice. My men outnumber yours; will you see them slaughtered for no gain, after all they must have been through to see you safely here? I understand perfectly," Hugh assured her, "all these years with that milksop Louis, you must have grown accustomed to making your own decisions. Well, all that is over now. I shall take care of you properly."

"You mean you will betray me and your oath of liegeance!"

Hugh's face darkened. "The betrayal was yours first, lady. As Geoffrey de Rancon's son-in-law, I should have been appointed seneschal to replace him, instead of that landless nobody who came out of nowhere to claim kinship and flirt with you until you forgot what was due to me. You have only yourself to blame if I decided to take my rights by force. It just shows how unfit women are to make decisions in affairs of state."

"If you truly desire the seneschalship, something can be arranged. I had no idea it meant so much to you. Let us sit down and discuss it in peace, and we can discuss the abbey charters as well. What exactly does Saint-Benoît require, my lord abbot?" *Bribe, promise, discuss, but most of all, delay.*

"Nothing I cannot supply," Hugh said. "Come! You wished to be at home before nightfall, and so you shall be, even if Lusignan is a little farther ride than Poitiers."

Eleanor swayed in his grasp. "My poor head! I feel faint. You will not begrudge me a moment of rest while I take all this in, my lord?"

"Rest on horseback," Hugh growled.

"My palfrey is not rested yet."

"I brought horses enough, and in any case you will ride with me; I'll not take my hands off you till the prize is fairly mine."

"Fairly!"

"Or unfairly. It makes no difference in the long run."

Eleanor tried protesting that she was too delicate to ride any horse other than her own palfrey, but the flash of anger had been unwise. Hugh declared himself perfectly willing to throw her over his horse and let her ride upside down to Lusignan, if she cared so little for her own dignity.

"Come with me willing, and be my queen, or unwilling, and be my prisoner. Your choice!"

Eleanor drew a long breath and glanced around the room. The abbot would not meet her eyes; the other men were all Hugh's. It was hard to tell through the thick stone walls what might be happening outside; men and horses always made a certain amount of noise. It might be more than it had been a moment earlier, or it might not. She preferred not to gamble on so slight a chance.

"Play a game of chess with me," she suggested, "as we did in Outremer."

"What, gamble on your freedom, when I have you in my hand? I think *not*."

"If you win," Eleanor proposed, "you will have proved your masculine brain the superior of my weak feminine mind, and I will accept your rule and obey you in all things. If you lose, then you will have to take me as a prisoner, and I will fight and make a scandal that will blacken your name." She smiled sweetly upward. "Come now, Hugh! You know your wits to be superior to mine, else you'd not have trapped me here. What can it cost you to demonstrate it just once, to have my willing submission instead of my enmity?"

Hugh slowly shook his head. "Women are not truly intelligent, but they are cunning. I remember how often you won those games in Outremer. I'll not play at chess to win what I already have."

The noises outside had died away, but Eleanor thought she recognized the light step coming down the hall. A blaze of joy lit up her heart and her face as she saw the man who paused just outside the door. Hugh misinterpreted the look.

"There now," he said triumphantly, "that's better. Give us a smile and a kiss, sweeting, and admit what we already know—women need to be mastered."

But Eleanor's smile was not for him. "You have already played," she said, "and lost. Raoul, did Hélie have to kill my horse to reach you in time?"

"The palfrey is well enough," said Raoul de la Faye. "I left it and Hélie to rest. My men are all fresh-mounted, and I brought enough that half of us can escort you to Poitiers while the other half see that this slime of Lusignan tries no more tricks."

"Check," Eleanor said sweetly to Hugh, "and mate." She turned to the abbot. "Did you really think me fool enough to stop here without sending a single messenger to Poitiers? But do not be concerned. I keep my promises. And I promise to examine your charter *very closely*."

The bishop of Lisieux was weary of receiving Norman lay lords and clerics by the time his young duke finally appeared in Lisieux, saying something casual about the need to extirpate a nest of robber knights on the way from Falaise.

"It would have been more proper," Arnulf said stiffly, "to have held your council first and then to have delegated one of your vassals to see to that task."

"Proper, perhaps, but much less efficient," Henry told him. "After all, it was right on my way—and what could I have done if I'd been here two days sooner? I'll wager that fat prating priest from Rouen has barely arrived."

"You are speaking," Arnulf said, "of one of your chief advisers."

"Yes," Henry said absently, "we'll have to do something about that. Damn shame it's so hard to get rid of an archbishop. I've it in mind to put Rotrou in his place; my mother always thought highly of Rotrou's abilities. You'll help me think of some excuse."

Snub-nosed and freckled he still was, but no one made the mistake of treating Henry as a boy when he entered the council room, nor did they take his lack of ceremony as license to interrupt him when he began talking before he'd even sat down, outlining his plans to revise the entire governing structure of Normandy. It was said that all the robbers had been hanged by the side of the road, even the two of noble blood and the one who pleaded his clerical tonsure. It seemed quite possible that he might hang a bishop for interrupting him, and while the pope would surely anathematize such an action, that would be small comfort for the bishop who provided the test case.

The council was hardly begun, though, when a page boy entered the room at a run. Arnulf drew breath to rebuke him, but the boy fell to one knee before Henry and handed him something too small for Arnulf to see clearly, a ring, it might have been.

The freckled face lit up. "Where is her messenger?"

"Waiting for your reply. He says . . ." The boy's voice dropped and Arnulf could hear only a confidential murmur.

"His horse will need rest," Henry said. "Give him a fresh one." Typical, Arnulf thought, he doesn't even think that the *man* may need rest. Or bother to tell the rest of us what's going on—there he goes now, ordering his men out, what on *earth*, he's taking a small army wherever it is, must be a rebellion, that younger brother of his, Geoffrey, I knew he'd make trouble . . .

"Gentlemen," Henry said, turning to his councilors, "we will resume this discussion at a later date. I must leave at once."

"But where are you *going*?" Arnulf demanded. "And why?"

"Poitiers," Henry said, and, as he pushed aside the door curtain, "to get married. I'll tell you all about it later."

*D*ear Raoul." Eleanor sighed as her seneschal finished the last in an exceedingly long series of verses celebrating the eyes, fingers, lips, and laughter of his countess. "You sing almost as sweetly as . . . someone I once knew." Her fingers sought the talisman bead. Cercle-le-Monde was long gone, and so was the innocent young girl to whom he had given this ancient stone. She felt a moment's sharp regret for that spring of innocence. At least she was wiser now; she would not give herself to a bloodless, pious man who longed to be a monk, nor to a bully like Hugh of Lusignan who thought he owned her.

Nor, for all the sweetness of his versifying, for all her gratitude for his loyalty and timely appearance at the monastery of Saint-Benoît, to her dear kinsman. But this she had avoided saying until this morning's messengers told her it was safe to do so.

"Such a pity," she said now, "that we are related. There is no man I trust more than you, Raoul, none other I would trust with the guardianship over my lands."

Raoul bent his head. "I would serve you forever and in all ways, my most lovely lady."

"I know." Eleanor permitted herself one fingertip touch on the yellow hair that reminded her of other golden, laughing, strong young men. But they always seemed to die young, these golden giants. The man she had chosen would outlast a dozen such. . . . Her heart beat quicker as she anticipated his arrival. At last she would be wed to someone who stirred her pulses, someone young and virile enough to satisfy the aching needs that had tormented her ever since one night in Constantinople.

And best of all, he was young enough to accept her guidance. She would teach him to rule by day, and together they would learn the arts of love by night, and together they would make an empire over half the world—yes, and many sons. All that was promised her by the vision in the fountain would be true now, even the crown; it was only that she had not interpreted it rightly the first time, had not chosen the *right* crown.

"This time," she said to herself, "I am doing everything right." And to Raoul, "There is something I need to tell you. . . ."

*H*er face lit with a light Raoul had never seen before, a blaze of joy that seemed like a torch lighting her way into the adventure of the future. He twisted his head to follow her gaze but could see nothing there to account for her happiness, only a short, redheaded boy in muddy riding clothes. He himself couldn't be any threat to Raoul's hopes. And he was not the advance guard for a great man, or there'd have been a whole train of mounted knights pouring into the courtyard instead of the three tired men behind the boy. A messenger? From whom?

Eleanor stood and put her hands into the boy's. He swept her into a joyous, crushing embrace, whirled her halfway around, and set her down again with mud on her flowing green gown. Neither of them seemed to think it mattered in the least.

"Raoul de la Faye, my dear kinsman and seneschal of Aquitaine," Eleanor introduced him first, as though this shabbily dressed boy took precedence. "Raoul, this is Henry Plantagenet, duke of Normandy, count of Anjou . . . and soon to be duke of Aquitaine."

"You left out England." The boy laughed. "We'll see to England soon enough, though."

Not a threat, Raoul realized numbly.

A disaster.

"You took your time!" Eleanor teased the boy now.

"My lady." Young Henry made a sketchy bow that ended, somehow, with his arm around her waist. "My very dear lady. I came as soon as I had the news. Your messenger went a roundabout way to find me."

"Hah!" exploded one of the men behind him. Raoul now recognized him, disguised by exhaustion and the mud of the roads, as that clerk of Eleanor's who usually tagged along behind her. Benoît, that was the name. "If *you* would stay in one place for two nights at a time, or travel at a reasonable speed like any other great man, a poor clerk might have a chance of catching up with you."

Still clasping Eleanor tightly, Henry laughed and clapped Benoît on the shoulder with his free hand. "I have a great many places to go, my friend. And you should have learned by now that I am not at all reasonable."

Benoît had the bemused face of a man charmed against his will. "In that, at least, you two are well matched. *Very* well matched."

Henry spared his attention then to Raoul, showing an interest in the details of his administration and an appreciation of how he'd handled the problems arising as he took over from Geoffrey de Rancon that almost charmed Raoul, too, into accepting this . . . interloper? Better not to think that way. His new lord, for Eleanor would scarcely expect to maintain personal control over Aquitaine now that she had a man to manage the realm for her.

And he was a man; Raoul appreciated that now. Young, but fitting his role so well that he must have been more than ready to rule Anjou before Geoffrey Plantagenet passed away. A man who loved ruling and understood what it took, a man who was accustomed to winning, a man who made up in charm and explosive energy what he lacked in height and dignity. Instead of two men who'd loved Eleanor being polite to the one who'd won her, somehow he had turned them into an alliance encircling and protecting her, taking their love for granted and assuming they would use it to her benefit.

And they wanted to be alone; that, too, was clear enough. Raoul pulled his ragged courtly manners together again and suggested that the count of Anjou might find it pleasant to walk with Eleanor in the gardens while his entourage—*such as it is*—was housed and stabled. He would see that some refreshment was sent to them there.

It was a relief to be out of the Angevin's presence; something about Henry made you feel as though he was using up all the air, even outdoors. Raoul hated to think what his effect would be in a small room. He asked Benoît, who had been riding with Henry long enough to form some impression, what he truly thought about their new lord.

"I was prepared to hate him," Benoît confessed as they went to see to the practical needs of the party. "I still could, easily enough . . . but not when he is looking at you. He makes you feel as if you are the only person who matters to him. He is so, so . . ."

"Intense," Raoul suggested. "Driven. Hyperactive. *Possessed*."

"There's demon blood in that race," Benoît agreed, "but I suspect it defies exorcism. I wonder . . . what it's like to be a woman he is looking at like that."

"I don't," Raoul said firmly, "even want to imagine it."

Eleanor had no need to imagine it. As the two of them paced decorously through the gardens, passing from the low herb knots of the outer garden to the flowering trees that scented the inmost one, she could feel Henry's hand on her arm and his eyes upon her face. He desired her. Not like Hugh of Lusignan, who wanted to get under her skirts exactly as much as he wanted to tumble every other woman under fifty; not like Thibaut of Blois, who would have married anything that held Aquitaine as long as it was female; and not like the men who had no hope of marrying her, men like Benoît who worshipped from afar and were really more comfortable that way. He desired *her.*

And the inmost garden, designed by that same Master Alluis who had built the duke's gardens in Bordeaux, was white with early-blooming trees. Under the white blossoms, Eleanor turned to Henry, placing both her hands in his as she had done in the moment of greeting.

It did not matter that he smelled strongly of sweat and horses, that his hair was untidy, and his short, common-looking cloak askew. It did not even matter that he had to look up slightly to meet her eyes. All she saw was that burning gaze that made her feel like the only person in his world.

Ab atraic d'amor doussana . . . a remembered voice sang in her heart. *At the call of sweet love to go into some garden or behind a curtain . . .*

Constantinople was very far away now, and instead of the autumn grasses of a dying world, here they were surrounded by the white flowers of spring, a spring in which all things were made new and fresh again.

The beating of the heavy pulse in her ears sounded like the rustling of birds, hundreds of white wings lifting like doves, the white flowers transformed, lifting her and Henry with them to hover between the blue of heaven and the green of earth. *Blue and green are the colors of the living world,* Cercle-le-Monde's remembered voice informed her as the flowering tree itself changed shape, transforming into a ship that sailed over gray seas into a misty green land.

Henry's hands touched her hair, freeing the heavy plaits into a cloak of shimmering amber whose light strands lifted about her face, as though blown by an unseen wind. . . . *The wind of heart's desire.*

He lifted the sheaves of her unbound hair like gold in his hands, kissed the flowing hair, and laid his lips upon the curves of her body revealed where he had lifted up the hair. She felt weak with delight . . . but no longer floating between heaven and earth. This joy of the senses was all of earth, and her feet were planted firmly on the green turf of Aquitaine, and she knew just how little privacy the pleasaunce afforded.

"We need a priest," Henry said between kisses that traveled up the long line of her neck, seeking her lips. "And a bed." He found and claimed her mouth in a long dizzying embrace that left her senses reeling. "Not necessarily in that order," he said, breaking free at last and breathing like a man who had been running with all his might toward some unimaginably desired goal.

This is what the visions meant, Eleanor thought again. *All the visions: the crown, the ship, the wind . . . I was too eager, before. I read into them what I could see before me.* This *is how it was meant to be. This union will be blessed with desire, unlike that with Louis; it will be blessed by the church, unlike that with Manuel; we will be together as we were meant to be.*

Shadowy figures passed before her eyes, not the army of skeletons that had tormented her dreams before Outremer but tall, proud men whose features mingled the Plantagenet fairness with the height and dignity of Aquitaine. *Sons. I will have sons, and they will live.* A part of her heart was buried in the wilds of Mount Cadmos, a greater part would grow up in Paris without ever truly knowing her, but this spring was the promise of a new beginning and new lives, many new lives. She and Henry between them would make an empire and sons to rule it.

All that was in the promise of the white flowers, the spiraling dance of the white birds, the force of the green buds opening into the warmth of spring. All that, and more . . . more that she could not read . . . but it must be good. *This* time everything would be right. It had to be.

A l'entrada del tens clar, eya,
Per Joia recomencar, eya,
E per jelos irritar, eya,
Vol la regina mostrar
Qui es si amoroza.

FICTION   Ball, Margaret,
BALL   1947-

           Duchess of
           Aquitaine.

$25.95

DATE			

7/06

BAKER & TAYLOR